Terrors of Time

Adventures in a Bygone Age
Volume III:
The Legend of the Extinction Stones

A novel by

Eric Skawski

Blue Cloud Publications.

ISBN 978-1-907407-87-1

THE BLACK LEAF PUBLISHING GROUP
13 Everard Court
Garrett Street,
Nuneaton, CV11 4QB
Warwickshire
England
www.blackleafpublishing.com

This book is firstly dedicated to:
My friends from my Grade 9 graduating class at F.E. Osborne Jr. High
You once joked about me riding dinosaurs through temples. I said it was too 'Indiana Jones' for me, but nevertheless it gave me the idea.

Secondly, to:
My friends from my first year of residence in the University of Lethbridge.
You know why

And lastly, but perhaps most importantly to:
Every paleontologist and archaeologist who loves their job.
Without the paleontologists, none of the information in this book would be possible.
Without the archaeologists, none of it would have been inspired

Also by the same author

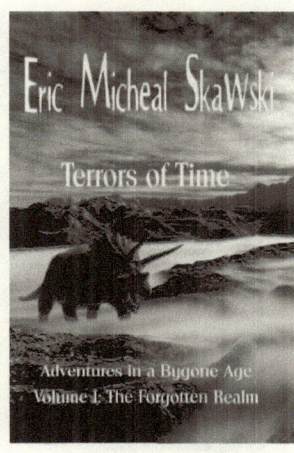

Terrors of Time I
The Forgotten Realm

Paleontologist Drake Burgess and his colleagues are off to Argentina for a dig when their plane crashes. Drake and the survivors shelter in a cave, only to find themselves trapped... or are they? They find an exit, but the world they find is not the one they left. It is a beautiful, thriving land where they meet, to their surprise, dinosaurs! Living, breathing dinosaurs! It is something Drake has only ever imagined, and he and his colleagues are mystified. But how are they to survive in a land full of prehistoric Terrors of Time?

Drake is thrown into an adventure across the vast land, on a journey through time, millions of years in the making.

Blue Cloud Publications
ISBN 978-1-907407-41-3

Avaiable at Amazon, Waterstones and all leading book stores

Also by the same author

Terrors of Time II
The Kingdom of Giants

John and Jorge face dangers of their own as they attempt to reach the Hekeni village, but it's nothing compared to the challenges facing Drake and Al, as they chase the Golarans across land and sea. They are driven by a desire to rescue their friends, and the Golarans are driven by a desire to keep them.

But what happens when the land fights back, and the Hekeni find themselves walking into the Kingdom of Giants?

Blue Cloud Publications
ISBN 978-1-907407-44-4

Avaiable at Amazon, Waterstones and all leading book stores

For those of you who didn't read the prequel

For those of you who didn't read the prequel (and hopefully, after this, want to), there's really only three things you need to know. Firstly, Drake Burgess, the main character, is not from the land of Prehistorcia initially but from earth, known to the Hekeni tribe as the Above-world. He is currently dating Jane, also from the Above-world, and it ought to be fairly obvious who is an Above-worlder by birth and who is not once you get into the story.

Secondly, and this probably answers some questions you're having about the first point, Prehistorcia is a land where nothing goes extinct, and also the primary god of the native tribes. This means, as you've probably already guessed, dinosaurs, mammoths, Neanderthals... well, anything, really. It's typically thought of as being beneath the earth, however it is not quite true. It is often said by the natives that the land is alive, and can only be found if it wants to be found. It is said that every Above-worlder has been brought down for a reason, and time slows down in the land, allowing people to live for hundreds of years without age. The largest tribe in Prehistorcia is the Golaran Tribe, a generally hated tribe with a reputation for robbing from other tribes (this was, in fact, the basis of the first books).

Finally, the Hekeni are one of twenty tribes in Prehistorcia, one of the largest, and among the most ancient of human cultures. They are also, by far, the best at training animals. This means – you probably guessed correctly again – domesticated dinosaurs. But *never* think of them as tame! To the Hekeni, training animals is a highly spiritual part of their culture, and to kill an animal for anything other than sustenance is among the highest of blasphemies. The Hekeni

Tribe's chief is Roggan Spinosaurus, and his second-in-command, Alan Triceratops, is Drake Burgesses (remember above?) closest native friend.

Everything else you need to know you'll read about.

If you enjoy it enough that you want the prequel, simply look in any major retailer for *Terrors of Time: The Forgotten Realm* and *Terrors of Time: The Kingdom of Giants*. Don't worry if you haven't read either of them yet, however. Like I said, everything you need to know for this one I've said above.

Tyrannosaurus Mtns.

Solg Tribe

Hehini Tribe

Cretaceous Forest

Thunder Marshes

Great Yellow Plains

Dark Forest

Drought Lands

Trantoll Tribe

Turtle Lake

Pachycephalosaurus Mtns.

Petrosaurus Mtns.

Tylosaurus Lake

Mt. Ash

Triassic Desert

Fertile River Tribe

Yaxog Tribe

Pterosaur Canyon

Fertile River

Dilophosaurus Shore

Wetlands

Golaran Tribe

Crocodile Peninsula

Sea of Prehistorcia

Green Islands

Sauropod Valley

Blue Fields

Brachiosaurus Mtns.

Xuanhanosaurus Mtns.

Zuniceratops Woods

Snake Isles

Amargosaurus Mtns.

Old Mayztec Empire

Valley of the Mayztec

Vulcanodon Valley

Ceradactylus Island

South Drought Lands

West Mtns.

Triceratops Mtns.

Rilowin Plateau

Velociraptor Basin

Narrow Valley

Rhinoceros Plains

Redwood Forest

Reef

Mountain Tribe

Hadrosaurus Mtns.

Great Lake

Mosasaur Bay

Ceratopsian Forest

Broken Valley

Great Forest

Swamp

Great Mtns.

Uncrossable River

Titanis Hills

Utahraptor Plateau

Quellorg Tribe

Preface

The history of Prehistorcia is vast and brutal, yet everything the natives were, are, or ever will be is based on those traditions which were built in the past. Living in Prehistorcia, they never noticed dinosaurs or mammoths were out of the ordinary for most Humans on the Above-World, but they always felt a certain magic about their home. The land wasn't always so peaceful... well, peaceful in terms of Above-worlders, which is a remarkably small bar to set, admittedly. Once, the land was owned by the mightiest tribe in history known only as the Mayztecs.

A year ago, when Drake's plane crashed with his colleagues and other civilians, he heard some things of these Mayztecs, and even through a foreigner's eyes he could see the influence they once held, but never once did the survivors from the plane crash bother to discover exactly who the Mayztecs were.

The Mayztecs, powerful engineers, scientists, and builders took their names from those Above-world places of Mesoamerica. But they were, in fact, descended from many ancients tribes – Incans, Mayans, Aztecs, Chinese, Japanese, Egyptians, Romans, Greeks, Native Americans and Arabic people from the Above-world all flocked to the great Mayztec Tribe. For nearly eight thousand years the Mayztecs dominated the land, building a civilization and making war on the rebellious northern tribes – Hekeni, Golaran, Yaxog, Trontoll, Fertile River and Solg.

As millennia passed, the Mayztecs grew more powerful. The six original tribes of Prehistorcia stood against their aggression, and waged war after war against the Mayztecs.

In their wars, several tribes formed. Many tribes were formed and wiped out and shrunken, but always the original six survived. In the time of the Great Revolt, when the Mayztec power was broken for good, twenty tribes existed in Prehistorcia: Hekeni, Golaran, Trontoll, Fertile River, Yaxog, Solg, Zolgaf, Mountain, Kluugon, Vorrog, Borchillian, Dark Forest, Quellorg, Flimzoak, Urallag (also called Shore), Klenkara, Rooloer, and the three nomadic tribes, Catteua, Enorrion, and Agaltrox.

Finally, in Mayztec Empire Year 7955, the last emperor of the Mayztec emperors was cast down! A broken empire was all that remained, and what remained of the Mayztecs became the twenty-first tribe, punished by the victorious rebels to be the nomadic Nemnar Tribe. The Rooloer were later destroyed by Golarans.

But what caused the Rooloer to be destroyed by the Golarans? Why, after eight thousand years, did the rebels finally beat the Mayztecs? And why does Prehistorcia exist in the first place?

The answer comes from their most ancient story. This story is as old as the land itself, the first of the first, from the very earliest days of Prehistorcia, as old as time, even older than the tribes themselves, and one that continues, even to this very day: the Legend of the Extinction Stones...

One for the Golaran, strong and proud,
One for the Trontoll under white clouds,
One for the Yaxog at great height,
One for the Hekeni with the animals' might
One for the River in the afternoon breeze
One for the Solg in the shade of the trees

– Hymn of the Extinction Stones
(Translated to English by Harold Dryptosaurus)

Chapter 1 – Newcomer

Drake Burgess, an unshaven man with blond hair and brown eyes; he had a soft chin, a stocky body, and was dressed in dinosaur skins. He was not a handsome man, but he wasn't particularly ugly either. Drake was kneeling on the soft ground in front of a small, feathery bird. But this was no bird, though his kind had eventually evolved into one. It had a tiny, sickle-shaped claw on its second toe that dwarfed the others. It stood on two powerful legs, and a stiff tail jutted out behind it. The creature had a slightly elongated neck, and a triangular snout with sharp teeth. Its arms had three claws each, and they, too, were covered in a brownish down.

The creature stared up at him adoringly. It was a Utahraptor, and this little male would eventually grow up to be the deadliest predator ever, even deadlier than the mighty carnosaurs such as Allosaurus, Tyrannosaurus Rex, and Spinosaurus.

Drake lived in a land as amazing as the baby Utahraptor itself – Prehistorcia; a land that endured throughout time, suppressing evolution, leaving everything that ever lived here intact and interacting. Al, a brown-haired, round-faced man slightly younger than Drake (at least physically – chronologically, he was much older) stood beside him.

"Well, Drake, Ahrzi is responding very well to you." he said.

"You think?"

A year ago, Drake had chosen an egg from a recent clutch of the resident Hekeni Utahraptor pack that would hatch, and he would train. Six months ago, that egg had hatched, and Al said it was important to let the baby see Drake first, as it established a connection from birth. Since then, Al had been teaching him all the secret Hekeni techniques.

"Well, he's learning to listen to you very well. Even better than Tenethax, when he grows up, I'd say."

Tenethax was a fully-grown Triceratops that Drake had developed an instant connection with, and seemed to train him on the spot over a year ago when the Hekeni had problems controlling him. But little Ahrzi had known no other trainer, unlike Tenethax, who had had many trainers but no real connection to any Human prior to Drake.

Drake remembered when he first named the Utahraptor, a couple days after hatching:

"Well, what's a good name for a dinosaur?" asked Drake to Al.

"Well, you know the names of some of them. There's no bad name. Dave called his Phorusracos Jimmy."

Drake thought. He looked at the sickle-shaped claw, which would eventually be a deadly weapon. He asked: "What's the Hekeni word for claw?"

"Ahrzi."

"In that case, I'll name him Ahrzi." said Drake.

"A bit odd, but alright."

Since then, Ahrzi had responded well to his name. Now, Drake stroked Ahrzi the Utahraptor under his chin, and the tiny thing chirped happily. He emitted high-pitched squeaks, which Drake had come to interpret as a demand for food.

"First you have to jump." said Drake.

Ahrzi crouched down and sprang surprisingly high, up to Drake's head. That was twice Ahrzi's body height! Drake took out a meat scrap from the wooden bucket next to him and tossed it at Ahrzi, who jumped up again and caught it. He began playing with it, enjoying himself.

"He certainly grows fast, doesn't he?" asked Drake.

"Yes, even with the extended time down here, the dromaeosaurs will reach adulthood in seven or eight years." replied Al.

"Really? That means that back in the Cretaceous, they'd have grown up in less than three years!"

Drake tossed Ahrzi another scrap of meat. Ahrzi was one of only three animals that would be raised to understand English. Even Tenethax, for more specific orders than 'run' or 'turn', needed to be told in Hekeni. The other two were Jimmy, the terror bird Dave had raised three years ago, and a Styracosaurus that John was trying to raise. It was a little thing, only a month old, though its egg was laid a year ago. Its horns were short little nubs poking out of the skin, and it was only as long as John's arm, but its proportions seemed to be the same of the fully-grown adult animal that Dazz, the Neanderthal, had raised some thirty or forty years ago. John had much more trouble choosing a name than Drake, and for now it remained nameless.

Gary, Jane, and Steven had no animals yet, though Gary had an egg picked out from a recent nest laid by a Stegosaurus. Jane was on the waiting list for a Parasaurolophus, but Steven said that while he loved riding them, he didn't think he was ready to raise one yet, even though he was thinking about it.

Drake looked up at the western sky. It was a beautiful day, cloudless. Yet something was wrong about it. What caught his eye?

Suddenly a flash as bright as the sun came and went, and a fiery object plummeted from the sky!

"What was that?" asked Drake.

"I don't know." said Al. "Should we check it out?"

"I think so."

They got up, looking at where the thing had landed. It was not burning anymore, though there was smoke blowing in the wind. They began to walk towards it.

"No, you stay, Ahrzi. Stay." commanded Drake, and the Utahraptor, looking sad, stayed there.

They walked out the Hekeni village and into the Cretaceous Forest. It wasn't long before they found what had happened, just two or three kilometres away, hidden by the trees. It also wasn't long before John, Jane, Steven and Gary showed up with Dazz, Tom, Harry, Dave, and many other Hekeni by them. There were some animals there, too, including a fully-grown Utahraptor, three Deinonychus, a few Hadrosaurs, and an Ankylosaurus named Edthax.

What amazed them was the object. It was an airplane! A US military craft used for transport. Based on the sand, Drake guessed it had come from Iraq, or whatever country the Americans had started a war with by now. It wasn't burring anymore, and it looked as though it had never been. One motor on the wing was blasted apart, and there were rocket markings al through the hull. The wing on the other side had fallen off from the crash, and hung limply downwards, crushing the jungle, clearing a path. Drake went around the other side, to the broken wing.

There was a Troodon, a thin, nimble dinosaur that looked somewhat like a dromaeosaur, only there was no claws, fewer (though more developed) feathers, the neck was longer, the tail wasn't as stiff, and the snout was narrower. The sickle-shaped claw on the toe was much smaller, proportionally, than those of dromaeosaurs.

It was sniffing at a crack in the side of the hull, large enough for a grown man to squeeze through. Al shooed it away, and looked in.

"What is this? It seems so familiar..."

Al had been lost like Drake, when his plane crashed in 1969. Could Al remember a plane, though? He had only been three at the time.

"It's an airplane. You were in one, once."

"Maybe that's why it's so familiar." he admitted. "Well, let's go in!" he squeezed through the crack. Drake followed.

It was dark in the hull, though it was large and spacious. What little light they got came from the crack and some puncture holes from the crash. There were things covered in tarps; or they were, but the crash had jumbled everything. Drake saw a military jeep standing on its wheels at the edge of the light. There was a crate that spilled open on the floor, revealing all sorts of things like flashlights, first-aid kits, and small army knives.

Drake wondered vaguely if there was anyone alive in there. He found the door to the cockpit, and opened it. There was the pilot, his face bloody on the wheel, clearly dead. The co-pilot was lying against his side window with a bloody face. Drake wasn't sure about him, so he poked him. His skin was still warm. His mouth moved, and unintelligible muttering came out.

"This one's still alive." he said.

"Yeah, but for how much longer?" asked Al.

Drake heard something that made his heart stop – the small, metallic click of a gun being cocked. He turned around, hands raised, knowing there was no defence against it down here.

There was a man, lying against one of the upturned crates. He had dark skin, and a shaved head. He had a square build, like a brick with legs, the right of which was bent out of shape, and his pants were covered in blood. He clearly had a broken leg. But he was still in good enough mind to point a gun at them, and probably in good enough shape to shoot them.

"We don't mean you any harm." said Drake, calmly and clearly. "Your leg is broken."

"I know my goddamn leg is broken!" he yelled. "You don't think it's shootin' pain into me every second? But Ah'll take y'all out first!"

"We mean you no harm." Drake repeated.

"Then why the hell did y'all crash my plane?"

"We didn't!" said Drake, forgetting his calm voice now. "Put down the gun, and we'll explain to you exactly where you are. We'll fix your leg, too."

"How do ah know ah can trust you?" he asked.

"Drake, what's taking so long?" it was John, wearing his silly fedora, which looked much too large for him and clashed with the dinosaur-skin shirt and shorts, who crawled through the crack. "There's a crowd gathering." The soldier pointed his gun at him. But as soon as he saw the face, the soldier seemed to relax.

"Ah've seen you somewhere before." he said.

"I doubt it. I've never been in the army." said John. "And at any rate, I'm Canadian."

"No, no, it's another face. From a book, or something. Something to do with dinosaurs."

"John, he's got a gun!" said Drake.

"That's it!" said the soldier, dropping his gun. "You're John Rockman, paleontologist! I just finished your book last year! You got me interested in paleontology in the first place! They said you died, over a year ago by now!"

John smiled. "I didn't know my book got so far. As of now, you're dead, too."

"What? But then... why is my leg broken? Why am I so weak?"

Drake laughed. "That's just John's sense of humour! You're not dead, but they'll report you to be! Because, as soon as your plane hit our ground, you're not technically on Earth."

"Not on Earth, but... isn't that dead?" he asked. "Or is this some hidden government alien base?"

"No." Drake laughed. "We'll get you out of here, and we'll explain."

They pulled him out of the plane, where he was handed over to a Hekeni doctor. Al turned to Drake, and when he talked, he sounded excited.

"Drake, with this modern equipment down here, do you know what it means?"

"Not really. So what?"

"An idea struck me! Isn't it possible, with the help of this Above-world equipment, that we can at last retrieve the Extinction Stones?"

"The... what?" asked Drake. "What are the Extinction Stones?"

Al looked as if he had been slapped in the face. "Drake, I can't believe no one's ever told you. The Extinction Stones are the whole reason Prehistorcia exists!"

Chapter 2 – The Extinction Stones

It took a moment for the gravity of the statement to sink in. Drake didn't know there was a reason for Prehistorcia to exist. He just always assumed it was there, like evolution, the sun, or moving forward through time.

"It's the reason Prehistorcia exists?" asked Drake finally.

"Yes!"

"But... how?"

Drake wasn't the only one listening. The paleontologists were all gathering around, with Tom (the co-pilot from the plane that brought Drake), and even some Hekeni who liked the story.

"I'll tell you." said Al, nervous under all the eyes. "But to understand it, you have to go back... way back... to before the Hekeni lived here. Sit down, it's a bit lengthy. You know of the five extinctions in earth's history, right?"

They all nodded in agreement. Throughout earth's history, there had been five major extinctions – one at the end of the Cambrian (or Ordovician – there was a bit of debate), 500 million years or so ago, one at the end of the Devonian 380 million years ago, one at the end of the Permian, 252 million years ago, one at the end of the Triassic, 204 million years ago, and one at the end of the Cretaceous, 65 million years ago. Each one had killed off a vast majority of animals, and often made way for a whole new stage of evolution.

Sixty-five million years ago, the dinosaurs had died to make way for mammals. Before that, the Triassic animals made way for dinosaurs to take over. Two hundred and fifty million years ago, the end of the Permian brought about the death of nearly 95% of life on earth, killing off most of the Palaeozoic animals to make way for the Triassic, a transitional time where the world was evolving to bigger things. The Devonian extinction and Cambrian extinction were the two scientists knew the least about, them being so old, but newer, more efficient animals evolved very fast out of them.

"Right, well, there is a sixth." said Al. "We, the humans, are the sixth. Each Stone represents a period of mass die-offs in earth's history, when a lot of life goes extinct very fast. It could be that the extinctions were created because the Stones were made and needed tremendous power – or it could be that the tremendous power of the extinctions made the Stones. We don't know. But there are six Stones, one for each extinction.

"Well, many thousands of years ago, close to twenty or thirty thousand years ago, there were only six tribes in Prehistorcia, as opposed to the twenty today. We, the Hekeni, were one. The Yaxog and Golarans were another two. The Solg, a newly formed tribe, was the fourth. There are also two tribes way out east, the Trontoll and the Fertile River Tribe, they were the other two. Well, there were five Stones back then, and the Solg, which split from the Hekeni for religious reasons, did not have one. But, around twelve thousand years ago, down south, where the Golarans lived, a sixth Stone was born, brought out of the sky by a fiery flash.

"It created a massive crater. The Golarans found the sixth Stone, and coveted it, but later gave it to the Solg. The tribes were friendlier back then. Now, these Stones, it is believed, were created by the Great God Prehistorcia himself, and whether or not that's true, there is no doubt that the Stones hold incredible power. We figured it out, eventually, that these Stones kept the time here frozen. When we used them, we were able to harness the power of the creatures of the time the Stones represented. We found that the Stones could not be broken or changed in shape, and any harm that came to them seemed to be reflected onto Prehistorcia.

"They are highly religious artefacts, and if you were to find the Holy Grail, all the Christians in the world would not revere it as strongly as one Prehistorcian revered Stones. But this is just the beginning of the story. Nine thousand or so years ago, the Mayztecs came. They built their own empire, and for a thousand years, it lay just in a small area which today is called the Valley of the Mayztecs. But their power, and empire, grew. We rebels fought them, but nothing could stop their expansion; they took over everything north of the Hadrosaurus Mountains, west to the West Mountains, east to the sea, and north to the Pillars of Shuy-Fromoth. The Golarans were forced to abandon their peninsula and go west, across the sea, to the Pachycephalosaurus Mountains.

"But that was thousands of years later. Well, the very last dynasty of Mayztec emperors had three kings. Elmoth had overthrown the fortieth dynasty, and called himself emperor. He continued the love of magic that his predecessor had, and had his royal servants give him the source of ultimate power.

"But, he died, some say killed by his son, Elmerik, who goes by the name of Elmerik the Extinctor."

"Extinctor?" asked Drake. "Is that a word?"

"It is in Hekeni." replied Al. *"Elmerik na Ergothar.* Elmerik had listened to many rebel stories as a boy, and knew exactly what would give him the ultimate power he desired – the Extinction Stones. For you see, it is said that anyone who could find and unite the Extinction Stones would have power over Prehistorcia; he could command the elements, the animals, he would be indestructible and invincible. If Elmerik had the Stones, he would be unbeatable, and immortal. For the Stones grant ultimate power over Prehistorcia, because they are what shaped it.

"Well, by that time, there were more than us six rebel tribes running about. There were twenty rebel tribes. But he knew what the six original tribes were, and guessed they were with us. So he sent attack forces straight to the tribes. We fought harder than we ever had in history to keep our Extinction Stone, but the Mayztec armies were too strong, and too many. We Hekeni, training animals, held on the longest, but even so, after years and years of fighting, we lost our Stone. We feared that Elmerik would try to unite the Stones, so we wasted no time in gathering an attack force.

"This was nine hundred years ago. All tribes everywhere united, and stood as one, and attacked the Mayztec Empire. We gave many tribes trained dinosaurs, and this was back in the days when we had an army of carnosaurs. We had Tyrannosaurs, Allosaurs, Spinosaurs, Neovenators, and a whole mess of sauropods, stegosaurs, ankylosaurs, ceratopsians and dromaeosaurs, all prepared to take down the Mayztecs. We began attacking – but Elmerik had already united the Stones.

"But Elmerik missed one piece of vital information – the Stones don't work for personal gain. You must want the Stones for the right reasons. The Stones' power worked individually, but they did not give him the power over Prehistorcia he had hoped. The tribes got in, and many were lost, but in the end, the great power of the Stones consumed Elmerik, and ate him alive. Witnesses say he died right then and there, dissolved to a skeleton. Others say he collapsed in blinding light. Still others say that lightning shot from the Stones and he was burned. But whatever the story, he died. His son and only heir, Elmork, inherited a kingdom in turmoil.

"The war continued, and Elmork knew that the Stones would not save the empire. As a final act of Mayztec defiance, he sent the Stones away, in secret, to places far beyond the northern borders, each one to be hidden in a separate temple, and the temple to be sealed. There were only four tombs of former emperors in the northern rebel part of Prehistorcia, so he built two more, his father's, and his own, and hid the Stones there. The Mayztecs fell, and Elmork was killed, but not before the Stones were hidden.

"The Mayztecs, their last emperor fallen, placed him in his tomb, and in doing so placed the final Stone with him. The last of the Mayztecs were hunted down and killed, and their only survivors are now a nomadic tribe in the deep south; they do trading with the Golaran, Mountain, and Quellorg tribes." Al finished.

"So that's it?" asked Drake. "What did you do once the Mayztecs fell?"

"Well, naturally, all tribes tried to get information out of surviving Mayztecs. It didn't take long. But when we opened the temples to try and get them out, we found surprises."

"What surprises?" asked John.

"Well, the Mayztecs set booby-traps all over their temples, to keep people from entering, but the biggest shock was one the Mayztecs did not expect – the Stones themselves had guardians. Each Stone had its own guardian, a powerful animal from Prehistorcia, to defend it. They were cursed animals, each sworn to protect the Stone. Each temple is guarded by a different one. There is the Dromaeosaur, the Carnosaur, the Ankylosaur, the Stegosaur, the Ceratopsian, and the Sauropod."

"So, you think the Stones are magic?" asked Drake, stifling a laugh.

"I *know* they're magic." said Al.

"Which Stone did the Heken used to have?" asked Jane.

"The Six Stones came in six colours – blue for Ordovician, brown for Devonian, red for Permian, green for Triassic, yellow for Cretaceous, and black for Pleistocene. The feathers on our arrows are reminiscent of the colour of Stone we used to have."

"So you had the green Stone." said Drake.

"And the Yaxog had the brown one!" said John, remembering his experience with them a year ago.

"The Golarans must have had the red one." said Gary.

"That's right." said Al. "The Trontoll had the yellow one, the Fertile River Tribe had the blue one and the Solg had the black one."

"And you believe these Stones were made by Prehistorcia?" said Drake.

"What other explanation is there for their power?" asked Al. "The Stones, be they magic or not, are still highly valuable religious artefacts, and they are the one thing we value above the land, considering that they made the land."

"They didn't make the land!" said Drake.

"They did, Drake, and if you come with us on this quest, you'll be convinced!"

"Well, even if they keep this land here, they can't be the life force of it. They're just stones, nothing more, even if they do keep this land what it is. Besides, why get them out now? Why haven't you tried before?" asked Drake.

"But we have." said Al. "Seven hundred years ago, when the Mayztec Empire fell, we searched far and wide for the Stones, and eventually found the temples they were hidden in. The tribes entered, in attempts to get the Stones back, only to be stopped by booby traps and cursed spirits. On the last expedition, five hundred years ago, we came very close to getting the red Stone. The expedition ultimately failed because the Golarans came to help, but the prospect of their old stone seemed to have an effect on them.

"They began squabbling amongst themselves and the other tribes. In sight of the Stone, the guardian beaten, they beat each other up over it, fighting for the right to take the Stone. The expedition was killed, and only one person survived, named Norral. He at last was able to grab the Stone. He removed it from the tomb, but as he turned around to leave, he saw everything that had been done. We don't know what happened after that. We only know that the Stone caused him great pain, and he dropped it, leaving it there, and ran back to his own tribe, the Rooloer, to tell his story.

"After that, it was agreed that the Stones must stay there until we had a way of grabbing them without losing our minds. No expedition has been sent since."

"But wait a minute, Al, the Rooloer Tribe is extinct." said John. "What happened to them? Did it have something to do with the Extinction Stones?"

"John, it had everything to do with the Extinction Stones! The Golarans never believed their story. They thought he had the red Stone and hid it from them, jealous that the Golarans had the right to it. They came in and slaughtered everyone, searching everywhere for the Stone which would never be found. That is why the Golarans are hated. Every other tribe severed communication and trade, so the Golarans began stealing from us to make up for it. But we are ready to forgive, and they have not taken it."

"So why do the tribes want the Stones so bad now?" asked Steven.

"Were you not listening? We've always wanted them, but we've been too afraid to try again! We want them safe in our hands." replied Al.

"But they're safe in the temples. Why not leave them there?" asked Drake.

"Because they are *ours*." said Al. "They belong to us, and we want them back. To not go looking for them is... well, there's nothing it's comparable to. It's entirely inconceivable. To leave them there and give the Mayztecs their final victory isn't just unacceptable, it's sacrilegious, and now that we have the technology to go get them it would be the greatest sin against our culture and our gods not to at least try."

Drake sighed. He doubted the Extinction Stones were magical, but they were obviously a very religious symbol. "Fine, I'll help you. When do we get going?"

Chapter 3 – The Council of Elders

Normally, being co-chief of the Hekeni Tribe meant that Al was pretty much able to do whatever he wanted whenever he wanted as long as it was not against the laws laid down by the Elders. He was allowed to take a rescue mission to Golarans without permission if he could find the volunteers. He was allowed to take a team of Hekeni hunting with him without notice. He was even allowed to train dinosaurs himself without permission.

But this was much bigger. This needed to be discussed with the Council of Elders; Al needed advice and permission. The Council of Elders were composed of the oldest, wisest Hekeni and they decided everything for the tribe, or at least every major thing. They decided who could be allowed to train dinosaurs (although it was usually everyone. You needed to do something pretty bad to get a 'no' on that), and assign people to find new animals to train. They even had to approve expeditions, although Al's adventure with Drake last year did not need to be passed, since Al was so high up and everyone was a volunteer that knew the risks.

The Council's most important job, however, was to choose a new chief should the old one die. They selected candidates, and the most qualified one would become the chief. The chief was allowed to pick his second, should he leave for some reason and needed a replacement, or die, so his second could fill in until a new one was found. But the chief didn't need to die for a new one to be selected. If the elders didn't like the way he was running things they could kick him out. Although it was usually from complaints brought to them about the chief that they made any decision to do that. The current chief could also decide he didn't like the role anymore, and resign. The current chief, Roggan Spinosaurus, had been chief for twenty years, after the old one passed away. Roggan was the second to the old chief, but from what Drake had heard, using the second-in-command to replace the chief was quite common.

Al and Drake entered the massive circular hut in the centre of the village. Inside there were two tables, each a half-circle, contouring to the walls, around a vast wooden platform. Behind the tables fifteen very old Hekeni were seated, seven women on one side, spots for seven men on the other (though there were only six present), and the Head Elder, a very old, bald, Neanderthal man with a long white beard and thick eyebrows sat in the middle of the two tables, wearing the pelt of a Tyrannosaurus.

"Alan Triceratops." said the old man.

"*Tehrah*, Head Elder Muthwag. I come to you with news." he said.

For the sake of the paleontologists, whenever they were present, the elders conducted the discussion in English, as most elders knew enough of it. The paleontologists were trying to learn Hekeni, and it was coming along well. Drake understood that *Tehrah* was a greeting, but not a normal greeting, it was reserved for those of high status such as these elders and the tribe leader. He could understand Hekeni well enough, too, but speaking it he was often clumsy. He had no ear for languages, and no tongue for it, either.

"Is it referring to the flash in the sky?" asked Head Elder Muthwag. "At first we sent Elder Skarg to look, which is why he is absent, but now we know it is a great sky machine your people use to get around." he said, turning to Drake.

"It is partly that, but there is another thing. It has much modern equipment." said Al.

"I see. And you want advice on how to use it?"

"No, actually, I had an idea in mind. It's radical, but it just might work."

"Please explain... what is radical? I have not heard this word before." Al put a word in Hekeni. The elders nodded. "Very well. What is the 'radical' idea?"

"Well, I was thinking, now that this technology is available to us, shouldn't we at least try to get the Extinction Stones?"

A deep silence reverberated around the room. Drake knew not all elders knew English, but they seemed to understand those two words. Drake heard muttering in Hekeni, elders whispering in their neighbour's ears, or else asking questions to the group. He asked Al what they were saying, but he said it was too mingled to translate properly. Head Elder Muthwag stood up, and he was quite tall, and held up a hand for silence.

"No one has suggested that in many hundreds of years." he said.

"Yes, but we've never had this technology. We also have more people than ever before who do not know of them, and do not worship them. They will not kill each other over them."

"The hearts of humans, even those who do not worship the Stones, can be corrupted."

Mutters of agreement went around. One ancient woman from the left-hand side asked:

"Can they be trusted not to lose them?"

Al turned to Drake. "Drake may not value the Stones as a religious artefact, but he knows that the rest of us do, and he would be as careful with it as he would be with anything else."

"That's true. I would take the Stones without wanting to kill my friends, and I would carry them safely back here." he said.

One old Australopithecus man from the right, the only Australopithecus in the room, spoke.

"We do nut doubt you conscience, Drake Torvosaurus, or you will. But we wonder eef you tooly know the value we hold the Extinction Stones to."

"I might not comprehend it, but I'll still guard them."

"None of us disagree that you'll bring the Stones back to us." said Muthwag. "Yet you have your Utahraptor. Have you named him yet?"

"I have."

"Good. However, the Utahraptor is very young, and he will need you with him if you want him to see you as his trainer. He is at a delicate stage. And your friend, John, his Styracosaurus is even more important. Your other two friends may not have dinosaurs, but Gary's Stegosaurus will hatch in a month. It will take at least that long to get to the final temple, if you skip everything else."

"Well, what if I took Ahrzi with me?" asked Drake. "What if John brought along his Styracosaurus?"

The elders looked at each other, and there was more muttering, but when Muthwag began talking, they silenced themselves.

"Training while exploring? That has not been done since... Alol, has it ever been done?"

An old *Homo sapiens* man said something in Hekeni. Muthwag turned back to them.

"It has not been done, apparently, since before the Mayztecs, back when the sixth Extinction Stone was found. We have no records of how the animals turned out, but as we do not do it anymore, it could not have turned out better. It is inadvisable to try."

"But elders, the expedition, probably, will only take two months, perhaps three. Those three months will not make a difference to training, will they?" asked Al.

"Not in all the stages of training." agreed an old woman. "But done this early, it could make a large difference."

"Well, couldn't Ahrzi have a temporary trainer for that long, and not make a difference to Drake?" asked Al.

"Yes..." the woman hesitated, "but the Styracosaurus will need John, if he wishes to train it properly to obey him. Otherwise, he will return in a few months, and the Styracosaurus may not accept him as the primary trainer."

"Well... could he try training it in the field?" asked Drake.

The elders began discussing. Muthwag at last looked back at them: "Yes. But if the baby does not show the usual signs at the right time, then it will have to be brought back, with or without John. Al, you are a good enough trainer to recognize these signs. Do you swear, by Prehistorcia, Zog, Hagoth, and the Extinction Stones you are about to seek, that you will send this baby back to be trained properly if the usual signs are not seen?"

"Yes."

"Then John may try."

"Another question, elders." said Al. "Should we tell other tribes what we are doing? Invite them to come along, or perhaps to come over and take their Stone back?"

The elders discussed again, this time for a long stretch. At last, Muthwag said: "It will be no secret what you are doing, should you be asked. But we think it better you set out alone, just Hekeni, and bring the Stones back here. When the Stones are retrieved, then we will send word to the other tribes to come and claim their own."

"Understood."

"Oh, and one moment." said Muthwag. He gestured for a thin man with shaggy white hair and a shoulder-length beard to stand up. He held many stone tablets and rolls of papyrus, and wore a coat of giant ground sloth skin. "You are to take Alol with you."

"Understood."

"Wait here a moment, though." said the elders. "We must see Drake's friends about this 'training in the field', and Steven has asked for you to be a witness to his training."

"Steven's finally going to train an animal?" asked Drake.

"Yes, but he must want a special case, or he would not ask for you to stay here. Nellmarie, will you get the door and let him in, please? He made an appointment earlier."

A grey-haired woman, the youngest-looking of all the elders, got the door. Drake assumed she was the newest member, as they had her doing trivial things such as opening the door.

Steven walked in, and nodded to Drake and Al. He looked more relaxed. Steven was of Chinese descent (though had been born and raised in Canada), with short black hair. He was not as clean-shaven as he once was, though his muscle tone had noticeably improved in his year here.

"What is it, Steven Thalassomedon?" asked Muthwag.

"Well, you have a fine collection of animals here, but none really call to me to train. I was hoping you could send an expedition, perhaps for a new animal?"

The elders began talking at this, too.

"Steven, there are many animals here. Is there really nothing you would like to train?"

"Well, I want to start easy, I guess." he said.

"Well, then, there are easy animals. Try a Dire Wolf, or a Hyenadon, why don't you? Dromaeosaurs are easy to train, too, as are the Ornithomimusaurs. Our small Troodon population is easy. Even our Pachycephalosaurus are easier than expected. Do you not want any of them?"

"I kind of liked the Pachycephalosaurus, but there are no others like it. I was kind of hoping for a smaller one, like maybe a Stygimoloch, or a Homalocephale."

"Al will have to explain what those are."

Al told the elders their names in Hekeni.

"Steven, just because animals are smaller, it does not make them easier, or gentler. Try a Pachycephalosaurus. But if you still want to try for a new animal, Al is taking you on an expedition. If you find an egg of your choice species that meets the standards, you may take it and train it. Have Al explain the standards to you. Now, if that's all, you had better get going! Those Extinction Stones won't find themselves!" said Muthwag, as the new woman got up to open the door for them.

"Why do we have to take Alol?" asked Drake.

"Because he's the Hekeni's official historian. Besides, the elders want to be in on all major expeditions like this." replied Al.

Chapter 4 – Kevin

It took a couple of days for the expedition to prepare, having to widen the crack in the plane and extract useful equipment. Drake was left looking for a replacement trainer for two days for Ahrzi that would, hopefully, allow him to be trained without losing his connection to Drake. John was going to take his Styracosaurus, which he still had not named, on the expedition with him. The little thing was less than a metre long, and weighted only a few dozen pounds. Its mouth was open as if in a smile as John lifted it up by his front legs, having his back legs and tail droop down. One day it would be too big for John to do that.

Gary, on the other hand, had the hard choice to make. Did he stay here, in the Hekeni camp, and wait for his Stegosaurus to hatch? Or, would he leave his egg to another trainer, and get a Stegosaurus on the next breeding round, and postpone the training for another year? He could not take his egg on the trip, it was far too delicate, but he could risk visiting the first temples, and try to return later, hoping he didn't miss the hatching.

Jane, who was waiting to train a Parasaurolophus, did not need to decide. The Parasaurolophus herd were only just now laying eggs, and according to the Hekeni, there would be a good three months before it hatched – more than enough time to take an expedition. And, of course, Steven was going to search for his animal.

The criteria for finding a new animal was quite simple for the rules. The Hekeni had a breeding population of almost every animal they train, except for the Neovenator, the Euoplocephalus (you-plo-sef-al-us), Zanor the Zuniceratops, and the Velociraptors. Every now and then, they went out to get a new animal, however, as the breeding populations never last forever in captivity. The animal had to have no parents, and still be at a young enough stage to be trainable. The age varied among species, but for Dromaeosaurs and other naturally social animals, the limit tended to be older, whereas Ankylosaurs and Tyrannosaurs, where independence came early, the age had to be younger.

Most animals were snagged as eggs from a nest, but they never dared take the eggs of social animals if there was someone looking, because often they would go to any measure to take it back. Most social animal eggs were taken while the parents were away from the nest. In many ways, it was cruel, but by taking the egg, they had massively increased its chance of survival, and parents were used to eggs being eaten or stolen. If they could not find the culprit, they were unlikely to try. But, if they did see the culprit – survival chances were slim.

So, Steven had to find a parentless infant or an abandoned nest before he could snag his animal. His eyes were opened for Pachycephalosaurs and therapods, but his eyes were open for anything that looked easy to train. Last year, Steven's problem was overconfidence with his knowledge – this year, it was the opposite.

Before the expedition left, however, Drake decided to pay a visit to the wounded soldier in the medical area, as it was his stuff they were taking. Apparently, there were four people on the plane, two of them dead, one of them unlikely to make it. When Drake entered the hut, there were two people on a bed of leaves, wrapped in a mammoth-skin blanket. The soldier who was awake looked at his thoughtfully.

He saw Drake. "This is mammoth skin, ain't it?" he asked.

"Yes, it is. They don't value it as much down here."

"Do they value anything as much as we would?" he asked.

"They value a great many things more. Their respect for the land and its inhabitants is staggering. They absolutely refuse to take an animal life if they will not use it for something, and their value of gold is much, much lower than their value of good, dry wood."

"Sounds like Native Americans." said the soldier.

"Hah. Native Americans wish they were as harmonious and peaceful as the Hekeni. They're altogether two entirely different people, even though a first glance might suggest otherwise. So, what's your name?"

"Corporal Kevin Shales of the US military." he replied.

"That means absolutely nothing around here." said Drake. "Now, you're just Kevin."

"No last name?"

"Not until you choose your guardian animal."

"What the hell?"

"Didn't they explain anything to you?" asked Drake.

"They explained that this place is called Prehistorcia, or somethin'. They explained that they're the Hekeni, and what this place is. They told me ah weren't the first, and that I ain't gonna be the last. They also told me that ah was brought here for a reason."

"Yeah. Well, they should explain more things."

"Were you here for a reason?" asked Kevin.

"Yes." Drake said. "But I'm more comfortable keeping that reason to myself."

Truth was, at first, Drake thought he was here for Jane. They began dating last year, but Drake had always felt the land wanted them together for more than the sake of happiness. There was some purpose he hadn't fulfilled yet, he could feel it in his soul, but the land wasn't yielding its plans.

"I understand." he replied.

"I only know that you don't know why you're here until you've already experienced it. When you find out you're here, you know that was the reason automatically. My friend, a year ago, Jorge, his reason was to listen to the land. Even if you told him that was the reason, he wouldn't believe it until it happened. Even if he did believe you, it's not something you can learn and automatically do once you know it. It has to come naturally."

"I don't understand."

Drake sighed. "You had to be there, I guess."

"What happened to that friend, anyway?"

"Jorge? He went home."

"You didn't?"

"I already was home. So did they tell you why they're taking the stuff out of your plane?"

"Yeah, and it makes a lot of sense. Besides, it's not like the US is ever gonna get that crap back. If they wanna use it to retrieve some lost, forbidden object from a cursed tomb, I say let 'em. It's a damn better use for it than what it was goin' to do."

"I agree with that." said Drake. "Well, I ought to get going now."

"Alright. Hey, what's your name? I never asked on the plane."

"Drake Burgess. But down here, they call me Drake Torvosaurus."

"A dinosaur name, huh? Do I get one?"

"You have to earn it."

"How'd you earn yours?"

"It nearly killed me." smiled Drake. "But that's not a requirement. You know, they let you ride the dinosaurs, if the animals will let you."

"Really?" asked Kevin, his face lighting up. "That would be somethin'."

"It is something. Get well soon, corporal, the sooner you do the sooner they'll let you ride one. Oh, and next time you meet someone who knows English, ask them about Spirit and Guardian animals."

"You can't tell me?"

"I have to go. But if no one's told you what's going on by the time I get back, I'll tell you. Or maybe I won't. If no one's talked to you in that long there'll be something really wrong with you."

"There's nothin' wrong with me."

"'Course there's not." said Drake. "It's the natives that can get screwy. Prehistorcia makes much better decisions than the genetics floating around in it, you'll find."

*****

For the expedition, there were so many volunteers people actually had to be turned away. They brought Nemeli the Neovenator, healed from her Golaran ordeal a year ago, and grown a few inches since. She would be a necessity on the trip, because, as Al always said, it comes in handy to have a carnosaur on your side.

Nemeli was light-blue, and nearly seven metres long. She was from a branch of Allosaurids, from the middle Jurassic jungles of Europe, meaning she had no feathers, unlike most other carnosaurs. The first appearance of feathers was in the Triassic, but they didn't become common until the Early Cretaceous. Tyrannosaurs and dromaeosaurs had feathers, but it seemed to vary with earlier animals.

They also brought Tenethex, Drake's Triceratops that shared a connection with him, and Dazz's and Dave's terror birds, since they shared a similar connection. Every Hekeni going that had such an animal was bringing it, meaning that there was about one animal to every two people, and there was an astonishingly high number of eighty people going. That's not much on earth, but to the Hekeni it was the largest force they had assembled since all the tribes united to destroy the Mayztecs.

Tom, the co-pilot from the plane crash over a year ago, had joined, though he was not training his own personal animal, but in fact helped everyone else trained theirs, as he was now highly interested in prehistory, but did not want to limit himself to learning about one animal.

All the paleontologists were going, along with much of the old Hekeni crew that had picked them up a year ago, such as Al, Harry, and Dazz; and there were some they knew from other experiences, such as David Karoo, whom the Hekeni knew as Dave Iguanodon.

Kevin, the soldier, wanted to go, but his leg was still in poor condition. He would have to stay.

Gary, meanwhile, was going to as many temples as possible, but in three weeks he would leave the expedition and return to the Hekeni village to watch his Stegosaurus hatch and train it.

Among the animals were three Triceratops, two Utahraptors, five Deinonychus, four Dire Wolves, the Neovenator, two Kentrosaurus, two Ankylosaurus, four Styracosaurus (three, if you did not count John's), six terror birds, a Stegosaurus, five Parasaurolophus, one Lambeosaurus, two Hadrosaurus, a Plateosaurus, three Ornithomimus, a prosauropod Drake couldn't identify on sight, a woolly rhino, and three Coelurus (see-lure-us), making their total number of animals forty-seven, which was three under the limit set by Al, or it would be too hard to control them through the trip.

They also packed military equipment, mostly things to be carried in bags. However, he saw a Styracosaurus (a Ceratopsian with six horns around the frill and one large nose horn) hooked up to a military jeep John had placed in 'neutral', and two Parasaurolophus tugging a second one, and each jeep held more supplies.

Ahrzi, Drake's Utahraptor pet, would be looked after by Al's wife and children. Al's wife was a surprisingly beautiful blonde, and the very first time Drake looked at her, he turned to Al and said:

"It's because you're second-in-command, isn't it?"

Al, of course, had denied it, saying that he also had brains, and skill with animals, and was funny, and gave Drake a whole list of things, until he said:

"You forgot modesty. And I was only joking, Al." and Drake was left feeling a bit ashamed.

Al had three children, though his wife had been pregnant four times, his second-born being killed of a disease at a very young age. Mortality was high in Prehistorcia, though if one could make it past childhood, survival rates increased dramatically.

Meanwhile, as the final preparations were being made, John dropped his little Styracosaurus, and tied a rope just behind his frill, so he wouldn't lose him. Hekeni rope was primitive, but strong. Al loaded the last of the provisions onto the backs of the dinosaurs.

"Alright, we're all packed. Let's go!"

He then placed a hat on his head, a bone ring with leaves stuck around it like a crown, and the tooth of a large carnivore at the front. Drake had seen him wear it only once before, in the forest and Drought Lands, the day they met and led the plane survivors to the camp. He wasn't exactly sure what it was for.

"Why do you wear that thing, Al?" asked Drake.

"This? It is a symbol. It means I am the Sekka, or leader, of this group, and it tells anyone we may meet that they are to talk to me."

"Is it a possibility we'll run into other tribes?"

"Not a possibility, a certainty. The Zolgaf will be our first stop!"

"Well, why the tooth? Where did it come from?"

"This?" he pointed to the tooth. "This belonged to Nemeli. You see the Sekka always wears a piece of or the likeness of his or her spirit animal on their head. They can wear their spirit animal, guardian animal, or family guardian on their Sekka-rings."

"So what are the leaves for?"

"Decoration." he replied.

"No spiritual meaning behind the leaves at all, eh?"

"Humans need to show power here, too, and if leaves makes it look more impressive or imposing, leaves will be added. I'll add bark and paint it, too, but both these things are itchy. Believe me, an impressive hat isn't impressive if the man wearing it is always scratching his head."

Alol, the Hekeni historian, approached Al. Drake listened as hard as he could as the man spoke Hekeni to Al.

"We need to leave, Sekka Al, the Hekeni are restless."

"Yes, of course." Al replied in like language. He replied to Drake in English. "Alol just says—"

"Get going. I heard."

Al smiled. "Hey, you're getting better! Well, if you heard him, we have to obey him!"

He sent a gesture down to a Neanderthal, Dazz, who had long black hair, a thick beard, and very little chin. His eyebrows were prominent, but his intelligence did not reflect his caveman appearance, being among the smartest humans Drake had ever known. Dazz nodded, and blew a gigantic horn of carved bone, setting the group in motion.

Chapter 5 – Zolgaf of the Thunder Marshes

The expedition set out, and Drake saw a forty-eighth animal, a Nemicolopterus (nem-ee-call-op-tear-us), a small, sparrow-sized pterosaur, that Al would probably use to send messages. Al was leading the group on the back of his Neovenator, Nemeli, a light-blue, seven metre, twenty-two-foot-long Allosaurid. Her final length would eventually reach to twenty-three feet, but she still had some growing to do. This time next year, she would reach adulthood.

Tenethax, the dark-green Triceratops Drake was riding on, was already fully grown at nine metres, or thirty feet long. Al moved down the eastward path, towards the Thunder Marshes. Drake wondered vaguely why they were going to there. They came to a place where a pathway split to the south, which Drake knew went to the Hekeni Swamp, where he liked to hang out sometimes. They passed it, taking the east fork. That path would take them past the Zolgaf Tribe; he didn't know much, but he knew where this path went by now.

The Hekeni lived in the Cretaceous Forest, where primitive trees and conifers grew abundantly. They lived in the shadow of the Tyrannosaurus Mountains, and when one climbed a mountain and looked north, they would see the Great Northern Shore, the northernmost border of their realm. Beyond it, no one knew what existed. Perhaps it was another continent of this vast world, or perhaps it was endless, and you sailed it forever. Or, as another myth stated, if you sailed far and long enough, you would touch on a southern shore, just south of the Great Mountains, which were the southern borders of the land.

Of course Drake found the new continent to be the most likely, especially since Prehistorcia, big though it was, was nowhere near large enough to hold a breeding population of every species that ever existed, even though it seemed to at times. The land would be overcrowded, bursting at the seams. The Hekeni, once they began receiving Above-worlders, began to theorize that, too.

Drake saw the Hekeni Elder, Alol, walking next to Al, riding an Ornithomimus. Drake didn't realize the Ornithomimus could carry a human, but Alol looked quite light, and the dinosaur was bigger than an ostrich (with more feathers, too).

"Hey, Harry." Drake called. Harry was leading his Ankylosaurus, stuffed with bags that seemed to be no burden at all to it. Of all the Hekeni, Harry had looked the most bookish, with freckles, short red hair, no beard, and a thin nose for an equally thin face and body. He had crashed with Al in 1969, when he was seven.

"What is it?"

"Who is Alol, anyway?"

"Alol Albertaceratops is the official Hekeni historian. He's an asset on this trip as he reads Mayztec, speaks Golaran, Yaxog, Trontoll and the language of the Mountain Tribe. He knows all the history, having studied old records and inscriptions, and is the current true owner of four dinosaurs and one Quetzalcoatlus. Only that one is with him on his trip, however."

"Does he know any Earth languages?" asked Drake.

"I'm not sure." he wrinkled his brow. "I don't think so."

"So he doesn't learn the one language that'll actually come in handy." said Drake.

"I suppose not." smirked Harry.

Alol looked backwards at them. Drake thought he heard, but a moment later he called for Harry.

"He knows your name?"

"I learned all my history from him. We're good friends. He's probably just looking for something."

Harry went over and began speaking to Alol in Hekeni, both of them were smiling, and Harry gave a small chuckle. Drake took to looking at the view, watching for interesting creatures. There was almost always something to see, though in a group this big it was hard, as most of the animals avoided groups this big. He remembered back to the Hekeni Swamp.

He had been there twice. It was full of reeds, and pine trees, and Drake had found a quiet, dry spot under a willow to sit. It was more like a wetland than a swamp, yet had the qualities of both. He remembered finding a Venus flytrap at one point, and fed an annoying horsefly to it. He had seen plenty of things there – a moose, birds, pterosaurs, and there was a herd of Hadrosaurs that made a home there. They were just small Secrenosaurus, no more than five metres, fifteen feet long, but the Hekeni did not have a breeding population of them, so Drake was interested because it was the only time he could experience the creatures. He had been making a mental list of every prehistoric animal he'd seen, and so far, for all the names on his list, there were more gaps to be filled.

The group walked on for a whole day, and finally set up camp at the edge of the Thunder Marshes. Below was a vast, swampy rainforest that extended for a very long way. To the north was a tall ridge of basalt, with more of the Thunder Marshes growing atop it, and to the immediate south, the Stegosaurus Mountains loomed over them. Where the Stegosaurus Mountains ended in the east, the Zolgaf would be camped under.

As the sun set, Drake saw their Nemicolopterus, which was scarlet red with rings of blue, fly off east, down into the Thunder Marshes. Al must have sent a message to the Zolgaf to alert them of their arrival.

A massive fire was started, and the eighty-four people and forty-seven animals gathered around it. Alol was staring out into the distance, somewhere northeast, with longing. Drake guessed that the first temple was in that direction. Drake sat next to Jane and put his arm around her. He looked back towards the Hekeni village, and wondered vaguely what was happening there.

Jane was not the classical description of pretty, and in fact, she was quite plain. Brown, wavy hair, hazel eyes, and nothing truly remarkable except her mind. But to Drake, she was the most beautiful girl in the universe. And her smile... that could always melt him.

Gary approached them. He was young, only twenty-two, a graduate student from Ontario who had gotten lost with them. He had looked rather geeky, but a year with the Hekeni had helped that, as did his very thin beard. He had otherwise a weak jaw, and shaggy brown hair.

"Going to miss the village?" he asked.

"It seems like my home now." said Drake. "Especially since I began training dinosaurs."

Jane shrugged. "We'll be back."

"I know what you mean. I feel like earth was just a dream, a distant memory, and that this place is all that is or ever was. Do you get that feeling?"

"I know that feeling." agreed Drake. "So you get a Stegosaurus now, eh?"

"I hope so! That'd be cool, wouldn't it? Oh, except you already know."

"I don't know how it feels with a Stegosaurus. I know that Ahrzi will grow up in a few years, I have no idea how long a Stegosaurus will take."

"Sooner than a sauropod, later than a therapod." he guessed.

"Well, there are only three orders of dinosaurs: Ornithopods, Sauropods, and Therapods. Why don't you try guessing how long it will take compared to other Ornithopods, hmm?"

"Well, it might be relatively the same length for all of them." said Gary. "I can't really imagine a Triceratops or a Parasaurolophus growing up any faster or slower than a Stegosaurus. But I could be wrong."

"I'll have to raise a Parasaurolophus soon. Maybe mine will grow faster than yours." replied Jane.

"Well, we'll see, won't we?" said Drake. "But Ahrzi will beat all of yours. Dromaeosaurs grow *fast.*"

"Not only that, he was hatched first. I'll have to leave you in a month. I wish I didn't have to, that'll be your second adventure I've missed."

"Gary, you were the *reason* for my first one. You took that journey too, you were just too upset to enjoy it. Won't it feel good to leave us for a better reason this time?" asked Jane.

"Yeah, that's true. It does feel good not to be the thing dragging you around Prehistorcia this time."

"You know, I heard that the Hekeni believe that once something is started, it must be finished." said Drake.

"I believe that's something parents told their kids so they didn't quit halfway through. But I never committed to the whole quest, and that's what saves me from that particular spiritual belief. I'm also safe because no lives are endangered if you quit." replied Gary.

Drake sighed. "I suppose that's true. But these are Extinction Stones. It is the one and only thing the Hekeni will throw all their beliefs away for. I'm worried, to be honest. With all this religious power guiding them, something is bound to go wrong."

"Look at mister negativity." said Gary.

"You have to have faith in the Hekeni." added Jane.

"The Hekeni have faith, and these Extinction Stones govern it. That should be a concern."

"Well, give it a while. They might surprise you."

"That's what I'm afraid of."

*****

The next morning, the Hekeni moved into the Thunder Marshes, a green, lush land with giant insects, and a 33% oxygen atmosphere, from the Carboniferous period, where the Zolgaf made a living. Drake wondered when and how the Zolgaf had come around. Were they a new rebel tribe that emerged to fight the Mayztecs? He didn't know. Perhaps he would ask Harry; he seemed to know everything about Prehistorcia's history.

The Zolgaf met them at noon, while clouds were starting to form over their heads. Living in the Thunder Marshes was like living on the coast – if it wasn't raining, it was going to.

The marshes were high at this time of year, and the trees were partially underwater, and the hills where foliage grew were small islands. But the Zolgaf lived up in the trees, in a series of interconnected huts, with wooden rope bridges between them.

"Did it look like this when you were here?" asked Drake to Steven.

"No, the water was lower. But the huts are the same."

The Zolgaf huts were now only as high as two men, and their village was at the edge of a large pool, beneath which swam a powerful amphibian; it looked like a crocodile, but it had the skin and snout of a frog, and the tail of a newt. Steven knew it was an Eogyrinus, which he had met last year.

"We trained the Eogyrinus as a special favour for the Zolgaf." explained Al. "We don't have a breeding population of any amphibian except those toads you have as pets on the Above-world. So it was hard."

"Why'd you do it for them?" asked Drake.

"They help us out. They have their own skills."

"Which are?"

"They keep captive scorpions, though they're nowhere near as tame as ours. They use them for poisoned arrows, and throwing at enemy tribes."

"They throw them?" asked Drake.

"Yes, by their stingers. Don't worry, the scorpions are well cared-for, and won't sting their keepers. It's a bit like zoo animals, which attack or are scared of all but their keepers."

"Can I see the scorpion cages?" asked Drake.

"Depends on what they say."

Al pointed up. Two Zolgaf men were lowering down a rope ladder. Drake recognized them as the species *Homo ergaster*, which, now Drake saw them, looked different from the *Homo erectus* they were now thought to be on Earth. Of course, the difference was very slight, but undoubtedly there. Drake couldn't blame the scientists for thinking this, as there was probably very little difference in the skeleton.

What perplexed Drake is that due to a difference in the neck, a species of Albertosaurus had been reclassified as a species of Gorgosaurus, when, for all the differences in sizes, shapes, and appearances, dogs were still all *Canis familiaris*. Meanwhile, species with such differences as Stygimoloch and Dracorex were now being thought of as juvenile Pachycephalosaurus, which Drake knew to be false, because he had seen Pachycephalosaurus of all ages growing up in the Hekeni village. He did admit, however, that Dracorex and Stygimoloch might be the same species. He hadn't quite developed the Hekeni knack for telling species at a distance.

Drake climbed the ladder. He wondered what the animals were going to do, and he looked down to see the Hadrosaurs settling into the pond, and begin eating the reeds. The two prosauropods did that, too. The heavier animals stayed on dry land, and he watched several Zolgaf tribesmen bring the Hekeni supplies for a tent to watch over them.

When Drake reached the top, he saw the Nemicolopterus on Harry's shoulder. Hekeni were being sent to different cabins and the military equipment, which consisted of two jeeps, each with a large gun, being towed by two Hadrosaurs and a Styracosaurus, were left on the ground until morning.

As the sun set, Drake was taken to see the giant scorpions. They were in a large, circular cabin. Lining the walls were bars and pens, each of which held one scorpion, a clay water dish, some foliage, and a food bowl, some of which were still full of things such as dead Meganeura (a giant dragonfly), giant cockroaches and even small amphibians. Things they would normally hunt in the wild.

There were some forty or fifty scorpions, the smallest being only a foot long, the longest being just a little shorter than Drake was tall. In the middle of the hut the tree trunk jutted through the roof and into the sky. But of course, Drake reminded himself, it wasn't a tree, just a tree-like ancestor of ferns.

"Are the scorpions always kept here?" asked Drake, who thought it might be a bit cruel.

"They kill ech odder unless alone." said the Zolgaf.

"No, I understand that, but are they always up in this cabin?"

"They take care uv. They happy."

Drake didn't ask how to measure a scorpion's happiness, but he was sure the Zolgaf could do it, if they had frequent friendly contact with the Hekeni.

"They here fo wet sesson." said the Zolgaf.

"You only keep them here for the wet season?" asked Drake. "Where are they when the water is lower?"

"In feld."

"Feld?"

"Feld. Big geen place."

"Oh, field." Drake assumed that since they killed each other, they were kept in larger, separate pens when the water was lower. Not that they looked too neglected in the cabin. When Drake looked around, he saw two keepers, one with a large, smelly, woven basket of dead insects and amphibians, and the second with a clay pitcher containing water. Right now they were sitting on the only bench in the cabin, built in a half-circle around the tree.

"You should really learn Hekeni, you know." said Jane, entering behind him.

"I understand it."

"But can you speak it?" she asked. "I'm sure the Zolgaf speak it quite well."

Drake rolled his eyes and looked into one scorpion's pen. Jane moved next to him and peered in as well. It was over a metre, or four feet long, with a large stinger.

"It's shiny green, not black or yellow like modern scorpions." Jane remarked.

"I suppose it's because they're so big they need camouflage to hide in the undergrowth. Everything was big in the Carboniferous."

"Probably." she agreed.

Drake and Jane left the scorpions when the feeders got up and began refilling the empty bowls, and climbed across a wooden bridge that led to a cabin that was supported by three trees (true trees this time, not fern ancestors). Soon, Drake saw why – in the middle there was an ornately carved hollow stone cylinder in the centre from which flames erupted. Most of the Hekeni were sitting there. Once again, Harry was surrounded by the paleontologists, plane survivors, and some Hekeni, telling a story. He saw Drake and called him over.

"Drake, Jane, you're just in time! Don't you want to know what temple we're going to visit?"

Drake sat down next to Jane. "Will this be a long story?"

"No, not long at all. Some people just had questions, and other people agreed with those questions, and now I have a crowd here to answer it to. I actually was not planning on telling a story today."

"Okay, then, get on with it."

Harry began in Hekeni, and Drake was able to understand most of it, and fill in the gaps of what he didn't: "We are visiting the tomb of –

yes, you're hearing this right – Emperor Zolgaf." Harry paused for effect, but it proved unnecessary. "I know, odd, isn't it? But let me tell you – originally, the Mayztecs sent thousands of soldiers to the Thunder Marshes, and those few hundred that made it through set up a camp here, in this very spot. It was a convenient outpost, as it gave the Mayztec kings access to scorpion and snake poison, and a good vantage point to spy on the Hekeni, one of the three most troublesome rebel groups at the time."

"What were the other two?" asked John, in English.

"Golaran and Mountain, but they were both close enough to be spied on from the Mayztecs own empire." Harry replied, still in Hekeni. "There were plenty of other reasons to be there, too. For three thousand years, they followed Mayztec orders, and we Hekeni waged war after war on them, and they stayed there even though, as years passed, the Yaxog and Fertile River tribes became more troublesome then us. Well, after a few thousand years, the Zolgaf felt ignored, and so Emperor Zolgrog sent them five hundred *Homo ergaster* soldiers, but it was a token gesture. They remained ignored. Well, along came his son, Emperor Zolgaf.

"Emperor Zolgaf not only felt the need to send a peace delegation, but he went himself. He talked it over with the Zolgaf, though at the time they were not called that. It was eventually agreed there would be two kingdoms, united against the rebels, the Mayztec to the south and the new empire, calling themselves the Zolgaf, to the north. It was a nice idea. Emperor Zolgaf was actually one of the better rulers."

"What happened, then?" asked Drake. "You didn't destroy the Zolgaf when the Mayztecs fell. Did they plead forgiveness? Did they switch sides at the rebellion?"

"No, nothing so cowardly. A couple hundred years passed, and things looked very bad for the rebels. Emperor Zolgaf goes and has a heart attack, and the Zolgaf Tribe places him in a tomb, not too far from here. But along comes his grandson, after the short-lived period of Zolgaf's son, to give us the advantage."

"What happened to his son?"

"We're not sure, but we're pretty sure murder by his own son. Emperor Zagog comes along, and begins to see the Zolgaf Empire as a threat, when none was present. Those were the two things Zagog was not known for: trust and kindness. He was a low point for the Mayztecs, even in their own history.

"Anyway, Zagog sends massive armies to the Zolgaf, which stand no chance of holding them off. The Zolgaf see them, and they know what it was for, because they had received a note asking for surrender. Not that it was really an option, as Zagog would have destroyed them anyway. No sooner did they see the army then they sent their fastest runner to the Hekeni. He was nearly killed on sight, if it weren't for the fact he was alone, out of breath, and unusually skilled at diplomacy.

"He begged for our help. Once he recovered, he literally got down on his knees and begged us, and on behalf of the Zolgaf he swore allegiance with us and whatever rebel tribe would accept it. Now, obviously, our better nature took over, as the Zolgaf are still around today. We sent two thousand Hekeni warriors and eight hundred animals to their aid, fifty of them large, carnivorous Allosaurs and Tyrannosaurs. The Yaxog and Solg Tribes sent help also, and it was with them the battle took place.

"It was one of the bloodiest battle in Mayztec Era history, up there with the defeat of the Mayztecs, and the Great War, which lasted four generations of kings, when the Mayztecs greatly expanded their empire. It was, however, the second-bloodiest in Hekeni history. We won, obviously, but barely, with one thousand, three hundred and sixty-one Hekeni returning home dead on the backs of the two-hundred and seventy-four remaining animals. The Zolgaf, greatly shrunk, concentrated here, further away from their tomb.

Nevertheless, they keep Zolgaf's name, for he was kind to them, even though his grandson was not. And here his tomb remains, unopened for seven hundred years, holding an Extinction Stone."

"What happened to Zagog?" asked Jane.

"After the battle? He was humiliated and lost some five thousand soldiers and a northern colony, but nothing else. He lived another twelve years, until he was assassinated by his own son. He probably had it coming. And in case you're wondering, Zagog's son went on an expedition to the Thunder Marshes to try and win the Zolgaf back, but he never returned. He died childless, and they used a cousin to replace him, though the dynasty would end with him. After Zagog, the dynasty could not hold the kingdom, and opened it for a new dynasty to take the throne." Harry turned to some of the Zolgafs that were listening. "We still don't know if it was the Zolgafs or the land that killed the last heir of the Zolgaf family."

"And you probably never will." smiled one of them in reply.

Chapter 6 – Through the Thunder Marshes

The next morning, as the sun was rising in a very cloudy sky, the Zolgaf refilled their provisions and gave them a map to the tomb. It was several kilometres north, and would take them two nights to get there. The Zolgaf were just as excited as the Hekeni to find the Extinction Stones, and hoped, no doubt, that they might get one instead of the original six tribes. It wasn't a baseless hope, as no one really wanted to go to the Golerans to give their Stone back to them, and many doubted that they really deserved it.

John set down his baby Styracosaurus in the back of one of the jeeps, the one being pulled by two Parasaurolophus, though those were still wading in the water with the other Hadrosaurs, prosauropods, and some Ceratopsians. The Eogyrinus swam around them harmlessly.

"Hey, John, that second species of prosauropod... do you know what it is?" asked Drake.

"Oh, sure. It's definitely *Lufengosaurus magnus*, native to China, early Jurassic, six metres or twenty feet long. I remember in the 90's I was on the Canada-China joint fossil project."

"Learn a lot from them?" asked Drake.

"Yeah. I was young, back then, hadn't made a name for myself." he began scratching his Styracosaurus behind the frill.

"What are you going to name him?"

"Mittens."

Drake worked very hard to suppress a laugh. "Really?"

"No. I was actually trying to figure out which name suits a Styracosaurus. I could call him anything. I narrowed it down to Bob and Rasputin."

"Are you telling a joke again?"

"Yes. I asked Al what the Hekeni word for 'spiky collar' is." said John. "He said: '*Edfellar*', but told me not to use it. Apparently the Hekeni word for a Styracosaurus is *Edfellar*."

"So you'd be naming him 'Styracosaurus', then?"

"Yeah. What about Horny?"

"Sure, there's nothing to make fun of there." said Drake sarcastically.

"Alright, fine, what name do *you* suggest if you're so good at this?"

"I don't know, but please don't name the poor thing after a tsar. Give him a name that you think suits him."

"Technically Rasputin wasn't a tsar."

"Whatever."

John looked at his Styracosaurus smiling up at him. It was brown with flecks of orange. He scratched it under its chin, which the Styracosaurus really seemed to enjoy. The Styracosaurus lay on its side, very happy.

"I know! I'll name you Sam."

"Sam Styracosaurus." said Drake. "Well, it's better than Mittens."

"Sam stays." John stated. "He looks comfortable here on the seat, too, so I think I'll leave Sam here for our trip." he took the end of the rope and tied it to the bars that made up the cargo area. The jeeps were opened to the air, so there was a small danger in him jumping out. The much scarier feature was the massive machine gun on the roof, and Drake was sure the Hekeni, thankfully, did not know what it was or how to use it.

Two Hekeni hooked up the jeep to the two Parasaurolophus, and moved it out. They walked north for a while, but turned northeast, using a little-known path. Eventually, they came to a river they would have to cross. It was wide, and deep. Many dinosaurs would not make it across.

However, the Zolgaf had prepared the Hekeni for this. Out of the back of the cars the Hekeni brought out cut wood, and an assembled boat. It was a flat raft big enough to carry Tenethax, which was the longest, and probably heaviest, animal they brought. Tenethax made it across with Drake, Jane, and four other people, and they sent the raft back for Nemeli, followed soon by the rest of the tribe.

It took them over an hour, but soon both of the jeeps, all dinosaurs, and all Hekeni were across. They continued along the riverbed, where the forest was thinnest.

It was muddy on the banks of the river in the high season, and in the tropical Carboniferous climate, it began to rain again. Drake looked up as lightning flashed across the sky, and thunder rumbled in a few seconds later. The terrain was getting tricky, and many times they had to move the logs so the jeeps could pull through.

After an hour, on the muddy riverbank in a downpour, the two Parasaurolophus and the Styracosaurus tugging the two-ton jeeps stopped. They looked back – the cars were stuck deep in the mud.

"Damn." said Harry. "Anyone know how to work these things?"

"Here, unhook the dinosaurs, I'll drive." said John. "Drake, you take the other one."

They unhooked the dinosaurs. Drake and John got into the two jeeps, started them, flicked on the four-by-four, and drove out. John turned to Drake:

"Welcome to Humans: polluting everywhere we go!" he said.

The jeeps splashed forward, and sprayed mud accidentally all over Alol, the Hekeni elder. Now that the jeeps were on solid ground, the two of them turned them off and got out, the gears set to neutral. Drake went to Alol.

"Sorry!" he called back in English. "But look at it this way, you're used to mudslinging!"

Alol smiled, and Drake smiled back. The Hekeni moved forward and hooked the jeeps back up to the dinosaurs, and kept moving.

As the day ended, they set up a camp at the riverside. There had been no animals all day, as they had been avoiding the large crowd.

The Hekeni seemed to find food anyway, and with help, they started a fire despite the downpour. Drake went to sleep under the shelter around midnight.

*****

He dreamed that they had reached the temple. It was a massive Taj Mahal structure, overrun with vines and the centre bulb replaced by a glowing moon. Al pushed him forward, telling him to go first, and he entered into a dark, stone passageway with ancient runes inscribed all over the walls.

As he moved forward, with Al following, they came to the end of the hall in a large square room where Drake saw a pedestal that looked as though it had been made in Ancient Greece. The stone atop it was dark blue, as smooth as a marble, and the size of a bowling ball. When Drake approached it, it had an inner light. As soon as he touched it, the light went out, the temple disappeared, and a great face appeared before him. It was Al! He looked down at Drake, and Drake looked at the Stone. Al reached for it, and as he touched it, the Stone shattered in Drake's hands! Al suddenly grew as tall as a tree, a giant, even though Drake was sure the roof of the temple was much too low.

"You've ruined the Stone!" yelled Al in a thunderous voice. "You've destroyed Prehistorcia!"

He turned around to run, and there was Nemeli, who he had not noticed before. She looked down at him, and because it was a dream, when she spoke Drake felt no surprise.

"You've shattered Prehistorcia!" she said in with voice in a clear tone that it might have come from a woman on the street. "You let Al touch the Stone! Al was not meant to have the Stone! No one was! They were lost for a reason! And you've retrieved it for him!"

"You belong to Al!" yelled Drake. "I didn't know!"

This time it was Al that yelled: "You know nothing! You are an outsider, an intruder! If you know what's best for this land you'll go back and never return!"

"I can't! I can't return!" he yelled.

He looked back at Nemeli, who was gone. He turned around again, and Al was gone, too. He was floating in darkness. A voice spoke to him:

"You are here for a reason. Jane was only part of it. You must believe, Drake. Don't let me down!"

"Who are you?" asked Drake. But he never found out.

*****

Drake was doused suddenly with water. He looked up – it was sunrise, and the rain had subsided. Al was standing over him with a wooden bucket, smiling at him. Drake could barely remember his dream. Was it a message? Or was he worried? Could he somehow break the Stones, and be banished forever?

"Time to get up! We're two days from the temple!" said Al cheerfully.

"Did you have any weird dreams last night?"

"No." replied Al. "Why?"

"No reason. I'm, just anxious I guess."

He looked around. Alol was creeping up on an Ichthyostega that was sitting on a log over the river. As he was about to grab it, the amphibian lazily hopped off into the river, swimming upstream. Alol, meanwhile, had pounced on nothing, and fell in himself.

"Nice catch!" called Drake. "How far away is the temple?"

"At least another night." said Al.

Drake got up, tired and sore. He decided to ask John about his dream, though he wasn't sure what the paleoecologist could do. He explained his dream.

"Well, there are a few theories on dreams." said John. "Some say they're visions of the future, which I doubt in your case. Sometimes, there are hidden messages, but science tells us it's just your brain spitting out familiar images and mixing it in with worries, hopes, and sometimes your own imagination. Dreams themselves are a tricky phenomenon in science, one I didn't much care to learn about."

"So you think my dream was just a random spewing of images?" asked Drake.

"Nothing else it can be." said John. "But... why not tell Jane about this?"

He shrugged. "You're more..." he struggled for a word.

"I get it." sighed John. He was more of a parent.

Drake dropped the conversation. However, if he had talked to a Hekeni, he might realize that there was profoundly religious significance in his dream, at least there would be to them. But then again, the Hekeni were very spiritual about everything.

"On another subject, though, do you know the legend of the Mayan underworld?" asked John.

"No."

"Well, they believed in a place called Xibalba, that existed underground and could be accessed by deep pools, holes, or caves."

"So?"

"Oh, come on, you had a friend in the archaeology department! Xibalba, the underworld of the Mesoamerican civilizations. They believed portals to Xibalba were found in caves! I think perhaps so many of their people got lost down here through those caves that it started a whole new concept of religion!"

"That's a little bit of a stretch, isn't it?"

"Is it? Perhaps 'Xibalba' has a similar meaning. Maybe it evolved from a word in very early Central American society? I'm telling you, it could have completely changed Mesoamerican religion!"

"Well, we'll see when we get to the temple, won't we?" asked Drake, not believing a word of it.

*****

They got up and moved along the riverside, continuing north-northeast to King Zolgaf's temple. Harry said they would find the old road soon. Drake looked into the river, and saw a large, innocent-looking log that Drake suspected was a crocodile. When he looked closer, he saw that it was much larger than any crocodile he'd seen before. It was almost as if it was a Sarcosuchus.

Then he realized it very well could be. He moved further from the bank.

"I think I saw a Sarcosuchus there!" he told Jane.

"Really? I've always wanted to see one!" she hurried to the riverbank, with the total opposite reaction of what Drake was expecting. She came back in a few seconds. "You're right, it is one! I'm going to go watch it!"

Drake sighed. "Love you, too." he mocked.

"Well, why tell me about it if I'm not supposed to see it?" she called back.

That night, Drake lay down again, next to Jane. They smiled at each other, and they fell asleep looking into each other's eyes. This night, he hoped to have no dreams. But, no sooner had he gone to sleep, than a lizard was trying to burrow into his cheek. Odd dream, he thought, and it felt so real.

Then he realized it *was* real. He sat up in alarm. It was late at night, and the stars shone brightly. He looked around at the source of the sensation.

"Ahrzi!" he exclaimed, looking to his right.

There was Ahrzi the Utahraptor, covered in downy protofeathers, looking up at Drake, looking immensely proud of himself. Jane woke up from his exclamation.

"What is it?" she asked in a tired voice.

"It's Ahrzi! He must have followed us here! You clever little dromaeosaur, you must have snuck out right underneath their noses! Forget Utah Thief, you could steal much more valuable things!" he turned to Jane. "He must have scent glands in his nose, making him better than a bloodhound!"

"We're not that hard to follow." said Jane. Looking back the way they had come, he saw the trees cleared and the undergrowth trampled.

"True."

"He must have missed you!" she said in that voice people use when they see a puppy. "Come here, little guy. You must be starving!"

"Clever little guy, isn't he?" said Drake. "I should get him some food."

He walked over to the bags on Tenethax and pulled out some dried meat used to feed the other dromaeosaurs at their mealtimes. He stripped a small piece off.

"Here, eat this." he said, throwing it at him.

Ahrzi jumped high and caught it in his mouth. He began gobbling it down voraciously. He finished in mere seconds, and started chirping for more. His chirping was high-pitched and annoying.

"Alright, Ahrzi, shut up, I'll find some more!"

But people were already beginning to wake up. The adult dromaeosaurs opened their eyes and looked as though they wanted to kill whatever was making that sound. Al got up, and took one look at Ahrzi. He looked towards Drake, disappointed.

"Drake, did you bring Ahrzi along?"

"No, he followed me!" Drake protested.

"Well, control him!"

"He's hungry! He hasn't eaten anything in days, I'd imagine!"

Al growled. He took out the whole slab of meat and tossed it down at the Utahraptor's feet. He chirped happily, and began eating, though the meat slab was bigger than him. Al and everyone else went back to sleep. One Deinonychus came over and laid down next to the infant.

There was a collective sense of parenthood, even towards other species, Drake thought. Though it was probably the Hekeni training that did it. He looked through the bags and found a thin rope. He tied it around Ahrzi's neck.

"Is that really necessary? Obviously he'll follow you." said Jane.

"Now at least I know where he is." said Drake. "What do we do with him, Al?"

Al rolled over. When Drake asked again, he sat up. "Well, it's one more mouth to feed. But obviously he'll have to come with us for the whole trip. It seems impossible to separate him from you. Oh well, if he was able to follow us, he'll be able to stay with us. Goodnight."

"What if we—?"

"He's coming with us. Now goodnight!"

Chapter 7 – The Temple of Emperor Zolgaf

When they got up the next morning, there wasn't a long walk ahead until they reached the temple, but it was still a hard task through the rain and thunder. Every time lightning struck, an explosion was triggered, but luckily no bolt had struck near their path, or they would have to turn around until the fire stopped.

Ahrzi was on a leash, but it wasn't as though he needed it. He followed Drake so close that the leash was always slack, and trotted at Drake's ankles looking pleased with himself.

Sam, on the other hand, John's Styracosaurus, was content to leave John to walk alone, as long as he wasn't left behind. He slept peacefully in the back of the military jeep. John asked Al if he was showing the signs of proper training yet, but Al said it was too soon to tell.

Now that John had named him, if he was being trained properly in the Hekeni way, Sam should know he was Sam in five to eight days, which was lengthened because Sam was a ceratopsian. For Ahrzi, he had to learn his name in three days. However, Drake liked to think Ahrzi was above-average in intelligence, and sure enough the Utahraptor learned his name in just one. When Drake tried to prove it, Al was ecstatic when Ahrzi seemed to respond to his name and ran for Drake. A few seconds later, though, it was apparent he was not running for Drake, but rather for John, eating a sandwich full of meat.

Soon, after an hour, they came to a stone platform on the edge of the river. It had grass growing between the cracks, and a stone pathway, also ancient-looking, tapered off into the trees.

"What is this?" Drake asked Harry.

"A sign we're not lost." he replied. "This, Drake, is the ancient stone pathway the Zolgaf would use to visit King Zolgaf's temple. They visited it regularly until the fall of the empire, and even so one or two

Zolgaf will take this trip to see their history for themselves. We're probably the biggest traffic to use it since the Search for the Extinction Stones seven hundred years ago."

Harry promptly turned the group away from the river and followed the path. It was narrow, and overgrown in many places. Drake felt like one of those explorers in adventure movies who was always hacking at plant matter with a machete.

Soon, they came to the base of what was clearly once a staircase leading up the hill. It was covered in a tangle of vines and jungle foliage, but it was still visible. On either side of the path at the base of the staircase was a small pillar of stone, which might have once been lit with fire. They walked to the top, some of the two-legged animals stumbling on the steps. Nemeli was especially clumsy, as her feet were too big for the tiny stairs.

When they reached the top, Drake saw another two things flanking the staircase. One was a rearing Arthropleura, a giant centipede-like bug that was longer than Drake. However only the legs and base were left, the top half, the one supposed to be rearing up, was laying in the trees a few steps away. On the other side was another Arthropleura statue, only this one was still in one piece. It was crumbling and overgrown with vines.

"We're getting close." said Al. passing Drake.

The path continued for a few more minutes, though to Drake it felt like an hour. Finally, they reached the end. In front of them was a narrow, steep cliff with water at the bottom, though it wasn't flowing very fast. It was high enough, however, that if Drake knelt down he could stick his hand in. The other side was not, in fact, another piece of land, but rather an island, oval-shaped, water flowing around it. Crossing from the shore to the island was a very old-looking, moss-covered rope bridge. What was on the island was the final resting place of Emperor Zolgaf.

The temple was nothing like the Taj Mahal. Actually, it was much more reminiscent of an Aztec or Mayan pyramid. It was low to the ground, and it was a step pyramid, going up layer by layer. On the centre of all four sides were what looked like staircases, all leading up to the top, which, on a Mayan pyramid, would end in a box with windows. On this one, however, it led up to a flat platform where a statue of a dromaeosaur sat perched. It literally sat, it a way that no real dromaeosaur would sit. Its legs were crouched down, as if to spring, with its tail long and straight, jutting out behind it. The top, however, was raised high, as if in a regal position, with the arms positioned together as though it was rubbing them together. The neck stretched way up, and the narrow snout looked down on them, as if surveying them.

"This is King Zolgaf's tomb?" asked Drake.

"Yep." said Harry.

Drake looked up at the dromaeosaur. The tip of the tail was missing, and one claw was snapped off, but otherwise it looked perfect, unspoiled, totally different from the temple itself. Worse than that, though, it was Aztec in design – proving John right.

"Why does it look so new?" asked Drake.

"Probably because the Mayztecs carved it and set it here after the temple was built." said Harry. "You see, they put it there hoping it would scare intruders away, because a spirit of one still existed there. The Mayztecs were brutal and powerful, but they were also deeply spiritual."

"So why a... what is that? Velociraptor? Dromaeosaurus?"

"It's a Velociraptor." said John. "I'd know it anywhere."

John would know it anywhere, Drake thought, having nearly been eaten by them last year. But John didn't blame them. They were just doing what predators were meant to do.

On the other side of the bridge was a very neat stone pathway, lined with vertical rocks with symbols and pictures on them. The whole island seemed clear of foliage, though small trees and ferns were coming up around it.

"What is that, ten, maybe twelve feet?" asked Drake.

"Fifteen." said Al.

"Well, I don't like that bridge. It's too rickety. Should we just swim for it?"

"No." said Harry. "Look."

He pointed in the river. Drake looked into the slow-moving surface. Swimming beneath were animals Drake had seen in aquariums and read about in books – a red-bellied piranha. More than one. There were hundreds of piranhas swimming below, in a deceptively calm state. They were barely moving now, but Drake knew that the moment he jumped in and began thrashing, the piranhas would frenzy, and strip his flesh from his bone. There was no way they could all make it across alive.

"Well... we'll have to use the bridge." Drake gulped.

"The animals will have to stay here." said Al. "Who's coming with us?"

"Al, I don't think any Prehistorcian-religion Hekeni should come." said Drake. "I have no religious connection to the Stone. I will not fight to keep it, though I will bring it back out to you. John, Jane, Steven, Gary and I should go. We won't kill each other over it."

Al looked back at some angry faces. "Well, he's right."

The Hekeni nodded in agreement, but still looked upset. Al turned to Drake.

"I will come."

"Al, no, you –"

"What? If I try to kill you, you can just hand me the Stone and it will be over." Al said, half-laughing.

Drake thought about it – he was right. "Fine, but Harry should come, too, and Alol, since they know the most about this place. And I trust Harry to stay sensible in a time of crisis."

"For the Extinction Stones?" asked Harry. "Well, that'll be tough, but I think I can keep my right mind."

"Good."

"Drake, a word of warning." said Al. "These Stones, while not valuable to you, have awesome power. Even someone not attached may be unwilling to give it up. We'll have to use extreme caution, and keep our wits about us. You might not believe in magic – but these Stones will blow your mind."

"Understood." said Drake, more scared and curious than before.

*****

After some disagreement of who should go first over a shoddy rope bridge made of moss-covered wood over piranha-infested waters, John stepped forward. He straightened his hat, and pulled up his mammoth-skin shoes. He began smoothing out his clothing.

"Just go!" yelled Drake.

He nodded, and put a confident step forward. He pressed down. The wood creaked, and he held his breath. It held. He stepped again, slowly, and though the wood creaked, it did not break.

After a few minutes, he called: "Alright, I'm across. Now you come, Drake!"

"I don't want to." he groaned, looking at the piranhas.

"That's okay, I'll go. There are worse things in this old world than a couple of piranhas." it was Dave Karoo who spoke, a man with light-brown, short hair, a slim face, blunt nose, and a patch of beard around his mouth. He was a British man who had gotten lost four years ago climbing the mountains of Switzerland, and found the Hekeni.

"Are you sure?" asked Drake.

"Yeah, mate. I'm sure the bridge is sturdier than it looks."

Dave moved forward. They all watched with their breath held until at last, step by step, Dave reached the other end. Drake turned to Tom.

"You want to go?"

"I ain't goin' anyway." he sa d.

Drake sighed. He moved forward. The wood beneath his feet felt as solid as concrete. He moved forward, gripping the mossy ropes tightly. He looked down – he was halfway there already! He moved forward still more carefully, skipping a couple of planks that had already fallen out earlier. There were just a few boards left between him and the island. He stopped.

"Huh. I guess this bridge is sturdier than it looks."

The bridge groaned. The plank cracked, and Drake was suddenly freezing cold. He swam to the island, and John and Dave pulled him out quickly. When he looked back, the piranhas were much closer, and very active.

"You jinxed it." said Dave.

"Yeah, I guess so."

Alol was next. He crossed easily, followed by Harry, and then Gary. Steven and Jane were both on the other side, but they didn't seem to go anywhere.

"Aren't you two coming?" asked Drake.

"I'm not. There'll be other temples." said Steven.

"I'm coming!" yelled Jane, "I just need to... uh... work up the nerve."

Al moved forward on the bridge, holding a sack. Jane followed him. They seemed okay, though Drake was a bit nervous when they reached the centre, which was dipped down further from the extra weight. But soon they were both across. Drake turned to face the temple.

The path here was overgrown with grass, but still plainly visible. The rocks lining it had pictures and symbols, one of a stickman fighting an Arthropleura, a pack of dromaeosaurs surrounding a clump of human children, a Tyrannosaur cornered against a wall by four humans holding spears, and a great fire coming from a crack in the ground scorching an invading army while the others bowed down before it. One was a man surrounded by Meganeura, some were of giant scorpions, and one had two spearmen fending off a giant crocodile. Drake assumed that these at least had to mean the journey they took.

"What are these?" asked Drake.

"Curses." said Al. "Most of them, anyway. But don't worry – the only real magic the Mayztecs ever possessed was engineering and the Extinction Stones. None of the curses on these stones have any effect."

"I don't believe temples have working curses anyway." said Drake.

Al looked at him with narrowed eyes. "You may not believe in curses. But last year you did not believe in this place. And six hundred years ago you did not believe in a North America. If truth were beliefs, then you'd be living in a flat Europe with the devil possessing all the left-handed people, all the non-Christians, all the women, and with the sun orbiting the Earth. Truth and belief are separate. You may not believe in the power of the Extinction Stones, Drake Burgess, but that doesn't mean it isn't there."

Drake was going to point out that it was Al's belief the Extinction Stones were made by the great god Prehistorcia himself, but thought better of it.

They reached the door. It was surrounded with symbols and the door itself held a large carving of a man with a pointed chin, a long hook nose, shoulder-length hair and beard, and holding a spear. Unlike the Velociraptor statue, this carving had never been painted, while the Velociraptor up top had faded paint over the feathers and snout.

"Was this Emperor Zolgaf?" asked Drake.

"Yep." said Harry.

Alol began reading the symbols out in the Hekeni language. Harry was the translator, and repeated Alol's words in English:

"Beware those who enter the tomb of King Zolgaf: the temple is protected by powerful curses you cannot comprehend. None but the gods may enter it, and not even the gods may remove treasure from it. Enter at your own risk, for those who enter do not return."

"What a load of bull." said Al

"Weren't you the one who was just saying curses can be real?" asked Drake.

"I also said that the Mayztecs had about as much magical talent as that rock over there. There is a terrible curse within, but it is the power of the Extinction Stone, not the Mayztecs."

"So how do we open it?" asked John.

Drake looked around. There had to be some clue. He found one stone, very close to the entrance. It was the painting of fire coming from the cracks, but it was a different version of it. This time people were bowing down to a great dromaeosaur that seemed to be made out of fire, and it was breathing fire on the enemy army, which was running. Was this some sort of clue that had something to do with the statue on top?

"Does this mean anything?" he asked.

Alol and Harry both looked at it. Drake knew there had been a campaign earlier to retrieve the Stones. How did they open it then? Did they open it then?

Drake walked up the pyramid to the statue of the Velociraptor at the top. It was much larger than a real-life Velociraptor, and Drake had to reach up to touch the snout. The picture depicted it with its mouth open. So, Drake moved to the chipped snout, with faded brown pain, and tried to open it. It didn't work. He tried squeezing the mouth, but it was no good. It was, expectedly, solid rock.

He tried getting down on both knees, as if to bow. He placed his hands on the front of the podium it was sitting on. Nothing. He actually bowed. He saw the Velociraptor from a new angle. And then he saw it – the way to open the temple! On the base of the curved claw were symbols. Drake grabbed the claw, and twisted it. The whole statue twisted, which seemed to turn a crank, and the door rolled open as the statue rotated!

"Drake, you did it!" called Al from below. He was halfway up the stairs.

Drake ran down excitedly, and saw that the great stone door was indeed open, moved by great iron chains coming from a hole in the roof. They moved into the passage. Al dropped the bag he was holding and pulled out four flashlights. Drake showed him how to work them, and soon the passage was filled with light. No sooner was it than an incredibly strong wind blew, nearly toppling them over, and the stone gate slammed closed.

"That would have put out torches." said Al. "With regular technology, we'd have been stuck here in the dark."

Drake shone the light around. To the right was a crack, filled with water. It looked like a puddle, but it was actually deep, with a crack going under the temple. There were several boomerang-shaped skulls of Diplocaulus (dip-low-call-us), a two-foot-long amphibian that resembled a lizard, but with a boomerang head. Drake assumed that they must have walked up here through the crack and then died.

John, meanwhile, shone his light around. There was a carving of a Velociraptor on the wall, lunging at them. One of the claws was actually sticking out. John pressed it.

The door opened a crack as a small stone tab poked out.

"Hey, I found the exit!" he said unnecessarily.

The door closed again when he took his hand off. They continued forward, but Alol stopped them. Drake, wondering why, moved his flashlight around.

On the floor just ahead was a series of connected tiles, small, each the size of pebbles, like a mosaic. However, to the far left, the floor had broken open to reveal a hole. Drake shone his light with Al into the hole, where he saw a human skeleton impaled on wooden spikes sticking out of the solid stone ground. Further inspection showed that the mosaic was actually thin, only one layer thick, nowhere near thick enough to support a human's weight.

"It's a trap." said Al.

"How long does this trap go until?" asked Gary.

John shone his light across the mosaic. The pebbled surface ended about three metres, or ten feet, away. After that was the solid brick used in regular construction again.

"Too far to jump." said Jane. "But the Mayztecs built this temple. How did they get out?"

"Maybe they built backwards?" suggested Gary.

"Not possible." said Jane, shaking her head. "They'd have to have some way across, or the floor wouldn't be built properly."

"You're right." said John. "Drake, look under. Is there some secret bridge or beam they built under that we can't see?"

Drake stuck his head through the hole. He saw nothing. "No." he said.

"Was it made of wood? Then it could rot away." said Harry.

"No, because the spikes are wooden too." said John. "Is there anything on that side? A bridge, or something?"

All four flashlights held by Drake, John, Al and Dave scanned the other side. There was a large block of mossy wood to the far right, just hanging over the edge. Drake saw it was very long – more than long enough to reach the other side. That was their way across!

"But how do we get to it?" asked Dave.

"It shouldn't be hard to move if we can get someone over there." said Drake.

"We'll have to throw somebody." said Al.

There was agreement. It was also agreed that Jane and Alol were the lightest, so one of them would have to be thrown.

"Throw me." said Jane. "I can move the block of wood."

"No." said Drake. "Throw Alol. He's the politician, here. He's also not my girlfriend."

"But you two are so close..." smirked John.

"No, we'll throw Jane." said Al. "Besides, Drake, I think Alol is too feeble to move it. John, Harry, you two get on the other side. Me and Dave will take this side. We're the strongest, so she has the best chance to make it."

All the better, thought Drake. He was not sure he could bring himself to throw Jane over the pit. The four men gathered around, picked her up, and began swinging her back and forth.

"On three, ready?" said Al. "One... two... three!"

Jane flew over the trick floor easily, and slammed her face into the floor on the other side. She got up and dusted herself off with her hands. Drake noticed her nose was bleeding. She moved to the back of the wooden slab, and pushed forward. The slab moved over the floor, and touched the other side. It was now safe to cross.

"Alright!" said Al, running over.

Drake went next. Jane was rubbing her hands on her clothes.

"What are you doing?" he asked.

"It's all slimy." she replied in disgust.

"And your bloody nose?"

She rubbed her nose, and saw the blood on her fingers. "Huh. It didn't hurt at all until you mentioned it."

They moved down the hall, which ended abruptly in a T-shaped fork. The picture over the left one was a scorpion, stinger reared, facing them. The second was a coiled snake. Alol began speaking. Harry listened, and translated:

"He says it's a riddle. The safest way is the right way – scorpion or snake?"

"Well, we're bigger than a scorpion." said Gary.

"Yes, but the snake could be nonlethal. All scorpions are poisonous, but not all snakes are." said John.

"So the snake?" asked Drake.

"No, the scorpion." said Al. "See, the snake has markings that make it lethal to humans. Not all scorpions are lethal."

"So the scorpion?"

"No, the snake!" said Harry. "See, these are neutral markings. They drew it to look poisonous, but it's not. You can tell because there are no teeth. It's a constrictor. This species is harmless."

"That sure sounds like something the Mayztecs would do." said Al. "Okay, we take the snake!"

The group ran down the right passage. They went another right, which would take them back the way they came. When they turned, there were two things blocking their way. One was a puddle of thick, gooey mud, probably there by accident. The second was a massive snake, thick and long. It was fifteen metres long, almost fifty feet! It had glowing red eyes, and a forked tongue. It reared up high above their heads, as thick as a small tree, the head the size of a pumpkin.

"What in the bloody hell is that thing?" yelled Dave, clearly scared.

"Titanoboa!" said John.

"What's that?" asked Drake.

John suddenly calmed down. "Yes, it's a Titanoboa. From Colombia in the Palaeocene. It's large, but it's not poisonous. So, I can do this."

John leapt at the snake before it could strike. He flattened it, and the group ran past. They reached the hall, which made a left turn, and coiled around so it went the opposite way. Drake stared back at John, who was now punching the snake.

"No longer afraid of snakes, see!" said Gary.

"Do you need help?" asked Drake.

"No, Drake, go! And I'm only afraid of the poisonous ones!"

Dave held Drake back. "I'll go, mate. You continue."

Dave then screamed, and leapt on the snake to help John. Drake saw them both wrestle with the strong coils. John dropped the flashlight in a corner, and Dave held his in his mouth. It was thanks to the two lights that they could see the snake to fight it. Drake followed the others around another turn.

There was another obstacle that had all three natives standing stone still. It was a massive wall, and there was only a little place to squeeze through at the very top.

"Do you think the burial chamber is behind there?" Gary asked.

"Without a doubt." said Harry.

"We need someone skinny." said Al. "Drake, you go."

"Am I really the skinniest?" he asked.

He looked around. Of everyone, he and Alol were the most stick-like. But, Alol was too feeble. Harry seemed to be second.

"Alright, I'll go." said Drake. "Maybe there's a way to open it from behind."

Harry and Al let Drake step up onto their hands. They hoisted him up. Drake held the flashlight in his mouth and crawled over. It was a tight fit. When he was half through, he held his flashlight in his hands again. He turned around, and landed on his feet. He then faced the chamber.

It was a large, square room, with a coffin in the very middle, covered in symbols. He looked around, but he didn't see anything that looked like an Extinction Stone. Just the bare coffin.

"I can't find the Stone!" he said.

"Are you sure?" asked Al. "What's there? Is there a secret door or something?"

"No."

"Then it must be in the coffin! You'll have to move it."

"I can't move a coffin! It's disrespectful!"

"Drake, move the damn coffin!" yelled Harry.

Having never heard Harry so impatient, Drake moved to the coffin, and pushed away the lid. Inside there was a skull and some ribs, and under the left hand was the most coveted artefact in Prehistorcia. Here was the Extinction Stone.

Chapter 8 – The Blue Stone

The Stone was not what sent the shiver up Drake's spine. Nor was it the skeleton of King Zolgaf. It was the fact that the Stone appeared, almost exactly, like the one in his dream. It was perfectly round, the size of Drake's head. It was even dark blue, almost like sapphire, just like in his dream. He shone the flashlight through it, and saw shadows moving inside the sphere.

"Drake?" called Al from the other side.

Drake did not respond. He picked up the ball, perfectly smooth, but heavy. As soon as he did a tingling sensation coursed through his body. He let the flashlight drop to the floor, where it clattered. He saw immediately why the Hekeni revered this Stone.

"Drake?"

"I'm here." he said.

"What did you see? Did you find it?"

"Yes." said Drake. "I found it. I have it here." he was talking softly. "I can see why you revere this Stone. It's… wonderful."

"I want to see! Open the door!"

Drake tucked the Stone under his arm and picked up the flashlight. First he closed the coffin – it seemed disrespectful not to. He found a carving of a lunging Velociraptor with its claw sticking out next to the door. Drake made to push the claw. When the claw was pushed downwards, like a lever, the door rotated ninety degrees, which allowed them to get in.

He held up the Stone for the Hekeni to see. Harry, Alol and Al were all in awe.

"Drake… give me the Stone." said Al, extending his hand.

Drake was about to oblige, when he remembered his dream – did he dare give it to Al? Would something terrible happen if he did? He wasn't sure. But he had to give the Stone to one of the Hekeni – he could already see the gleam of intense desire in Alol and Al's eyes, and just a flicker from Harry.

"I... I think I should give it to Alol... the Hekeni elder, you know."

"I'm the co-chief!" said Al. 'Besides, he's a politician! He can't be trusted!"

"Al, I really think Alol should at least *hold* it first."

Al closed his eyes, and sighed. He gestured to Alol. Drake was relieved, because for a brief moment he thought he saw a gleam of rage in Al's eyes. Alol accepted the Stone with great reverence. He went down on his knees, staring at it with all of his concentration.

"Alright, now give it to me!" said Al, taking the Stone out of Alol's hands. Alol looked upset, but accepted it. Al placed it very carefully in the bag he had used to carry the flashlights.

Drake heard a screech. They looked around – standing on top of the coffin were two red-eyed, metre-high, feathered, mean-looking Velociraptors.

*****

John and Dave wrestled with the Titanoboa, the light from the two flashlights aiding them. The Titanoboa had gleaming red eyes, and was surprisingly strong. Its body was as thick as John's, and when it got around his leg it squeezed. John screamed in pain, and pounded at the snake's head.

Dave, meanwhile, found some rocks and began tossing them at the snake, causing it to loosen its grip. It turned on him, its jaws opened wide, as if to swallow Dave whole, which, John thought, it was big enough to do.

John took this moment of freedom to grab the snake's tail. He wrapped it around the Titanoboa's head, and it attempted to squeeze him. Instead, though, it squeezed itself around the neck, and began choking. By the time it untangled itself, John and Dave were already on it. They slammed the Titanoboa's head against the wall, and it slumped down, unconscious.

*****

The Velociraptors were only the height of Drake's waist. They were as long as he was tall. They had a covering of white down, and their arms were long and tipped with three claws on dextrous fingers. Their tails were stiff behind them, and their snouts were long and narrow, like a crocodile. But they most closely resembled birds.

"Velociraptors." muttered Gary.

"Where did they come from?" asked Jane.

"There!" said Harry.

He pointed to a partially closed door that Drake had not seen on the far right. The Velociraptors were now in front of the sarcophagus, snarling.

"Al, give me the Extinction Stone." said Drake.

Without waiting for a response, Drake took it. He took the Stone out of the bag, and held it up, hoping to keep the Velociraptors away. They paused, but they did not stop. They snarled and leapt at the group. At that moment, Dave and John came around.

"What's u – Holy crap!" yelled John, ducking as the Velociraptor jumped over him.

There was now one Velociraptor at the end of the hall, and one at the beginning. Drake held the Stone, hoping it would reveal its power.

He shut his eyes. A fantastic blaze of white pierced his eyelids, and when he opened them, the approaching Velociraptor was on its side. Everyone looked at him as though he had shot lightning from his hands. The Velociraptor at the other end of the hall charged, but didn't care for the others. It aimed right for Drake. It jumped at him, and he barely missed.

He tossed the Stone to John.

"Run, John, get it out of here!"

John nodded, and ran, the Velociraptor chasing him. The second one stirred. Drake, thinking fast, picked up the Velociraptor and threw it into the partially opened door, and shut it. The Velociraptor could be heard banging against the wall, but it was making no progress.

Drake ran. The group ran. They all went down the hall. At the end, Drake stumbled, and the flashlight slipped out of his hands. He heard the click-clack of claws on stone. He didn't dare pick up the flashlight from its hiding place.

The Velociraptor walked up to the flashlight. Drake noticed its eyes were no longer a gleaming red. It bent down and sniffed it. It picked up the light in its jaws. The Velociraptor was not big. Drake took the opportunity to leap on it and flatten it, and the animal was knocked out. Drake looked at the animal. It actually looked rather pathetic now. He took his flashlight, and ran down the hall, leaping over the Titanoboa.

He finally reached the trick floor. He saw the group running across the bridge, away from the Velociraptor. Drake waved the light in the dromaeosaur's eyes, and irritated it. The red-eyed Velociraptor turned and charged. Drake threw the flashlight down the hall.

Distracted, the Velociraptor followed the light. Drake ran across the wooden bridge and then they pushed it over to the other side, cutting off the way across. Meanwhile, they heard a crunch and the light emitting from the hall went out. The Velociraptor had crushed the flashlight. It came back towards the floor.

It approached the edge. It seemed to know the floor was a trick. But it stepped on it anyway. Drake thought they were safe, but as the foot came down – no split. Nothing! It didn't fall through! It stepped lightly forward again, and it didn't fall through. The trick floor didn't work!

Drake looked around. He saw a boomerang-shaped skull of a Diplocaulus, and picked it up. He threw it with all his might where the

Velociraptor was standing. It worked! The floor broke, as did the skull! The Velociraptor fell through, somehow avoiding the spikes. Drake watched it weave around, its feet splashing in the thin layer of water that leaked in. It jumped at the existing entrance, but it was too high.

"Quick thinking, Drake!" said Al, over the snarls of the Velociraptor. "Now let's get out!"

They hit the claw. The door opened, and a powerful wind blew them out.

When they looked back, the Velociraptor was back up!

It snarled and ran at them, but the door closed before it could reach them. They ran down the path for the bridge, Al stuffing the Extinction Stone and the flashlights back in his bag. It was now a downpour in the Thunder Marshes, and the river was flowing faster.

"Wait, look!" said John.

They looked. The Titanoboa seemed to be crawling out of a hole in the roof. Only there was no more of the red gleam in its eyes. It flicked its tongue out, and descended the temple, away from the Hekeni.

"Why isn't it attacking?" asked John.

"Because we won." said Al. "I don't think it's cursed anymore."

"It was never cursed!" said Drake.

"Cursed or not, we still need to get off this island. There's the bridge. Let's move!"

Drake did not hesitate this time. He ran across the bridge lightly, reaching the other side in a few seconds. Alol followed him, and then John, and Jane, and Gary, and Harry. Al was the last one there. He stepped on the wood, the Extinction Stone over his shoulder. He stepped down. The wood cracked.

"Al, the Stone is too heavy!" said Drake.

"Well, how am I supposed to get it back there?" he asked.

"Throw it!"

Al looked at Drake as though he just suggested killing a child for fun. "Are you crazy? It could fall in the river! It would be lost forever!"

"Just throw it, Al, we'll catch it!"

"No!"

"Throw it, or you'll stay there for the rest of your life!" the temple behind Al opened. The two Velociraptors stumbled out. They saw Al and raced towards him. "Which may not be very long!"

"Fine! But you have to catch t!"

Al swung his arm around in a circle, picking up speed, until the Stone was thrown over the river. Al ran across the bridge, boards cracking under him. Drake lunged forward. The sack fell in the river! He reached for it, and grabbed the end of it. He tugged it out of the water, the piranhas swarming where his hand was a few seconds earlier. Al reached the other enc.

The Velociraptors looked at the bridge, and sniffed it. They didn't seem too keen to cross. They turned around to look at the other side of the island.

Drake looked inside. There was the dark blue Stone of the Ordovician, innocently sitting there.

"That was close." said Gary.

"What now?" asked John.

"Now we cast it into the fires of which it was created." said Dave.

"The way they talk about it corrupting people, it may not be such a bad idea. I sure hope this Stone is worth it, Al." said Drake, putting it in a bag on the back of the Lufengosaurus.

"Oh, don't worry. It is." Al replied.

Chapter 9 – Leaving the Temple

They left the temple, heading back down the path the way they came. When Drake looked back he saw the two Velociraptors scamper across the bridge, and run into the forest. He wondered vaguely why the Velociraptors had stopped chasing them. Al said it was because they had won. Perhaps it was true. However, the other guardians were much bigger than the Velociraptors. If that was the first one, he didn't want to see the other five.

"So where's the next one?" asked Drake.

"The Drought Lands." said Al.

Drake thought back to the Drought Lands, so long ago now. It was a vast expanse of sandy desert, incredibly hot and very dangerous. He had witnessed a Tyrannosaurus and an Alxasaurus fight. He had seen a Gorgonops, and a whole herd of Protoceratops. He remembered one man very nearly lost his life to a Euchambersia, a poisonous species of mammal-like reptile.

The rain came down hard now. The path wound its way back to the river, and they began following that south, towards the Zolgaf camp site. Soon, night came.

Drake, John, and Gary were all on night watch. John, between the two of them, held the Extinction Stone in his lap. It was at Al's request that the Stone remain in the hands of someone at all times. It was just paranoia, thought Drake. No one knew what the Hekeni were doing. John and Gary approached him.

"So, that was some light show, Drake." said Gary.

"What do you mean?"

"In the temple."

Drake was puzzled. "What happened in the temple?"

"You mean you didn't see it?" asked John. "It was incredible! It was an Anomalocaris, pure white, and massive!"

Anomalocaris (an-om-al-oh-car-iss) was a Cambrian arthropod that lived in the water. It had a body shaped like an oval, with hard, triangle-shaped plates sticking out the sides, and a forked tail, like the antennae of a bug. Its head had large insect eyes, and its mouth was long believed to be two animals. The mouth was round, and thought to be a jellyfish, and the jaws were two worm-like appendages that were once thought to be worms. It was the largest predator in the Cambrian seas, but quite small compared to modern predators.

"What?" asked Drake. "I never made any Anomalocaris!"

"Yes, you did." said Gary. "It was huge, too! You know that model Anomalocaris in the Tyrell? It was at least that big, maybe bigger!"

The Tyrell Museum had a massive Anomalocaris model, about ten feet long, much bigger than the real thing. Of course, they had to make it bigger, as most animals from five hundred million years ago were so small. Drake could already picture it. But he was sure he didn't make it.

"What happened?"

"Well, you were holding the Stone, and it just kind of... happened." said Gary.

"Yeah, it glowed white, and all of a sudden this massive Anomalocaris shows up, just for a second, and blasts the Velociraptor right off its feet!" said John.

"Well, I swear, I had no idea how I made the Stone do it!" said Drake. "In fact, I'm not sure I could do it again if I had the chan-"

At that moment, two animals appeared across the river, and bent down to drink. They had a long neck, a triangular head, long, slender hands, slender legs, and a long tail. It was only about two metres long, just over six feet. Drake had absolutely no idea what it was. There were little horns over its eyes. Drake's immediate thought was perhaps they were baby Carnotaurus, but no, it was not right.

"John, what are those?" he asked.

"I have no idea... wait. I think they're Kakuru."

"Kakuru?" asked Gary.

"From Australia. Though I have no idea why I thought of them."

"What are they?" asked Drake

"Kakuru was thought to be a small Therapod, but very little is known about it. In fact, it's known only from the tibia that… that's it! That's how I know it! The tibia turned to opal!"

"Opal?"

"Yeah, through an extremely rare fossilization process, the bone of Kakuru turned to opal. Although I have no idea how I can know they're Kakuru, but they are, I'm sure of it."

The two Kakuru lifted their heads up from the water. They stared across the river at the group, and went off in another direction. Drake was amazed that such a rare and little-known animal could survive here in Prehistorcia, and that he got to see it. He stared around at Ahrzi, suddenly very glad he was a part of this land. He looked at the Extinction Stone. Could it really be the reason Prehistorcia existed?

*****

The next morning, it was raining again, and the thunder could be heard in the distance. Every Hekeni was crowding around the Extinction Stone, all wanting to touch it, all reluctant to give it up. They were all bowing before it in worship, staring at it with awe, and the paleontologists were always getting many thanks and hugs for retrieving it for them.

"Hekeni, we must get going." said Al. "You'll all get a chance to touch the Stone, don't worry, but we must get going now, or we'll never get the second one!"

They put the dark-blue Ordovician Stone back in the bag over the Lufengosaurus. All the way walking, Hekeni were reaching in and touching it, praying to it, and one man even kissed it. At that point Al felt it better to keep the Stone away from the group, as it was distracting them from their own mission.

After another night, they returned back to the Zolgaf camp. The Eogyrinus stared at them like a motionless log, swimming away when a Zolgaf called for it.

A Zolgaf came up to Al, and looked around in the group. "*Meh u mellef mah?*" he asked.

"We got it." replied Al.

"Can I see it?" asked the Zolgaf, forgetting the Zolgaf language and speaking Hekeni.

Al pulled a bag out of a pack, and took the Extinction Stone out, holding it in the palm of his hand. The Zolgaf's eyes twinkled in awe, and he reached out for it. Al put it back in the bag, the Zolgaf having a rather disappointed look on his face.

"Can we not have it? It is not the green one."

"No, but it is blue, which means it belongs to the Fertile River Tribe." replied Al. "If the Golarans do not settle things with the rest of us peacefully, we will consider you for the red Stone."

"May I hold it?" asked the Zolgaf.

"I think it's better if you don't." said Al, putting the bag back in the pack.

The Zolgaf looked very disappointed, but let them through. Harry, meanwhile, was on the back of an Ankylosaurus, writing a letter with the Nemicolopterus on his shoulder. He rolled it up, tied it to the Nemicolopterus, and it flew off to the west.

"Isn't the Fertile River Tribe east?" asked Drake.

"Yes, it is, but I was writing back to the elders." replied Harry. "They'll write to the Fertile River Tribe and tell them to come here and retrieve their Stone. The River Tribe is too far away for that poor thing to make it."

"Will they let the Stone go?" asked Drake.

"I hope so, or we're going to have a major war on our hands."

*****

They set out the next day from the Zolgaf camp, after allowing the Zolgaf to admire the Stone, and every Zolgaf in the area ran to see it. They were still getting panting sprinters from other villages asking to see the Stone, even as they ascended the hill, away from the Thunder Marshes.

Drake could see already that the Stones had a great power over the land, even if it was just the power of religion. He knew that that could often be the most dangerous power that existed. Even if the Stones had no powers of sorcery or weren't made by Prehistorcia, all the tribes worshiped it as though it had one sixth of that incredible power. He had never seen a more potent religious force.

He often imagined as a child what he could do with the incredible power of time, being able to control all the animals that had ever existed. But that was a dream. He was older now – there was no such thing as magic. Not in that sense.

He believed in magic in some things. This land itself had some indefinable force that Drake considered magical in its own way. But the Stones, there was no way. The Stones were very pretty, yes, but they did not have power over Prehistorcia. They were not made by the almighty God, and they were not the entire reason Prehistorcia existed. How could they be? Things like that just didn't happen.

They reached the Cretaceous Forest and set up camp. Next night, they would rest back home in their village, as they would have to pass it anyway to get to the Drought Lands.

Al was digging in the ground, searching for edible roots by digging with a stick. He found a large bulge in the ground, and began yanking it out.

"What have you got there?" asked Drake.

"I don't know, but I hope it's good!" replied Al.

He gave it a tug, and the stone popped free. It was a diamond the size of a potato! Al cleaned off the diamond, and examined it.

"Ah, damn, not these things again."

"Al, that diamond is huge!" said Drake.

"Well... so?"

"Do you know how much that thing is worth?" asked Drake.

"What does it do?"

"Well, it... uh... it's obviously... uh..."

"Uh-huh." said Al. "Why do you people value these things again? They can't start fires, fill your stomach, quench your thirst, train your animals or bring you happiness. If it was sharp it could be useful, but nothing can break it into a point. I see no value." he threw the rock behind his back into the trees.

It was times like this that Drake really appreciated good old Hekeni wisdom. They had their values right. They spent more time caring for nature than they did making themselves beautiful. They valued things for their use in the real world, not their shininess. Drake shrugged, and laid down to sleep. Cavemen really were more sophisticated than people gave them credit for. In fact, thought Drake, they might just be the most socially advanced society on or under Earth.

But the Extinction Stones, he thought, were another matter entirely. That was the one thing the Hekeni valued above natural beauty and their animals. That was what worried Drake most. Could Prehistorcia take what the Extinction Stones would bring? There were only six, which was fine for six tribes, but today there were twenty. Even so, would the Hekeni be willing to give up the Stones they already had?

*****

They reached the Hekeni village by mid-afternoon the next day. The Hekeni all wanted to get a glimpse of the Stone, but it was kept hidden, away from prying eyes.

Drake saw Al's wife running up to him.

"Drake! I am so sorry! Ahrzi, he got out, I don't know how, but —"

"It's fine, Tjella, he followed us to the Thunder Marshes." said Drake. "We're just going to keep him with us from now on."

Tjella looked relieved. "Oh, good. So, I heard you found an Extinction Stone?"

"No, you can't see it." said Al, walking up. "Not yet, anyway. Sorry, Tjella, but I must be equal with everyone. If you see it, the whole village will have to see it."

"And why not?" demanded Tjella. "Why not let everyone see them?"

"Because, if we do, we'll never get out of here. They'll all want to touch it, to pray to it, and it'll take weeks for the whole village, time we don't have. Not to mention the Hekeni from the other villages. But now, I need to see the elders." When Drake turned away, he heard Al whisper: "I'll show it to you at midnight."

So, Drake found himself that sunset in the Hall of Elders, with Al, John, Gary, Harry, and Alol beside him, the Extinction Stone in a sack at Al's side. Chief Roggan Spinosaurus was there this time, too.

"Bring forth the Stone." said Chief Elder Muthwag.

The rough-hewn stone table in the middle now had a wooden circle over it. Al turned over the sack, and the dark-blue Extinction Stone landed with a dull thunk on the table.

The elders muttered excitedly, each smiling, talking to each other in Hekeni.

"So it is true." said Muthwag in his slow voice that could not hide surprise and enthusiasm.

"Yes, we retrieved the Cambrian Stone." said Al.

"This Stone belongs to the Fertile River Tribe." said John. "With all respect, elders, I believe we should send it back to them."

There was muttering at this, some of it angry.

"That is a possibility." said Muthwag, quieting them all down. "Interesting. It would certainly give us eternal friendship with them. However, if we don't find the Triassic Stone…"

"We will!" said Harry. "Their equipment worked once!" he gestured to John and Drake. "It will work again!"

"But can we be sure?" asked Muthwag.

"I am positive of our abilities." said Al. "We *will* get the other five Stones. We will return them to their rightful owners, except perhaps to the Golarans. I don't really think they deserve theirs."

"I like your confidence, Alan, but it does not change the fact that we still only have *one*."

"By right's it's ours!" yelled a woman.

"Now calm down!" yelled Roggan. "John and Harry are right. Stone belongs to Fertile River."

Muthwag silenced all arguments. He paused. "I wish to hear your account of the temple."

They promptly told their tale, speaking in clumsy Hekeni for the elders to understand better. The Titanoboa, the Velociraptors, and even the door handle as being a claw on Velociraptor carvings. When the tale was finished, many elders gave their opinions to Muthwag. He nodded, and then silenced them.

"For now, I am only interested in one elder's opinion. Alol, what do you believe?"

Alol began speaking to him in Hekeni. Muthwag nodded, and occasionally shook his head. He asked questions. Alol seemed to be the only one he cared about at this time. After a while, he turned to consult only with Roggan.

"Very well. Roggan and I have reached a decision. We will have a vote." said Muthwag. "We have three options: we keep the Stone, we send it to the River Tribe, or we keep it until the green Stone is found. All those in favour for keeping it?" asked Muthwag.

The elderly woman put her hand up, as did two men. A vast minority.

"Send it to the Fertile River immediately, taking Al's word on faith?" he asked.

One elder put their hand up, as well as Roggan and Alol.

"Keep the Stone until we find the green Triassic one?"

The last nine elders put their hands up. A majority by two. Muthwag, who did not vote, announced this, and dismissed the meeting. They were all welcome to go to bed.

"Oh, elders, before we go, may I ask how my egg is doing?" asked Gary.

"It has not hatched, and it will take some time more." said Muthwag. "You have time to go to the Drought Lands temple, however I suggest you return here after, if you want to witness the hatching. In fact, you should not miss the hatching, for the first one it sees it will assume as a parent."

"Very well, elders, thank you." and Gary left the room as well with the customary bow.

Chapter 10 – Back to the Drought Lands

The same group left the next morning with fresh supplies. They didn't pack much last time, knowing they would return, but now all the packs were stuffed full of provisions and materials, and there were only five empty, brown hempen bags for the Extinction Stones.

The trip to the Drought Lands was short, taking just one night, moving along the ridge of the Bactrosaurus Mountains, until it went into the Drought Lands. The Bactrosaurus Mountains turned southwest upon entering, and then made their way due south, finally making a sharp turn east until it ran along the coast. It was the longest mountain range in northern Prehistorcia, and a major travel route, as six tribes lived in or near the Bactrosaurus Mountains.

They reached the centre of the Bactrosaurus Mountains at night, and Al stopped them, staring out into the distance. He turned to the group.

"It's that way." he pointed towards the open desert.

Drake had never been in the west end of the Drought Lands. He had been in the east side, which was much smaller, but the west end stretched on for weeks over open, barren desert, so wide that it marked the northwest border for Prehistorcia. It was rumoured to be much hotter, though Drake thought that was just because one could see the end of the east end, and the mind made it slightly cooler.

Many animals were also reputedly coming into and leaving Prehistorcia through this entrance, the animals finding some way to go through the desert. Though perhaps no one cared enough to try making it all the way. There were only two kinds of Drought Land explorers – those who came back dying with no new information, and those that never came back at all. Drake was positive that the vast majority of the second kind had died, but he was equally sure that at least one of them must have made it, but for some reason did not make the journey back, because they were too weak, or died after.

Harry started a fire with a match from the pack brought from the plane. He had seen them before, but Dazz marvelled at how easily they could start a fire. Not that they really needed matches. The Hekeni could start a fire, rain or shine, with just two rocks and a stack of wood and kindling.

"So who's temple are we visiting now, Harry?" asked Drake.

"Well, I'm going to get more questions. You'll have to wait until everyone else is gathered around."

So Drake waited. More people did come and ask, and Harry invited them to sit. Alol sat next to Harry. He was about to begin when a horn sounded in the distance. They looked east, towards the open desert.

"Oh, I forgot about them."

"Who are they?" asked John.

"Borchillians."

Four Arabian-looking men came up, three riding on Bactrian Camels, and one, their leader, riding on an Iguanodon. They stepped off.

"Just in time, guys, I'm about to tell the story of Queen Klefferniti." said Harry, again in Hekeni.

They seemed to recognize the name. The three other members sat down. The leader, though, a harsh-looking, desert-worn man, went to Al, who was giving Nemeli a bowl of water, the man wearing the Sekka hat. They began discussing in another strange language that sounded surprisingly like Zolgaf.

"So, we will not be visiting a king tomorrow." said Harry. "No indeed, this one is Queen Klefferniti, last ruler of the thirteenth dynasty, a dynasty with seven rulers total, and she ruled for a total of five years before her advisor killed her and claimed the throne for himself."

"Why'd they kill her?" asked John.

"I'll get to that. There are two reasons why she's buried here. You see, like the Zolgaf, our Borchillian friends here were once a Mayztec colony, a last remnant of a military outpost sent here to explore and find the other side of the Drought Lands. They failed, of course. Borchillian is a Mayztec name, I forget what it means, but unlike the Zolgaf, they were never a second province, and unlike the Zolgaf, they turned much quicker. In fact, they were formed a thousand years after the Zolgaf, and turned fifteen hundred years before.

"Queen Klefferniti is not an iconic symbol like King Zolgaf. In fact, in Mayztec history, she was one of the most unremarkable rulers, except for her legendary beauty. The rebellious tribes sent a total of three assassins to kill her, last of a dynasty that had caused us much pain, but none of them could do it. Our final one almost did, but when he got close, she seduced him. She was not a dumb woman, you must realize, she knew exactly who this assassin was, and used her beauty as a weapon. When he was close enough, she pulled out a little trick of her own, and stabbed him in the back, quite literally.

"But I'm off topic. The Borchillians once received a visit from her, three hundred years before they became rebellious. She did not visit the Zolgaf, which led to the whole ignored thing, but you've heard that story. Well, they loved her, but it had very little to do with her beauty. She came because she respected their work, and how hard it was to stay there. She brought with her several doctors, many of which stayed to treat heatstroke and extreme dehydration, and even today Borchillians are still the most skilled in medical techniques.

"So, they loved her. But her advisor killed her a couple of years later. You ask why. It's quite rude, and ladies if you'll forgive me for being so blunt, it's because she was a woman."

"You're kidding!" said Jane.

"No, I am not. But Jane, remember, these Mayztecs came from the upper-world kingdoms of Egypt, Rome, and China, and included the people of Latin America and the Native Americans. They loved their queens, but not as rulers. Queens were always second to the king, not rulers; it was a shame on the kingdom. We Hekeni have had woman chiefs in our time, though I admit it's a rare occurrence. When she died, everyone knew the murderer, but who were they to protest? He was a man. She was a woman.

"The Borchillians, being stranded here for so long, loved the attention, even if she was a woman. They offered to take her. The Mayztecs, not wanting her in so high an honour as to lie at peace with the valiant kings before her, decided it would be fine. Borchillians don't hold Klefferniti to the same extent the Zolgaf hold their ruler, but the Borchillians took her and gave her a nice burial out in the desert all the same. Normally, queens who outlive their husbands and have no son are buried with their husbands when they die.

"No Borchillian, at least not very many, travel to her tomb, not since they joined the rebels. To them, her temple is there, just a mark on the unchanging desert, to be respected, sometimes cleaned, yet ignored. I'm surprised Elmork even remembered her to hide the Extinction Stone here. Then again, he was more of a 'Rilowin' king than an 'Elmerik' king."

"Who was Rilowin?" asked Drake.

"Valued knowledge as the ultimate source of power." said Harry. "But that's another story."

The leader of the Borchillians who came finished talking to Al. He turned to his crew and summoned them to get up. They mounted their animals, and rode off, without looking back.

"What was that about?" Harry asked Al.

"Well, I forgot we were in their territory." said Al. "I explained everything to them, and apologized. They like what our quest will accomplish, and they've given us five days to retrieve the Stone and leave."

"What did you reply?" asked Harry.

"I told them it was more than enough, which it is. We'll be in and out in two days no problem, maybe three. Then it's off to the Falls Rainforest."

*****

Drake watched the sunrise over the desert. He sat on a ledge of a mountain, higher than the scrub brush and small trees growing on it, but not high enough that the group could not see him. He was lucky to be up so early... it was his turn on the night shift. When the sun got too bright, he turned west and stared out over the desert as a herd of sauropods walked past, going south. They were not near the group, but they were close enough that Drake could make out their heads, that they were dusty brown or grey, and that they had relatively short tails, long, upright necks, and longer front limbs.

He looked down, and saw John climbing up to meet him. John was the second person on night watch for the last couple of hours, so he was already awake, too. He had binoculars around his neck.

"Hey, you got a good view of the sauropods here." he said.

"Yes, I do. Am I to assume you've already identified them?" asked Drake.

"Almost. They're definitely a species of Bothriospondylus, though I'm not sure what species. But yes, this is a much better view." he put the binoculars to his eyes.

Drake looked at him. "Bothriospondylus? What is that?"

"Oh, a brachiosaur from Madagascar and western Europe, between fifty-five and sixty-seven feet long, middle Jurassic era. Yes, I see it now. This is definitely a *Bothriospondylus Madagascariensis*, Excavated Vertebrae from Madagascar. Although it looks like these guys are all on the long end."

"Is there any dinosaur discovered you don't know of?" asked Drake.

"Oh, certainly. I have no idea of the existence of Agilisaurus, Valdosaurus or Othneilia."

"Oh, come on, everyone knows about Othneilia."

"Seriously, I probably do know all the names, but I can't put a picture to all of them. I'm sure you know your fair share of unheard-of dinosaurs." said John.

"Perhaps." said Drake.

He and John worked in the same museum, but John was the one that had his picture on the wall. Drake wasn't considered quite as qualified. As a matter of fact, John was the only paleontologist down here who was good enough to be considered the revolutionary paleontologist, or a paleontologist that made such a large discovery or theory that it changed the entire paleontological community's view on prehistory.

Once in a while, there were people who changed the face of the fossil record. Gideon Mantel, first man to discover dinosaurs, Georges Cuvier, the first man to come up with the theory of extinction, Othneil Marsh and Edward Cope added hundreds of dinosaurs between the two of them to see who would win, Mary Anning, first woman paleontologist (and, in a surprising twist, the first real paleontologist, man or woman), discovered one of the first pterosaurs, and, in the recent generation, Phillip Currie and Jack Horner, who proved once and for all that dinosaurs were, in fact, related more closely to birds than to reptiles.

The Bothriospondylus had skin that was like leather, only scalier, and their heads were held high, against the current belief sauropods were straight-necked and level. Many paleontologists were beginning to adopt this view, thinking that perhaps the veins in the neck had flaps that allowed the blood to go only one way. Perhaps they were right.

Dinosaurs, as Drake and John both suspected, were warm-blooded, with the blood of birds rather than mammals. However, the bird-hipped ones seemed more sluggish, and possibly cold-blooded, but as John argued, a cat was just as lazy. But they weren't willing to cut open the dinosaurs to solve the debate.

"How many are there?" asked Drake. "I counted twenty-two."

"Did you count the babies?"

Drake looked down. There were some babies, only a third the length of the adults, some half the length. They seemed fuller in colour, as if the adults got some of their colour scratched off.

"No, I forgot. What do the babies make it?"

John counted quickly. "Twelve. So, added to twenty-two, there's thirty-four Bothriospondylus." he said proudly. "They all seem to follow a female, too, like elephants. Do you see any males?"

"Doubtful." said Drake, who knew the only female-led animals led all-female herds, perhaps some juvenile males that left when they got older. Some kinds of dogs had a head male and female, but that was as close as it got. On the other hand, some female dinosaurs were bigger, whereas in mammals, the males were almost always bigger.

"It seems you're right." said John. "But I'm really not looking that closely."

Drake looked down. There was a light-blue carnosaur glaring hungrily at the animals. It was Nemeli the Neovenator, but Drake knew she wouldn't do anything.

Even so, the youngsters moved to the middle, and the older animals surrounded them, away from the Neovenator threat. As long as Nemeli didn't attack and risk either a stampede or vicious fight, everyone would be fine.

"Nemeli!" called Drake. Her head twisted back. *"Lo greht na shuy-lars!"*

In just over a year, Drake had learned enough in Hekeni to say 'no eating the sky-necks'. Nemeli was the only trained carnosaur in Prehistorcia, not counting the dromaeosaurs. There used to be a great many Hekeni-trained carnosaurs, but the necessity for them dwindled, and Nemeli was the last. Carnosaurs were also hard to kill, so whenever an expedition went to search to train one, the mother or father of the eggs or hatchlings was always present. Plus, carnosaurs looked for stolen or missing hatchlings. The two parents worked together, so there were rarely any abandoned babies, and certainly no abandoned nests.

All those added together, and there were not many carnosaurs at all. Nemeli's mother was killed by a Polocanthus, and her father was missing due to some other circumstance. So Al took Nemeli, last egg of the litter, and raised her as a Hekeni Allosaur.

Nemeli turned away from the herd and stood next to the ledge Drake and John were sitting on. Her head was below them, but not by much.

Nemeli was fed large scraps of meat from the hunting, and she was perfectly well-fed. Drake didn't think she would do anything to the Bothriospondylus more than tease them, and have some fun, without intending to kill them. But it was best just to let them pass uninterrupted.

"I heard the temple is deep in the desert." said Drake. "That means we'll have to leave soon. I wonder when Al was intending to wake up."

"Oh, crap! I was supposed to do that!" said John.

He hopped off the ledge to look for Al. Drake stared down at three little dinosaurs scurried around at the base of the ledge. They had longish necks, triangular snouts, long, grasping hands and thin legs with birdlike toes. They were Coelurus, just over a metre long, trained by the Hekeni. He wondered if they could survive the trip over the desert.

But it wasn't only the Coelurus. Parasaurolophus, Hadrosaurus, and the Ceratopsians were all used to lush climates, not this Sahara-desert-like landscape. The woolly rhino would die. The Lufengosaurus and Plateosaurus could probably make it. Drake knew that the dinosaurs, under Hekeni care, could probably make it a day in the desert, but still, would they be willing to take that risk? Wasn't there some failsafe plan they had?

"Hey, Drake, ready to go?" called Al.

"Yeah." he called back, as the last of the Bothriospondylus passed. "How are we getting the animals across without killing some of them of dehydration?"

"Oh, we're only taking three animals."

＊＊＊＊＊

Drake was then sitting in the driver's seat of the military vehicle, John sitting in the other. They squeezed five people in each jeep. The ten included all five paleontologists, Al, Alol, Harry, Tom, and Dazz. Dave said he was too tired from fighting the Titanoboa to do much else.

"Are we really only going to take these as a transport?" asked Drake.

"Have to. Otherwise we wouldn't reach it until sunset." replied Al.

"Well, will we at least have people following behind?"

"Oh, sure, they're following. But we brought this equipment for a reason, didn't we? Now, let's set off!" Drake shifted into drive and hit the gas.

"Ha hah! Riding in car fun!" said Dazz in broken English, as Drake thumped down the sands.

"Yeah, but the ride will be very bumpy." replied Drake, hanging onto the sides.

In the back of John's car was Sam the Styracosaurus. In the back of Drake's was Ahrzi. Both were sitting on a lap, as there was little room for much else. They had two lengths of rope, six flashlights, food and water, spears, and a crowbar. The third animal was an Ornithomimus, and Drake was surprised how it was getting there.

Drake and John must have been going roughly eighty kilometres per hour over the sands, as fast as a major city road, and there was the Ornithomimus, running level with them! It had some light supplies on its back, but it was still following – at eighty kilometres per hour! And it didn't get tired, either! It wasn't as fast as a cheetah, but it certainly had a lot more stamina!

"That thing is fast!" said Drake.

"Isn't he?" replied Al with a smile.

John pulled up right close to it. Alol pulled out a water canteen and held it at the head level of the Ornithomimus. It opened its mouth, and Alol poured water in it, the Ornithomimus looking considerably happier once the canteen was emptied.

It took them forty minutes, but soon Al was telling them to pull up around a patch of desert vegetation. They parked the jeeps on top of a dune, took out the equipment, and followed Alol.

They were led to a bare stretch of dune. On the hillside ahead, Alol bent down, and Harry bent down next to him. They began brushing away the sand. Soon, Drake saw, they uncovered a massive rectangle of stone, with a Mayztec drawing of a Stegosaurus on the door.

Drake sighed. "I think I can guess this one's guardian." he said.

"Stegosaurus?" asked Gary.

"Who knows?" said John. "All I can tell you is that it has no shoulder spikes. Not that it says much. The Velociraptor at the last temple said nothing about a Titanoboa."

"Well, we now lift it." said Dazz, the Neanderthal.

He held up the crowbars. He and John both stuck it under the stone, between the two cracks between the entrance and the rest of the temple, and pushed. The stone began to lift. Drake came to help. The stone lifted, and the others helped pull it back, and flipped it upside down, like opening the cover of a book. They looked down into darkness.

"Well…" said Harry, "here we are."

Chapter 11 – The Yellow Stone

This time there was no fight over who would go first. Drake got a jeep, and pulled it up to the temple. They tied a rope around the bars; not a weak, easily cut Hekeni rope but military-grade bungee rope. It reached the bottom of the temple, barely. The end hovered just above the sandstone bricks. This tomb was very Egyptian, Drake thought, over the last one which looked Mayan.

"Alright, I'll head down first." said John.

He tied the rope around his fist, and slowly lowered himself. The bottom wasn't far, just three and a half metres deep, twice his height.

Next, Alol was carefully lowered down. Drake went next, followed by Jane, Harry, Steven, Gary, Al, Tom, and coming in last was Dazz. The entrance was wide, but the temple was very, very dark. The entrance shaft was placed in such a way that very little light was let through. Drake noticed the corner of the temple entrance, even after all this time, was sharp, rimmed in obsidian. Only a strong rope, stronger than the Hekeni could make, would be able to bear the weight of the climbers.

The burial chamber was small, at least compared to Emperor Zolgaf. It was a large rectangle, longer ahead than it was sideways. At the very end were two doors, one on the left of the far wall, one on the right. Drake began to step forward, but Al held him back.

"Did you learn nothing? Take this, scan the floor!" he thrust a flashlight into Drake's hands.

The square of light from the open entrance was not enough to light the whole temple. Drake scanned the walls first. All around it were pictures, mostly of brave warriors riding chariots to battle, while the queen directed. There were some where the queen tamed a whole pack of Deinonychus just holding out her hand, but more than anything, it was a Stegosaur depicted, sometimes with the queen's head, sometimes the queen with the stegosaur's plates.

"Hey, Al, did the Mayztecs believe in spirit and guardian animals, like the Hekeni?" asked Drake.

"They believed every person channelled a spirit, yes, but they did not believe in guardian animals. In case you didn't figure it out, Zolgaf's was a Velociraptor."

"I got that, yeah. And Kleffe-niti was this stegosaur?"

He looked at the stegosaur pictures. It was odd, this was one he'd never seen before. It looked like a Stegosaurus, except instead of the usual diamond-plates, this one had rectangular ones, as though wooden two-by-fours were sticking out of it. Did the Mayztecs make a mistake?

He scanned the floor. There was open sand right in front of them, though Drake was willing to bet it wasn't open sand. He picked up a rock and threw it over. The rock sank.

"Quicksand." said Al.

"How deep?" asked Drake.

"You can bet they built it deep enough for us do get stuck, but not die. The true magic of the Mayztecs was in engineering, not sorcery."

"But not even the best engineers can keep the sand wet." said Drake. "How'd they do this?"

"They maybe built it on underground well." said Dazz.

"Look there!" said Tom.

Drake pointed his flashlight. There were two human skeletons, up to their shoulders in quicksand, their arms at their sides as though they were raised to grab a rope before they died.

"Luckily, there's an easy way across this." said John. "A trick I learned from an old prof."

He got on his belly, and crawled forward, evenly distributing his body weight over the sand. He crawled over, sinking slightly, but staying up. Soon, he was up on the other side, his front covered in wet sand. He faced them, smirking.

"There must be an easier way." said Al. "They Mayztecs must have had a way to avoid their own booby traps, didn't they? The architects and builders certainly didn't die in here."

"Maybe they knew that trick." said Jane.

"Possibly," agreed Al, "but there must be another way anyway, in case they didn't."

Drake scanned the walls. He found nothing, and scanned the floor. As it turned out, on each side of the quicksand pit, there was a gap between it and the wall. It was wide enough for two humans to walk side-by-side.

"Hey, John, you got dirty for nothing!" said Drake.

"A day in the dirt is never for nothing." he smiled. "Just get over here so we can finish this!"

They walked along the sides of the wall. Drake thought that arrows would pop out of the walls. When he looked, there were no holes in the walls.

Drake scanned the floor again. There was a round stone, slightly elevated. Could they get any less subtle? He knew right away he was no supposed to touch that. They walked around the stone, splitting the group, five in front of each door.

"Which one is it?" asked Steven.

Alol read aloud the writing on his door, the one on the left, and Harry, as usual, translated:

"Here lies Queen Klefferniti the Beautiful, greatest queen of the Mayztecs, ruler of the Marthax-Nugruth." he said. "That means 'square-backed spike-tail', or a stegosaur with square plates. Have any of you heard of such a thing?"

Drake was expecting John to know, but he shook his head. To Drake's surprise, Gary nodded.

"Yes, I've heard of one." sa d Gary. "Wuerhosaurus (wir-ho-soar-us)."

"Of course!" said John. "I can't believe I forgot about that one! But Gary, why don't you explain what it is for a change?"

"Wuerhosaurus is a stegosaur from the Early Cretaceous, a hundred and twenty million years or so ago." explained Gary. "It was native to China, and the last known stegosaur on the fossil record. What makes this dinosaur odd is that it has rectangular plates on its back, not the spikes or hexagon-shapes commonly found on other stegosaurs from earlier times. R ght?" he turned to John.

"Well put." said John.

"What does our door say?" asked Al, who was on the right with Drake. He called Alol over.

Al translated this time: "The treasures of the queen are the treasures of a god. May a curse fall upon all those who dare to touch it."

"So... is it in the burial chamber or the treasure room?" asked Drake.

"We'll have to open them both. Whichever one has the guardian obviously must have the Stone, right?" asked Al. "That was how it worked with Zolgaf."

"Maybe... how do we open them?"

"Just push, they don't look locked, just heavy." said Harry.

With John on the left and Al on the right, the two teams pushed. Drake looked in the right door. It was incredible! Gold lining the walls, paintings, clay pots! What wealth! Where was this in Zolgaf's tomb?

"Why didn't Emperor Zolgaf have any of this?" asked Drake.

"Klefferniti was the last of her line. Zolgaf wasn't. She received the wealth of her family buried with her, of course her husband would have a vast majority, her keeping only what was needed to survive." said Harry.

Drake shone the light in the room. Suddenly, from the back of the room, a large animal popped out. It was a lion! They had a lion in this tomb! It roared menacingly, with glowing red eyes.

"Shut the door, shut the door!" yelled Drake.

The door closed, the lion locked in. "Drake, the Stone's obviously in there!" said Al.

"No, it's not!" said Harry. "It's in here!"

The other five people backed off, as a scaly, reptilian head moved out the door. A massive stegosaur emerged, as long as Nemeli, its back as tall as Drake. It was dark yellow, with vertical brown stripes, like a zebra or tiger. The plates on its back were rectangular, laying across the back. The plates were alternating, like a Stegosaurus, one row ahead of the other. Its long tail was held high, tipped with two pairs of sharp, lethal spikes. Its feet were like tree trunks, its small triangular head dwarfed by the body, only as high as Drake's hips, with two small, red eyes. It was a Wuerhosaurus, a deadly stegosaur no one had seen for a hundred and twenty million years.

*****

"How do you know the Stone is in there?" asked Al.

"I saw it, just before this Wuerhosaurus popped out!" replied Harry.

"Where was it?"

"On a podium. It's the yellow one, Al, the Cretaceous Stone!"

They ran to the other door. The Wuerhosaurus swung its tail. Drake hit the floor, narrowly avoiding it. It swung again, and John was hit by the blunt end, narrowly avoiding the spikes. He stumbled backwards, and fell into the quicksand. Drake rushed to help.

"John! Are you okay?"

"Help me out!"

Drake pulled, and John was dislodged from the quicksand, only to duck as the Wuerhosaurus swung another time. John's hat was nearly knocked off! He looked at Drake.

"We have to get that Stone!"

"But I don't know how to use it!" said Drake.

"Does it matter right now?"

Drake ducked again, as the group ducked and dodged the tail. One spike hit Tom, scratching his arm. Drake was right at the door.

"You okay?"

"Fine!" he said, clutching his arm.

Drake was in the room. There was the sarcophagus, lying face-up, with symbols on it. At the very back of the room was a pillar, it looked Greek or Roman, and on top of that pillar was the yellow Extinction Stone.

He got excited. It was the exact size and shape as the other one, only this one was bright yellow, and the shadows that seemed to move within it were no longer swimming. They seemed stationary, moving around the sphere. But there was no time to think of that. He ran to the room and picked up the Stone. He turned to leave, and saw Dazz with him.

"You found za Stone!" he exclaimed.

"I guess I did. Do you know how to work it?"

But Dazz just pointed at the pillar. It had sunk into the wall, and a door opened to the gold room opposite. The lion prowled in, eyes glowing red.

"Dazz, try to work it!" said Drake, shoving it into Dazz's hands.

"I try, but I not know how!"

Dazz closed his eyes, his knuckles white clutching the Stone. Then Drake saw what everyone else saw in the Thunder Marshes – a great, white animal. It was a Tyrannosaurus, glowing white, actual size. It existed for a lot longer than Drake's did, though. It roared and smashed the lion. Dazz opened his eyes to stare amazed at the T-Rex, which ran out the chamber. The two of them followed it.

The Tyrannosaurus confronted the Wuerhosaurus. It slammed forwards, and the Wuerhosaurus was thrown back, into the quicksand. The others looked amazed at the T-Rex, which disappeared as Dazz lost concentration.

"God almighty." whispered Tom.

"No. God didn't make them." replied Al.

Dazz looked just as surprised as everyone else in the room. The Wuerhosaurus guardian did not sink in the quicksand, but instead tumbled out to the other end, not making a dent in it. When it opened its eyes, Drake saw that the Wuerhosaurus was now normal; its eyes were no longer glowing.

Drake turned to Tom. His cut was deep, and losing blood fast. Dazz placed the Extinction Stone near the cut. The blood flow seemed to stop. His cut became shallower. Soon, there was only a scab. Dazz removed the Stone.

"What the hell was that?" asked Tom.

"The power of Prehistorcia." said Al.

"Well, there's no denying the Stones hold power." said Drake. "But come on, made by Prehistorcia? The reason for the land's existence? They're obviously some powerful stones that, I don't know, channel the electrical current of the mind, perhaps by some geologic anomaly, and make the user's thoughts known."

"Or you could stop being a closed-minded scientist and start opening your eyes to the true power of the land." said Al.

"I don't know, Drake, these Stones have some kind of power." said Jane.

"Maybe, but it's certainly not the power of a god."

"You know, those who don't believe in magic are doomed never to see it." Al retorted.

The Wuerhosaurus snorted, and began sniffing the ground. It was no longer a guardian; something in the Stone changed it. But Drake could already see a red light returning.

"Guys, I think the Wuerhosaurus is becoming the guardian again." said Drake.

They turned. The Wuerhosaurus had its eyes closed, shaking its head. They walked towards the rope, but the stegosaur stayed calm, and let them pass.

Al took the Stone and placed it in the sack. He climbed up first. Suddenly the Wuerhosaurus roared and turned, its eyes red again. It ran for Al, and swung its tail high, narrowly missing him. He threw the Extinction Stone over the lip and scrambled up himself. Drake looked up, but Al did not return.

They dodged as the Wuerhosaurus slammed its spikes against the wall. Its tail was embedded in the stone. Drake climbed up, closely followed by everyone else. When Drake got to the top, he saw Al with the stone in the bag, sitting cross-legged at the entrance.

"Oh, good, you made it." he said.

Drake knelt down to help pull the others up. Drake saw the Wuerhosaurus pull its spikes free at last and roar up at them. They grabbed the entrance, and flipped it over, sealing the tomb.

"You could have helped us." said Harry.

"You made it up here alright on your own." answered Al.

"Let's get out of here." Drake grunted. The rope was still tied to the jeep, and the end was still beneath the entrance. He cut it free, as the others closed the entrance. "Good thing we brought extra."

Al got into the jeep with Drake. They drove off, John getting everyone in the second and following. Once again, the Ornithomimus ran next to them. He wasn't sure why they brought it now, but he supposed they had needed to prepare for every eventuality.

"So where to next, Al?" asked Drake.

"To the tomb of King Elmork, in the Falls Rainforest."

"Where's that?"

"It's a branch off of Pterosaur Canyon."

Chapter 12 – From Desert to Canyon

They returned in the jeeps the very same day they left. They met the rest of the group a little ways away from the mountains; they were in no hurry to leave. When they all heard of the Cretaceous Stone being found, they were all overjoyed, and just like the Ordovician Stone, but not to the same extent, they wanted to see it and touch it.

But now this was the second Stone found. Harry sent a message to the elders, asking what to do. This Stone technically belonged to the Trontoll Tribe, which lived on the Great Yellow Plains in the central east. Drake, he now realized, had only ever been west, and not even very far south. There was still so much of Prehistorcia to see!

They decided to stay one more night. As predicted, the Borchillians came back, however this time there were five of them, the one on the Iguanodon leading. When they arrived, they were not the harsh desert-men they were the previous night, but they were jittery, excited children as if they were about to receive a bag of candy. Their leader confronted Al. Drake already knew what they were asking for.

Drake pulled out the sack. As he walked up, he could already see Al denying them the sight of the Stone. Drake thought it was a bit unfair, as they had stayed on their land, and this Stone meant as much to the Borchillians as it did to anyone else.

"Why can't they see the Stone, Al?" asked Drake.

"Well, I just don't think it's a good idea. We don't want the whole tribe delaying us the way we were held up by the Zolgaf."

"There's only five."

"There's five now, but what about when we show them?"

"We bring no more!" said the leader, understanding some English. "We bring no more! Just five, promise, OK? No more dan five!"

"Well… alright, fine." said Al. "Drake, show them the Stone."

Drake brought out the yellow Stone. The Borchillians smiled in awe at it. As they had promised Al earlier when Drake was grabbing the Stone, they did not touch it. They just stared at it to admire it. They were on their knees, staring into its depths, where Drake could almost see a light in the centre.

"Alright, I think that's enough." said Al.

The Borchillians closed their eyes, and held their hands together. When they rose, they thanked Al and the Hekeni, and turned to leave. However they did not stop looking at the Stone until Drake stowed it back in the bag. They rode off, talking excitedly in their own language.

"They remind me of high school girls, talking like that." said Drake.

"Well, this is a potent religious artefact. But this is where it gets both easier, and harder." said Al.

"Why?"

"From now on, we don't have to cross into any tribe's territory, because the other tombs are in secluded places. Unfortunately, this means inaccessible, barren terrain that makes our journeys through the Thunder Marshes and Drought Lands look easy. We must pass through only two other tribes, but that is because they are in the path, and the tombs are far away from both the tribe and their land. We must prepare. The hard part of the journey is about to begin."

"But, where are the other tombs?"

"East." said Al, vaguely. "The nearest one is in the Falls Rainforest, in Pterosaur Canyon, but from there we go east. We leave tomorrow."

*****

As promised, the Borchillian Tribe had left them alone, at least when it came to the Extinction Stones. Those five were the only ones to see it, and they had kept the rest of the tribe away. As Al explained, it was a small tribe anyway, with a much larger territory than was manageable. Unlike the Hekeni and other tribes, they could not position people on all borders indefinitely, but rather had lookouts on high peaks to warn of intruders or visitors. However, the Borchillians did see them off, leading them through the easiest path out of the Drought Lands.

They worked their way east for two days through the Bactrosaurus Mountains into the Cretaceous Forest. Once again, they reached the road to the Hekeni camp, but this time they did not take that road. They would continue south, until Pterosaur Canyon.

They saw the road that led north.

"Well, I guess I leave here." said Gary. "Bye, guys."

"Bye, Gary." said Steven.

"Hey, Al, do our animals have to go back now?" asked John.

"Obviously Ahrzi has not lost any attachment to Drake. He's staying for now. And I guess Sam is staying, too, since he's responded to his name."

It was true. John had called for Sam, and he raised his head in curiosity. He didn't come, but Al said that was typical, much the way a cat will respond to its name, but not care. This was not behaviour unique to Styracosaurus, nor was it all Styracosaurus' that did it. This behaviour varied among species by personality, and John had been lucky enough to get that one.

"Sam, come here!" called John. The Styracosaurus, chewing on a fern, looked over at him. It smiled and squeaked, but went back to eating.

"I think he just lipped you off." said Drake.

"He's doing that a lot. Are you sure it's normal?" he asked Al.

"Oh, yeah. This is an excellent sign, don't worry! Tenethax, before Drake tamed him, was very poorly behaved, but you'd never guess it when he was a hatchling. Sometimes the dinosaurs that don't behave well as kids can be the best companions when they grow up."

"So was Nemeli like this?" asked John.

"Oh, no, she's always been well-behaved. But don't worry, this behaviour is normal, too."

John sighed. He went over and grabbed Sam, who hung onto the fern until it broke off. He stared up at John, as if he should be impressed by his strength.

"Persistent little thing, aren't you?" asked John, placing the rope-leash around his neck.

Gary, meanwhile, gave Sam a little scratch just under his frill, in the section just below his ear. He waved goodbye and left the group.

"Hey, Gary, take the Plateosaurus as well. I think we have a bit too many animals after all." said Al.

"Is that possible for the Hekeni?" he asked.

"Apparently. Here, take it."

Gary hopped onto the Plateosaurus. "Alright, well, I'll inform the elders of your progress, I suppose. Have fun, Drake. John." he nodded.

"What are you going to call your Stegosaurus?" asked Drake.

"Don't know. We're not even supposed to name them until two weeks after hatching. I don't know why, but it seems to work."

So, Gary left the group. The rest of them continued on towards Pterosaur Canyon, a vast canyon that in some places was deeper than the Grand Canyon. It had rainforests and deserts and badlands and rivers, forests, plains, lakes, and animals. It was incredibly long, spreading across the entire north of Prehistorcia, the major route to almost every tribe to the north. It was wide in many places, sometimes so wide that one wall could not be seen, and sometimes it was so narrow that you felt trapped, enclosed. But it continued all the way to the Fertile River, filled with all sorts of weird creatures.

So, they continued south, for three days. They went along the southern side of the Bactrosaurus Mountains, passing the Rookail Hunting Grounds, where Drake and his friends had first been seen by the Hekeni. The very first thing of the Hekeni they saw was Nemeli. Drake could still remember the terror of that meeting.

The vast yellow grasslands were to their right, and the forest that sat beneath the mountains was on their left, as they walked between the barren foothills.

Drake saw a herd of prancing Macrauchenia, deer with short trunks. Over a year ago they had hunted them with the Hekeni. It was when the Hekeni agreed to take them back to their camp, and they began building fences to keep the dinosaurs in.

"Ah, remember when we found you here?" asked Al.

"Hard to forget." said Drake.

They turned south. Drake saw the peaks of Allosaurus Pass off in the distance, to the northeast, and looked southwest, but could not find what he had dubbed 'Cyclotosaurus Rainforest' where he had originally entered Prehistorcia. He almost laughed at himself. Back then, he wanted nothing more than a way out. He thought this land would make his life a horror story. Then he realized that the land, while it was dangerous, was amazing.

That was a different Drake, though, it seemed, the one who wanted nothing more than to leave Prehistorcia. Now he wouldn't leave even if he had the chance. And he did have the chance, a year ago, he remembered.

Back then, a new entrance had opened up, and they were all given the choice to stay or to go. Drake had stayed, as had his paleontologist colleagues. He still remembered Jorge, who had flown the plane that crashed, and came to Prehistorcia with them. Jorge had been attacked and nearly killed by a Cryolophosaurus, and had no interest in paleontology, yet even he saw the beauty of the land, eventually. He had gone up the entrance, though, and Drake couldn't blame him. He had a family. His child must be two years old by now. Was Jorge even now thinking of Prehistorcia? Drake was sure he remembered, at least; it was impossible to forget.

He wondered vaguely how Jorge would have fared through this adventure. He wondered a lot about Jorge, sometimes. Was he still flying planes? Did he regret his decision? Did he have a new respect for the past?

But such things were of little relevance here in Prehistorcia. Drake did know that, wherever he was, Jorge was happy. He was where he needed to be.

Jane put her hand on his shoulder. He smiled and spoke to her.

"Just think… where we were a year ago."

She nodded. "Think about where we were two years ago." she replied. "It seems almost laughable that we ever wondered about dinosaurs."

Drake nodded in agreement. "And last year, you and I… we weren't together. I know I wanted to be, but…"

"I wanted to be too. You just couldn't make a move!" she smiled. "Where do you think we'll be next year?"

"Oh, I hate this talk…"

"No, not that." she rolled her eyes. "Just… if that's where we were a year ago, think about a year from now. Do you think we'll have aged a year by that point?"

"Maybe, it's hard to say." admitted Drake. "You *want* to get old?"

"Well, I can get used to this 'retaining my youth' thing." she chuckled.

"Yeah… and you never see a truly fat Hekeni. There are big ones, a little chubby, but nobody truly fat. I guess all the physical exertion forces you to stay healthy. We'll be in good shape even when we get old." he smiled, thinking of it. Being decrepit due to age been one of his worst fears about time passing.

"You think we'll still be together when we're old? Are we in that sort of commitment?"

"Now you're just trying to annoy me." he playfully pushed her away while she laughed.

As the sun began to set, they walked through a familiar patch of forest. When they emerged on the other side, to a darkening sky, there it was – a great, withered crack in the land, very deep, and very long. It was the mightiest feature on the Prehistorcian landscape. They had arrived at Pterosaur Canyon.

Chapter 13 – Pterosaur Canyon

Drake had very vivid memories of Pterosaur Canyon from a year ago. It really was filled with thousands of pterosaurs, all looping and twirling through the sky, pterosaurs of every species, many of which Drake was sure had not been discovered on the Above-world.

The Hekeni set up a tent in the shade of the trees, although the sky was so dark by now there was no shade. The northernmost point of the canyon was still some way to their left, to the north. Here, the canyon was bordered on their side by trees, except the last few paces from the trees to the cliffside, where the terrain was grassy, with the plants growing between the rocky ground, until great stone spikes thrust sideways over the sheer cliff, with many ledges where pterosaurs and birds made their nests. There were a few caves which attracted bats.

At the bottom were more coniferous forests and a river running a little west of centre. Currently, the other side of the canyon was just a hazy grey line touching the horizon. Drake could just make out long, moving necks from there, though they were as small as flies. There were large sauropods directly across from them.

The canyon was some five kilometres deep, in a sheer drop, until it abruptly levelled out to terrain that looked like a wrinkled green blanket covered in trees until it reached the river. However Drake knew the cliffside got lower as they went south, the height changing the further they went, sometimes higher, sometimes lower, and not as steep. He also knew that the trees would eventually disappear into rocky terrain, with sparse vegetation. Even further down, where he had never been, was desert, and beyond that, at the other end, was lush, tropical forest around three lakes that the river emptied into.

Drake watched as a pterosaur with a massive head crest like a sail flew by. It was a Nyctosaurus. It swooped down and out of view. Drake turned to Al.

"Maybe you had better tell me where the other tombs are now."

"Oh, we'll get there. King Elmork is the only temple south of Pterosaur Canyon, though. Even then, it's on a south branch, not actually out of the canyon."

"Well, where are the others?" asked Drake.

"Nowhere you'd know. But the three locations are: Mount Ash, the Icy Peaks, and the Triassic Desert."

"I don't really like the sound of any of those places." Drake responded.

"True, they don't have all the comforts of the Falls Rainforest, our next destination, but they're actually safer. We won't be battling the animals, just the Mayztecs. And the elements."

"So are we going down the same way we did last time?" asked Drake.

"I'd assume so."

"But last time it took us four days!"

"So? We have provisions. Besides, this time I think we can cut it down to two."

*****

They walked very far the following day, and rested in a familiar sight. It was a large semicircle, completely treeless, covered in grass and dirt. The surrounding trees looked as if they had been in a fire, but they were all blooming for the first time. Many were trampled. Drake knew this place.

"This is where we saw Camarasaurus last year, isn't it?" asked Drake.

"Yes, it is." said Al. "Although they're not here anymore. They stripped the forest and went away."

"A lot of memories here." agreed John.

Last year, John and Jorge had gotten lost here, escaping the Golarans. With help from a native named Tok (who would later be killed by a Baryonyx), they made it to a tribe friendly to the Hekeni, the Yaxog, who, they now realized, were the owners of the brown Devonian Stone.

The next day they continued their walk south, searching for the ramp down. Last year they found a way, but it was only wide enough for humans. This time, however, they needed to get the animals down, too. The other temples were on the other side of the canyon, and they could not afford to wait for the animals to go all the way around. As it turned out, however, there was a much wider ledge that allowed for the animals to walk down, too, just past last year's path. The canyon was also shorter and less steep here.

"Time to head down." said Drake.

"Yes. Alright, it's wide enough for the Triceratops." said Al, eyeballing it. "Barely. Everyone will have to go single file. Let's move!"

The Parasaurolophus went first, followed by the Lufengosaurus, and then a Hekeni trainer. Al and Drake were about to follow when there was honking coming from the trees. A car horn! Drake had forgotten what those sounded like. But who was driving a car?

"Al, wait here for a minute." said Drake, holding him back.

A few seconds later, a military truck crashed through the trees. It was the typical military truck, painted green, with a green canvas over the storage area. At the passenger seat was Kevin, the soldier, and in the driver's seat was the twenty-two-year-old with short brown hair named Gary.

"Gary? Why are you in a truck?" asked Al.

"And how did you get it out?" asked Drake. "Isn't the crack in the plane too small?"

"We managed to get it wider." answered Gary, who helped Kevin out of the passenger seat. He was still limping, but he seemed much better. "Kevin here wants to join you."

Gary hopped back into the driver's seat, shifted to park and turned off the engine. Kevin was now in Hekeni dinosaur-skin clothing.

"Y'all have a problem with me joinin' ya?" he asked.

"No, the more the better. But, Gary, I thought I made it clear that there was too many people as it is." said Al.

"Yeah, well, Kevin will take my place. He's from Earth, too, so he won't kill anyone for the Stones, either. I, on the other hand, have to get back. Have fun, Kevin!"

Gary turned the engine on again and drove back. Kevin waved goodbye.

"Gary, wait!" yelled Drake. "You're driving home?"

"No, I thought I'd take the truck for fun, maybe walk for six days instead of drive for three hours." he replied sarcastically. "Well, see you! The Stegosaurus' are hatching earlier than expected!"

Gary drove off into the woods. Kevin walked up to Al, looking out of place, because he was the only one who looked like he knew nothing about this place. But, of course, he didn't know anything yet. One of the things of living in Prehistorcia, Drake learned, was that everything you thought you knew on the Above-world made no difference whatsoever here. It was like starting kindergarten again.

"Okay, Kevin, so has Gary filed you in on everything so far?" asked Drake.

"He told me a' the Mayztecs and Emperor Elmerik, and the Extinction Stones. Only thing ah don't know is what they look like."

"Well, we should change that. Al, where are the Extinction Stones?"

"I don't want to take them out." he replied.

"Come on, it's Kevin. He's from the Above-world, he won't spend hours gawking at it."

Al snorted. "Fine. The blue one is in the Lufengosaurus, going down the cliff, but the yellow one is on Tenethax's back. Sorry I didn't tell you about it, but I thought it safer to leave it there."

Drake walked over to Tenethax.

"Why's he sorry about puttin' it on this Triceratops?" asked Kevin.

"Because he's mine. When you return to camp, I'm sure the elders will be happy to give you a dinosaur of your own. Well, here it is. The Cretaceous Stone."

Drake held out the smooth yellow Stone. Kevin gave an audible gasp; he could see why the Hekeni valued it, too. "That sure is some rock." he said.

"*Stone*. They get offended otherwise. Right now we're going to Elmork, King Elmerik's son."

"Elmerik had a son?"

"Yeah, didn't Gary tell you? Who did you think hid the Extinction Stones?"

"I never thought 'bout it." Kevin admitted.

"Well, Harry will explain it. He spends a lot of time around Alol Albertaceratops, the official Hekeni historian. So far he's told us of King Zolgaf, Queen Klefferniti, and a year ago he would tell us stories, some that were religious, others that were true, and some that were stories little Hekeni children grew up hearing."

"Drake, you're falling behind!" called Al from the back of Nemeli.

Drake saw he was last in line. He invited Kevin to hop on, and kicked Tenethax forward.

"This Triceratops is yours?" asked Kevin.

"Yep. His name is Tenethax."

"Tenethax. What's that name mean?"

Drake was suddenly struck dumb. All the time he had known the Hekeni and Tenethax, he had never once asked what the name meant.

"I don't know. Hey, Al, what does Tenethax mean?" he called down.

"Hekeni have six names for green, and 'Ten' is the name for Tenethax's shade, or closest to it. The 'e' is just a connector, and Thax means 'back'. So Tenethax means 'green-back'." he called back.

"There you go. I wonder what 'Nemeli' means."

They moved five kilometres down Pterosaur Canyon, taking only half an hour. Soon, they were back in a large group, and set out for the river, through the trees. Drake had gotten off Tenethax to let Kevin take a turn, who was, if it was possible, more excited than Drake first was at the prospect of a trained dinosaur.

Kevin, Drake learned, was enthusiastic about dinosaurs, thanks to John's visit to his school in Houston ten years ago. John remembered he was on an exchange, and only visited three schools in that area. Kevin had gone to college, only to drop out because of family pressure. His father and grandfather were military men, not 'college nerds', as were his two older brothers. So Kevin had been pressured into joining the army. So he settled for a two-year minor degree in economics, and was shipped off to Iraq shortly after.

Also, his plane hadn't exactly 'crashed' until it hit Prehistorcian ground. It was shot at, and he flew into some clouds. The fog enveloped them, and they came out over a jungle, at a complete loss as to how that happened. Their instruments failed and they smashed down. Another mystery of Prehistorcia.

The Hekeni group exited the forest and came onto vast, open plains of yellow grass that expanded all the way to the river. Drake remembered this from a year ago, too, and wondered vaguely if their old path was still visible. Unlike last time, there were no longer Diplodocus here eating the trees. There were, however, leaping 'gazelle dinosaurs', such as Hypsilophodon, Dryosaurus, and Lesothosaurus. They looked like dromaeosaurs, only herbivorous, without the claws and teeth, and with a beak instead of a snout. Their arms were longer, but their fingers were shorter, and instead of the three found on dromaeosaurs, there were four or five fingers, depending on the species.

They stood in the grasses grazing, until the group began approaching. Then one lookout animal sent up a sound, a bit like a honk, and the dinosaurs scattered to the other end of the plains.

It wasn't a long distance to the river. From the forest to the river took just two minutes, and Drake remembered that Gary had run across it, or so he said, and reached the river in just a few short seconds. When they reached the river, everyone took the opportunity to fill their water bottles, and the dinosaurs drank up.

"Well, we might as well stay here." said Al.

"What? Why?" asked John.

"Well, there's nowhere more suitable than this to sleep tonight, at least nothing we can reach in the three hours of daylight left. Enjoy the view, guys."

Drake was happy that Al was able to take it easy for once. Normally, when he went on a journey, it was the destination only that mattered. Cover as much ground as fast as possible. But Drake wasn't going to complain. He'd wanted to watch a scene like this for a long time.

He walked up to Edthax, an Ankylosaurus, who was grazing on the grass.

"Okay if I sit on you?" asked Drake.

Edthax snorted. Drake sat down on his knobbly armour, which didn't feel much different from asphalt. He stared out at the plains.

There were two species of dryosaurs, or so he guessed. Dryosaurus, and Lesothosaurus. Dryosaurus was longer than Drake was tall, about eight feet long, but Lesothosaurus was only a metre, or three feet, long. Lesothosaurus lived in the Early Jurassic named for the country it was discovered in, Lesotho, whereas the larger cousin, Dryosaurus, lived in the Late Jurassic in North America.

The two herds had settled down, the Dryosaurus on the far right, near the trees, and the Lesothosaurus some distance away. Nevertheless, they seemed to coexist, as it was a Dryosaurus that put up the warning, but the Lesothosaurus had run, too.

John had occasionally talked about behavioural evolution, which was something he thought Prehistorcia couldn't suppress. He said that these species had been around so long that while their appearance remained the same, their behaviour couldn't possibly have done. This happened with many things, as John learned last year, and wasted no time in telling Drake about.

While John and Jorge were lost in the wilderness, they had witnessed what John called 'conclusive evidence' of behavioural evolution – such as the Alvarezsaurus depending on the Futalognkosaurus for protection, the fact that the Iguanodon on an island set up night guards for jaguars and other nighttime hunters, and, the largest thing in John's opinion, that a Baryonyx had swam between islands like a Komodo dragon. Drake still wondered, though, if John was right. There certainly were some instances of behavioural evolution, but was that really the reason for *everything* John saw to be right?

Of course not. John just hated to be wrong. But nevertheless, there were undeniable instances of behavioural evolution, such as these Dryosaurus working together with the Lesothosaurus.

"Cool. Fabrosaurus." said John, sitting down next to Drake.

"I thought they were Lesothosaurus."

"You did?" asked John. "Well, they're the same genus, at least, Fabrosaurus being the valid name. It might even be the same species. But I suppose you're right, for now they're still *Lesothosaurus diagnosticus*."

"Uh-huh. Dryosaurus, too."

"Yep. Those are definitely Dryosaurus. See how they seem to live together, even though they're from two separate periods and on opposite sides of the world? Just what I was telling you, Drake. Behavioural evolution."

Drake snickered, despite himself. "Funny, I was just picturing your views on that."

Drake turned left. He saw fourteen previously unseen animals there. They had the typical dinosaur body, with a long tail and strong legs, standing on two feet, with tiny arms. These ones had four fingers, and their arms were slightly longer. Their heads, though, were what drew Drake's attention – thick, heavy domes made of solid bone, with very tiny spikes that circled it and went down their snouts. They were called Pachycephalosaurus, and they were about five metres, sixteen feet long.

Edthax snorted and shook. Drake and John took this as a sign to get off. The Ankylosaurus moved to another patch of grass to eat, towards the river.

"Hey, here's an excellent chance to observe pachycephalosaur behaviour!" said John.

But as they watched them, the Pachycephalosaurus were depressingly dull. All they seemed to do was eat. A couple were even lying down, taking a nap in the evening sun.

"I think that one just blinked." said Drake. "But it could have been a trick of the light."

"Ha hah." said John sarcastically. "Actually, this is good. People view these things as always butting heads, but it's clear very little of their time is spent doing so. Actually, they look a bit lazy. I wonder how they'd respond to a predator in this apathetic state."

No sooner had he said it than an ear-splitting roar issued from behind them. Nemeli ran at the Pachycephalosaur herd, causing them to get up and begin snorting at her. They shook their heads, but Drake was sure it was for pure display only. A few more steps and Nemeli would scare them away. Shame, actually, Drake was enjoying them.

"Nemeli!" yelled Al. Nemeli stopped dead.

"Nemeli, come here! *Komak*!"

Nemeli bowed her head and turned back towards Al. He was speaking to her in Hekeni, and gave her a massive hunk of meat, which she tore at happily.

The Pachycephalosaurus returned to normal, though they were much more vigilant now.

Drake was sure there would be no predators. There were eighty humans and forty-eight animals, all of them large and many armoured or armed. It would take a pack of Tyrannosaurus to even pose a threat, and even then they stood a good chance.

*****

Night came and went, and the sun rose over the lip of the canyon, turning the sky orange and red, outlining the pterosaurs soaring in the early morning dawn.

Drake woke up on the bank of the river. He must have rolled there in his sleep.

He got up, and looked towards the Pachycephalosaurus. They were still there, though the Lesothosaurus moved on, leaving only the Dryosaurus chewing.

All the animals seemed to have calmed down, and were now mingling with each other. Drake could see small baby Pachycephalosaurus, only half as large as the adults. There weren't as many baby Dryosaurus, but a couple still existed. Drake was sure this meant that the Dryosaurus were easier to hunt. They would run, not display, and therefore the carnivores could kill the babies, which were weaker than the adults.

Al was getting everyone up. They walked along the river bank, through the trees that continued some way up. They would be doing this for a while, if Drake remembered correctly. He followed along,

Tenethax in the water, not sure exactly where the Falls Rainforest was.

There was little room for the cars to move between the trees, but they managed to do it somehow. They met no animals once again, which Drake found upsetting. He liked to see the animals, and last time he was here there was no shortage of them. But then again, back then they were in a smaller group. The lack of things trying to kill them, however, was rather refreshing.

"Hey, look up ahead!" said Steven. "Remember this place?"

The group had come out of the forest, which began retreating from the river. Now, instead, it was rocky hills with grass and small bushes cropping up between the cracks. As they continued, they saw sparse clumps of trees, usually conifers, sometimes standing alone. Some trees had fallen, leaving bare logs to rot on the ground.

"Yeah. This was where we saw the Sinosauropteryx!" said Drake.

Last year, a pack of Sinosauropteryx had crossed the river to hunt a hadrosaur. They were the only dinosaur with a known colour on Earth – rusty brown or ginger feathers with white rings around the tail.

"You actually saw a Sinosauropteryx?" asked John.

"Yeah, a whole pack of them! Hey, John, do you know if they're poisonous?"

"Poisonous? No, you're thinking of Sinornithosaurus –"

"I know what I'm thinking of! But the two are related, aren't they? Is it possible that Sinosauropteryx is poisonous like Sinornithosaurus?"

"Oh, I see. Well, despite what names suggest, the two animals aren't closely related. Also, Sinornithosaurus may not be venomous, as the pouches may have been made by loosening teeth from the jaw during handling. Thirdly, Sinosauropteryx has no evidence at all of poison pouches or grooves along the teeth, and therefore we must assume it is not venomous."

"But we saw them take down a baby hadrosaur of an unknown genus!" said Drake.

"Really? With just one bite?" he asked, surprised.

"Well... no, it might have been blood loss. But there was a chance it was poison."

John frowned. "Well, for now we'll assume it was just blood loss."

They walked along the river, and Drake could not see the old hadrosaurs he had last time. In the distance, where the pine forest continued, there were five Diplodocus, their heads level with their bodies, feasting on the lower branches. One of them looked young. Drake wondered if one of them was the Diplodocus he had seen more than a year ago. He decided it didn't matter much anyway.

On the other side of the river was a four-legged dinosaur, about fifteen feet long, covered with nodules and bumps like chainmail that continued all the way down to the tip of the tail. Drake knew it immediately as a Nodosaurus, from the Late Cretaceous North America.

There was only one Nodosaurus, bending down to drink, but it was surrounded by five smallish Hadrosaurs, only about four metres, or twelve feet long, with duck bills and no crests.

"Hey, John, what are those?"

"Claosaurus (clay-oh-soar-us), or else something undiscovered." he said.

Of the five Claosaurus, three looked young, but only one was noticeably a baby. Whether the Claosaurus and the Nodosaurus were here by coincidence, or because they travelled together, was completely unknown to Drake.

But, from behind the rocks, a pack of dromaeosaurs appeared. They had the classic dromaeosaur appearance, but they were smaller, with a smaller claw. They were covered in downy, ginger-coloured feathers, with white rings around the tail. It was Sinosauropteryx (sign-oh-soar-op-tear-ix).

In fact, thought Drake, it could be the exact same pack from last time. There were thirty or forty animals, all surrounding the small group from the other side of the river. The Claosaurus herd ran across the river, wading up to their arms, half-swimming, and came out, cutting across the Hekeni group. The small baby still struggled, and the adults paused, unable to do anything. The baby made it out and ran off with the adults.

The Nodosaurus, meanwhile, turned to face the dromaeosaurs. He swung his tail, though he lacked the side spikes common on other members of his family, and there was no club as there were on Ankylosaurs. One of the Sinosauropteryx leapt on the Nodosaurus, biting its back, but its jaws just scratched the surface, having no effect. The Nodosaurus shook. Despite all the Sinosauropteryx leaping onto him, he held his ground, and shook them violently off of him. The Sinosauropteryx, giving up, let the Nodosaurus walk away.

"I thought them raptors always killed their meal." said Kevin.

"No. Actually, most of the time, a hunt is unsuccessful, especially with the Ankylosaur and nodosaur group. Although, with dromaeosaurs, the chances of making a kill are greatly increased." said John. "And it's dromaeosaurs. *Always*. Never raptors, unless you're talking about a bird of prey."

"Ain't dromaeosaurs technically birds? And being predators, don't that make 'em birds of prey?" he asked.

John growled.

"Don't anger the paleoecologist." Drake warned, but laughing all the same.

Chapter 14 – The Falls Rainforest

The group walked for two days more, reaching an old part of the forest where the trees were tall and thick, and a fog hung in the air, as it did last year. Nothing could be seen but shadows more than a few steps away, and the river, a long, wide shadow that resembled a snake, was the only recognizable feature.

However they left that section of forest rather quickly, only to find Pterosaur Canyon's shallowest point – just over seventy metres, about two hundred feet deep, in a section full of dusty, desert hills, and large lumps of dried clay. There were sparse pine trees, and grass grew only on flat surfaces. It looked remarkably like the badlands, the region spreading from Alberta to Utah where thousands of fossils had been found since paleontology was born.

As the sun began to set, they continued following the river, until they came upon a familiar sight. Lying in the bushes, at the side of the river, were two large rafts, broken by time, decay, and animals. But they were unmistakably the rafts Drake and Al had sailed on a year ago, when they rode the river.

"Well, that's it, then." said Drake. "From here, we go into unknown territory."

They followed the river. Drake looked back at the rafts. To think it was then that a Torvosaurus, the animal Drake had chosen as a guardian, had once nearly killed him in that very spot. He had come from those pine trees, the ones the group was just now passing. He looked into them – no Torvosaurus. No anything.

They set up the tipis and army tents along the bank of the river, built some lean-tos, and started a fire. Crickets chirped as Harry once again sat down to tell stories. Drake was not listening, tonight, however.

Instead he looked across the river, towards the other side of the canyon. There, he was certain he saw a tyrannosaur prowling. The Torvosaurus still held this territory. But it was not uncommon – predators often stayed in one spot, while herbivores moved on. It was because herbivores could strip a place of plant matter before it could regrow, and had to find new spots, while a carnivore could just hunt on whatever animals were in the land, which there was never a shortage of.

He heard the Torvosaurus roar. It sounded a long way away. He looked up and saw the scarlet Nemicolopterus returning to the Hekeni. It looked injured. It landed on Drake, the closest Hekeni perch.

"Al, I think we have a hurt pterosaur, here!"

"Well, throw it away! Let nature take its course!"

"Uh, you don't really understand. It's one of ours. The Nemicolopterus."

Al walked over. Drake held the tiny pterosaur in his cupped hands. One of its wings was bleeding, and it looked as though it had been through a hail storm. It was shivering violently.

"What's happened to it?" asked Drake.

"I was hoping you knew." said Al. "It looks as though he's met Gherroz. I don't see a note anywhere. He came from the north, right?"

"Yes."

Al grunted. He hummed, and began thinking. "He must have been intercepted."

"It wasn't a hail storm?" suggested Drake.

"No, a hail storm couldn't cut his wing. Besides, he's been through the worst storms, and sheltered through it. If a storm did this, he wouldn't have returned to us."

"So who could have intercepted him?" asked Drake.

"Well, based on how long he was gone, he was intercepted with the elders return letter. We're not on great terms with the Catteua, but they wouldn't do this. The Yaxog and Zolgaf certainly wouldn't. The Golarans are too far south. I suppose it could have been Solg, but they have no interest in our affairs – or at least, they didn't when we left. Poor guy, he's shaking in fright." Al hugged the pterosaur gently.

"So who did it?"

"I don't know. But you can bet whoever knows isn't kind towards the Hekeni."

The sun rose the next day without incident. The Nemicolopterus was given a break from its work to heal, and sat in the back of the truck keeping Ahrzi and Sam company. Despite the fact it was small enough for Ahrzi to eat, the Utahraptor didn't think of it as food.

They walked along for several hours, until Drake was able to see their destination.

Pterosaur Canyon suddenly dropped down from the badlands, which were getting steeper anyway. It was an angled drop down, the water flowing over it in a large torrent. Beneath them, the semi-arid climate continued, until off to the right, south of their position, was a second canyon splitting off, full of tropical vegetation, like an oasis in the desert. The Falls Rainforest was in that segment of canyon.

As they descended the drop, which was not as steep as Drake originally thought. It did, however, continue for some two hundred metres down.

As they got closer to the canyon, Drake saw that the rainforest, while on relatively flat ground, was elevated from the rest of the canyon by a sheer drop, which the mother of all waterfalls streamed down. Only at the sides was the wall gentle enough to climb.

So that day they did climb t, and as the sun set, with dozens of Pteranodon flying overhead, they had made it.

Walking in the canyon was like walking on the side of a hill, though the slope was gentle as they got closer to the river. Here, either canyon wall could always be seen. Al explained that this was called the Falls Rainforest because fourteen waterfalls fed into eleven rivers which fed into this one they were walking next to, which was deep and wide. Al also explained that the tallest one was over a kilometre and a half tall, which was about twice the size of the tallest waterfall on Earth, Angel Falls in Venezuela.

That night, however, on the riverbank around a fire, Harry explained what Drake had been waiting for – the story of King Elmork.

"Well, if you could say one thing about Elmork, it was that he was the best of his dynasty." Harry said. "He, unlike his father and grandfather, felt that knowledge was mans' greatest weapon. He was crowned king at what you Above-worlders would consider fifteen, after Elmerik's unfortunate end, and he had just inherited a kingdom in chaos. Now, he had his father's bones, the Extinction Stones, and an empire everyone knew was doomed to fail. So, in our eyes, he committed the most evil act, an act that leaves the Mayztecs victorious to this day – rather than admit total defeat, he hid the Stones, leaving his kingdom in ruins.

"When he was twenty, he had fled the kingdom with fifteen servants, the Extinction Stones, and a trained Deinonychus. The Mayztec Empire was already falling by that point, and in his absence, it fell. Not that it was going to survive if he stayed; but it might have held on a year or two longer. But, as I said, Elmork was a thinker, not a fighter. And his brilliant yet terrible act is, as I said, what keeps the Mayztecs victorious over us.

"He knew it wouldn't be long before the rebels found out that the Stones, along with the emperor, were missing. So, he came here, the nearest secluded place north of the sea. His servants chiselled out his tomb from an existing cave, placed in a coffin, and put an Extinction Stone there. Then, to three servants each, he gave them the other four Stones, because one of them was already in his father's tomb. He sent them away, telling them exactly where to go, and warning them that they'd find no help anywhere anymore.

"It wasn't long after that the rebels found him and his remaining three servants. His Deinonychus put up a fight for him, but in the end and to this day the dromaeosaur lies dead on a hill a ways up there" – he indicated further into the canyon – "with six dead rebels around him. His servants fled, and King Elmork was captured, and tortured right there. But he never gave up the location of the Stones. He said only 'I have hidden them where none can reach them.' and then he was shot with an arrow.

"But it was his servant that shot him. We've guessed that Elmork knew he would be found, and ordered his servant to shoot him at the right time. His servants were tracked down, many of them slaughtered, and we got them to talk. None of them were ever given the full plan – but we guessed it. Of all Elmork's servants, just two remained to bury his body, when the rebels left this place. So, they placed him in the pre-made coffin, and so he was buried at the age of twenty-one. Eighty, in Prehistorcia time.

"But he didn't ensure Mayztec victory, as we now know. He just delayed their defeat. Because now, we have two Stones, and soon we will have the third. By this time next year, all six will be in our possession, and the Mayztec Empire and the terror it brought will truly be over, Prehistorcia restored to what it was intended to be. I can't wait! Unfortunately, we must. Goodnight to all of you. We wake at dawn."

Drake went to bed again, with a lot to think about. The Hekeni hated Elmork, but Drake (though he would never admit it to any Hekeni) admired him a little. It seemed that Elmork could have been a great king, in another time. Drake thought to himself, in that position, he'd have done the same thing, too.

*****

When morning came, they walked southeast, further into the canyon. They crossed two rivers that fed into the major one, and passed an elevated cliff with a mossy mound beneath it.

"See there?" asked Harry. "That's where Elmork's servants fled and his Deinonychus died."

Drake noticed that on the cliff were markings, carved into the rock and overgrown with the roots from above, along with seven animals, one of them a Deinonychus.

"You left a grave marker for the Deinonychus?"

"Wasn't his fault for being a Mayztec." shrugged Al. "Hekeni respect and value all animals. It loved his master, even if his master wasn't loved, and it died for him. That's something to be honoured, in our opinion. In the tomb of Elmork I hear there's actually a painting depicting the battle."

"That's probably a myth." said Harry.

Soon, they crossed from the right side of the river to the left, when it was shallow enough. After a few minutes, they stopped. There was a large pool, with a river flowing out into the main one. The waterfall feeding it was high, nearly two kilometres above them, and splashed down creating a foggy mist around them.

"Why are we stopping?" asked John.

"Because we've reached the tomb." said Al.

Alol Albertaceratops was knee-deep in the pool, checking behind the waterfall and looking up. He beckoned Harry over.

"Well, look at that!" said Harry. Drake and John moved closer. Drake looked up behind the waterfall.

About forty feet above their heads was a large, square stone jutting out of the cliff, but it was a wide deck, connecting to the cliff at the sides, while allowing the water to pass through a rectangular hole in the middle which looked thin enough to jump over.

"How do we get up there?" asked John.

"We need an experienced climber." said Harry. "Hey, Dave! Do you still like climbing?"

Chapter 15 – The Tomb of Emperor Elmork

Dave was an experienced mountain climber before he came to Prehistorcia. Drake had almost forgotten that. Dave climbed up quickly, never missing a step. He was certainly an expert, and he had scaled the thirteen metres to the cave in just a few minutes. He took the rope he was carrying in his mouth out of his mouth. The rope had a small grapple attached to it.

"Well, I'm up, but I can't seem to find anything to hook this to." he called.

"No stick, or loop, or anything?" asked Al.

"No, not... wait, I see something, But I'm really not sure if it will hold. I suppose it's worth a try, but if you fall, try and aim for the pool."

Dave crawled onto the square and disappeared. A few moments later he poked his head out over the cliff. He called down to the crowd below.

"It's hooked up! Who's coming first?"

Al decided he would be the guinea pig. Drake had no objection. Al climbed the rope, which seemed to hold. He sat down on the stone square, calling for the others to go up. John went next, with no fear, followed by Kevin, Dazz, and Alol, with help from Nemeli. Soon, it was Drake's turn to climb up. When he looked down, no one else was coming up. It seemed Jane, Steven, and Harry decided to sit this one out.

"Jane, you're not coming with me?" he asked.

"No, I think I'll stay here and survive!" she replied.

"Please?"

"What, you can't spend one hour away from me?" she laughed. "Actually, that's kind of flattering."

He growled in response, determined to climb alone now. Drake was not afraid of heights, but it was hard not to be in this position, especially when the guy who tied the rope said 'I'm not sure if it will hold'.

He reached the top. He saw that above the waterfall was another artificial rock, which seemed to be a funnel with a rectangular end. It diverted the water so it fell in an even sheet through the hole in the rock. The massive tile he was standing on was carved with a scene which had a Deinonychus screeching at an army of rebels, surrounded by them, and standing on two or three that were already dead. But that was the edge of the stone.

Around the left and right ends were further carvings, of Mayztec and rebel soldiers, fighting each other. In the middle, made up of a dozen tiles, was a square-frilled Ceratopsian; it looked like the frontal view of a Pachyrhinosaurus.

Drake stared through the sheet of water which was the tomb of Emperor Elmork, last king of the Mayztecs. The entrance was perfectly square, but there was a shadow. It too, was square, but odd, as if it had horns. The bottom part of it was triangular. Then Drake realized what it was.

He was too late. The guardian charged through the waterfall, Drake watching the water splashing off of its snout, and he leapt out of the way – narrowly.

The Ceratopsian grazed Drake and he tripped over, but relatively unhurt. The frill of this dinosaur was large and square, with skin stretched over the windows in the frill. It had long, curved horns on the corners of its frill, two small ones over the eyes, but the most noticeable feature was the massive, bony lump on its snout, which looked like there should be a horn there, but it was sawed off. It was a Pachyrhinosaurus (pack-ee-rhino-soar-us), about seven metres long, as long as Nemeli! It was as tall as Drake, and it had the usual glowing red eyes.

The Pachyrhinosaurus turned, and charged at Dazz. People scattered. Dazz was tossed high in the air by the blunt horn, and landed on his chest near the edge of the cliff. The Pachyrhinosaurus roared in triumph and anger.

Drake and Al ran to Dazz. His arm moved, and he tried to get up, and stayed down. Dazz was a Neanderthal, built to take heavier hits and stronger crashes. But of course, just because he could take harder crashes, didn't mean he wanted to.

"Dazz, are you alright?" asked Al.

He made a sound of pain. "Me okay. Get Stone." he grunted.

The Pachyrhinosaurus turned and charged at John. He was too quick, and dodged, but the dinosaur hit the outcropping of rock Dave had hooked the rope to. The grappling hook shattered and the Pachyrhinosaurus screeched in pain as the rock shattered into dust, the rope falling down to the ground below. Its snout had begun to bleed.

The Pachyrhinosaurus shook its head in annoyance. It faced outwards, its right side on the edge of the stone. Dave, Kevin, Alol, and Al charged it and slammed into it. It got angry, and prevented itself from skidding.

"Drake, John, we need your help!" said Al.

"Will it survive the fall?" asked John.

"Who cares? It's cursed anyway! Just help us!"

Drake and John slammed into the Pachyrhinosaurus's side. Its skin felt like leather, only lumpier. All five of them pushed, and the front right foot went over the edge. It groped for traction, and came in under the dinosaur.

They pushed harder. The back leg went over. Success! As soon as the back leg went over, the Pachyrhinosaurus shrieked and went over itself, tail first. It seemed to grope on with its front feet, but it didn't last long. It was over, giving out a final roar as it fell through the mist, from a splash after a few seconds.

"If it survives, the Hekeni down there are going to have a hell of a time." said John.

The five of them leant back. The waterfall was now void of all guardians. Drake decided to step beyond the sheet of water first to the chamber beyond.

It wasn't as large or lavish as the other temples, but it was pretty good for the work of just fifteen servants. The cave went way back, some twenty or thirty feet until it came to rest at a stone sarcophagus. The chamber had a square entrance, but the smooth square became rough and cave-like near the back.

Over the coffin there were diamonds stuck into the roof and walls. Around the edges were carvings of Mayztec writing. Those parts of the wall seemed smooth, but they made no real effort, carving it in only a year before their master died, possibly less. Drake began counting the diamonds as Alol walked in with Al and John by his side. Kevin followed a little behind.

"Where's Dave?" asked Drake, still counting.

"With Dazz." replied Al.

Alol began translating the writing on the wall. Al translated that to English:

"King Elmork, last king of the Mayztecs, may his victory over the Stones be eternal. But what Alcl has said was 'stones' in the sense of Extinction Stones, not some old rock just lying on the ground." Al explained as Alol moved to the other side. Al proceeded to translate: "Fifty diamonds for fifty stars, may the great Emperor Elmork forever sleep under them."

Then Al began talking as himself. "Incredible, those fifty stars perfectly mimic the exact position fifty brightest stars above this point on the date of Elmork's ascension to the throne!" he exclaimed.

"Except there's fifty-one." said Drake.

"What?"

"Fifty-one. Count for yourself, but there's one extra."

"That can't be right." said Al. He counted himself quickly. "Huh. It is right! The Mayztecs wouldn't make a mistake like that, unless... unless one of them opens the way to the Extinction Stone!"

"I don't get it, Al, there's no sign of the Stone, and there's no way this rock cave is sophisticated enough to have a whole secret passageway, or fancy mechanics like King Zolgaf. In fact, it doesn't have much technology of any kind, really." said Drake.

"Yes, but there's a reason we never found this Stone. It could be no one ever counted the diamonds, too intent to look for the Stone or distracted by the guardian. They assumed there were fifty, while the fifty-first was a trigger!"

"But Al, look around!" said Drake. "Is this cave big enough to have a secret passage?"

"No, but it is big enough to have a secret compartment, which is all it needs. Everyone, start pressing diamonds, see if any of them open a cabinet!"

All five of them began pressing the diamonds as though they were buttons. None of them went down. Every gem Drake touched was solid, and it seemed the same way for everyone else. Then, as they were running out of options, John pressed the diamond close to the ground, near the back. It seemed to sink into the wall like mud. Something triggered, and a small crack appeared. John pulled on it.

"It's not opening!" he cried.

"Hold on, I brought something for this." Al pulled a massive crowbar out from the bag.

They jammed the crowbar through the crack, and Al and Drake pushed it towards the wall. The stone split and the door opened! The cave seemed to growl as dust and a couple of diamonds rained down. It was not a large door, and it was more of a secret compartment than a passage.

It was only the size of a kitchen cupboard, touching the ground, but jammed inside it was clearly the light green Triassic Stone of the Hekeni.

"Al! This is it! This is the Triassic Stone!" exclaimed Drake.

Al knelt down. Drake saw a light come into Al's face, and a sense of awe as he gazed upon the Stone that his tribe, the Hekeni, had once owned, a thousand years ago. No Hekeni had touched this Stone in over a millennium. Al reached out for it.

"Uh, people... could we hurry this up a bit?" asked John.

The diamond button fell out of its socket, and rolled across the floor. Out of it poured thousands of honey-coloured ants. One of them crawled up John's leg. It bit him.

"Ouch! That's no ant sting! That's a bee sting!" he said.

"What's the big deal, man?" asked Kevin "They's just ants."

"Those aren't just any ants!" said Al.

"So, what are they?"

"A carnivorous species of *Ciahrzemmar*!" he yelled.

"What?" asked Drake.

Al grabbed the Stone and ran away with it. Drake saw him leap through the waterfall, not even glancing back. Drake had no idea what the ant was, but he knew that wasps evolved from ants sometime in the Eocene, so whatever these were, they were an extinct genus of ant that bit like a wasp.

"We need to get out of here!" said John, swiping ants off of his leg.

"Funny. No one really finds insects all that dangerous." said Kevin, backing off towards the waterfall.

John, Alol, and Kevin backed off. Alol went out the waterfall. John leapt out, still swiping ants from his legs. Drake, however, to avoid the ants, had stood on the coffin.

"You need help?" asked Kevin.

"Thanks, but unless you have a thousand hands each with a flyswatter, you can't. I'll find a way. You go!"

Kevin exited the waterfall. The ants began climbing up the stone coffin, abandoning the entrance for their fresh meat. Drake leant against a wall. An ant crawled onto his arm.

He squashed it, but not before it bit him. He cried out in pain. It did feel like a wasp sting! But then a thought occurred to him, one he never had to worry about:

'I'm allergic to bee stings!'

He jumped off from the coffin, jumping all the way over the ants, and sprinted to the exit, jumping through the water. He collapsed on his stomach, breathing heavily. He looked up at John, who was staring down at him. Looking at John's fedora-like hat made him speak his thoughts aloud.

"Since when did I become Indiana Jones?" he asked.

John laughed and helped him up. Drake stared at the place where the ant had bit him. It was possible the ant was not evolved enough for its venom to take as much affect as a bee sting.

"I'm allergic to bees and wasps. Will I be all right?"

"I'm sure you will." said John. "They're still ants, not bees, though the pain of their bite suggests otherwise. But there are still some living ants whose bites will hurt, and more than a bee sting. Also, bees have no relation to wasps or ants, despite appearances and common belief. Even so, people allergic to bees can get bitten by an ant and have no consequences. I wouldn't worry, Drake, unless it was an actual wasp or bee."

"What happened to Al?" he asked.

"I'm here." said Al. He was standing on the edge staring at the stone in both hands. "Look, Drake, we did it! See? The Triassic Stone!"

"You didn't do anything." said Drake. "*I* realized there was one extra star. *I* was the one who took the first hit from the Pachyrhinosaurus, and let's not forget that *I* was the one you abandoned for the rock!" yelled Drake. "Why did you just run out on us like that?"

"Oh, quit complaining! You're still alive, aren't you?"

"That's not the point!" said Drake. "You Hekeni preach friendship and unity, yet the moment you get your hands on the Extinction Stone you leave us there!"

"What could I have done?"

"Calm down!" said John. "Al, it wasn't that you abandoned us. It was how you abandoned us. No backwards glance, no offer to help, just grab the Stone and run."

Al sighed. "Look, I'm sorry you feel that way, but you all got out fine. I knew you would."

"I barely did." said Drake.

"Uh, people..." said Kevin, "there, uh, there ain't no way down."

The three of them stopped fighting. Kevin was right; the Pachyrhinosaurus had broken the rock the rope was tied to, and the metal hook. Drake wondered what happened when the Pachyrhinosaurus landed down there.

"Well, there's a pool at the bottom." said Dave. "Did anyone think to get the depth?"

"Who would have thought to?" replied John.

"Well, I guess I'll have to climb down and see." said Dave. "I will come back up with the rope."

Dave clung to the canyon ledge and scuttled down, until he disappeared in the mist the falls were throwing up. In a couple of minutes he was back up with a rope in his mouth. He hopped onto the stone platform and removed it. "Well, I'll be holding the rope while you go down, I suppose."

Drake agreed to go first. He stepped up to the edge. "Hey, Al, you could give me the Extinction Stone." he said.

"No, I'll keep it."

"If you let me have it, the Hekeni will have it sooner." said Drake. "Come on, Al, you know you'll get it back."

Al hesitated. "Fine." he handed the Stone over quickly, and without looking at it.

"Alright, Drake, I'm going to lower you down." said Dave. "Hold on tight. Just shout if you need a minute to regain your grip."

Drake wrapped the rope around his right-hand wrist, and grabbed the spot above it. He carried the green Stone under his left arm, and lowered himself off the platform. Dave lowered the rope slowly, and Drake reached the bottom in five minutes. He landed knee-deep in the pool.

"Alright, I'm at the bottom!" shouted Drake.

"Excellent! Now tie the bottom of the rope to something sturdy, for more support." replied Dave.

Drake found a tree root and tied it to that. He pulled to show it was done. Then he turned to face where everyone else was standing – only to find out they had all gone.

Chapter 16 – The Falls Rainforest (Again)

Drake couldn't believe it. No one was there! No one had waited! That was unusual.

"Hello?" he called. "Anyone?"

There was no reply. He walked through the mist, seeing the trees. Then, he found where everyone had been – or all that was left of it.

One of the army jeeps was on its side, with a dent in the door. There was one dead Hekeni smashed into a tree, and all the animals seemed to have disappeared, except for Tenethax, who grunted and came to Drake. He also saw Ahrzi bounding up behind him.

"Tenethax!" he said. "Where is everyone... er, uh... *sulluh mel na Hekeni?*" he asked, trying to say it in Hekeni.

He grunted, and faced the remaining jeep.

"No, no, that's not the Hekeni. *Sulluh mel na Hekeni*, Tenethax?"

Tenethax walked up to the jeep and nudged it. Drake walked over and looked inside. It there were some fifteen Hekeni, including Harry! They seemed to be packed in there tightly, as well as hiding behind it. They were all lying cramped on the floor, a tarp over all but Harry, who was only half-covered.

"Harry! Where's everyone else?" he asked.

"Drake, I can't hold on!" came a voice from the waterfall. It was John. "Drake, you'll have to catch me!"

"Drake, the other Hekeni are hiding with the animals." said Harry, pulling the tarp off. "That Pachyrhinosaurus emerged here and went on a real rampage!" there was a splash in the distance. "It survived, but its eyes were still red. It upended a jeep, killed one of us, and the animals and Hekeni ran off, trying to drive it away from the camp. Don't worry, they'll return. So did you guys find the Stone?"

"You bet we did! And it's yours! Take a look!" he held up the Stone.

The Hekeni stared at it with reverence, more so than the other two, if it was possible. They began jamming into each other for a closer look.

John came up soaking wet. "Hello, Drake."

"Hello – what happened to you?"

He sighed. "Nothing. Everyone else is coming down now."

Harry grabbed the Stone, but as soon as he did other people began grabbing it. Soon, they were fighting over it, except for Steven, Jane, and Tom in the far end.

"Whoa, whoa, hold on there!" yelled Drake. "Give me that!" He wrenched the Stone from everyone's hands. "This is important to you, I get it, but you are Hekeni! Hekeni do not fight other Hekeni! You will all get to hold the Stone later!" he repeated it in broken, accented Hekeni. "John, do you have the bag?"

"I have it." said Al, appearing out of the mist. "Here, put it in."

Drake dropped it into the open bag. Al threw the bag into the pack on Tenethax's back.

"I see what you mean about wars being fought over the Stones." said Drake.

"I told you they're dangerous. You may not believe they have power, Drake, but you have to admit, they do have a terrible religious power."

"Hey, do you reckon the jeep will still run?" asked Dave.

"It might. Tip it over and find out." said Drake.

Dave and Kevin pushed hard, and the jeep tilted back onto its wheels with a thump. Kevin got in and started it. It seemed to work fine.

"Good." said Harry, getting out of the jeep. "That leaves our losses at one."

Soon, other people began turning up out of the forest. One Hekeni managed to get the Pachyrhinosaurus to chase him, and then he doubled back and lost it. Besides, as he explained to Al, the red glow was fading from its eyes. Soon, all the animals and most of the people were back.

It took a while for roll call, but Al managed to do it. He determined that all the animals were safely back with them, and that there were only three people unaccounted for. Al sent Nemeli to look for them. The large allosaur stomped off in search of the other tribesmen. Meanwhile, Al took out the Triassic Stone and placed it on a flat rock near the camp. All the Hekeni gathered around it.

Drake, however, remained behind. He kept his distance, thinking.

"Hello, Drake." said Jane, behind him.

"Hi." he smiled, suddenly immensely happier.

"We haven't spent a lot of time together lately." said Jane. "There's a part of me that finds it refreshing. Something on your mind?"

"Just the Stones... the Hekeni seem to forget all their beliefs for them."

"Well, it's their religion." said Jane.

"Yes, but the Stone's miraculous power – they say it holds amazing abilities. They say the Stones keep Prehistorcia alive, that they were made by the Great God Prehistorcia's hand. I mean, they can't really believe it, can they?" he asked.

"Drake, I honestly don't know what the Stones are." she admitted. "But after witnessing the events in the tombs of Emperor Zolgaf and Queen Klefferniti, I'm inclined to believe them, too."

Drake looked at her incredulously. "Come on. You really think they were made by the Great God Prehistorcia?"

"Well, no, maybe not that part."

"Do you really believe that they're magic? That they keep Prehistorcia alive?"

Jane shrugged. Drake looked more sceptical.

"My scientific mind tells me that they're not magic." admitted Jane. "But, Drake, look at this place! Remember how we got here?

This shouldn't exist. Maybe the Stones aren't the reason Prehistorcia exists, and maybe they were never made by their god, but come on, Drake, you have to admit they have some power science can't explain."

"But... they can't be magic. Everything has an explanation."

"Really?" asked Jane. "Take sleep. Why do we even need sleep? You may think the answer is obvious, but from a scientific perspective, how do we gain energy by sleeping? Why do we need to do it at all? Shouldn't gaining our energy from food be enough? And what about water? Earth was a dry wasteland four billion years ago – where did we get our water? There's only so far the 'comets' theory can go. And how does the complex human system function so perfectly when our much simpler computers fail all the time? How does this place exist?"

"So what, you think that all those things are magic?"

"You've missed my point." said Jane. "But there are some things science has no explanation for. There are some things that will never be explained. There are some things that don't need to be explained. We can look our whole lives for a logical explanation of things – or, we can just let it *be*."

"You sound like Al."

"Well, Al's smart on a lot of things, even if he is impulsive." said Jane.

"So what, are you saying you believe the Extinction Stones are magical?"

"What I'm saying is does it really matter if they are? You dwell so much on the facts, Drake, that you miss what's in front of your eyes."

"But there has to be a logical explanation!" said Drake.

Jane sighed frustratingly. "Fine. I can't convince you. You'll have to learn it for yourself. But like Al also says – Prehistorcia's alive. Not the god, but the land itself."

Drake kissed her. She smiled, almost condescendingly, and walked away. He continued to dwell on what the logical explanation for the Stones could be.

*****

Soon, all three missing members were back with Nemeli, and the group set out again. They missed a lot of time with the Hekeni worshipping their Stone, so they had to camp at the edge of the Falls Rainforest for the night.

Harry was soothing the Nemicolopterus slowly that night. He tied a small note to it and set it out. He was hoping that the pterosaur would be safer delivering a message at night than during the day. This was important news, or so the elders would see it as such. Drake supposed now they'd have to give the Stones back to their rightful owners; it was all for the best.

He listened around the camp. He was surprised how few people agreed with him. He couldn't speak Hekeni fluently, but he knew enough to catch phrases like 'we shouldn't give the Stones back', or 'I wonder what we'll do once we have all six'.

He sat down next to Dazz, who was stoking the fire.

"Dazz, you think we should return the Extinction Stones to the proper owners, right?" he asked.

"It is right." agreed Dazz.

"Glad you think so. You seem to be in the minority."

"I not." he said. "Many Hekeni agree that it is proper. Many Hekeni will not return Stone, however. We talk big, but we not deliver Stone to owner. We not practice what we preach."

"If we met a Trontoll right now, would you hand over the Cretaceous Stone?"

"I say yes to others and to myself. But I not so sure actually. I wish to return Stone, but I not sure I could do it. Understand, Drake? I know Stone must be given to Trontoll – but I not want to do it."

"I can understand that." said Drake.

Dazz nodded, and stared into the fire. "You know that when time comes, it must be Above-worlders, and not Hekeni, that must return Stone, right?"

"Oh, I know that, Dazz." Drake sighed. "Unfortunately, I've known it all along. That's not what worries me."

Chapter 17 – Pteranodon Cliff

Drake awoke the next morning to loud squawking and ear-splitting caws. It sounded like seabirds, only it was a hundred times louder, and a hundred times more numerous. He was amazed he had slept at all with this racket! He sat up to see that he was not the only one awake. In fact, almost everyone was awake, except for a few deep-sleeping people. Those that were up looked like they had gotten up recently, too, also woken up by the ceaseless squawking. Drake walked over to Harry.

But he didn't need to ask. Standing on the edge of the cliff, looking out into the main part of Pterosaur Canyon, Drake saw hundreds upon hundreds of Pteranodon! Large animals with massive wingspans, a long, straight beak and a curved crest jutting out the back of their heads. They had a very small tail, with two tiny legs. There were thousands, stretching on both sides of the river to the jagged hillside the group had descended three days earlier. And every Pteranodon seemed to be screeching.

Flying high above were nearly a hundred more, shrieking at each other and circling the entire group.

"Holy crap, what are they doing?" Drake yelled to drown out the noise.

"There's a territory war!" replied Harry.

"What?"

"Pteranodons are very territorial!" Harry yelled in explanation. "Like lions, there's usually only a few males and a lot of females! Right now it's mating season, and like turtles, the Pteranodon all come to the same place every time to breed. That means it builds up like this from time to time, were just unlucky enough that they all decided to mate at once here! It happens every twenty years or so!"

"So what's going to happen?"

"A battle! The males of the groups are going to fight each other for the right to breed!"

"I didn't know they mate like this!" Drake said.

"Oh, yeah, they're always here! We just forgot about them, we were so focussed on the Extinction Stones! But don't worry, it'll die down in a couple of days!"

"Do all pterosaurs mate this way?"

"No! Some of them gather together and mingle. Some of them do it the dinosaur way, and just try to attract whatever female comes for them. Some of them are decorated exotic colours to try and get females!" shouted Harry over the noise. "All large ones but the Quetzalcoatlus do it this way! I don't know why, maybe it's because they're predators and can't have bright colours!"

Drake saw that all the Pteranodon were not brightly coloured, but rather camouflaged, coloured blue, light-blue, grey, and dark grey, to blend in with the sky's colours.

Drake also knew that all pterosaurs were carnivorous. Yet small ones like the Nemicolopterus had brightly coloured skin and fur. Perhaps that was because they ate insects, and maybe berries, like birds. These Pteranodon, however, would go for bigger prey, like fish or small dinosaurs.

Drake covered his ears and went into the trees, towards the river. It was only a minute or two away from the camp. But the honking, while it was a little quieter, still drowned out all other noises.

Drake dwelt on the pterosaur situation more. He decided that he could picture a Pteranodon descending down on some small animal to eat it. He was already imagining one of them picking up a Dryosaurus and eating it, or dragging it into the air to drop it. He looked out over the cliff again, and this time noticed something he hadn't before.

There were two species of known Pteranodon, *Pteranodon longiceps* and *Pteranodon sternbergi*, the difference being the size and crest shape. There were what Drake guessed five species down there – but none of them were mingling. They were all in their own groups. Drake also guessed that each had a different call. The *P. sternbergi* were on the far side of the river, and *P. longiceps* was on their side, with an unknown species. When he looked further down, he saw the other two species in large groups. No two species of Pteranodon were fighting each other.

The female Pteranodon had shorter crests. While the males had glowing crests of red, green, and yellow, the females' crests were bland.

Drake got closer, the scientist in him telling him that he'd never get another chance to observe this. Two rival males of *P. longiceps* confronted each other up above. The two males descended, just hovering over the river, and attacked each other!

It was an actual, brutal attack! Wings beat at each other, beaks jabbed in and out like spears, the tiny claws on their feet scratched out like needles! There were loud shouts and honks, until the wing of one knocked his opponent down into the river! The disgraced animal hauled itself up and shook off, and the winner went off to the rival's group of females.

Then Drake saw, on the far side of the river, his old friend, the Torvosaurus. It might have been the exact same one from a year ago; it was the same territory. It looked like a Tyrannosaurus, but it had three fingers, not two, and it had the wrong look to be an Allosaurus. It was the same shade of light-grey as the one from last year.

It ran from its hiding place in the trees towards one of the *sternbergi* Pteranodon. It must have roared, because Drake saw its mouth open and the nearby Pteranodon scatter, but Drake never heard it. The Torvosaurus found one pair mating. The male flew away, beating the female down in fear. The Torvosaurus leapt, but the female Pteranodon was away, too, just barely. It turned again and chased the Pteranodon. It was relentless. Certainly it would catch one of them soon. And it did!

Two Pteranodon were fighting again. The Torvosaurus leapt up and seized on the larger one by the wing! It yanked the screeching animal down, stepped on its wing, and ripped out his throat.

The Torvosaurus dragged his meal to the edge of the mating area, and began to eat. The other Pteranodon continued as though nothing had happened. The smaller Pteranodon kept his spot and began honking, challenging his rivals, adding his echoing voice to the rest of the din.

Drake watched the Torvosaurus eat and walked back to the Hekeni camp. They were already frying breakfast: Pteranodon bacon (no surprise where from), some primitive bread for toast, and they had out a large bucket of squashed berries for jam.

Drake saw the Lufengosaurus over by the trees, chewing leaves. For some reason this dinosaur always seemed to draw his attention, unlike some of the other exotic animals they brought. He looked near the back of the group, in the deepest part of the rainforest, and there were Hekeni shaving the woolly rhino's hair and placing it in buckets. He guessed they used it for blankets or clothing.

Drake found Al quickly. He walked over.

"Al, can't we just go through them?" asked Drake.

"Nope, sorry, it's too dangerous." he replied. "But it'll die out in two or three days, don't worry! We'll just rest here. Or all the rest we can get over this din."

Drake saw Dazz dragging another Pteranodon, this time one of an unknown species, with two arrows in its back. This made it the fourth one brought down, but there was a large group to feed. This one, Drake recognized, was a female. It was easiest to hunt females because they were the ones on the ground.

Dazz dumped it in the pile with the other uncooked pterosaur. Drake noticed four thin sheets on the ground. He went to look at them.

They were the wing membranes from the Pteranodons!

"Dazz, why don't you cook these?" he asked.

"They bitter." said Dazz. "And they strong. Make better clothes than food."

Drake left the Pteranodon bodies. Over the next few hours they were cooked and eaten, and everyone had eaten their fill. The carnivorous dinosaurs were fed the leftovers, but there was not quite enough to feed them totally. But, in a couple of days, all the Pteranodon will have left, and they could be fed properly. At first, Drake wasn't sure how this was to be done, but then he realized that dozens of Pteranodon must die, whether from fights, heart attacks, or simply being too old.

The honking continued all day, but Drake found that the more it continued, the less it seemed to bother him. He was getting deaf to the noise as the day went by. Yet, not so deaf that they did not keep him awake that night.

The next morning he woke up in one of the military tents, stretched, and walked outside not to the chirping of birds but to the honking of pterosaurs. However, now that he had slept on it, he realized how lucky he was to actually hear this sound, a sound that had not been heard except in Prehistorcia for ninety million years. Pteranodon once lived on every continent, but, like all animals, they went extinct eventually.

He walked over to the group and sat down next to Al and John. They were discussing something, but he tried not to eavesdrop. He heard anyway, and soon enough he was asked to participate.

"Drake, we understand extinction, don't we?" asked John.

"Why?"

"Because Al says we don't."

"Well, Al, I can say that as paleontologists we totally understand extinction."

"No, you don't." said Al. "You understand the *concept*. What you fail to realize is the actual thing. Humans know what extinction is, but we can't comprehend it happening to us. We assume that we are the indestructible species, that we will remain on Earth forever, but we won't! Human society does not understand extinction. They do not realize that someday humans will be extinct just like the other ninety-nine percent of all life."

"Hmm." said Drake. "Sorry, John, I gotta go with Al on this one."

John waved his hand in scepticism.

Drake began thinking of extinction. They were as sure as they could be that the dinosaurs were killed by an asteroid, but the other four major extinctions were a complete mystery. Current belief on the Permo-Triassic Extinction was drought, volcanoes, or possibly a comet, and the Devonian Extinction was thought to be a comet, too. No one really had any idea what extinctions were.

There weren't just five extinctions total, though, even though there were five major ones. Every period in Earth's history – Silurian, Carboniferous, Jurassic, Eocene – they all had extinctions at the end of them. And even within the periods there were minor die-offs – every Ceratopsian except Triceratops and Torosaurus were dead five years before the dinosaurs were. Stegosaurs were dead twenty to thirty million years after the Jurassic. Dimetrodon was dead nearly thirty million years before the Permian Extinction. What, then, caused a single species to die off, several species to die off, and almost all the species to die off? There were theories, but no one would ever really know why some extinctions were larger than others.

By far the largest extinction was the Permian Extinction, killing off 95% of all life on earth. It was so devastating that it ended the Palaeozoic era and began the Mesozoic era. It killed off Trilobites, a crablike creature that had lived since life first began. The second-largest was the Cretaceous, which destroyed some 70% of all life on earth, including the mighty dinosaurs. Of course, the Ordovician Extinction must have been devastating, but so little was known about it, because it happened so long ago – half a billion years ago, as a matter of fact. This was assuming Humans weren't an extinction.

The scary thing? If you considered the humans as an extinction, they would be the most devastating one *ever*. Species are dying off faster than any other extinction since the Permian, and if it continues at this rate, humans will have destroyed all species quicker than any other thing has ever done so. Faster than the Cretaceous extinction, faster than the Ordovician extinction, perhaps even faster than the Permian extinction. Humans say they are getting better, but they aren't. They were getting worse; they expanded and demolished the wild without even walking into it and seeing what the Hekeni were able to see.

But extinction could also be a good thing. It allowed for new development, better animals to evolve to harsher conditions, different climates, and ultimately allowed life to continue. Without extinction, there'd be no evolution. Without destruction, there would be no construction. Hence, the weakness of Prehistorcia.

*****

The Pteranodon continued their honking the following day. Drake decided he would walk back into the rainforest until their sound was down to a bearable level. However the mating days were almost over, this being day three, and there were now only a few dozen females of each species, and all the live males that remained (which was almost all of them) kept jostling and fighting for them.

He found he didn't have to go far to escape the honks. When he reached a river cutting across his path from a waterfall, the honking seemed above him, not around him.

He knelt down and began drinking from the river. The thing with Prehistorcia was that the rivers always ran clean, and the pollution was purely natural. He washed his face in the cool water, feeling relief. He looked around to make sure no one was looking, and then he rolled in himself.

He splashed around a bit until he was soaked. He let the water flow around him. His mind cleared, and he closed his eyes. Then, he actually felt the land.

Many Hekeni could do this, but Drake never had. It surprised him when he began hearing it. It didn't tell him anything, but it gave him feelings, but not all of them were good.

He had a feeling that many angry footsteps were marching his way. He wasn't sure what they were, but he knew they meant the Hekeni harm. He felt the spirits of the land; that the Mayztec spirits were angered about the Hekeni truly defeating them, but he also felt that the spirits could do them no harm. Prehistorcia wouldn't let them.

Then he felt a truly awful feeling in his gut — he suddenly felt foreign, like an outsider. He didn't belong here, and many people felt that about him. He felt his full purpose was not yet served, that there was still more he needed to do. Why, then, was he here?

He remembered the old Hekeni knowledge — ask the land.

Ask the land? How dumb was that? But, it was worth a shot. He thought, in his head: 'why did you bring me here, if not for Jane?'

He waited and held his breath. He received no answer. He sighed. His breathing sounded loud now, heavier. Then the truth hit him:

It wasn't his breathing.

He opened his eyes. There stood a tall, mottled green carnivore, surprisingly like Nemeli. It was as long as her, with a thin, oval snout, and long forearms with three claws, or at least long for a carnosaur. It was taller than Drake by a head. Drake placed it by the skull immediately — Abelisaurus, from Cretaceous South America, named for the discoverer, Abel.

It was bending down to drink, but there Drake was in the river totally motionless, like a little dessert. He rolled over, got to the other side of the river and stood up.

The Abelisaurus roared. Drake turned and ran, but the Abelisaurus pursued him. Drake did the only thing he could think of:

"Nemeli!" he shouted.

He got closer to the camp. Then the pale-blue Neovenator smashed through the trees, shielding Drake. Nemeli was larger than the Abelisaurus, but not by much. She was certainly more menacing, however, and when she lunged forward with a roar, the Abelisaurus growled back, but backed off. Nemeli roared again. The Abelisaurus walked into the trees, disheartened.

"Atta girl, Nemeli. Thank you." said Drake, patting her leg.

Nemeli turned and nudged her nose up against him affectionately. Drake pet her nose. He chuckled, remembering the very first time he met Nemeli – he wouldn't have dared pet her nose. Now he couldn't imagine not petting her. She was so affectionate, thought Drake, as long as you were her friend.

Drake walked with her back to the camp, which wasn't too far away. He sat down next to John and watched the Pteranodon again. There were even fewer females above than before, the rest being dead or flown away. These females seemed to be the old or withered ones, and the males above were the runts.

"Where were you?" asked John.

"Listening to the land." he said.

"Oh? What did it say?"

Drake now remembered that feeling of a foreigner. Is that how the land viewed him? How the Hekeni viewed him? As an outsider, or even an intruder?

"It, uh... it said nothing." he lied.

"Too bad." said John. "I've listened to it a couple of times. It didn't tell me much either."

"What feeling did you get?" asked Drake.

"I got a feeling of acceptance." John sighed happily. "I felt that Prehistorcia wanted me here as much as I wanted to be here. I felt that everything in my life from now on would turn out the way it was supposed to."

This added to Drake's anxiety. Well, he thought, John was like a father at this point, and Drake looked to him for advice not only on science but also when he was feeling nervous. If he couldn't tell John, who could he tell? Jane? She would understand too. But, he thought, since John was here, he might as well come clean.

"Alright, I lied." said Drake.

"What?"

"The land did speak to me. But I felt like I was an intruder, and outsider that it didn't want here. I felt that my purpose wasn't fulfilled."

"Hmm. I guess my saying I felt I belong here didn't help much then, did it?"

"Not really."

"Well, Drake, the Hekeni don't view you as an intruder, and neither, obviously, do their animals. Are you sure you got your feelings right?"

"I'm pretty sure."

"Yet you also felt that you still haven't realized why you're here. That means that Prehistorcia still has you here for a reason. Could you think at all of what that reason would be?"

"Nothing. But we've been through all this before, last year."

John sighed. "Drake, if you have not completed what you were brought here for, then the land wants you to stay. You are not an outsider; your feelings of unfulfillment may have been mistaken for feelings of intrusiveness. You're your own worst enemy, you know. But if you don't think you've found the reason you're here, then obviously the land wants you to stay here until you do. And that, Drake, ought to be a happy thought."

Drake smiled despite his feelings. It made him feel a little better, but he still couldn't help but feel, for the first time in a very long time, that he didn't belong there.

Chapter 18 – Pteranodon River

The next day all the Pteranodon had left, except for a few desperate, weaker males with straggling females that were also growing too weak to make their journey. There were only a handful of males left of three species, all of them too old or too young to fight, and they sent across desperate calls to the two or three females that were too young or too old to last long on a journey.

Al decided it was time to head out, there were few enough Pteranodon that they could move through safely. He then placed his Sekka hat back on his head and got the Hekeni to pack up.

They went down the side of the cliff, at the point where the slope was gentlest. They came up the west slope, and descended the east slope, and had to cross the river at the first possible point. Drake looked back and saw the river they camped near fall down the drop and then form a small lake, which flowed into the main river.

There were dead, rotting Pteranodon littering the ground, and Nemeli and the other carnivores bent down to eat them. Ahrzi was with the other trained Utahraptors, and they accepted him as if he was their own baby. Then again, as Drake thought, he was a youngster of their herd, which was completed at the Hekeni camp far away. Unlike the wild dromaeosaurs John saw last year, Ahrzi did not have to wait for his turn. Then again there was enough meat that even wild ones wouldn't have to wait in a group that small. This wasn't the greatest way to observe if the Hekeni had gotten rid of deep-seated hierarchical instincts.

Drake saw that of the five species of Pteranodon, there were only three species left, minus an unknown species and the *P. longiceps*. The others were still there. Of the three remaining species, however, there were only a very few left, still stubbornly trying for a mate they never got in the last three days. The most numerous were still the *P. sternbergi*, the last remaining species on the other side of the river.

The main difference between the two known species was crest length and shape. The *longiceps* had rounded cone-like crests while the *sternbergi* had flattened ones.

They moved east, as the canyon continued that way for a long time. Al said there would be a place to cross the river a few kilometres up. Meanwhile, Drake saw a pack of seven little Dromaeosaurs, no more than a metre long, and covered in feathers. There were five adults and two children, all standing around a cluster of rock, with three pine trees.

"John, what are those?" asked Drake.

"Atrociraptor. I saw another group with the Yaxog last year, they're the same animal."

Drake had heard of that one, discovered in Alberta, Canada recently. All seven of the Atrociraptor were eerily silent, and all staring in one direction. He followed their line of sight.

They were looking at an unknown species of Pteranodon still desperate enough to try and mate. It looked old, and it was one of only six living ones in the area that still hung on.

Drake suddenly realized what they were about to do. So did John, because he stared towards them and watched, too. The five adults ran from their hiding spots and leapt on the Pteranodon, which tried to take off. But the Atrociraptor pinned her, and slashed at the wing membranes, tearing them. Then they moved to the body, and broke her neck. The two youngsters emerged to feast with their parents.

"John, did you see that?" asked Drake. "They went for the wing membranes first!"

"Yes, I did see that. They learned that the pterosaurs can't fly without the membranes, so they learned to slash them first. Now they've taught their children the same thing!"

Dromaeosaurs really were the smartest of the dinosaur families. They had the intelligence of birds of prey, or of large cats, which learned swiftly. He saw two remaining Pteranodon take off out of fear. As Drake suspected, the two young Atrociraptor did not need to wait for the adults to finish – there was more than enough meat and space for everyone.

They walked for two hours along the riverbank, passing the carcasses of Pteranodon, but they were becoming scarce, too, and the few that still remained were being eaten by scavengers and large carnivores that preferred scavenging to hunting, or else they were already eaten. Drake wasn't used to the quiet after three days of hearing nothing but loud squawks and honks.

They crossed the river at a shallow, but wide point, and all the animals and vehicles were able to cross as well. Drake saw that the land was vast and grassy, with rocky hills, and sparse trees.

They continued to walk along the canyon, but it would be some time until they came to their next destination, a place called Karandagga Canyon, which was, like the Falls Rainforest, a branch off of the main Pterosaur Canyon. Drake asked Al what a Karandagga was.

"Well, it's the Hekeni name for a genus not discovered on Earth." said Al. "Or so it was according to the books Dave and previous Above-world travellers have lost down here. We've determined it was probably native to Australia, Central America, or possibly Antarctica."

Drake wondered what it could be. But he had plenty of time to think. With the green Triassic Stone found, the Hekeni's pace seemed to drop in urgency. They took it easy, sleeping late, camping early. But they were on no set time, like they were last year, when every day increased the risk of being too late. With this quest, however, the Stones had been in the temples for a thousand years, and they could wait a couple of days longer. There was still the anticipation, and the tension of what would happen when all the Stones were found, though.

Another night came and went, with the Hekeni baking bread and cooking meats with spices and vegetable juices. The Hekeni were quite good at cooking, when they could pack the material.

When they woke up the next morning, they continued due east on the northern half of the river, as Al and Harry explained it would be two more nights before they reached the canyon, and then a third night in the actual canyon, at this pace.

Drake was content for now as they continued walking across the vast grassy plains on which wild horses and herds of buffalo munched on. They passed a small pond, and a large rocky mound which was, apparently, a memorial for a great battle. A Mayztec general, General Agaltrox, was a powerful general sent north to fight rebels. But when the time came to go to war, he took many slaves with him as well as soldiers, and hid in the canyon, defecting to the rebels. They settled in the grassy plain, but the emperor sent a massive army to kill them. They fought, and Agaltrox died in the battle, but his tribe, which would later become one of the current four nomadic tribes, built the memorial there and moved on.

The next night they settled under a grove of leafy trees, next to the powerful river, and slept under the full moon. When Drake woke up, all he could see from it were the Hekeni animals and a large group of wild Gallimimus grazing on ferns in a valley below.

The Hekeni got up and walked east again, the canyon walls looming high and sheer above them. Here, they went up in what looked like large steps only a giant could climb, but leaving the clefts open for thousands of nesting pterosaurs and birds.

They left the grassy fields to a wide, shady forest, where the trees grew far apart, but high and healthy.

A small pterosaur with a wingspan of just over a metre flew by. It had a great, banana-shaped beak which curved upwards, and wire-thin teeth. It was brightly coloured green, with brown blotches. It landed by a pond to the right of the group, and began dipping its beak in, as if it was a pelican. Drake watched as water spilled out between its thousand teeth. Then he realized – it was filter-feeding!

"John, what pterosaur is that?" he asked, not expecting proper answer.

He looked at it. "Hey, that must be a Pterodaustro (tear-oh-dost-row), it's been thought to filter-feed like that! That's kind of cool."

"You mean you've actually heard of it?" he asked.

"Yes. Come to think of it, I've probably heard of everything."

*****

Soon enough, the Hekeni came to the entrance of Karandagga Canyon. It was a vast, flat entrance that touched the bottom of the canyon. Drake saw, however, that it sloped up and got narrower as it went further in, and the walls of the canyon seemed to go down, too, greatly reducing the height.

However, also at the entrance, was a group of people blocking the main path, preventing the Hekeni from getting in. Drake saw that some of them carried sharp, Clovis-point spears, while others carried heavy axes with the blades made of stone. All of them had a hunting bow and quiver of arrows over their shoulders, except for two, which were holding crossbows with the arrows made of bone.

"Who's blocking us?" asked Drake.

"I thought you knew!" said Al. "Look at their arrows!"

Drake looked at the feathered arrows in the quivers – all of them had red feathers.

"Golarans!" he exclaimed.

The Golaran Tribe was the largest in Prehistorcia, and the most violent. There were some thirty Golarans all together, and all looked ready to kill. The leader began speaking in Golaran.

He walked over the Harry. "What are they saying?"

Al began yelling back. Harry began translating at the Golarans reply.

"We know you have the Stones, Hekeni! We know you are looking for them. We demand to have our Stone now. Hand it over, or we'll raid you, and take them all from you. We only want our Stone, but if you are not willing to hand it over, we will take them all."

"You can try!" Al yelled in Hekeni, making Harry's translation unnecessary. "But look around you – eighty Hekeni and fifty animals against thirty Golarans. I like our odds! Besides, we don't have your Stone, and even if you could kill us all, you'd see that! But go ahead! Attack us! We'll just do to you what we did to your prison camp a year ago, and this time we'll leave no survivors!"

The Golarans held their spears. Hekeni hated to kill animals, especially their fellow human beings, but for the defence of the Extinction Stones, they would not hold back. Even if the Hekeni did hold back, however, the dromaeosaurs and Nemeli certainly wouldn't.

"Move, Golarans, or we'll push our way through!" Al shouted.

The Golarans didn't move. Al called Nemeli and the dromaeosaurs, and the animals charged forwards as everyone else ran behind them. The Golarans stood no chance against the might of the Hekeni, and the remaining ones backed off A Golaran stared at Al, who was now walking at the back of the group.

"*Lel tur murhah zill, Hekeni.*' he said.

Al smiled back. "*Rahalah*, Golaran." he replied.

"What was that?" asked Drake.

"He told me it wasn't over." answered Al. "So I told him 'rahalah'. It means... well, it means a lot of things. It can mean we are superior and we will cause your extinction. It means we will always be victorious. It's kind of a formal goodbye for an enemy, and our battle cry when we warred with the Mayztecs. It's just a way to say 'you are finished, I have won'."

There were a lot of meanings in one word, and Drake didn't like any of them. He decided that it wasn't his place to voice it out loud, though. Instead, he looked around the canyon. It was a red-sand desert, like that of Arizona or Australia. Cacti grew out of the ground, and small creatures lurked under rocks.

"So this is Karandagga Canyon?" asked Drake.

"Yes it is."

"And the Golarans aren't done yet, are they?"

"No, they are not. But when next we meet, we will be done. And then they will be sorry."

Chapter 19 – Karandagga Canyon

The Hekeni walked along the canyon with brownish-red layers jutting up the sides. The sun began setting, but today the Hekeni travelled as far as they could, until the western sky was pale blue, and they settled down in the middle of a clearing, in the light of a full moon.

Yet again, Harry was going to tell them of the Mayztec emperor, with Alol at his side. Many Hekeni gathered around for this, as well as those not familiar with Prehistorcian History, such as Drake. Ahrzi sat on his lap, while Sam was asleep next to John. A great green Parasaurolophus yawned, stretched, and laid down comfortably behind Harry. He began the story:

"This next Mayztec building is the tomb of Emperor Rilowin the Wise." he said. "Rilowin is perhaps the greatest king to ever rule the Mayztecs. He believed in knowledge above all else as the ultimate power, and luck seemed to favour him because of it. When he first took the throne at the age of fifty, seventeen to you Above-worlders, he sent spies into the rebel camps, and had the rebels return to him, ten years later, with information. You see, we rebels used a secret form of communication, to avoid Mayztec ears.

"But his spies ruined us! They cracked the code, and taught it to Rilowin, who then proclaimed it the official language of the Mayztecs. All the rebel tribes formed after still speak that language – Zolgaf, Borchillian, Agaltrox, Quellorg, and Nemnar to name a few." then Drake realized why the Zolgaf and Borchillian language sounded so similar. "Next, he was thirty years old, and sent a massive force into the Thunder Marshes, a force that would later become the Zolgaf Tribe" Harry continued.

"However Rilowin was hated by us rebels, naturally. Why do I call him a great king, then? Because he only started out hated by rebels and loved by Mayztecs. He would later find a way to make both groups love him. Many native historians call this short-lived period the Golden Age of Mayztec Prehistorcia.

"He sent himself north. That's right, he actually went north in person, the first Mayztec emperor to do so, and the only, except Queen Klefferniti, to return alive. He came first to the Golarans, with a small defensive force, and spoke to their leader, asking him to spread the word. It took a few years, and a few more to trust him, but eventually his grand unification plan was accepted when he was a hundred and thirty years old.

"Right under the Supersaurus Mountains, where we are going tomorrow, he and the rebels teamed up to build a master school, which attempted to bring all tribes of Prehistorcia together in peace and harmony. It was a nice idea, and it seemed to work.

"At the age of one-sixty, Rilowin took a wife, but this was not what angered the Mayztec people. She was a Trontoll, a rebel, unfit for one so noble as their king. It was a disgrace; a rebel was below a slave! However the people accepted her, and Rilowin made her a queen. They had three sons and two daughters, and Rilowin raised them to his beliefs in knowledge, equality and unity. His oldest daughter was given to the chief of the Hekeni at the time as a peace bond when she was older.

"However, Rilowin grew old, and there were many dissidents who hated that he'd associated with rebels, most prominent among them his oldest son. His oldest son was talking to the Mayztec people, and ignored his father, each with differing opinions. He held back, though, because Rilowin had raised enough goodness in him that he could not commit murder, and besides, he was half-rebel himself.

"When Rilowin was the ripe old age of five hundred and ninety, his wife died at the age of five-sixty-four. Rilowin used all his power to help heal her, but it was no good. A year later, he was still grieving, and sent his wife, as per her wish, to be buried in the north. A kilometre away from the school, they built the building we will visit, and buried her there. They say his last words to his wife were 'you've spent your life in my realm. We'll spend the afterlife in yours'. His oldest son, who was now eager for his dying father to give him the throne, hired an assassin to kill him.

"But in the end he could not kill his father. He tried to stop the assassin, but it was too late, Rilowin had died. The son simply shrugged, and got ready to take the throne. But Rilowin was smart enough to see what occurred in his oldest son's heart.

"He left the throne to his second-born."

Harry finished, chuckling a little bit. "King Rilowin's body was sent north, as per his request, and there he lies next to his Trontoll wife."

"So what happened to the school?" asked John.

"Oh, things don't last. The school was disbanded by Rilowin's great-great grandson, and abandoned, although its remnants can still be seen." replied Harry. "The tomb, however, remains intact beneath Mount Ash, and there lies an Extinction Stone."

"Is this building very big?" asked Drake.

"It was built as a branch of the school, the Memorial Building, and he was buried in the basement. I think it's a safe bet the building is a fair-sized one."

Drake looked north towards the end of the canyon. He could see large mountains looming in the distance, one prominent and forward of the others. It looked unpleasantly familiar.

"Harry, Mount Ash isn't a volcano, is it?" he asked.

"Oh, don't worry, Drake, that thing hasn't blown in two thousand years, and it's unlikely to blow tomorrow."

"The fact that we're climbing it raises the odds exponentially." said Drake.

*****

Drake woke up the next morning with the sunrise coming over the horizon, brightening the sky, but leaving the canyon in shadow. He stretched and got up, seeing that he had been sleeping next to Tenethax. He looked around and saw Jane still asleep elsewhere. He felt a little guilty, it was the first time on the trip they hadn't slept next to each other. Looking around, many Hekeni were already up, but taking it easy, on no fixed schedule.

"Hey, Drake, you up now, too!" said Dazz. "Come! I will show you Karandagga!"

"You've found a Karandagga?" asked Drake.

"Yes, he not far from here. I went out looking just for palentolojists to see."

"You didn't have to do that." said Drake.

"But I did anyway. You follow, and I show you. Perhaps you know Engliz name. We wake John!"

Drake looked over at Jane as Dazz shook John to explain. He considered, for a brief moment, waking her, too. But she looked too peaceful. Ahrzi was asleep, head resting on her arm. He sighed, hoped she wouldn't be mad, and followed Dazz without waking her.

Dazz led them northwest, until they came to a small cliff overlooking a desert. The cliff wasn't high; Drake could jump down and not hurt himself.

"Look over." said Dazz.

Drake and John looked over. There was a small carnivore, about six metres or nineteen and a half feet long. It was as tall as Drake was standing up, with long arms tipped with three claws. One of them looked like a dromaeosaur claw, except that it was on its hand, not its feet. Its tail was stiff for balance, and it had an oval head with strong jaws; its feet were the three-toed birdlike feet found on almost every other Therapod.

"So that's a Karandagga." said John. "Where have I seen that before?"

"You mean it's actually discovered on Earth?" asked Drake.

"Yeah. That claw reminds me of the Baryonyx, but this certainly is not that. It was a really new find, oh, what is it? It's on the tip of my tongue! Oh, what was that carnivore found in Australia?"

"Oh, that one!" said Drake. "Australovenator!"

"That's it!" exclaimed John.

"So in you world it called Australovenator?" asked Dazz.

"Yes, and that was surprisingly well-pronounced for one who has such a strong accent." said John. "As the name suggests, it's native to Australia, a hundred million years old, and the very first of its kind found there. This put Australia back on the dinosaur map."

"Well, point is, we now know what a Karandagga is." said Drake. "No wonder Al didn't know its English name! This animal wasn't described until 2009, after Dave got lost here in 2007. He was their largest knowledge source, until Al got some new names and descriptions from your book. But Australovenator was even too new to go in there. I remember your book was already being published by the time it was discovered. It never went in there, along with the other two sauropods found with it."

"Yeah, that was one of the digs I didn't go on." said John. "Too bad. That would have been something to be a part of."

"Dinosaur history for sure." agreed Drake. "Shall we go back to the camp?"

The dark-brown Australovenator stopped sniffing the ground and began leaping up at small pterosaurs that began waking up. The pterosaurs were too quick.

"Maybe in a minute." said John.

Drake noticed that the Australovenator used its hands as a primary weapon, not its feet or jaws, as many other related carnosaurs did. In fact, the legs were much shorter because of this, proportionally. It was having some trouble jumping.

It leapt up, swiped its large claw at the sky, and tore the wing membrane of a Dimorphodon. The pterosaur went down, and the Australovenator was on it in an instant, ripping it apart with his hands. It roared and began eating.

"Alright, let's go now." said John. "Dazz, do you remember the way?"

"I always know way." he replied.

They got back to camp, and announced the name of the Karandagga in English to Al. Jane, Drake noticed, was still asleep.

*****

The Hekeni group got up and began moving north, looking for a good spot to take the animals and the equipment up the canyon without straying too far off their path. The canyon looked a lot like the Grand Canyon, but there was no river running through it, just barren desert.

A tarantula scurried under a rock as Ahrzi chased it, trying to catch it. It was incredible how fast the dinosaurs were being trained, considering it was in the field. Drake was sure Ahrzi was already more obedient than other dromaeosaurs his age. Sam was the same way, too. Sam was playful and curious, and he was looking for fights, a stage that didn't come until a year or two later. He was able to take orders and follow directions very well, at least if he wanted to.

As they moved further down the canyon, the desert began to show more life, with tufts of desert grass, cacti, and small animals leaping out of places. Pterosaurs stalked overhead, hoping to catch an unwary kangaroo rat or large arachnid – not that any arachnids would be large here compared to the Thunder Marshes.

Soon, at the northernmost part of the canyon, they found a great ramp leading upwards, wide enough for ten people to walk side-by-side. The outside of it was crumbling, and the inner wall was caked with dirt, but it was still a very efficient way up.

"Did the Mayztecs build this?" asked Drake.

"They sure did." said Harry. "You couldn't have all the Mayztec and southern rebel students walk all the way around the canyon, could you?"

"And it's still standing?" asked John. "Shouldn't it have eroded away?"

They stepped up onto the ramp, which was very solid. Al answered this time:

"If you look, John, they shaved down the side of the cliff to make this ramp, it's not like it was some clumsy brick structure. This ramp will still be here for a long, long time before it's totally useless."

"And it is eroding." said Jane, pointing to the outside edge. "See? It's just doing it very slowly, just like these canyon walls will one day erode backwards, slowly."

"I can just imagine this back in Mayztec times." said Harry. "This would have been very crowded.'

"Maybe in the peak of its progress." said Drake. "But you said yourself it only lasted four generations. What is that down here? Two hundred years? Three hundred?"

"Typically, for a Mayztec king, it averaged about two hundred Earth years per generation." said Harry. "In this case, the school lasted just over a thousand years. Rilowin's sons were not gifted with Rilowin's long life; royal intrigue and assassinations eventually got the better of them."

They walked up to the top of the canyon, until they stared across another brownish-red desert landscape, with high peaks jutting up in the distance. There were pine trees slowly beginning as the mountains got closer, along with all the desert rocks and hardy plants. The forest ahead wasn't particularly thick or lush, but it wasn't barren, either. But the Hekeni weren't going that way.

Harry led them east, but he took them along the edge of the canyon, which was northeast for now. Drake looked around, hoping to see some sign of a structure.

"Al, where's the school?" he asked.

"Look closely in that general direction." he pointed towards the mountains.

At first Drake couldn't see a thing, but then, as they got closer, he saw a layer of bricks, waist-height, outlining the old school area. There were statues, toppled pillars, and a half-collapsed arch, but that was down the paved road. Al turned them away from it, heading due east now that the canyon had bent off and away east as well. The wall was still visible for a long time afterwards.

Drake also saw remnants of the old courtyard, with stone tables and benches, and hardy desert grass still growing from where the old stuff was well-watered and fertilized.

He tried to imagine it, thousands of years ago, as a student just coming to see the school for the first time. Drake imagined seeing huge walls, which encompassed a building, perhaps with a second floor. He pictured a huge brick rectangle, and there was the first floor, held up by mighty stone pillars, and maybe two stairways to the second floor. He pictured the building as having a huge rectangular hole in the centre of it, for the courtyard, and perhaps the second floor even had a third above it. Then there were hundreds of students, all mingled, learning about the same things, trying to share cultures.

But that was reduced to a pile of rubble. He'd never see it, and no one would ever see it again. It was a shame, really, to have the mighty ruins fall, to have that school that tried to preach acceptance torn down. He could relate to Rilowin, what he was trying to do.

Tribes in Prehistorcia claimed to get along, but really the only thing they did was ignore each other until it suited them. The Hekeni and the Zolgaf were the only ones on truly friendly terms. The tribes made their own little alliances against the world, letting others live in peace, but not really caring about their problems. The tribes needed to practice what they preached. At least Golarans didn't try to hide their indifference.

They approached one section of mountains that jutted out from the rest of the range. At the very edge was a large volcano, and underneath the volcano was the most extravagant tomb yet.

"Welcome to Mount Ash." said Al.

Chapter 20 – Beneath Mount Ash

The tomb of King Rilowin was the most extravagant one yet. It was a two-story-high black, rectangular box carved from igneous, or volcanic, rock. He could tell it was two stories tall because there were six windows, three on each floor, but they were bricked up, so no one could see in them. Flanking the building was one high tower on each side, each tower ending in a giant sauropod head, its mouth opened, one facing east, one facing west. Behind the tomb was a half-circle of wall, extremely thick, and twice as tall as Drake, or so he guessed. Surrounding the giant wall at the very back was hardened, flowing rock, and Drake suddenly knew what it was – the wall was a barrier to lava, and that flowing rock had gone around the wall, and avoided the tomb.

"They actually built a lava shelter!" said Drake.

"Yeah, but I'll bet that wall won't last forever." said Al. "It was probably thicker when it was originally built."

"So this is the tomb of King Rilowin." said Steven.

"Yes, the tomb of King Rilowin the Wise." said Harry. "You see on either side of the tomb, or so Alol tells me, these are called the Pillars of the Sun, because–"

"Because they face the rising sun in the east, and the setting in the west." said Drake, starting to get the idea behind Mayztec architecture.

"That's right." said Harry. "This is an extravagant tomb, even for those tombs they built in the south, where most of their emperors are buried."

"What do the normal tombs look like?" asked John.

"Typically like the one Emperor Zolgaf was laid to rest in." answered Harry.

"So where will we find the Extinction Stone?" asked Drake.

"I suggest we check the burial chamber." said Al. "But this is a large tomb. Elmork may have found that predictable, and hidden it someplace else."

"I suppose we'll just have to enter it and find out." said Dave. "Do we go in today?"

"Might as well." said Al.

"We'll need a bigger group for this." said Drake.

"You're right." said Al. "It'll be all the paleontologists, Dave, Kevin and Tom, me of course, Dazz, Harry, Alol, we'll bring in a fully-grown Deinonychus and one other volunteer." he ordered. He then asked for a volunteer in Hekeni, and all the hands went up.

Al chose the owner of the Deinonychus they were bringing. With that settled, they went into the tomb of Emperor Rilowin the Wise, with Al in the lead.

They approached the entrance, which was an eight-foot-high stone arch with two great stone doors in the way. Alol read the writing on the door, and Harry translated:

"Here lies King Rilowin the Wise." he said. "And then there's a song. Alol doesn't want to read that."

"Oh, come on!" said Drake.

Harry asked him in Hekeni. He replied: "He says no. It'll sound stupid in Hekeni, because it doesn't rhyme, and even stupider in English."

"Fine. Let's just enter then." said John.

They pushed back the stone doors, and walked into a large rectangular room with a perfectly flat floor. At the back of the room was one staircase on each side going up. Then, on the inside edge of the upwards staircases, were two sets, one on each side, of staircases going downwards. There was rotting wood at the edges of the room, stone benches knocked over or thrown against the wall, and four pillars holding up the second floor at key structural areas. It really was a miniature castle. It was dark, and silent.

"Here." Al handed Drake one of five flashlights.

Al took the second one, gave a third to John, gave the fourth to Dazz, and the fifth to Kevin. They all switched them on, which threw the room into sharp relief.

All over the walls were carvings, obviously supposed to be there, carved at head height between two small bands. They depicted Mayztecs and rebels shaking hands, hundreds of people walking from all different paths walking up to the school, Hekeni standing next to giant animals, welcoming several Mayztec visitors to try and ride it. There were Mayztecs teaching a small group of rebels how to build things sturdier. The whole room had an air of friendliness, and to Drake it certainly *felt* like a school.

But this building was long-gone. There was writing, he saw, just above and below the bands, in six different languages, or so he assumed because some symbols were so different from others.

"What are those languages?" he asked Harry, indicating to the walls.

"Mayztec, and the languages of the six original tribes. You probably only see five, but remember, the Solg broke from us, and they use the same writing and generally the same language as us... us being the Hekeni."

"Yeah, I got that. So the languages are those of Hekeni and Solg, Golaran, Trontoll, Fertile River, Yaxog and Mayztec?"

"Pretty much, yeah."

"So where do we go from here?" asked Jane. "Up or down?"

"Well, the burial chamber is down." said Al. "So I guess we'll try that first."

The large group went down the stairs, half on one side, half on the other. But it didn't matter anyway, because they both made a U-turn, and opened up to the front of the temple basement, in the same room. The room was exactly like the one above it, only there were no downwards stairs, no carvings, and the stone benches were intact, carved into the wall. There were also two stone coffins, side by side, in the middle of the room.

"The Stones can't be here." said Drake. "There's no guardian."

"Yes, but history tells us the people who found the red Stone beat the guardian." said Al. "Maybe this tomb is where the red Stone is."

"Then it would be seen in plain sight!" said Drake. "Remember also that you said he dropped the Stone, leaving the dead bodies. Well, aside from the king and queen there, I don't see any dead bodies. What would have happened to them?" he asked.

"I don't know. But we should, at least, look." said Al.

The two groups crammed around the coffins. Drake's team lifted up the lid of the queen. There was nothing but bones, in tattered royalty robes. There were a few bronze possessions, but beyond that, nothing. Next, he looked into the coffin of King Rilowin.

The same thing. His robes were much more royal, with jewels and a stronger fabric that made it less tattered, but there was no Extinction Stone.

"Let's try upstairs." said Dave.

"Agreed." replied Al.

They closed the coffin lids and ascended to the main floor, and then went one above that. There were two statues of a man on each end of the room. They were the same man. He was fat, dressed royally, and held his arms wide with a big, welcoming smile. He looked like a happy, grandfatherly figure, sitting on a throne as if it were grandpa's armchair. Both statues were pure gold. Drake was sure this accepting look was intended.

Drake knew that it must be Emperor Rilowin here. There were two stone statues of a sauropod, the frontal view of it, standing between wide arches. They were in the opposite corners from the Rilowin statues. There were no carvings or stairs here, either, and there was a large lump in the middle of the foor.

The group moved around the room. Drake peered behind a stone sauropod, and leaned on it. To his surprise, it began sliding backwards. Excited, he kept pushing. The other Hekeni helped, and soon they heard a thump. The sauropod was as far back as it could go. They pushed harder, and found that the sauropod swung backwards, revealing a spiral staircase, full of light.

"The entrance to the east pillar!" said Drake.

"The Sunrise Tower." said Harry. "Quickly, see if the Sunset Tower is an entrance!"

Drake ran forward. His foot caught on something and he tripped. He picked up his flashlight, and pointed it at what he tripped over. His heart nearly stopped.

A tail.

He moved his light up the tail. What he thought was a lump was actually a body! It was pure black, like the tomb itself, which threw him off the first time. But he was looking closer now.

He saw the thick leg, crouched inwards. He kept moving his light up. He saw the front legs, the shoulders, and followed down a tapering neck that curved inwards, away from the entrance, which ended in a small head. The whole animal was six and a half metres long, or twenty feet. He shone the light at the animal's head, and saw the piercing red eyes.

The eyes were opened! It was watching him!

"Hey, Drake, this one's a door, too!" called Al.

"Al..." he gulped, finding his voice, which was weak and shaky.

"What?"

"It's a, uh... it's..." he gulped.

The massive sauropod stood up, the roof high enough for it if it didn't stretch its neck. Everyone was now watching. This was a small sauropod, leaving them room to manoeuvre, but that meant it had room to move and attack as well.

"It's a Vulcanodon." said John. "It means 'volcano tooth'. But that shouldn't be taken literally!"

This sauropod was from the early Jurassic, one of the earliest, if not the earliest, sauropods discovered. It lived in South Africa, and lacked the whip-like tail its descendants would have. This was slightly better, as it gave the Vulcanodon one less weapon.

Al yelled at the Deinonychus to get it, and it leapt on the Vulcanodon with a shriek. The Vulcanodon roared in retaliation, smashing against the walls, until the Deinonychus was thrown off!

The two animals faced each other. The Vulcanodon was much heavier, and slightly larger, though the Deinonychus was much deadlier. The Deinonychus tensed up and hissed, preparing to pounce. The Vulcanodon faced this new menace, and began waving its tail back and forth. Drake saw a curved claw on the foot of the Vulcanodon, too. He guessed it would kick at its enemies, or else rear up on its hind legs and smash them. In this case, it would kick – there was no room for it to rear up.

"Which turret is the Stone in?" asked Al.

"Is this really the time for that?" asked Drake.

"Yes, this dinosaur can't fit up the pillars!"

Al sent Dazz, John, Dave, and Kevin over to Drake's side. He then came over himself, leaving five on one side, and six on the other. The Deinonychus ran through the side with five, and the others followed. Al led his group up the spiral staircase of the second turret, leaving the Vulcanodon roaring.

Drake reached the top of his tower – it was the one facing westward. It opened up onto a balcony from inside the stone sauropod's mouth. It was spacious, enough for the six of them to stand comfortably inside it. Drake faced backwards, into where the gullet would be. The spiral staircase entered from where the throat would be, but the mouth went further back, towards the back of the head. It ended with a stone pillar, upon which sat –

"The Extinction Stone!" said Al.

There was another Extinction Stone, spherical, shiny, and light brown. It was the Devonian Stone – the one that used to belong to the Yaxog.

"Wow, we got it right? What were the chances of that?" asked Drake.

"Well, technically, one in two." said John.

Al picked up the Extinction Stone.

"We need to get to the other tower to tell the others." said Al. "Funny, though. Usually there are two guardians. What happened to the second?"

"You really want to question that, or do you just want to get out of here?" asked Drake.

They ran down the spiral staircase and back into the room with the Vulcanodon. From the other side, Harry and the others came down. The Deinonychus leapt up while the Vulcanodon had its eyes on Al, and tore at the skin and ligaments. The Vulcanodon roared with rage and threw the Deinonychus off of him. The two groups ran down their respective staircases, the Deinonychus following.

The two groups faced each other at the bottom of the steps.

"We got the Stone!" said Harry and Al together, each holding up a brown, spherical stone. A look of utter confusion appeared on everyone's faces.

"Didn't I get the Stone?" asked Al.

"No, this is the Stone!" said Harry.

"Let's see if we can figure this out." said Drake.

They passed the stones to Drake, who held one in each hand. They weighed exactly the same, perhaps one only slightly lighter than the other. They certainly looked exactly the same.

"Do we have another Stone for comparison?" he asked.

"Outside." said Harry.

"Not enough time, then, I suppose." said Drake. "What attributes did you say the Stones had? They were spherical, had an inner light, and... anything else?"

"Neither of those has an inner light." said John.

"No, but the inner light has faded from the other Stones from time to time, too." said Jane. "If you believe the Hekeni, perhaps the Stone wants us to figure it out for ourselves."

"The Stones are indestructible." said Al.

"Nothing is indestructible." said Drake.

"Well, the Stones can't be carved, dented, chipped or otherwise harmed by any tool we Hekeni possess." said Al. "We could try chiselling the stones, and seeing which one takes damage. That way we can determine which one's fake and which one's real!"

"Anyone have a chisel?" asked Drake.

"I got a knife." said Kevin, pulling one out of his pocket.

"I suppose I'll have to do this, then." said Drake. "Seeing as how no one among you is willing to stab the real Extinction Stone."

The native Hekeni muttered in agreement.

Drake took the heavier stone first. The natives looked away. He raised the knife high, and plunged it at the rock. The knife slid away, leaving a long scratch.

"That one must be fake!" said Al.

"Not so fast. Look." Drake wiped away the scratch until it was barely noticeable.

"Try other one!" said Dazz.

Drake raised the knife high again, and plunged it down on the lighter rock. There was a blinding flash of light, the sound of shattering glass, and a shape made of smoky light emitted from the Stone; it took the form of a massive fish with a heavily armoured head. A Dunkleosteus (dunk-lay-oh-stew-us), the largest predatory fish on the fossil record from the Devonian. It vanished in a silver mist, which disappeared in the air, as thunder rumbled, even though the sky was clear, and at that moment outside, lightning struck the mountains.

Drake held up the knife – it had shattered! Pieces of metal were scattered all around the Stone, the knife hilt useless, retaining only a jagged edge of the original weapon.

"Well..." said John, "I guess it's that one."

Drake picked it up. "I guess so. Well, here we'll give it to Alol, our resident idiot politician."

He handed the Stone to Alol. The old man smiled and tucked it under his arm. Harry picked up the fake stone, the scratch much more noticeable now they knew it wasn't real.

"What do we do with this one?" he asked.

"Leave it here." said Al. "Who cares?"

"Well, it's still a good piece of craftsmanship." said Harry. "Ah, well, you're right." he dropped the stone. "Come on, get going." he called to the Deinonychus.

They walked out of the temple, Harry following the Deinonychus. Harry had a sack in his hands. Drake had the suspicion that Harry couldn't just leave the stone there. They walked back down to the group, Al holding the Devonian Stone above his head, descending to cheering. There were no prayers of reverence or bowing with this one – perhaps because they revered the Triassic Stone more than any other.

Al placed the bag the Extinction Stone was in on Nemeli, with Drake thinking Al had not changed his attitude in this temple. He was relieved – until he realized the stone he had found in their tower was the fake one. He wondered where they were going next.

"Al, where are we–?"

"The Icy Peaks, my friend, the Icy Peaks." he replied. "The name for a particularly cold branch of the Mammoth Mountains."

"Are these the MM?" asked Drake, using the abbreviations the Hekeni used for their mountain ranges.

"No, these are the SuM, or Supersaurus Mountains. But this isn't a large mountain range. We'll be where we want to be in four days, if we travel at our current pace, which is pleasantly relaxing yet surprisingly fast. Just be patient, young paleontologist."

"Hey, I realized what the second guardian was after all!" said John. "Logic!"

"He's right." said Jane. "That certainly sounds like a Mayztec thing."

"So whose tomb is it next?" asked Drake.

"Harry will explain everything, as usual." said Al. "Four down, two to go."

Drake sighed, and patted Tenethax on his shoulders. "I'm worried what those last two Stones will do, though." he said to Tenethax. "You don't think my fears are misplaced, do you?"

The Triceratops snorted and shook his head.

"Well, that's good. At least you understand me." he replied.

Chapter 21 – Leaving the Volcano

The Hekeni group camped away from Mount Ash, underneath the Supersaurus Mountains, Pterosaur Canyon no longer visible – not that they were far away from it. It was just an optical illusion caused by flat land, and Pterosaur Canyon could not be discerned from the ground until one got close enough to look down.

The mountains, on the other hand, were surprisingly short, both in height and range size, considering their being named for the longest dinosaur on the fossil record.

Trees were scarce, but a forest would begin to spring up in a few kilometres. Their next destination was four more days of travel away, and Drake, who found joy in even the simplest things of Prehistorcia, thought that this journey, where there was no sense of obligation or a certain time limit to it, seemed the best he had ever been on. He was including all his trips on Earth with that thought, too.

When the group woke up, Al led them into the mountains, northward. The mountain range didn't seem particularly thick, either, as Drake could see the end of it through the first pass. There was a forest on the other end. Why were these called the Supersaurus Mountains? Was it some sort of joke?

"Hey, Drake, look at that!" yelled Jane.

He was the last of the paleontologists to see it. Perhaps the last person to see it... or... them. A great sauropod herd thundered around the mountains! They were diplodocids, holding their heads out straight ahead, with a long, whip-like tail tapering behind.

Supersaurus! They were huge! They had to be at least forty metres long, or a hundred and thirty-five feet! That made it twenty-five feet longer than the 'biggest animal ever', the Blue Whale.

These animals were huge! They were all brownish-green, and they dwarfed the Futalognkosaurus John and Jorge had ridden a year earlier. The Hekeni stopped as the majestic animals walked by. Drake saw one of their young – it was longer than Nemeli and Tenethax standing end-to-end! Many of the Supersaurus were even longer, too!

"How big are they?" asked Drake.

"Some scientists theorized up to a hundred and forty feet long." said John. "I think that's ridiculous. It's much longer. Some of these animals are a hundred and fifty feet!"

"Well, when they get to that size, the only thing that kills them is age!" said Al.

"Supersaurus is thought to not have existed, you know." said John. "Like Seismosaurus, Supersaurus could be an unusually large Diplodocus. That might be the case with the skeletons we've found, and we're looking at a totally undiscovered species."

"Fine, call them unknown if you like." said Tom. "I'm calling them Supersaurus."

They moved slowly across their path. They didn't even take a second glance at Nemeli – she was much too small to pose any kind of threat. The fortunate thing was that this didn't slow their progress – the Supersaurus were so big and so slow that they could actually move beneath their bellies! Even the tallest of their dinosaurs, the Triceratops and the Hadrosaurs, could just fit under their tails.

Many people said that the biggest animal to ever live was the blue whale – that was a lie. These were the biggest animals that ever lived, and Drake had a feeling some other species got bigger. A blue whale may have been the heaviest animal known to have existed – but it was in no way the biggest. Dinosaur-age animals broke through all boundaries, and set every record, except, perhaps, most intelligent. All the niches filled in the modern world were not only filled by dinosaurs – they were created by them! Even so, there were some niches that no longer existed, but did in the dinosaur age.

Drake put his hand up as he rode Tenethax under the belly of a very large adult, and touched the underside easily. It gave the most miniscule of flinches – it didn't even know he was there! Or perhaps it did know, but he was of no more interest than an ant crawling up its leg.

The entire group was through, pausing only for legs to stomp by. They made it across in twenty minutes, and continued their journey. Drake turned around, riding Tenethax backwards to get a better view of the Supersaurus – they were still coming!

"That's the only herd in Northern Prehistorcia." said Al. "That's why they're called the Supersaurus Mountains."

"How can you possibly know that's the only herd?" asked John.

"Did you see the size of them? You don't think we all went looking for them? An animal of such size is heavily worshipped among other tribes! We've checked – there is no other Supersaurus herd north of the Great Sea."

"How many are in that one?" asked Drake.

"About four hundred, but we've never actually taken census." replied Al.

"How long does it take for them to cross the whole range?" asked Jane.

"You people sure ask a lot of questions." said Al. "I don't know. I'd guess about three or four months, and then the same way back. They live to about two hundred and fifty years of age – on your world, that's about two thousand years. Those larger animals were around to see the Mayztecs fall."

"Wow. That's old." agreed Drake, still gaping at them.

"Where'd them things live?" asked Tom. "'Cause I think I've seen one somewhere."

"It lived throughout North America." said Drake. "It's skeleton was found by Jim Jensen in Wyoming, in the 1980's. You could remember it from tabloids about ten years ago, when its size was authenticated. It stands as, legitimately, the world's largest known animal."

The Above-worlders and even most Hekeni stared at the animals for a long time. Those animals would have been alive through so much – the oldest of them would have been born at the same time as Caesar! The history they had lived through!

The Hekeni entered the forest, putting an end to the desert, and opening up a wider variety of plant and animal life, and, more importantly, more access to water and edible food. Drake did not want to drink water from a cactus; it seemed like a desperate last resort, and their stores were running low.

The sun began to set. Low rumbling grunts could still be heard from the Supersaurus. But they were likely the most high-pitched sounds, as a Supersaurus probably had hearing much lower than a Human's.

At night the rumbling actually seemed soothing, because it cleared the mind of all thoughts. It helped Drake relax as he listened to the rumbling. It just didn't seem like night without listening to an extinct sound. The last thing he remembered before falling asleep was thinking that it was a sign he'd spent way too much time in Prehistorcia. He also didn't have a problem with that.

*****

When they woke up the following morning, faint rumbles of the Supersaurus herd were still coming. They got up and moved further away, and the rumbles faded altogether, and new wonders of the forest began to appear. It was a mixed forest, filled with leafy trees and evergreens. The ground was mossy or grass-covered, and the forest was wet, but it was not a rainforest.

Soon, the group came to a river with a rocky bank. It was wide, but shallow, and they followed that upstream, north towards the distant, much larger mountains it originated from.

Drake urged Tenethax forward. Soon, he was next to Dave, who was leading Jimmy the Phorusrhacos along with a rope tied around the massive bird's neck. Jimmy was dark yellow, and Drake wondered vaguely if that was to camouflage on the open plains where these birds hunted.

"So, Jimmy grew up fast, considering you trained him and you've only been here five years."

"I guess so." said Dave.

"How did you get him?"

"When I first came down here, the little bird took a liking to me. He was half-grown already, and being trained by a team of trainers. I guess he felt neglected, and never took to the name they gave him."

"What was his name before?" asked Drake.

"Can't remember." he said. "I only know he's only responded to 'Jimmy' since."

"Why did you choose that name?"

"Thought it would be funny." Dave admitted. "You know, I've always been slightly interested in dinosaurs. I've never liked them to your extent, but I was fond of them."

"Well, I suppose you're much more interested now... or are you less interested?"

"A bit of both." he replied.

"Did you ever find out why you were brought here?" asked Drake.

"No, but I've never felt I was brought here for a purpose." he said. "I think I just got lost, and Prehistorcia found me. I won't go so far as to say I found it, because that's not what happened. The land is—"

"Yeah, yeah, the land is alive. I've heard that preaching before." said Drake.

Dave smiled. "Well, perhaps there is a reason people are preaching it." he said. "The Hekeni are not wrong... in fact, they're rarely ever wrong. They are the only Humans I know that do not believe they own the land. And to be honest, it's worked for them! The Prehistorcian tribes have lasted about a hundred times longer than any culture on the Above-world!"

"What about native Americans, or Australian aborigines? They don't believe they own the land."

"Drake, have you ever *listened* to their stories? They preach that the land belongs to everyone, but that entails that it belongs to somebody! The Hekeni, and even the Golarans, they don't believe that! They never have! If you ask them who owns the land, they'll say that the land owns itself! If you hear Hekeni stories, they tell of how the animals and the land are all smart, and how we Humans are mere children! Every religion on earth preaches respect for the land, but these tribes are the only ones who truly practice it!"

"I'm not sure if everyone will agree with that view. Don't you think it's a little overdramatic?"

Dave sighed. "No. My statement might be opinionated, but it's still true. These people love the land so much that all the hippie, Greenpeace, love the earth stuff going on above us is just an act. The Hekeni would consider them imposters!"

"Oh, come on."

"Seriously. They all still drive gas cars, they still live in massive, polluting cities, they can't last four seconds without a cell phone, and they hold massive environment protests by shouting cuss words into the atmosphere and killing trees to make the wooden signs! Though, in their defence, wood is better than plastic..."

"You've had a lot of time to think about this, haven't you?" asked Drake.

"Not much else to do when you're surrounded by the real thing. I once asked Al how the Hekeni learned to be so respectful of the land. He replied to me with another question."

"Sounds like Al."

"How did we not learn to do it?"

"That definitely sounds like Al." said Drake. "As I look around, I have to ask myself that same question. What jerk would look at this place and say: let's build a noisy highway with cheap motels and fast-food chains?"

"Yeah. Fortunately there is some real protection going on in greener parts of the earth. But believe me, no matter how many good things you hear about them, the Hekeni do it much better."

"So, if you believe the Hekeni, do you believe the Earth is alive, too?"

"It was."

"You hide your cynicism well. For a moment I thought you were being positive."

"Well, we all make mistakes." he shrugged.

"Yeah, and I think Al made a mistake at the map. How did he plan to get us all up this?"

Ahead of them was a rocky cliff with a waterfall flowing down it, into the river. The cliff was steep, and there was no way an animal could climb it. Drake looked left and right. Across the river was a place to climb up, but the river was deep and fast-flowing here.

"Hey, Al, how did you plan to get us up this?" called Steven.

"I knew this was here, if that's what you mean." said Al. He turned around to Dave and Drake, just behind him. "I heard you talking of the beauty of this land. Well, this is a nice place. I thought it would be a good place for all of us to camp for the night. What do you think?"

"You don't have to stop on our account." said Dave.

"We'll never get up the cliff before sundown anyway. Go ahead and look around. What do you think?"

The rocky cliff had a deep gouge in it filled with flowing water, with moss and twig-like trees growing from the rocks. It opened up into a much wider river from between the rocks, and the river flowed deep and swift. It was surrounded by a beautiful forest. The scene was indescribable, and as most things in Prehistorcia were, they had to be seen to be believed.

"This is a nice spot." agreed Drake.

"I thought so, too. We'll set up camp now?"

"Okay, but what do we do tomorrow, when we do need to get up the cliff?" asked Drake.

"There's a way down there." said Al, indicating to the west, on their side of the river. "We can get everyone up the cliff easily there."

Drake was momentarily distracted as their Nemicolopterus whizzed past his nose, delivering another note. He chuckled, remembering there was once a time pterosaurs never flew past his nose.

*****

As the sun began to set, a herd of sauropods came to the other side of the river and began drinking. The four Extinction Stones were out of their bags, and Alol, Harry, and Al were placing them in a square. The blue and brown Stone were on one side, the green and yellow on the other. The blue Stone was at the bottom left, the brown at the top left, the green at the top right, and the yellow at the bottom right.

Drake saw what they were doing. He walked up to them. "What are you doing?" he asked.

"Placing the stones in a circle." replied Al.

"Looks like a square to me." said Drake.

"Yeah, well, you try making a circle out of four dots. It's a coincidence. You see, the Ordovician came first, so it's here, at the bottom. Next was the Devonian, so that goes here. Up here" – Al indicated to a space above the square in the middle of the line – "Is where the Permian, or red Stone, will go. Next, there's the Triassic, and the Cretaceous stones, and the Pleistocene should go here." he indicated to the bottom of the square.

"Any reason you're doing this?" asked Drake.

"If the Stones are united, they must be united in the proper order, oldest to youngest." said Harry. "It took Elmerik days to figure it out."

"What happens when the Stones do unite?" asked Drake. "I mean, I know what's supposed to happen – but how do you know if you've united them correctly?"

"Legend says they're supposed to rise up and orbit around the user." said Al. "That is, if the historical texts from witnesses are to be believed. But witnesses can't agree on how the Stones killed Elmerik – I wouldn't trust their testimony on that, either. But they do let us know when we unite them correctly."

"Okay..."

Drake got a very bad feeling in the pit of his stomach. Why were they rehearsing how to unite the Stones? Weren't they giving them back? Drake went to their sleeping area with Jane, Ahrzi and Tenethax.

"Something wrong?" Jane asked.

"Maybe." he replied vaguely. "Nothing you need to worry about."

"I'll decide what I worry about." she frowned.

"I misspoke – nothing to worry about *yet*."

He lay down and tried to fall asleep. Jane did not attempt to engage him in conversation again, and Drake felt a little bad for that. He spoke with concern, not impatience, though he may not have been clear. The result was that he was trying to fall asleep with *two* things to worry about.

Chapter 22 – A Night with the Klenkara

When the Hekeni woke up, Al led them west, along the ridge, and a few minutes in, they came to a steep hillside. It was crumbling, and the angle was sharp, but it was enough for the dinosaurs to climb up with some help. The Hekeni had to tie ropes around the equipment, and pull it up manually, as it was cruel to subject their towing animals to that kind of weight on an incline. They used a series of pulleys to pull the jeeps up the hill with help from the heavier animals, and they rolled their two vehicles up to the top of the hill in about an hour.

That day, they approached the Mammoth Mountains, coming up on the northern horizon, and the Hekeni continued to follow the river towards them. They spent one more night in the forest, and then continued northward. Drake knew the next temple was in the Icy Peaks, part of the Mammoth Mountains, but he saw no ice.

They spent another night in the woods, after driving off a Cave Bear. All that day, Drake saw no sign of a tomb, or, for that matter, any ice. They had just reached the foot of the mountains, a boreal forest full of poplar, maple, oak and cedar trees, and others like them. It reminded Drake of something peaceful, the kind of forest one would find in the Maritimes.

"Al, where's the tomb?"

"The tomb?" he asked. "That's still days away, Drake, deep in the mountains!"

"But you said we'd be there in four days, four days ago!"

"I said we'd be where we want to be in four days. And we are. I wanted to reach this place, just a little further up the road. You'll see."

Drake saw that they were actually following a dirt path. Soon, they came to the riverbank, in a spot where there was a wide opening over to the other side, which had a wide dirt trail leading into the forest. Al yelled something across the water.

Drake nearly jumped when he heard an answering cry. Al gave another answer, and eventually a man appeared from the trees. There were two bulky Neanderthals, each with short hair and a bow. The Neanderthals emerged on the forest edge, and each yanked on a rope hung from the trees and were tied to something in the water. Drake thought, for a ridiculous moment, that they was trying to pull the riverbank up.

That is, until they did just that! The two men pulled the rope, each rope tied to two massive hooks, which raised a large stone platform under the water. The technology was so advanced for a land so primitive! But they had actually made a kind of canal! Together, they tied the ropes to the trees, holding the bridge up.

"Who are these people?" asked Drake.

"Klenkara." replied Al. "They're very reclusive, and don't normally allow visitors. But we're lucky. But you were wondering about the bridge, weren't you?"

"Crossed my mind."

"This is technology 'borrowed' from the Mayztecs. Pretty cool, isn't it?"

Drake got off Tenethax and stepped on the bridge. It seemed solid enough. Water still flowed over it, up to his shins, but the river was at least crossable now. Al went forward, followed by Drake. The bridge seemed to hold all the Hekeni animals, too. In the middle of the bridge, there was a wide arch allowing the toughest parts of the river to pass under them.

"So what's the story behind the... Klenekaria?"

"Klenkara." corrected Al. "They were founded by a rebel who assassinated Hemeblar the First. They've always been a thorn in the side of the Mayztecs, which is how they got the technology."

"Who was Hemeblar the First?" asked Drake.

"Grandson of Ragoth the Great, founder of the first Mayztec monarchy." explained Al. "Ragoth was the first king of the empire, about four years after it began. Hemeblar was his grandson, and was killed year ninety of the Mayztec Kings, ending the first dynasty. Actually, you'll be hearing more about the first dynasty from Harry, as they concern our tomb in the Icy Peaks."

"So his assassin fled up here and formed this tribe, always fighting the Mayztecs?"

"Yep. His name was Klenkara... hence this tribe's name. Official records say that his ancestry was as a Fertile River tribesman who was banished, but this tribe is now a mix-and-match of the descendants of all tribes, including some of Mayztec slaves and traitors."

"Klenkara was banished, and then fought against the Mayztecs?"

"Klenkara was old when his tribe was formed early in the Mayztec history. He may have been young when he was banished, the Mayztecs gained power, and then he did what he thought was right."

"Why didn't the Fertile River take him back?"

"He was still banished. No matter what deed you do after banishment, you are still banished. Besides, the records don't say what kind of person he was." said Al. "He could have been a jerk, and he gathered other bandits and criminals to form a tribe. Just because he assassinated the emperor doesn't make him a good guy. It wasn't until about two thousand years later, when the Mayztecs became a serious threat, that we began to think that they were either with us, or with the Mayztecs, not neither, as Klenkara was."

"But this is just guessing, isn't it?" asked Drake.

"No, that is what happened." said Al. "I'm guessing he could be a jerk, but who knows? Maybe he was falsely accused, or a good man who did a bad thing."

"Ve like to think it is zat last one." said a voice.

They had stopped just before a massively tall man, if he was a man. He was eight feet tall! Surely he must have been a man, but his features just didn't resemble that of a *Homo sapiens*.

"Uh... who are you?" asked Drake.

"I don't know what species you are!" said John, stupidly.

Did Humans have ancestors this big? Or was he just a regular, modern-day Human born to be a basketball player or a wrestler? His nose was short, like a Neanderthal's, but his brow was not as thick. His hair was red, and seemed to be everywhere from a long beard and tangled hair. If he had been wearing a shield and carrying a broadsword, Drake could have sworn this man was a less-evolved Viking.

"He's not a species discovered on the Above-world." Al smirked. "There aren't many of your people left, are there? But he's a direct ancestor, somewhere before the time we moved out of Africa. At least, that's what I think. Obviously, I can't know for sure."

The large man smiled, and chuckled. "I am zee leader of zee Klenkara Tribe." he said in a Transylvanian accent. "I am Ulkar, and I vill accommodate you Hekeni... you know for vat price."

"You'll all see the Stones, Ulkar." said Al. "We'll take them out tonight."

"Good, very good."

The Klenkara chose a beautiful patch of forest, in Drake's opinion, on the south of the Mammoth Mountains, in a boreal forest. As they moved down the path they saw the Klenkara pens – not as diverse as the Hekeni ones. There were mostly canines of breeds found on Earth – border collies, bloodhounds, sheepdogs, saint bernards, and golden retrievers; all the dogs that could be trained to do something useful, none of those rat-dogs that people kept in purses. They also had a couple of Deinonychus, and one large, vulture-like bird Drake knew to be a Teratornis. He avoided that one's eyes, though its head twisted to follow them.

After the pens, which were very small compared to Hekeni ones, they reached their place of living. It was a large village, houses arranged around a clearing backing onto the forest, around a great campfire. There were some rocky caves that large, Ulkar-like children were playing in front of beyond the villages, just at the edge of sight.

"The Klenkara are very small." said Al. "Only one or two thousand members, not all the same species."

"Ve are small, but ve manage." said Ulkar.

"Yes, you do." agreed Al. "No need to give us guest arrangements, we brought our own shelters."

"Good, because I am not sure ve have enough room for you eef you did not."

Drake helped the Hekeni unpack the military tents and sleeping bags that they had been using. Drake saw at the far end of the village, on the side of a tiny dirt path, was what appeared to be a fence blocking access to a vineyard.

"If it's not a secret, Ulkar, would that be a vineyard?" asked Drake.

"Yes, it is."

"You make wine?"

"The Klenkara are the best in Prehistorcia for wine-making, though most of us prefer the grapes." said Harry. "They also make beer, but from barley grown by the Kluugon and Vorrog Tribes."

"Wahoo!" said Tom. "For once a specialty I can agree with! Break it out!"

"It might not be as strong as your stuff on the Above-world." said Harry.

"You think I care? That just means more for me!"

The sun sank swiftly into the west, and the Klenkara brought out the beer as the massive campfire in the centre roared with heat and light. It was so warm that many Hekeni just pulled out the mammoth-skin blankets and stayed on the floor. Drake drank the wine and it was good, and despite what Harry said, a little strong.

Knowing this was one thing he could win, he offered a drinking game with Al, who was terrible at holding his liquor. Drake drained his fifth glass, which was actually a clay mug, and set it down, ready for more.

"How're you doing this?" asked Al drunkenly, setting down his fifth mug.

"It's not too strong. I'm only a little drunk." he chugged the sixth, sour glass. Al didn't get to his. He passed out onto the ground.

Drake held his arms up to applause from the Hekeni and Klenkara. "It appears I've won, Al!" he said.

"Do you even feel drunk?" asked Jane.

"A little, but like I said, it's not strong. Didn't you have any?"

"Yeah, two mugs. On Earth, I'd need a ride home by then."

Drake stared at Al snoring on the ground. "Yeah, and you thought *you* couldn't hold your wine. But then again, he's grown up sober."

Jane smiled. "It's no German beer, I admit, but it's better than that American piss-water we had when we crossed into Montana, remember?"

"Oh, yeah." Drake smiled. "I forgot that night. I won a drinking game with a local then, too. The only two times I've ever won a drinking game." he sighed with a smile.

Some Neanderthals near the fire, having fun with the Hekeni, took out their instruments and began playing on them. It was a tune that seemed to suit the place; it wasn't very slow, but it wasn't that fast, either. Music was one of the most vital parts of Prehistorcian beliefs, and every night in the Hekeni village there was someone playing somewhere.

"You want to dance?" asked Jane.

"I thought I was supposed to ask." Drake replied.

"You never ask sober."

"Well, I'm drunk now, I might have eventually." he snickered.

The grabbed each other's hands and began dancing as best they could to the speed and tune of the music. It ended up looking so silly that both tribes ended up laughing at them.

"Well, you try something better!" yelled Drake.

Ulkar the Klenkara chief came up, and stared doing a one-man dance that actually looked very good considering the music and absurdity of his appearance darcing to it.

"Zer you are, Hekeni." he laughed, leaving the floor.

The crowd chuckled and applauded appreciatively. Drake and Jane began dancing together agair, this time much more coordinated. Some Klenkara men and their wives or girlfriends came up and began doing the same. The musicians slowed down the song a small bit, making it easier to find the right steps.

"You dance like you sing – terribly." said Jane.

"Look who's talking! Like you've ever taken a dance class outside of PE?"

They both chuckled.

"You know, I don't think there's anywhere else I'd like to spend my life." said Drake. "With no other person. I'm glad we both chose to stay."

"So am I." smiled Jane.

They leaned forward, about to kiss. They were interrupted by a large burp, and the sudden presence of Al standing up beside them.

"Oh, sorry paleo-people, I'm interrupting, I think." he said drunkenly. "I'm think I need back to sleep. Time to sleep in bed." he laughed loudly, stumbled off, and collapsed in a tent.

"You know, I've never seen him drunk." said Drake.

"Neither have I." said Jane. "He's kind of…"

"Weird?" Drake suggested

"Yeah."

"Yet, even drunk, he always seems to come in at the worst time."

Jane sighed. "I can agree to that."

*****

Drake woke up the next morning beneath a mammoth-hair blanket at the edge of the fire. When he looked around, he saw Jane sleeping not too far away, in a tent. He saw Ahrzi sleeping up against him, breathing deeply. Drake began scratching his pet Utahraptor, and the dromaeosaur rolled over to have its belly scratched.

"Hungry, Ahrzi?"

The baby got up and chirped happily. Drake got out of bed, removed some food from Tenethax, and tossed it at him. Ahrzi ate it gratefully.

He noticed that all the members of the Klenkara tribe, including the chief, seemed gathered around four Hekeni — Harry, Alol, Dazz, and a fourth person, each of them holding an Extinction Stone. They were allowing the Klenkara to come close, to touch them, to mutter prayers to them. This was what the Hekeni promised in exchange for letting them camp here.

"Ooh, Drake, I've got a splitting headache." said Al, walking over to him.

"It's called a hangover, Al, and you shouldn't get one from that tiny amount of alcohol." said Drake, who, unlike Al, had no hangover whatsoever.

"You mean this stuff is stronger on the Above-world?"

"Oh yes, but there's weaker stuff, too. We call it 'American Beer'. But we use machines that would take you several thousand years to invent, and another thousand to get the hang of. That's assuming you ever choose to develop."

"I don't care, long as you know a cure."

"My uncle would cut a potato in half and tape it to his forehead to 'let the starch absorb in'." he chuckled.

"Does it work?"

Drake knew perfectly well it didn't — but he had to see if Al would actually do it. "Sometimes, I think, yeah." he worked hard to keep his laughing concealed.

He walked over to the Klerkara group around the four Hekeni. Harry saw that Drake wanted to ask something, so he called them over, putting the green Stone under his arm.

"What's on your mind, Drake?" he asked.

"When are we leaving the camp?" Drake asked.

"In an hour or so." replied Harry. "But you'll be one of the ones following me to the Icy Peaks."

"Aren't we all following?"

"What? Weren't you told? Never mind. The Icy Peaks are far too cold to allow our animals to pass through them. We'll be taking Yaagol, the Woolly Rhino, and our Dire Wolves with us, and some of our Terror Birds. Other than that, we can't take anything else."

"Not even the jeeps?" asked Drake.

"Our next temple is up a mountain, and a steep one. You want to try and get the jeeps up them? I doubt even in all-wheel they could drive up the peak."

"I don't know. Much as I was making fun of their beer, Americans build some good military equipment. It might just be able to get up the mountain."

"Even through knee-high-snow?"

Drake shrugged. "I suppose it's better to just take supplies and not worry about the jeep." he admitted.

At that moment, Al came rubbing his head, holding half a potato to it. Harry smirked and tried to hold in his laughing. "What is that?"

"A headache cure."

Harry laughed. Harry had been lost in Prehistorcia since the age of seven, while Al was three, so he often got more of the stuff the Above-worlders tried to elaborate on. "Al, you realize that it doesn't actually work, right?"

"Drake said it did!" he exclaimed.

"Yeah, I did, but only because I was wondering if you would believe it!"

Al dropped the potato. "You're a jackass." he grunted.

"It was harmless." Drake smiled.

"Yeah, it was. I was wondering why the Klenkara were snickering when they handed it to me. Let's get going. I'll find a way to get you back someday."

"I'm sure you will."

Chapter 23 – Mammoth Mountains

The Klenkara gave the Hekeni fresh fruit and bread for the trip, and sent them on their way. Ulkar waved goodbye to them as they set off down a dirt trail, past cave-like stone houses, vineyards, and small gardens for vegetables and flowers. The Mammoth Mountains loomed ahead of them, with clouds gathering for rain.

After a few minutes, the groups parted. Al removed his Sekka-hat, and Dazz placed on his, a ring of bone with large, painted wood spikes to resemble the horns of a Styracosaurus. Al sent Dazz to lead the group going around, which included all the dinosaurs, including Ahrzi in the back of the truck being looked after by a capable-looking Hekeni Trainer, and military-grade rope as a leash.

With Drake's group went all the people who would not kill each other over the Extinction Stone – Drake, John, Jane, Steven, Tom, Kevin and Dave. They were led by Al, who was with Harry, and they brought Alol along as well. They had three of the five Terror Birds – Jimmy, Dave's Phorusracos, Flutt, Dazz's bird of an undiscovered species which he had lent to them, and a Titanis, one of the animals Harry trained. Yaagol the Woolly Rhinoceros (which John said was a Coelodonta) was a communal animal, which meant he belonged to the tribe, not to one person, and it was the same situation with the four Dire Wolves.

"So we're heading north, through the mountains, and meeting them on the other side as they go around?" asked Steven.

"Yeah." said Harry.

"Because the dinosaurs can't get that cold and make it through?"

"Correct." said Al.

"I want to go with that group!" proclaimed Steven.

"Too bad, you're one of the few people we have who will not kill for the Extinction Stone." said Harry. "You are one of the most valuable people on this quest, Steven."

"I don't feel that valuable." he grunted, hoisting his bag higher onto his shoulders.

"We're Canadian! We can handle colder than this!" said Drake, hoping he would not regret those words.

They travelled all day northwest, following the natural curve of the mountain range, passing some fourteen mountains before settling in for the night when the sun began to set. Without Nemeli, large dinosaurs, or a vast number of people moving with them, Drake was able to see a lot more wildlife for a lot longer. They were still in the boreal forest, but Al said it would be ending soon.

A herd of Kentrosaurus lumbered past them as they got a fire going. The Kentrosaurus were over four metres, or fourteen feet long, with spikes instead of plates, and two spikes jutting out of their hips. They were yellow-green, which would blend in with an autumn forest, as this was no doubt becoming.

Al found and cooked a Moa, a large herbivorous bird that died off on New Zealand sometime in the thirteenth century. Drake was surprised at how good it actually tasted, though he still preferred the modern meats. Alol got the first pick of the Moa, even though Al was leader. It appeared there was a small hierarchy in the Hekeni after all.

The next morning when they got up, they came to a large clearing in the forest. The hills were bare, and growing on it were clovers, growing and sprouting a healthy green colour. Eating them and the flowers mingled in with them, were large Ceratopsians some twenty feet long, with an oval-shaped head with spikes, and instead of the three horns on Tenethax, they had just one nose horn, which was long and white. Drake knew them immediately, as did Kevin and Dave. It wasn't the least-known dinosaur out there. In fact, it was probably mentioned in every dinosaur book, though many people didn't know of it.

"Centrosaurus!" exclaimed Kevin.

"A whole herd of them!" said Steven. "Hey, look at those ones!" he pointed.

Two Centrosaurs were facing each other, scraping the ground with their nose horn, snorting and grunting. One was beige, and one was blackish-grey, but both their frills were splashed with bright colours.

"They're males," said John, "and those are the females."

On the far side of the two fighting males were three females. Drake knew they must be females, because they were only slightly smaller, their frills were noticeably smaller, and they weren't coloured.

"So you think they're fightin' over females?" asked Tom. "I thought they just butt heads."

"Well, I can imagine some species doing so." said John. "But look at their horns – they could kill each other in that position! It's a display war, and the first one to run is the loser."

"See, there goes one now!" said Drake.

The beige Centrosaurus backed away, and the black one walked over to the females. But they weren't the only ones fighting – all the males' frills were brightly coloured, and many seemed aggressive. There were at least four pairs fighting, and it wasn't long before the winner of the one they watched was challenged again, this time by a dark-green one.

"Seen all you wanted to?" asked Al.

"No, but all I need to." said John. "We can leave now."

"Yeah, we'll have to." agreed Tom.

"Good. Well, it'll be hell getting across that field of testosterone-fuelled aggressive males, but fortunately, we won't have to. Our path from here is east, or perhaps northeast. Either way, it's around here. Follow me."

Al led them around the field, on the edge of the forest, which continued into the mountains, and still further along their ridge until it ended on the Mammoth Migration Lands. Drake did not know it, but several kilometres north was where Jane had gone over the mountain forest to get to the Hekeni camp. The Mammoth Mountains got much thinner until they reached the peak Jane climbed, west-north-west of their current position, and then they tapered off into the southern Thunder Marshes.

The wolves went ahead of them, sniffing the ground, though they weren't likely to find danger. As the sun began to set on another day, the group had made it into the mountains, and camped out with the military tents under the shadow of a snow-capped ridge.

There was a lake at the bottom of this mountain, which meant clear, clean water, and it was already chilled, since the lake was glacial. They wouldn't find large fish in it, though, so Al and the wolves went out hunting. Flutt brought back a dead rabbit, which he wouldn't let anybody take, but Al and the dogs brought back another Moa, as well as a mountain goat.

Drake noticed as they cooked the food that the nights were getting colder, and the animals were getting more modern, ones adapted to cold environments.

*****

As a new day dawned, there was a slight chill in the air. It wasn't actually that cold, about fifteen degrees, but Drake had lived in near-tropical temperatures for a long time. It felt more familiar, like home, for there to be a slight chill in the wind.

However Al diverted their course east, and this time there was no denying that the temperature was getting colder. It dropped some ten degrees in just ten kilometres. Drake was sure this was too cold for any dinosaur to survive. Al took out the warmer clothes, which were mammoth-skin, not the traditional dinosaur-skin, and they wore pants, not shorts or skirts, with sweaters. As the travelled further,

Drake saw some unmelted snow, just half an inch of it, in patches of forest.

Therefore, it was a surprise when they came to a large lake to see none other than Parasaurolophus, drinking from it! The Hadrosaurs were long, as long as Tenethax, had two slim front legs that they reared up on to reach branches or run faster. They had large tubes coming out the back of their heads, and made honking sounds to one another. Some of them were even wading in, eating seaweed.

"How can they be in that water?" asked Tom. "It must be freezing!"

They reached the lake shore, and John stuck his hand in the lake. "Actually, it's not. This lake isn't glacial. So it must be volcanic, getting deeper at some point. Or it could be an overflow of a volcanic lake attached to it. Often volcanic lakes, even in cold environments, are warmer."

Tom stuck his hand in. "It ain't warm!" he said.

"I said warmer. It's not warm, but it's warm enough for animals such as moose, caribou and, apparently, Parasaurolophus to wade in and drink from."

"That means they must be warm-blooded!" said Steven.

"But we've suspected that. These things have been found north of the Arctic Circle. Even in warm, lush times that was cold."

"Yeah, and they're not the only ones found north, either." said Drake. "There's Pachyrhinosaurus, found in Alaska, Alaskacephale, which is a Pachycephalosaur, and even some carnosaurs like T-Rex, while they've never been found there, have been thought to go up there. They may have followed a Parasaurolophus migration, from north to south, just like modern-day birds."

"Parasaurolophus migrated?" asked Tom.

"Maybe, maybe not." said Steven. "We don't know. It's all theory. I think they did, but it's impossible to know for sure... unless you want to sit here for three months waiting for them to move."

"We don't have that kind of time." said Al. "But we can stay the night here, if you like."

The sun was getting low, but it wasn't low enough to stop. It seemed too soon.

"Okay, but let's do it on the other end of the lake." said Drake.

*****

The next day, Drake woke up and got out of the tent to see a Pachyrhinosaurus eating a bush. This one was, happily, not cursed. There was more than one Pachyrhinosaurus. There were actually seven of them, most of them green or brown, but one was deep yellow. Drake went out to get closer, but the nearest one grunted and moved to a different bush.

Al was already up, on the other side of the tent, gathering berries and roots for breakfast. Drake could tell this morning was cold, because he could see Al's breath, and his own. The Pachyrhinosaurus' snorted, and steam issued from their nostrils every time they did. These Ceratopsians had to be warm-blooded, unless there was some source of heat they knew how to get that Drake didn't.

The ten of them left after breakfast, under a cloudy sky. Later in the day, it began raining, but the rain was cold, and unpleasant.

"How far to the temple?" asked Drake.

"Two more nights." said Al.

They moved across a lot of ground, and left the rain behind them, though the clouds still hung over. Soon, they walked along the side of a mountain, and when they got to the top, they were overlooking a large field, full yellow grass and tall prairie flowers.

The forest continued on their immediate left, but to the right was nothing but open field, until the edge of a lake could just be made out. Far away the mountains began again, with the forest. It was just a large valley surrounded by mountains. It was a valley in the Hekeni sense of the word, which meant a field or open gap surrounded by mountains, not the spaces beneath them.

But it was what filled the field that held their attention – Triceratops, wild, untamed ores. There were literally hundreds of them, all of different ages, colours and sizes. Drake could tell male from female, but that was because he had trained them with the Hekeni and could tell at a glance. Their frills were not splashed with bright colours, so they must have run on a different mating schedule. Youngsters were ramming their heads together, but it was just play, practice for when they were older.

"See, Tom, there's your butting heads!" said John, pointing out the youngsters.

"So are these guys matin', too?" he asked.

"No, their frills are plain, with no colours." said Drake.

"We might see some action, though." said Harry. "See there, in the trees? You'll have to look closely, their camouflage works so well."

Drake looked. A Tyrannosaurus! No... five Tyrannosaurus! At least! There were five T-Rex hiding in the trees, dark-grey and -green, and Harry was right, they naturally blended in very well. What was more, they were feathered! Like dromaeosaurs, the tyrannosaurs were covered with thin feathers. They were all watching the Triceratops herd, and forming some kind of silent strategy. There was one large one – the leader, he guessed. There was one small one, too, which must have been an adolescent It was too large to be a baby, but too small to be a full-grown adult. There were two males and two females, roughly the same size, but Drake could tell the difference with careful concentration.

Now he really knew he had been in Prehistorcia too long.

"What are they gonna to do?" asked Kevin.

"Probably hunt." said John.

"I knew that! I meant how're they gonna do it?"

"I don't know. We're about to see, I think."

"You know, on Earth, Jack Horner now thinks that Torosaurus and Triceratops are the same animal." said Kevin.

"Uh-huh. Nice try, but Jack Horner's too smart for that."

"No, man, I'm serious!"

"Really? That's dumb! Look at those – they don't look anything like Torosaurus! The Hekeni have all kinds of young Ceratopsians, and the Torosaurus babies look different from the Triceratops ones! Triceratops is larger, the frill is solid, and eye-horns are longer, even the build is different!"

"Yeah, if he really said that, I've lost a lot of respect for him." said Drake. "That's too bad, he's supposed to be a good paleontologist."

"Ah, come on, he ain't that bad." said Kevin. "Everyone makes a mistake in their career."

"Alright, but if some other guy comes down telling me a Parasaurolophus is the same thing as a Lambeosaurus, I'm going to smack him." replied John.

"It's not that bad." Jane frowned. "It's kind of bad, but not career-breaking bad."

"You know, John, getting off the topic of stupid theories, do you notice the direction of the wind? It's blowing towards us, so the Triceratops have a small chance of smelling them. Yet they sit hidden in the trees, as if they're more worried about being seen." said Drake.

"So?" asked Kevin.

"So it means that the Triceratops have good enough eyesight to spot them out on the open." said Drake.

"Was there ever another theory?" asked Tom.

"Well, in the Jurassic Park books, Crichton suggested that Triceratops' eyesight was very poor. It wasn't a bad guess, either, because rhinos have notoriously poor eyesight, and will charge a butterfly as if it were a lion. They navigate by scent, so a predator would do better to sneak up on them from an open clearing downwind than an enclosed forest upwind." said Drake. "Of course, the most obvious mistake he made is that Triceratops and Rhinos, though they seem similar, are in no way related."

"But these Tyrannosaurus are not doing so." said Steven. "That means the Triceratops has eyesight good enough to see them, and they would rather risk getting smelled."

"The weather is cold enough, and the wind weak enough, that their smell will be very faint." said Al. "Even for the sensitive noses of the Triceratops."

The T-Rex began fanning out, surrounding an old Triceratops (which looked nothing remotely like a Torosaurus). The juvenile stayed with the large female – it was possible that the leader was its parent, and it was the luckiest of a clutch of young to survive. Drake noticed one Tyrannosaur went way over to the far side, the female, in a position that was sure to get her smelled.

It did. One Triceratops sounded the signal, and the young Triceratops got in the middle of the herd, while all the adults faced the T-Rex. The old one they were hunting was exposed. The other four jumped out from other angles, causing the adults to shift position.

The old female confronted the target Triceratops, avoiding the horn swipe, and lunging her jaws into his neck. But the Tyrannosaurus missed. The old Triceratops, surprisingly nimble, avoided her, but just barely, and swiped at her with his spike.

She roared in irritation and backed off, a bleeding cut across her chest. The two males rushed in, but they, too, were deterred by the horns. All five T-Rex backed off, and the Triceratops herd continued grunting and snorting until they ran back into the trees.

Not every attack was successful. They couldn't afford to waste energy on a lost one. Hopefully, all five of them would live to hunt another, easier meal.

*****

The ten Hekeni worked their way through the Triceratops, but it was easy, as they did not consider Humans much of a threat. Some of the adults, when they got near the children, stood in front of them, but no aggressive actions were made. With Triceratops (the way Drake preferred it), it was live-and-let-live. The Triceratops didn't need the fight, and the Hekeni didn't need the scars.

They reached the far side of the field, and walked back into the forest, where they camped under a mountain. Drake saw high, white peaks in the distance, and the clouds seemed darker, more foreboding.

"Those are the Icy Peaks, Al?"

"Yeah, there they are, in all their glory." he said.

"Any reason why it's called that?"

"I think you already know."

"People have crossed it safely, haven't they?" he asked.

"Oh, sure, all the time. Have you ever heard the children's tale 'Why the Mammoth gave us Clothes'? Well, that story is set in the Icy Peaks. Basically, the humans were freezing to death, they found some mammoths who were starving, so they gave the mammoths food and we got their fur for warmth in return, and the expedition made it out safely."

"That's good for a tale, but what about in real life?"

"In real life? The truth behind that story is probably that the expedition slaughtered the mammoths to save them from coldness, and lured them there with food. Either way, they got out. But they're not the only account."

"No?"

"No, we've sent hundreds of expeditions to retrieve the Extinction Stones, and while almost all of them died in the attempt to reach this temple, some made it, and got inside. And a very few got out and lived to say they failed. Those are just the famous examples, too. The

Catteua, Klenkara, and Flimzoak use these routes all the time! It will be very cold, and the journey is hard, but don't worry, it is doable."

"That makes me feel a little better." said Drake.

"Besides, if we really get that cold, we still have those military-issue parkas. Why they were going to a desert country, who knows? But, we have them."

"I suppose we have those, too." said Drake. "Okay, I feel a lot better."

Chapter 24 – Icy Peaks

The sun rose over the mountains. They moved further into the Icy Peaks, Al giving them the thickest mammoth-skin clothes yet. As they moved on, they noticed that there was always snow on the ground, and getting thicker. But what Drake found surprising was, an hour into the trip, he saw yet another dinosaur.

Only in Prehistorcia would this fight be seen. The carnivore was feathery, small, and pale-grey, about the size of Nemeli, but Drake couldn't identify it. Neither could John. It was confronted by a solitary mammoth its own size, with massive tusks.

The mammoth was obviously a male, or so Drake thought. Males generally travelled alone, while females remained in large groups, much like modern elephants in Africa and Asia.

The carnivore confronted the woolly mammoth, and roared. The mammoth raised its trunk and honked, and it's trumpet sounded just like that of a modern elephant, only it was deeper. The mammoth waved his tusks threateningly, taking a step back, as if preparing to charge. The dinosaur stepped back, too, its side facing the mammoth.

The mammoth charged. The carnosaur dodged and sunk his teeth into the mammoth's fur. But his skin was thick – he wrenched himself away, and, using his tusks, rammed the dinosaur, and shoved it over. The mammoth sent the dinosaur tumbling a short way down the mountainside, landing ahead of the group. The mammoth walked off without a second thought. The dinosaur got up, shaking off his fall. It looked injured, but its arm was limp. Luckily, it was a short-armed carnosaur, and a broken arm usually didn't mean death.

"That was kind of cool." said Steven.

"Come on, we need to leave before the carnosaur considers us an easy meal." said John.

"We have Yaagol, the wolves, and terror birds. You really think he'd attack?" asked Al. "However, I think we should move anyway. I'm not willing to take the chance."

They walked all day, and reached the Icy Peaks by lunch. They were a full-blown Antarctica mountain range, in Drake's opinion, not only topped with glaciers, but covered by them. They were pure white, and the snow was up to their knees. To make matters worse, the snow had finally started coming from the overcast sky. Even in the warm mammoth-fur clothing, the thick leather boots, and the warm, mammoth-fur socks, they were still freezing.

"Al! D-do you think it might be time to bring out those cloaks?" asked Dave, shivering violently.

"I think you're right! Let's stop here!"

The group stopped. Al brought out the thick winter coats from the plane, and handed them out. He also pulled out hats, and handed them around.

"Made from musk-ox!" he announced. "Some of the warmest fur around!"

He also handed out gloves, again from the airplane, far away with the Hekeni Tribe. Alol, who was old and weaker than everyone, got on the back of Yaagol. But this didn't add much extra weight, as the weight of Alol was almost equivalent to the weight they had removed and eaten through the course of their trip.

"Well, we're warmer now." said Dave. "But we still might die of frostbite."

"Oh, quit complaining! This is average where I come from!" said John.

"It is not." Drake grumbled under his breath.

They trundled forward. The heavy winds picked up, and it got hard to see. However, they were able to determine when it was getting dark, and they found a clearing, and set up a fire. Drake could not see their surroundings, but Al and Harry were carrying back some wood, and laid it in the ground.

"Great, but how do we light it?" asked Steven.

"With that fire-in-a-tube you have!" said Harry.

"Harry, it doesn't work that way!" said Jane. "They don't set fire to just anything!"

"No, but they might with the right fuel." said Kevin. "Hey, Harry, check in that third bag, on the rhino's left side. That oughtta help!" Harry searched, and found bullets. He dropped them like poison.

"I know what those are." he said ominously. "What exactly did you think we needed these for?" he asked, appalled.

"Well, this, actually. Chill, man, when I heard it was the Icy Peaks, I took them bullets from the jeep."

"Why?" asked Al.

"So we can use the gunpowder to start a fire! Here, I'll show ya. Just pour the gunpowder on the wood, light it, and it should provide a good enough spark to start the fire."

"Will it work?" asked Drake.

"I ain't sure, but what other chance do we have?"

"You have a point there. Alright, open them up."

Kevin carefully opened up the bullets with a knife. There were twenty bullets, all from the ammunition strip of the machine gun mounted on the jeep. Kevin only opened ten, saying they'd need the others to start future fires, if it was needed. Al and Harry found the strategic spots to place the gunpowder, and ignited it.

"Oh, one more thing, it might produce a –"

BANG!

There was a small explosion, causing everyone but Kevin to jump back. Al and Alol positively freaked out, and it took a few seconds for them to calm down. But it worked! The dried leaves, the small pieces of wood and the large pieces caught fire, a small fire, and soon it widened into a large, warm campfire. Harry sat down on the used fire logs, ready for a story.

"Well, it's only right you hear the story of this temple, too." said Harry. "This one is of another woman, Queen Gralea, and this is the oldest tomb we'll visit."

"Who was Queen Gralea?" asked Jane.

"Well, for those of you who don't know, the Klenkara Tribe was founded by a man banished from the Fertile River Tribe, a man named Klenkara. Now the Mayztecs were a small tribe, they had been around for four years, all people competing for leadership, but one, Ragoth the Great, came out on top. He began the real Mayztec Empire, and it was his reign that would set the stage for the future.

"He spread out his armies, and uniting either by peace or by force all the tribes that lived there, all of which were descended from your earthly kingdoms of Egypt, Rome, Turkey, Mesopotamia, Babylonia, Greece, Maya, and, well, you get the idea. He did not coin the name 'Mayztec', although that would become their name in a few hundred years. Well, Ragoth eventually died in battle, but he gathered a lot of land, and his heir was able to hold it. His son built a huge army, though he himself would never use it.

"But, moving further along, eventually Ragoth's great-grandson, Hemeblar, took to the throne. He took a wife, by the name of Gralea. Well, we northern rebels began to view this new tribe as a threat, as his father and he himself had taken a lot of new land for the Mayztecs, and managed to unite two tribes descended from ancient Peru, and seven we believe may have been Aztecs. They all flocked to his cause. Well, Klenkara struck hard, early in Hemeblar's reign, just a year after marrying Gralea.

"Gralea had tried once to get pregnant, but it did not work. Then, Klenkara, as fate would have it, shot an arrow through Hemeblar's heart, and he was dead in minutes, childless. Gralea was heartbroken, but there was no heir to take the throne. She became queen. Her advisor kept her... advised, and he was very friendly and considerate to the queen... until he killed her."

"He killed her?" asked John. "Why?"

"Again, because she was a woman." said Harry. "This was early in the empire's history, they were small, and the people accepted the shift in power from Gralea to her advisor readily. But a woman was not worthy to be buried alongside kings, even that early in history. So, the new emperor chose a remote, uninhabited spot on the northern map, and here they sent her, losing several workers to the cold, despite this place being warmer back then. This was before they had slaves. Then, the new emperor sent his armies west, to take still more territory. That, however, is a different story.

"But, the Klenkara Tribe settled here, so they could ambush the funeral party coming back. Only a handful made it back to tell the king. Her tomb was marked on the records, for Elmork to find. However this part of history also signified a new age for the Mayztec Empire – the first dynasty was finished, but a new, lasting war with us rebel tribes was about to begin."

"So her tomb is up in the mountains?" asked John.

"Yeah, that one over there." Harry pointed. "The one with the wide ridge. It's kind of high, so it'll take us most of the day to get there, but we can be in and out by this time tomorrow."

"Let's hope so." said Drake.

They set up the tents, making sure to close the curtains completely. They could hear the wind howling, but it was warmer inside the tent, and certainly safer. All four of the wolves were in Drake's tent with him, and they curled up, just like modern dogs, at the feet of the sleeping bags.

*****

In the morning, the snow and wind had stopped, but outside the tents, the entrances were half-full with snow. Drake made sure his clothing was as warm as it could possibly be before he went outside.

The snow was up to his waist, and the whole clearing was covered in snow, with a round dent in the centre where the fire had been the night before.

Al, Alol, Harry, Steven and John were all up as well. The forest around him was partly the conifers he had always seen in the mountains, but in with them were also extinct plants, adapted for the freezing-cold environment. The wolves followed Drake out, and came bounding to their owners when Al whistled. Drake looked at the mountain they were supposed to climb. It actually wasn't too far away, though it was high. They had camped under the mountain ahead of it, and would reach the mountain the temple was on in an hour.

They didn't attempt to get a fire going. Drake was sure it was a mistake to bring the Terror Birds, which were freezing, but they seemed to survive. Yaagol had proven valuable for carrying supplies. The rhino could take on a lot of weight and still have some to spare.

Al stared up at the mountain. He whispered a song under his breath, which Drake had never heard him do before. The Hekeni often liked to invent songs, but Al had never been part of that group, until now:

"In the mountain way up high,
On the ridge, touching the sky,
We see the mighty mountain's face
The Extinction Stone's last resting place,
Many walked into that tomb,
They challenged death, and met their doom,
Their skeletons lie on the temple's floor,
There to sleep forevermore."

"Dark." said Drake.

"What?"

"I heard you under your breath. Isn't that song a bit dark?"

"Not really. It's mostly just something I thought of. We won't die, though, not with our modern technology. I can feel it! This time we'll be successful, just like in all the others."

"I didn't know you were into the whole singing thing."

"Music is a large part of Hekeni culture. Every Hekeni native needs to sing."

"Are there really skeletons on that tomb?"

"As much as there were in all the others. Great groups were sent here, and we know at least some of them died in the tomb."

They reached the foot of the mountain, and began their climb. The wolves sniffed out the way, chasing away a few extinct, furry mammals, but they weren't that big a threat. Soon, at the top of the mountain, there was a sheer cliff, with the ridge running along above it. A large glacier sat on the top of the cliff.

"Do we need to get up there?" asked John.

"No; come this way." said Al.

This high up, no trees grew, and the snow-covered ground was rocky. Al led them to a small square sticking out of the mountains, the size of a doorway, with a triangular roof. The rock the temple was built in was smooth, and the tomb itself was higher than the eight-foot-high cliff it was built into. It had a triangular roof, surrounded by a glacier, and it looked almost Mesopotamian or Babylonian in design.

"This is the tomb of Empress Gralea?" asked Drake.

"Yep." said Al.

Alol walked up to the door. There was one line of faded, carved writing, which had very nearly disappeared. Beneath that were two lines of freshly-carved lines – the writing the Extinction Stone carriers had carved onto the tomb when they hid it. Alol began reading it.

"I'm surprised a man that frail can even survive up here." said Drake.

"I know. I'm surprised he's made it this far." replied Al.

Alol began reading, and Harry translated:

"The first line says: here lies Queen Gralea, last in line of King Ragoth's family. The second and third lines, added afterwards he says, say: All hail Ragoth the Great and those of his line! May all seekers of the great Stone perish within, so proclaim the Mayztecs, masters of the land. Hah!" added Harry. "Them, the masters? They certainly were full of themselves!"

"Yeah. Well, it's time to enter." said Drake.

Al hooked up a line to Yaagol, and the other end to the temple door. He got Yaagol to walk forward, and slowly, with a lot of effort on the rhino's part, the door slid open. It wasn't all the way open, but it was cracked open enough to enter.

"Well," said John, "I guess this is it."

Chapter 25 – The Frozen Crest Returns

Al took out the flashlights, and handed one out to everybody. He took an empty sack, and was the first to look inside the tomb. He squeezed in. For a moment, there was silence, but soon his arm came out and beckoned them inside. Uncertain of what to do, Drake went first.

He looked inside – the whole temple was a flat grey, carved from rocks taken from the mountain. It was clear that not a lot of thought had gone into it. The walls were caked with dust, and there were faded carvings all around the walls. They went floor-to-roof, not small like those of other temples. But, Drake reminded himself, this was built when the Mayztec culture was still in the early stages.

Drake squeezed in, and shone the light around. Near the walls, there were blackened skeletons, some grasping charred wood, others lying at the side. There was one crouched just in the corner, a mammoth-skin blanket still covering him. The cold must have got that one in his sleep.

"Hello, Drake." said Al.

Drake jumped with fright. He had almost forgotten Al was there! "What?"

"Nothing." replied Drake. "I wonder what burnt these guys."

"Beats me."

Dust crumbled from the roof, and covered Drake's shoulder. He brushed it off. When he faced it upwards, he saw cracks it the places where the wall met the ceiling, packed full of what Drake thought was dust.

John and Dave squeezed through. Drake shone the light ahead on the floor, and saw a large strip of eerily familiar floor. It was the mosaic pattern from the tomb of King Zolgaf. Unlike Zolgaf, this one could easily be jumped over, though in the dark it would be impossible to tell it was there. There were holes in places of it. Drake sent his light down the nearest one.

It was just a chute, but it had no end. Drake did not want to know how deep that went. He turned to see Steven squeezing through.

"Hey, I know this." he said, taking some dust from the walls.

"Isn't it just dirt?" asked Drake.

"No... this is black powder!"

"Are you serious?" asked Drake.

"Yes, look. The Mayztecs must have had some Chinese in their tribe, and got the secret of black powder. Of course, based on timelines, it would have to have been added after the tomb was originally built."

"So that's what burnt these men." said Al, looking at the charred skeletons. "These charred bits of wood – they must have been torches. When the dust fell on them, or if they absent-mindedly brought it too close, the powder ignited, and they died. If they didn't light torches, this floor would get them.

"What's beyond the trapdoor-floor anyway?" asked John, as the last of the Hekeni squeezed in.

They shone their lights across. It was a bare stone wall.

"That... that can't be right!" said Harry. "I know it's hidden here! I know it!"

"It isn't right." said John. "Even without the black powder, these walls are old and faded. But this wall looks too new. It was built after the temple, to keep out intruders."

"Even so, that's it." said Al. "We can't get past that! I'll bet this was why all the expeditions were failure!"

"Don't we have grenades, or something?" asked Drake. "Didn't we bring any explosives at all? Didn't you anticipate anything like this?"

"Oh, yeah, they're on..." Al slapped his forehead. "They're on Nemeli."

"With the other group." sighed Harry.

Alol slapped Al in the back of the head. "*Nilahoh!*" he yelled.

"What?" asked Drake, not familiar with that particular word.

"He called him an idiot." said Harry.

"Stop it, stupid old man!" said Al, shaking him away.

"Well, we need to get past this wall somehow!" said Harry.

"How do you think we do that?" asked Al.

"People, people, shut up!" said Kevin. "Look, I got an idea. We use the Mayztecs own traps against 'em. Take as much of this black powder as we can, and place it near a structural weak point in the wall!"

"Not bad." said John. "But where's the structural weak point?"

"I'll look for it." said Jane, jumping easily over the trap floor. "I learned how to look for them, my dad taught me what to look for."

"What does her dad have to do with it?" asked John.

"He was a detonator, or whatever they're called." said Drake. "He looks for the weak points on commercial buildings that are set to be demolished."

"Ah, I can't find one." said Jane. "I'll bet my dad could."

Drake jumped over, and pushed against the wall. The bricks were not set in mortar. But there was never anyone on the other side to help build it. The bricks themselves were loose.

"I'll bet these bricks would just go with a big enough blast, anyway. Come on, gather up as much gunpowder as you can!"

They all began scraping fistfuls of black powder from the walls, Al placing his in the empty sack. They all went over the floor and dumped it at the foot of the wall, near the centre. Soon, the pile was up to Drake's knees, and twice as long. They made a kind of ridge along the wall, ready for detonation.

"Now we need a fuse." said Kevin.

"Do we even have a reliable one?" asked John.

Harry went back outside, and brought back in a lighter. "How long do these things stay lit after you turn them on?" he asked.

"None. That's a campfire lighter, they go off as soon as you let go." said Steven.

Harry looked deep in thought. He saw the skeleton wrapped up in the mammoth-skin blanket. He took it off, and placed it over the black powder pile.

"Mammoth fur burns well." he said. "You might want to leave the tomb, just in case."

They all squeezed back out. Drake was back in the cold for only a minute until he heard a small bang, and felt the tomb rumble. When they came back in, they found Harry at the far end of the cave, looking scared. They shone their lights across to the wall.

It was down! The bricks on the bottom seemed to have been shot backwards, leaving the top ones to collapse.

"What's wrong? The wall is down!"

"Look again." he whispered.

They all shone their lights back. Then they saw it. It was a huge, three-toed carnivore, with a crest jutting up from the back of its head. It was black from head to toe, except its crest, which was orange. The eyes glowed red, the arms were short and three-fingered, and the jaws were oval-shaped and filled with teeth. Its long tail went back into darkness, and it stood with one foot placed on the pile of rubble. John stepped back in fright, too. He had known this animal before, and feared it as a result.

"C... c-c... Cryolophosaurus." he said. "I know it means 'frozen-crested reptile'... but does it have to be so damn literal?"

"Well, Cryolophosaurus did live below the Antarctic Circle." said Tom.

"No, it lived in what is below the Antarctic circle *today*! The continent may have been on the equator back a hundred and eighty million years ago!"

"Oh..." said Tom. "Then yeah, the meaning is a bit too literal, ain't it?"

The Cryolophosaurus roared, but it didn't seem to want to pass the trick floor. But they had to get past it somehow, or their quest would be over.

"How do we get past him?" asked John.

"I don't know..." said Al, "we'll just have to run for it."

"Run for it?" asked Drake.

"Yeah... ready? On three... one, two, three!"

They all ran and jumped the trick floor. They ducked under the Cryolophosaurus, which snapped and snarled, confused by the numbers.

Beyond the wall, there were six pillars, three on each side. They lined a long, grey room shaped like a rectangular box. The walls had floor-to-roof faded carvings of Mayztec tribes allying themselves with one another, with armies throwing down their enemies, and brave soldiers fighting back dinosaurs and other prehistoric monsters. At the end of the room was a stone coffin, and the wall behind it had a faded carving of the frontal view of a Cryolophosaurus, crouching down to eye level and roaring at them.

Drake grabbed Jane and hid her behind a pillar with him. John and Steven ran and hid behind another pillar, Alol hid behind the pillar across from Drake, Al and Harry hid, while Dave and Kevin hid together, leaving Tom to go behind the sixth pillar as the Cryolophosaurus walked backwards, and began searching.

It turned and sniffed. Al and Harry were behind the pillar next to Drake and Jane. Drake looked at them.

"Where's the Stone?" he mouthed.

Al moved his mouth, though no sound came out: "Coffin."

The Cryolophosaurus peered around the first pillar, seeing Drake and Jane, followed by Al and Harry, followed by Tom, all lined up. It roared with rage.

"Run!" yelled Harry.

They ran from behind the p llars, and ran further into the temple. Dave and Kevin emerged from their pillar, stood ahead of the wall, and began shouting at it.

"Hey, you, come here!" yelled Dave. "Come on then, get me, you great ugly brute!" the Cryolophosaurus turned. "That's it, monster! Come get me, you scaly coward!" he waved his arms.

"I think we got his attention." said Kevin.

The Cryolophosaurus roared and ran towards them. John, Steven, and Alol emerged, too, knowing it was no use to hide.

"Come on, let's open the coffin!" said Al.

"Dave, Kevin, run!" yelled John.

Kevin tried to run, but Dave held him back. "Not yet, Kev... wait for it..."

"Wait for what?" the Cryolophosaurus came closer.

It was just one step away from devouring them, when Dave pulled Kevin out of the way, and they ran for it. The Cryolophosaurus turned abruptly, and skidded into what remained of the wall. The bricks fell across it, and it tripped over sideways, leaving a cloud of dust, the wall completely knocked over.

"We don't have long before he recovers." said Dave. "Get that Stone!"

John and Harry grabbed opposite ends of the heavy coffin lid and pushed it aside. The lid remained on the coffin, but they didn't need to push it off until they saw it. Like all the others, it was perfectly round, lying next to the bare, partially dissolved bones of a skeleton. It was the black Pleistocene Stone of the Solg.

"The black Stone!" said Al. He picked it up.

"Close the coffin." said Drake. "The dead, even the Mayztec dead, deserve respect."

Harry and John closed the coffin.

The Cryolophosaurus was getting up, shaking itself off. They all turned to look at it. Seeing what they were doing, the Allosaur charged forward at them. They ran behind the pillars, running from it. It stuck its head between the pillars, though it was really too large to get through. It snapped at them, and they all fled over the remains of the wall and over the floor before the Cryolophosaurus backed itself out. The opening to the door was too slim – they needed to go out one at a time.

"Me first." said Al, pushing them away and squeezing through with the Stone.

"That was rude." said John.

The Cryolophosaurus roared and ran towards them. The group all ran forward, and tried to squeeze out all at once. Realizing this wouldn't work, they backed off.

The Cryolophosaurus paused at the wall, growling. Did it not want to cross the floor? Did it realize that the Stone was gone, and killing them would not get it back? Or was it just pausing to consider what to do? Drake didn't want to wait and find out.

Alol went out while no one was looking, but he was so thin he didn't need to squeeze through. They all went through without really agreeing on an order – first John, then Kevin, then Steven, then Harry, then Tom. It was just Drake and Jane in the tomb. The Cryolophosaurus, realizing it was running out of tomb raiders, jumped across the floor and ran at them.

"Drake, you go first!" said Jane.

"I'm not even going to argue." he said. He grabbed Jane and forcefully shoved her out. He ducked and ran as the Cryolophosaurus slammed into the wall where he had been seconds earlier.

He ran the other way, and the Cryolophosaurus charged at him there, too. He dodged again, reaching the door, and getting himself out, just as the Cryolophosaurus slammed into it. The door rattled, though stayed in place, and Drake got up, feeling a sudden rush of cold air.

He saw looked up and saw Jane, both angry and relieved. "You're such a chivalrous moron." she said.

"At least we all got out." he said. "Where's Al?"

"I'm here." he said. "And we have the Stone!" he exclaimed, smiling.

"Can I see it?"

Al hesitated, but handed the Stone over. It was black, and unlike the others, there was no inner light. It was cold, not glowing with inner warmth. Was this supposed to be a sad metaphor on Humanity?

"Okay, that's enough!" said Al, taking it back.

"Did that Stone ever have an inner light?" asked Drake.

"It used to. But about ten thousand years ago, it stopped glowing, and no one's seen it glow since. I'd like to say it was the fault of the Mayztecs, but it wasn't." said Al.

"Do you think it will glow now?" asked Drake.

"I'm not sure." said Al. "All the other Stones glowed, even after this one stopped. Even so, you can see the other ones glow. I hope it starts – but it doesn't look like it."

"Where to next?" asked John.

"One more night here in the Icy Peaks." said Harry. "Then, we meet up with our group on the east side of this mountain range, and we head over to Turtle Lake and from there, it's over to our final destination, the tomb of Elmerik the Extinctor. I won't be explaining that one – no explanation should be required."

Chapter 26 – Teratornis Hills

As they left the tomb of Queen Gralea, the Icy Peaks began to grow warmer the further east they went. As they left, they came to a massive clearing, and saw dozens of woolly mammoth, mixed in with woolly rhinos, muskoxen, and on the far end Drake saw a pride of Smilodon, looking out with longing on the mammoths. Smilodon was Jane's guardian animal, he remembered.

They marched through the field unnoticed, though Yaagol spent some time frolicking among the wild rhinos. They were mostly Coelodonta (see-low-don-ta), like him, but some were rhinos with just one long, man-sized horn called Elasmotherium (ee-laz-mo-theer-ee-um).

The Hekeni didn't keep Yaagol back too much. In fact, they encouraged their domestic animals to spend some time with their wild brethren, at least for a little while, if they wanted. Often times, it is an easy way to get new genes in their domesticated group if it was female, and both genders were generally better-behaved if they got companionship. At least that's what Al said, and Drake took his word for it. Of course, when they did pass the clearing, Yaagol was called to come.

As two days passed, the mountains got shorter, the skies again became clear, the wind died down, and the snow got shallower as they left the Icy Peaks, the name for a group of mountains in the Mammoth Mountain range. The conifer forest returned, and they came upon a glacier lake for a place to camp, when the sun was just on the verge of going down.

"Productive day." said Al, looking west towards the sunset.

"Yeah." agreed Harry. "Five down, one to go. I wasn't sure on that one."

"You know, simply getting past the wall means we had already gotten further than anyone else, if you think about it." said Steven. "But that temple was certainly the hardest."

"Oh, I don't know, Steven, King Zolgaf was pretty difficult." said John, remembering the Titanoboa.

"I wasn't too fond of Emperor Elmork's tomb." said Drake.

"Yeah, but that one wasn't that difficult, if you think back on it." said Al. "But King Zolgaf was the only true tomb we visited, and by that I mean that's relatively what a true tomb looks like. Queen Klefferniti's was a good size, but it was simple, straightforward, though the style of tomb, while uncommon, is known in the place where Mayztecs typically buried their emperors. Rilowin was buried in a school. And as for Queen Gralea, she was just dumped there in a stone box. The obstacles were added some eight thousand years after her death. Elmork, of course, had his tomb hastily built by a handful of workers."

"So only Zolgaf is typical of a Mayztec emperor's temple?" asked Drake.

"Like I said, Klefferniti had a good style, and a good size, but typically those styles are much more complicated. So yes, you could say that."

"What 'bout Rilowin?" asked Tom. "He had a good tomb."

"It was a good size, yes, but the style, while elaborate, was wrong." said Harry, cutting in. "That was a school building, not a tomb."

"So what about Elmerik the Extinctor?" asked John.

"He has a proper Mayztec tomb, though it might be a little small." said Al. "That shouldn't make much difference, though, it will still have all the glamour of Zolgaf's tomb."

"Oh boy." said John sarcastically.

*****

The next morning, the sun rose over the mountains in the east, bathing the world in light. The group got up at the crack of dawn, eager to meet Dazz and the other Hekeni and give them the good news. While they packed up, Al boiled some breakfast over the fire, with water from the lake. It was the last of their provisions, consisting of fruit and Prehistorcian noodles, which were as primitive as the bread.

As soon as they ate, they set out, heading towards the bare foothills of the mountains. As they came towards the last mountain, where its snow was as shallow as ever, they met another unexpected animal.

It was a bear, but a bear larger than anyone had ever seen! Its snout was short, though its teeth were long. On its hind legs, it would be twice, maybe three times as tall as Drake; it was brown from head to toe, and when it saw them, it became angry.

Generally bears don't get angry unless someone sneaks up on them – which is what the Hekeni did. They had been walking silently, and had the unfortunate fate of sneaking up on the Short-faced Bear, the deadliest bear to ever evolve. It weighed over 1500 pounds, and was the top predator of the ice age. It died out from North America eleven thousand years ago, and even on all fours, it was almost as tall as any of them.

It growled, and they could see its warm breath condense in the cold air. The humans backed off, as the bear stood on both legs.

It roared, and ran at them. The three Terror Birds snapped at them, as did the wolves, but it paid them no attention, swiping them away, and it was thanks only to their quick reflexes they weren't killed.

"Yaagol! *Rahka!*" yelled Al.

All of a sudden, Yaagol went into a rage! He snorted, and growled, targeted the bear, and charged forwards. The bear turned tail and ran on all fours from the massive rhinoceros. He turned, still in a mad frenzy, sniffing the air madly! Drake, for the first time since he had first met them, felt afraid of a Hekeni animal.

"Yaagol! *Lok-rahka*!" said Al.

Yaagol calmed down. He walked back over to Al, who slung his arm around the rhino and patted him. The rhino was calm again.

"What was that?" asked Kevin.

"*Arctodus simus*, or the short-faced bear." said John.

"I think he meant the rhino." said Drake.

"No, I meant the bear. But the rhino ain't a bad question. What happened to Yaagol?"

"John, remember me telling you all Hekeni animals had a kill-command in case anyone captured them?" asked Harry. "And how they would only take commands from the voice and smell that gave it?"

"Yeah." he replied.

"Well, that was the command." explained Harry. "*Rahka* is a made-up word to send the animal into a rage. *Lok* means 'anti', or 'reversed', so saying '*lok-rahka*' is the command that everything is fine again."

"They are exceptionally trained." said Dave, in wonder. "I have never heard that command before."

"We don't need to use it that often." said Al.

"Back to mah original question – that bear was a short-faced one?"

"Yeah, it was." said John. "It was top of the food chain, at least in the Pleistocene. Clearly, a woolly rhino could scare it off – but then again, the modern rhino is immune to attacks from every animal except Humans. It's logical that they would be here, too, like the moose of the ice-age world."

"Well, thanks for the information." said Al. "With that, we continue."

*****

Over the course of the day, the snow disappeared, the mountains shrunk into hills, and the temperature got higher. As the sun went down, they had reached a large expanse of foothills covered with short, yellow grass, expanding far into the east, out of sight. They continued walking.

As they walked further east, a small pterosaur buzzed like a hummingbird from the sky, and perched on Harry's shoulder, with a note tied to it. He took it down, and opened the letter.

"It's from Dazz." he said. "He's giving us his location. This little pterosaur must have waited for us."

"Where is Dazz?" asked Al.

"He says he'll be waiting for us roughly nine kilometres southeast of here, and he'll be there by sunset tomorrow. That works out nicely for us. We can camp here, sleep in, and meet them there tomorrow."

"That sounds good." said Jane.

The group nodded in agreement. Yaagol, when he saw they were setting up camp, laid down for the night, along with the Terror Birds. The wolves, however, two of which were injured from the bear attack, seemed to know they were going to be asked to hunt. Al said something to them in Hekeni, and they laid down, too.

"I am finding us dinner, but I'll go alone." said Al. "Well, without the dogs, anyway."

"Ah'll go with ya." said Kevin. "Ah'd like to see a hunt."

"Y'know, so do I." said Tom. "But I know how to do it, too, so I can be of more help."

"Alright. We'll all be back in an hour." said Al. "Harry's in charge."

Al came back an hour later, when the campsite and fire was set up, each of the three men carrying an animal. Kevin and Tom held deer apiece, while Al held a Smilodon.

"You killed a Smilodon?" asked John.

"Little bastard tried to kill us." said Al. "I had to."

"It's true." said Kevin. "Then Smilodon were huntin' the same deer we were."

"Well, I'm glad you got away, at least." said John.

"You know, I remember a time when killing Smilodon wasn't so common." said Drake. "Besides, if it was hunting, it was probably a 'her'."

"Usually, yes, but this was a male, solitary." said Al. "Not that it would matter much. They make great meat. Come on, let's get this guy cooked!"

They ate their fill, and had enough left over to feed the dogs and birds. There were no leftovers, however. The sun was at its lowest point, and there were only a few minutes of light from the western sky left before it disappeared completely. The mountains looked oddly distant, a trick of the light.

Harry hummed a little, and then he formed words. Unlike Al, he did not bother to whisper them:

> "In the mountains of the cold,
> We sought a stone so very old,
> It was hidden in a tomb,
> And inside a hidden doom,
> But we came out alive and well,
> Emerging from the freezing hell,
> Victorious with the stones we seek,
> We've turned our backs on the Icy Peaks.
>
> We were stuck in the frozen snow,
> But from the cold our strength will grow,
> At last we found an Extinction Stone,
> Though it chilled us to the bone,
> We came back, the last Stone we still seek,
> But we've turned our backs on the Icy Peaks."

"Let's hope we can stay out, too." said John, when Harry finished.

"What was the song for?" asked Al.

"What was yours for?" smiled Harry. Al had not been as quiet as he thought.

Al sat silently. Darkness fell, and they all slowly fell asleep. For the first time in four days, Drake didn't feel at all cold, and he slept all through the night.

*****

The next morning, they got up, had a lazy morning, and ambled along in the general direction. They didn't have far to go, and they reached the hill by the mid-afternoon. Harry had sent their Nemicolopterus ahead telling Dazz they'd be waiting for them. They took turns watching the southern horizon.

"Oi! Here they come!" yelled Dave, two hours later, on his watch.

They got up and looked. The large Hekeni group, dinosaurs and all, were moving between the hills, with Dazz riding Nemeli in the lead.

"Hey, Dazz!" yelled Drake. "Dazz!"

Dazz looked up, and waved. After a few minutes, when they were within earshot, Dazz called out again.

"Did you find the Stone?" he asked in Hekeni.

"Yeah, it's here!" called Drake in English. "It's the black one!"

The Hekeni walked up around the hill, and the ten expedition members went down to meet them. Dazz took off the Sekka hat, and Al placed his back on. But Drake knew it was only ceremonial — everyone knew Al was the leader. They set off down the plains.

"Where are we?" asked Drake.

"A long stretch of land between the Mammoth Mountains and Turtle Lake, called Teratornis Hills." replied Harry.

"Teratornis Hills?"

"Yeah, you know, like the bird."

"I know what it is!" said Drake. "So is that where Emperor Elmerik lies? Turtle Lake?"

"No, are you kidding? That's a beautiful place, easily accessible, provides good food. That's not where you want to place something you don't want found!"

"I suppose not." said Drake.

"We're going to the Triassic Desert – yes, Drake, another desert." he said, seeing the disbelief cn his face. "This one is actually an extension of the desert surrounding Mount Ash, although it's considered a totally different region. The Icy Peaks was a necessary detour, we could have done them last, but this way we get the kindness of the other tribes to help us."

"Is there a tribe on Turtle Lake?"

"Yes, the Flimzoak, which means 'many mixed' in Hekeni. I'll tell you their story when we get closer."

Drake hopped up onto Tenethax, and Ahrzi chirped at him. Drake told him to jump, and the Utahraptor leapt into his arms. Sam, meanwhile, was growing quickly, and he was now as long as John was tall. The young Styracosaurus weighed about five hundred pounds.

They had been walking for about half an hour when they ran into a large group on the horizon. Drake feared more Golarans. Al shot an arrow in the ground ahead of the man in the Sekka-hat.

A yellow-feathered arrow shot into the ground in reply. If the tribes used the colours of their Extinction Stone on the backs of their arrows, then logically, this large group was Trontoll. Drake had seen the map – the Trontoll were several hundred kilometres north, in the northern half of the Great Yellow Plains, living on the shores of the Forked Lakes.

"*Tehrah*, Trontoll!" called Al. "What are you doing so far from the Forked Lakes?"

Al had either forgotten that the Trontoll didn't speak Hekeni, or didn't know any words in Trontoll. Fortunately, that didn't matter.

"We could ask you Hekeni the same thing!" called the Trontoll leader in Hekeni. The two groups met.

"What brings you so far from the Cretaceous Forest?" he asked.

"We're on an expedition!"

"Oddly enough, so are we. We're on our way to Pterosaur Canyon, an exploratory mission. Our tribe's maps are outdated. You?"

"Oh, uh… same thing." Al lied.

Drake looked at him with a look of confusion and anger. Al gave him a look that said 'if you tell the truth, I'll kill you'. Drake didn't stop looking at him, but he didn't call out the lie, either.

"We're on our way to the Flimzoak, improve some relations, catch up with each other." said Al.

"Good, good, they've been wondering about Hekeni visits." the Trontoll said. "Awfully big expedition! Well, good luck to you!"

"You too." said Al. The Trontoll and the Hekeni went their separate ways.

"Why didn't you tell them the truth?" asked Drake.

"Because they don't need to know." said Al. "We'd have to give the Stone back."

"Uh… isn't that the whole *point*?"

"They don't need to know yet. Relax, Drake, everything will work out in the end."

"It had better."

This had been exactly what Drake was worried about. But he didn't have to worry for too long.

They came up to another group, this time it looked as though they meant business. They had four Deinonychus, and a Triceratops, and there were some three dozen men holding spears or bows, and the odd one holding a crossbow. They were Golarans.

They came up to the Hekeni, pointing their arrows and spears at them.

Al yelled: "What do you want, Golarans? Do we have to beat you again?"

"Listen to us, Hekeni! You will not keep us away from the red Stone. We demand to see all your Stones! Let us see them, and you can go free."

"Al, in a time like this, it's best to avoid the violence." said Drake. "Just show them we don't have it."

"But Drake —"

"Al, the road to peace is a two-way street. If you ever want to cease Golaran hostility, one of you must make the first move. Since they won't, you must!"

"Fine." he ordered the Hekeni to show them all the Stones. They dumped all five Stones on the ground before the Golarans, who looked at them with awe.

"As you can see, we were just on our way to retrieve the red." he said.

"I suppose you are telling the truth." the leader admitted. "We would like you to seek us out when you find it, you know... we can maybe make peace."

"Wait, Sekka! What's that bulge there?" asked a Neanderthal.

The bag was turned upside-down. The brown duplicate stone tumbled out. The Golarans looked appalled. The leader stared up at Al.

"So! You're making duplicate Stones, are you? Trying to deceive us, give us false Stones so you can keep the real ones for yourselves? Typical Hekeni! How shameful!"

"It was made by the Mayztecs in the tomb of King Rilowin!" said Al, though he could not keep the desperation out of his voice. "It was a fake to trick us! We weren't sure which one was real, so we took them both, and figured it out later!"

The Golaran did not look convinced. "I do not believe you." he said. "However, in the spirit of..." he spoke the word with intense hate "*forgiveness*, I will choose to. But I can't be wrong. You will take my right-hand man, Nikhall, with you." he pulled forward a wiry, dependable-looking man. "You will give him the red Stone. He will send us a report every day."

"If we don't?" asked Al. "We can just kill you all here."

"One of us will escape." said the Golaran. "We will tell all the tribes what you are up to. You may defeat us, but you can't defeat every tribe in Prehistorcia! Consider this the first action of peace!"

"We can kill you all without a single survivor." he crossed his arms.

"Are you willing to take that chance? We may get a note out, even if you do manage to kill us all. In fact, my scribe's been writing one while we've been talking. What shall his conclusion be? Can you kill us before he finishes that? Take Nikhall and we will leave your expedition in peace. Kill him, and we'll know."

Al looked at Drake hatefully, as if it was his fault. "Fine, we'll take him. But you, Golaran, will leave us alone forever. Leave every tribe alone forever!"

"We shall see."

Nikhall walked into the group with three trained Golaran Nemicolopterus on his shoulder, looking overly confident. The Golarans walked away. The leader turned back and yelled:

"Remember, write *every day*, or there will be open war against you! Mark my words, Hekeni!"

Chapter 27 – Shades of Grey

The Hekeni took the Golaran, Nikhall, into their group, looking miserable at this prospect. They did not engage the Golaran in conversation, which worked out nicely, as the Golaran didn't care to be spoken to. He walked up behind Al, between Drake, John, and Alol, as if he thought he belonged with people of such high influence to the Sekka.

"Drake, we have the Golaran here." said Al, riding Nemeli, a little ahead.

"I'm aware of that. But you heard them – it's this or open war."

"We should have never shown them the Stones!"

"And then what, Al? Would we have fought them over it? Would they have not threatened us with open war with the tribes?"

"We'll never know now."

"Just give the Golaran the red Stone, and they'll be gone!"

"No."

"Why not?"

"The red Stone is the most powerful of all Stones." said Al. "Just as the Permian was the most powerful extinction. The black and red Stones equal each other in power, and the tribes who have the powerful Stones are said to be blessed. Based on the size of the Golaran Tribe, it's hard not to believe."

"So you're denying them their own Stone just because the Prehistorcian tribes hate them?"

"They do not deserve it, not for what they did."

"Hey, Hekeni, shut your mouth!" yelled Nikhall.

"You speak English?" asked Drake.

"Yes, I speak it, Above-worlder." said Nikhall, in a perfectly normal voice. "Yes, I can tell you are an Above-worlder. You have the look of wonder on your face when you view the land, and the Hekeni have not yet crushed your perception of right and wrong."

"You may have a right to the Stone, but that doesn't mean Golarans are innocent." said Drake. "You plunder and cheat to get what you want."

"We were abandoned! We would not have to do it if the tribes were willing to help us!"

"You still destroyed the Rooloer Tribe." said Drake.

"Yes, Above-worlder, I'm not denying Golaran guilt. But are the Hekeni so innocent? Have you ever heard our side of the story?"

"He doesn't need to, Golaran, you're liars anyway." said Al.

"You know, Al, something I learned long ago is that history is written by the winners, and the truth is always skewed to make the teller look innocent." said John. "I think we should hear the Golaran side of events. I still won't like the tribe, but let me draw my own conclusions."

"I don't like this!" he replied.

"You don't like anything." said Drake.

"You are wise, Above-worlder." said Nikhall. "I will tell you the story, though I, too, will skew it, this time in favour of us. But that is unavoidable."

"Just tell it." said Drake.

"You've heard the story of the Extinction Stones in the first place, right? About the six tribes, and the expeditions to find them?" Drake and John nodded. "Good, then I can start from there. You see, the story goes that an expedition recovered the red Stone, but when they got there, they fought amongst themselves, and killed each other. Soon, a man named Norral was left the only one alive, still holding the Stone. I will not deny that part of the story. They say he looked upon the carcasses, and was horror-struck by what he had done. He dropped the Stone and ran back to his own tribe in shame.

"But first some Golaran history, and the Hekeni Sekka would do well to listen to this, too. Norral used to be a Golaran, whether or not you Hekeni knew that I do not know. But he was banished from our tribe nearly ten years before that famous expedition."

"Banished for what?" asked John.

"Oh, please, what a lie!" said Al.

"You would do good to listen to your open-minded tribesmen, Hekeni." said Nikhall. "Norral was banished for raping and then murdering the daughter of a powerful village chief. He then lied about it, saying he was wrongly accused."

"How do you know he wasn't telling the truth?" asked Al.

"I thought you weren't listening. He was lying, we all knew it. It didn't help that her older brothers walked in on it, and Norral fled out the window. The daughter died a few days later from her bruises. If you think she consented, and Norral just went too far, keep in mind the girl was twenty, your equivalent of nine. He would have been banished, but on the day of his trial, he fled. He went to the Rooloer Tribe.

"We sent a message of his crime to the tribes, but the trial never having taken place, he was able to convince the chief he was guiltless. He lived there for years, building up trusts, making friends with the right people. He cheated, lied, and stole to get his way, and reached the top. Soon, as luck would have it, he was announced leader of the largest expedition to retrieve the Extinction Stones yet. He volunteered to lead a group of a hundred people, all from mixed tribes, into the red Stone's tomb.

"He had changed his appearance, so the four Golarans on the trip didn't immediately recognize him. When they learned his name, they remembered his crime, and had it not been for the Rooloer Tribe, the bulk of the expedition, he would have died right there. But they followed him with consent, thinking they would at least get back our Stone out of it.

"Well, they got to the temple, and fought over the Stone. Norral may have picked up the Stone and used it against us – but we can't know for sure. All we know was that when he came out, he was alone. So imagine our disbelief when we hear from the Rooloer Tribe saying that this scoundrel, this murderer, this piece of slime from the ugly underbelly of the land felt *remorse*... we just couldn't believe it."

"You might not believe him," said John, "but couldn't you believe the Rooloers?"

"Yes and no." replied Nikhall. "There was great debate on that. However in the end we assumed that Norral had kept the Stone for himself, not telling the Rooloers he had it. We sent forward three hundred armed warriors, and one hundred animals, with armour as best we could make. It was a tad excessive, but we wanted that Stone."

"You still killed the entire tribe looking for something that wasn't there." said Al.

"We did, but at the time we were sure it was there. Besides, that's a mistake given to children to make you hate Golarans. Many Rooloers survived. But the Rooloer Tribe was dying anyway, as many of them began breeding with their cousins, and there were only a few hundred left."

"You think that makes it okay?" asked Al.

"No, but let me finish, Hekeni fool!" he yelled. "There were three small villages in the Rooloer Tribe left, the largest by the shore of the lake. We said to them we only wanted Norral, but they refused to answer. We invaded, ripping apart all the houses, searching every nook and cranny for it. Many of them fled away on boats, only to get eaten by the Tylosaurus'. Those that survived went to the Yaxog.

"The second village, it so happened, was the smallest, with what our records say only two dozen people. But I will admit that was a lie. There were probably about a hundred. We killed all those who opposed our search, though our search went overboard. We burned all the dwellings to the ground, leaving the remaining living people with nothing. You were told they died, but it's more likely most of them fled to other tribes.

"The last village was beneath the mountains, and we knew Norral was there. So was the chief of the Rooloer Tribe. He told us to leave, and that he wasn't giving up Norral without a fight. And fight we did. Unfortunately, the chief happened to be Norral in disguise – he had killed the original chief just minutes before, when he saw us approaching. Norral knew why we had come, and we wouldn't accept what was, as we learned the hard way, the truth. We thought he was just avoiding us because he did have it.

"So we burned and smashed our way through the town, and when Norral, disguised as the chief, fled the camp; or so we believed, but he probably just perished in the flames and was never identified. Those we didn't kill fled to other tribes, and we searched through all the wreckage we had created, but in the end, the only thing we found of interest was the body of the chief, too long dead to be killed by us... his throat was slit.

"It took five months before we were happy with our search, and the other tribes, the ones who accepted Rooloer refugees, fearing the same fate, searched the survivors, with no results. You were probably told that Norral's expedition was the last. But that's not entirely true, either."

"What do you mean? Of course it is!" said Al.

"That's what *you* think!" replied Nikhall. "In fact we Golarans sent another, secret search party, a small one of five, to the tomb of King Elmerik, and they discovered the red Stone there. Of course, they only had time to see it, before the guardian killed all but one and chased him back. We had to accept the truth, strange as it was. We apologized to the other tribes, but they did not accept it. So we began our plundering and murdering to get what we needed. And it's worked out fine for us."

"What guards the tomb of Elmerik?" asked Drake.

"An Ankylosaur, but that's not the point." said Al. "That's quite a story, Golaran, but why should we believe it?"

"Because I am not telling it to *you*, Hekeni. What will I gain from telling a lie? What can I lose by telling the truth? I am telling it to the Above-worlders, not because I am hoping they will take my side, but so they, and you, know our side of the story."

"But Norral was never a Golaran!" said Al.

"How do you know? Every record of the Rooloer Tribe was lost when we killed them, and you haven't had access to *our* records in seven hundred years!"

"Well, it doesn't change my opinion of Golarans." said Drake. "But it does put their situation in better perspective. I choose to believe it's the truth. It matches the Hekeni story well enough."

"But we are ready to forgive." said Al. "Why did you not take it?"

"Old habits die hard." said Nikhall. "But we can never be sure. You think it's a trap if we ask for an alliance. How can one apologize when every time we get close to one of you we are considered a threat? How do you approach with peace when everyone else sees war?"

"If you can figure that out, you'll solve all the Above-world's problems, too." said John.

"It's the universal conundrum." agreed Drake.

"I'm not asking for peace on behalf of the Golarans, anyway." said Nikhall. "I am here to get the red Stone for the Golarans, and then, perhaps, we can have peace. But the Golarans want peace as much as you, Hekeni, believe it or not. We believe in equality and honesty, too."

"Then why is it I have such a hard time believing you?"

"I'm not asking you to. I've just told my version of events. Make of it what you will, but I already feel like peace is closer just for telling it."

Chapter 28 – Turtle Lake

The Hekeni camped by one of the many rivers flowing from the Icy Peaks to Turtle Lake, and Drake was sure Nikhall stayed up all night. In the morning, he sent a Golaran-owned pterosaur out with his message telling them he was alive, and they set off again. He had five pterosaurs, presumably enough to send out each day and return before the fifth one had to leave.

The next day, there was minor snow, which cleared up by afternoon. For two days following the winds blew fiercely, and John had to hide his hat in a bag or lose it entirely. The Golaran-owned pterosaur also returned to Nikhall without a reply, looking windswept. But finally, as they approached Turtle Lake, it was down to a gentle breeze.

Turtle Lake was so named because from above it looked like a turtle. It was a massive lake, the largest body of fresh water in Northern Prehistorcia. All the rivers formed from glaciers on the Icy Peaks drained into it, and Turtle Lake itself, seasonally, would overflow over a low, soft part of ground, creating a massive river flowing through the Triassic Desert. But then the Icy Peaks would freeze again, the water level would drop, and the river into the desert stopped flowing.

Of course, the Triassic Desert wasn't its only drainage pipe. There were rivers going north to the Great Yellow Plains, and east, to what the Hekeni called the River Hills, and even on a different route south, away from the Triassic Desert.

Drake saw the line of trees draw closer. It was a wonderful forest; it looked lush, mixed with pine trees. On the western shore of Turtle Lake (or the head of the turtle-shaped lake) lived another tribe Drake had barely heard of – the Flimzoak.

As they approached the lake, Drake again began to think of them. He decided to ask Al... no, wait... Harry knew more history. He backed up and asked Harry.

"So what's the story of the Flimzoak?" he asked.

"Them? They're not too long a story. You see, sometime in the middle of the Mayztec Empire, the Mayztec emperor Taik IX sent an army of Mayztecs north to Turtle Lake. It being the largest body of fresh water, he thought holding it would be a powerhouse. At the time, the Klenkara were still south of Pterosaur Canyon, and there was no way across. So the three tribes that were actually in good enough shape to spare troops to dislodge them did just that. The Trontoll, the Fertile River, and the Hekeni. The Solg were too far away, the Golarans were hiding, weak, in the mountains, and the Yaxog just couldn't afford the expedition.

"So, the three armies met up in the Forest of Carnivores... or, the forest we're about to enter. Don't worry, it's just a name. They marched south, towards the Stone Hills, where the Mayztecs made camp.

"The Mayztecs, however, saw them coming. They clashed here, at the head, and fought for days. Many soldiers were tired, and when the prisoners got talking to one another, they found they had more in common than previously thought. It was a true 'fact is stranger than fiction' moment, that the prisoners, after being let go, told their armies to make peace with the other.

"This concept wasn't part of Mayztec culture, and wouldn't be until Emperor Rilowin. However, the four armies made friends, and agreed to split the lake. When the king heard this, he was outraged, and sent an army to them again. The four tribes teamed up and defeated the Mayztecs, and decided to integrate.

"Unable to decide which part of the lake to settle on, they both lived here, where they first clashed. That's why they are called 'many mixed' in Hekeni, because they are a mix of four tribes. One Hekeni soldier suggested the name 'Flimzoak', and the four armies agreed that sounded like a good name. That day they struck a victory for friendship; sadly, a much rarer sight than a victory through war."

"So, what, this tribe stands as everything you want to happen in Prehistorcia?"

"In a sense, yes." replied Harry.

"Okay, but this 'Forest of Carnivores' thing. It is just a name, right?"

"There are higher than average carnivores here, to be honest." he said. "But relax, the Flimzoak are very good at keeping them out."

They came to the edge of the forest, which started gradually with stunted trees. They paused there. Almost instantly, a pygmy came out to meet them. *Homo floresensis* was just over a metre tall, and had more hair proportionally than the modern man, with a slightly more ape-like face. Nevertheless, he smiled as he came out to meet the group.

"Drake, that's *Homo floresensis*!" said John.

"I know. You see their skeletons in Indonesia, but it's hard to imagine them with flesh and blood."

The pygmy came out and greeted Al, who had kept on his Sekka hat, first for the change in power, then for the Trontoll, then for the Golarans, and now for the Flimzoak. They spoke some words in what Drake recognized as Hekeni, and he led them forward.

"Why do they speak Hekeni and not Trontoll, Fertile River or Mayztec?" asked Drake.

"The Mayztec language died after a while, since they were considered rebels to them, and because they had the option, they chose to switch languages. Zolgafs and Borchillians were pure Mayztec, and never got that option. Today, most Flimzoak know Trontoll and Fertile River, as those are the two closest tribes, but a few still speak the language of the Hekeni." explained Harry.

"Will any of them speak English?"

"Count on it. We get more Above-worlders landing here than you realize."

The forest really was a nice place to settle in. It was only in half an hour or so that they reached the shore of the lake – it was clear blue, stretching out into the horizon. The shore of the lake had professional docks, with canoes tied to the posts, and wooden sheds at the end.

Drake saw four Flimzoak – two pygmies, and two *Homo sapiens* – holding a giant net, one to each corner. When they pulled it up, there were several dozen wriggling fish.

"The Flimzoak have only one village." said Harry. "But it is large, and they use Mayztec technology. The Flimzoak are also the one hub for Hekeni-Trontoll-Fertile River relations. The tribes themselves rarely communicate directly, but the Flimzoak keeps contact with all of them, and they all keep contact with the Flimzoak."

"That's good, I suppose." said Drake. "Will they let us stay the night?"

"If they weren't going to, we'd have been rejected immediately. But we are Hekeni, we're always accepted by the Flimzoak." he explained. Drake felt a tap on his shoulder.

He turned and saw Dave. "What?"

"Just letting you know – Prehistorcia is much less united than they would like you to believe."

"More cynicism?"

"Not cynical this time. They are friendly – but they aren't united."

"Whatever." Drake replied.

Drake watched as a Neanderthal brought back an amphibian that looked like it came from another age. He walked into his wooden house with it.

They showed the Hekeni to their sleeping quarters. After Al finished talking, Nikhall was taken aside and placed outside the boundaries of the village. When he demanded to know why, he was ignored. Al, however, walked up to him, and said plainly:

"You may travel with us, but you will never be one of us. *Rahalah*, Golaran."

Drake was not there for that however. He was at the northern end of their territory with John, Jane, and Steven, staring into the pens the Flimzoak had for trained animals. Three small sauropods called Opisthocoelicaudia (oh-pis-tho-seal-ick-caw-dee-ah) were in the pen. They were twelve metres, or about forty feet long, and they had round, almost boulder-shaped heads. They were a smaller version of Camarasaurus from the Late Cretaceous of Mongolia.

Another animal there was Nigersaurus, from Niger, which was a sauropod with a duckbill, and its head was kept low to the ground for grazing on low-lying plants; there were five of them. Also in the pens were dromaeosaurs, an Ankylosaurus, and a whole herd of Corythosaurus, a large Hadrosaur with a half-circle crest.

"They sure have a lot of animals here." said Jane. "I haven't seen this many since we left Hekeni land."

"Well, they are descended from Hekeni." said Steven. "They probably inherited their talent. There's more animals around here than these, too. I actually saw an Artiocetus tied up to a beach-front house outside."

"Really?" asked Drake.

"I need to see that." said John. "That's a critical animal in whale evolution."

"It is something to see." said Steven. "His owner speaks Chinese, though I don't. He seems like a nice guy, though. I'll bet he'd let you see it."

"I do know some Chinese from that Asian expedition in the nineties." said John.

"Great, don't get John switching tribes on us." said Drake.

"Oh, come on, there's much better variety in the Hekeni." said John. "Even so, I'd like to see that Artiocetus. I'll be back around dinner time."

John left. The three remaining paleontologists stared at the animals in the pens, all well-fed and looking well-trained. Drake began chuckling.

"What?" asked Steven.

"I just realized that John, a red-necked white-skinned Albertan, knows more Chinese than the Chinese guy."

"Oh, shut up. My family hasn't lived there since the first world war." he replied.

"It's still a bit funny." said Drake. "You know, I'll bet these aren't even all the pens they have. They must have ceratopsians and other animals around here. If they did inherit the Hekeni gift, they're not going to stop with just these guys."

"That's a good point." said Jane. "I wonder where they keep the rest of them."

"Well. I don't really want to go looking for them." said Steven.

"I'll agree to that." said Drake. "I'll bet the Flimzoak have something planned for us, too, like the Klenkara did. I wonder what it will be."

*****

As night fell, and the Hekeni gathered around the fire, it was clear that the Flimzoak, in fact, didn't have anything special planned, but just listened as Alol told their story in Trontoll, the common language of the Flimzoak Tribe.

"You still need to learn English!" called Drake.

Alol turned on him, shrugged, and went back to telling the story. The Flimzoak were very interested, and stayed with the story until its end. Alol took some questions, but they seemed to be yes or no. Judging by the response the Flimzoak were getting, they were all 'no'.

"What're they asking?" Drake asked Harry.

"They're volunteering to help us with Elmerik's tomb. They're also asking if we'll show them the Stones. Alol is just telling them they can see them in the morning, when it's lighter out."

Drake was still worried about the Extinction Stones. He still didn't think they had any real power, but the Hekeni thought they did. As did every other tribe. This was becoming an obsession. If they did not give back the Extinction Stones, didn't they doom themselves to war anyway, despite the Golaran threats? He kept telling himself it wouldn't happen, but he had seen Al at the Teratornis Hills. Drake always assumed Al would have the will to do the right thing – Dazz even said he would – but no one did anything.

"Drake!" called Al happily. "Have some *Buzwhit!*" he said joyfully.

"Uh... what?"

"Here!" Al shoved a ball of bread into his hands. His hands became sticky, and he realized that the bread-ball was covered in honey, and studded with berries. He had not first realized it in the dim light of the fire.

"This is buzzit?"

"No, silly, *Buzwhit!* It's delicious, made all across Prehistorcia. Try it!"

He bit into it. It was actually quite good. He wondered why the Hekeni never had this... he didn't have a problem eating this.

Harry looked over. "Ah, sticky-bread! Al, where's mine?"

"Sorry." he handed it over.

Harry bit into it with satisfaction. "Ah, you know, we can't make this in the village very often. It goes so fast, and it's so hard to get honey! Bees are one animal we haven't learned how to train. Ah, well. We're all praying for a beekeeper to come down to us someday."

"You've never had a beekeeper?" asked Drake.

"We never had one. The Yaxog did, but they won't give us they're secrets. Neither will the Trontoll. The other tribes take a certain satisfaction in being able to train what a Hekeni can't. Rather the same way we take satisfaction in making endscrapers better than the weapon-making Kluugon and won't reveal our secret. But the beekeeping secret they've obviously given it to the Flimzoak. I'll have to ask."

"I'll save you the trouble. Just catch a queen bee." said Drake.

"We know that much. But how do we extract the honey once we have one?"

"Well, on Earth, they use, uh... I can't remember. I used to know."

"It doesn't matter anyway. If it's chemical, chances are remote we can make it correctly and indefinitely. Ah, well, this makes it more of a delicacy anyway, I suppose." he ate the rest in one bite.

"So... an Ankylosaurus guards the tomb of Emperor Elmerik?"

"No, an Ankylosaur. I think it's actually a Euoplocephalus. We have the best records on him, obviously, us getting so close."

"An Ankylosaur... I can't picture us getting past that, to be honest."

"We will. We always do." said Harry.

Drake nodded, unconvinced, and got up and went to bed. His dreams were filled with a massive Ankylosaurus beating at temple walls, with a fiery crack from the Extinction Stone, and with thousands of spiders pouring from the walls and exploding.

When he woke up he didn't remember much, though he tried to make sense of the nonsense. Al got all the Hekeni up, and Nikhall was given back to join them, having spent a night outside the camp. They set off south, down along the shore of Turtle Lake, and eventually into the Triassic Desert. According to Al, there was still three more nights until they would enter the tomb.

Chapter 29 – Stone Hills

Down Turtle Lake they went, following the shores of the great freshwater lake. Al and the Hekeni took the opportunity to fill all their pouches with the water, so they wouldn't go thirsty in the desert, which, while it was colder than the Drought Lands, would still be hot.

"You know, this place reminds me of the Green Sahara theory." said John.

"I suppose it does, a little." said Drake.

"What was the Green Sahara theory?" asked Tom.

"The Sahara desert, the hottest place on the planet, not too long ago, was actually mangrove forests. In was lush and green, and the entire desert was coated in a shallow sea where whales were thought to evolve." explained John. "Same thing with the middle-east."

"What dried it up?" asked Tom.

"We can't really know. There are theories, but in reality, we act smarter than we really are."

"You, as in, paleontologists?"

"No, we as in scientists. Paleontologists, ecologists, biologists, archaeologists, and especially astronomers and physicists. They all act like they know more than they really do."

"Why?"

"It's all guesswork, there's no shame in not knowing. Everything those fields do is guesswork. We can never really know... well, I can, but look at where I was dumped! When I was on Earth, I was perfectly willing to give the answer 'I don't know', but so many of my colleagues weren't." Drake snorted in disbelief – John ignored it. "Even with my being here, there are thousands of questions that remain unanswered. What scientists know can fill a library. What they claim to know could fill ten. Modern knowledge is just as modern as 17th century knowledge, just of a different kind."

"But there are some things we know that they didn't." said Tom.

"Yes, but you'd be surprised at how few of those there are, especially in paleontology and astronomy. Look at Jack Horner – brilliant man, but a stupid theory."

"Ah, the famous John Rockman rant." said Drake. "The Green Sahara is a known fact, and it simply means that it was lush and green at one point like the badlands. You don't need further elaboration."

"I gotta agree with that." said Tom. "But I like hearin' opinions, too. I ask John 'cause I expect the rant."

Drake laughed, and John looked a little taken aback, but shrugged it off, smiled, and continued walking.

They met no animals in the Forest of Carnivores, at least none that gave evidence for the name. They did, however, see a large herd of Corythosaurs wading in the lake and in the trees, but they avoided Nemeli and the dromaeosaurs. This must have been where the Flimzoak got their trained Corythosaurus' from.

They followed Turtle Lake all the way south, around the lower jaw, and down the front leg until they came to the southern tip of it, a place in the Stone Hills.

It was evident upon arrival that this used to be a Mayztec place of dwelling. The trees were all pine now, widely spaced among hills of cracked rock, on which only, occasionally, moss grew. The Mayztec remnants included partially-standing walls, rotting, collapsed houses or fences of wood, and evidence of a pathway, long overtaken by forest, was visible as well. Some of the stronger stone cottages were still standing, but they were overgrown with the forest, and the roofs had collapsed.

By this time there was still three hours of daylight or so left, but Al told them to rest and make camp here, so they could reach the temple the next day with a well-rested team. Nikhall, the Golaran, was led out behind a still-standing stone fence, green with mould, where he was told he would stay for the night. They gave him supper, but nothing else, except a piece of papyrus and charcoal for his daily report.

As the sun began to set, Drake noticed that the air was getting cold. Compared to the Icy Peaks it was quite warm, but compared to the usual weather it was cold.

He picked up a mammoth-fur blanket and brought it over to the stone wall, which was only as high as his hips. He looked over, and saw Nikhall sheltering as best he could from the wind. He looked up at Drake.

"Hello, Above-worlder." he said.

"Hello. Are you cold?"

"It's nothing I can't handle. Besides, what do you care?"

"I thought you might be cold. I brought you a blanket. It'll warm your body, but not your attitude." he handed it over. Nikhall took it.

"Thanks." he grunted, though it was forced.

"You know, I may be Hekeni, but I also respect their values – all their values – which include friendship, peace, and equality. The first step to peace has to begin somewhere. I'm taking the first one. I was hoping you could take the second."

Nikhall sighed. "I hate conceding arguments to Hekeni. Consider yourself privileged."

Drake decided to take it for a compliment. He had to remind himself that there was a lot of old hate between the two tribes.

He looked at Drake. "It is dim. A warning, Above-worlder, it is dim."

"What is?"

"The *shay*. I know not the Above-world word."

Drake sighed and changed the subject. "You people live, what, seven hundred years here, right?"

"I suppose I have heard that from the elders, yes." he agreed.

"Well, from all the stories, you all say this battle happened seven hundred years ago. If my calculations are right, then that means even the babies of that time must be dead, or close to it."

"What's your point?"

"My point is that it wasn't your fault for the Rooloer Tribe. It wasn't these Hekeni that shunned you. It was your grandparents and great-grandparents, not your generation. It wasn't their generation that shunned you, either." Drake pointed to the Hekeni. "The oldest member there is an elder, our historian, and even he must have only been a baby at the time. I think you need to forget what each other's grandparents have done, and create a legacy for yourselves." he said.

"That makes a good point." said Nikhall. "But we're still shunned. Not one tribe had offered us peace. Last year, I'm not sure if you know, but the Hekeni pulled a major raid on one of our northern villages."

"I might have heard of it." he said, careful not to tell him he was part of it. "So? You took members of their tribe. What were they supposed to do?"

"Well, did they ever ask us for peace? Did they ever say 'hey, Golarans, let's be friends, we don't want to fight'? No, they never did, they came in, and just destroyed us. Did they ever make any offers for a permanent, lasting peace between the two tribes?"

Drake suddenly felt ashamed of himself. Not once did they ever assume the Golarans would have wanted peace. But if they did, would the Hekeni still have offered it?

"Of course they didn't." said Nikhall. "I think if they did, there was a slim chance we would have taken it."

"Really?"

"Yes. You raise a good point, Above-worlder, that both our tribes are holding on to their ancestors' grudges. But once again, we come to the unanswerable question: how do you bring peace, when all the world sees is war?"

"On my world, before any nation has peace, they need to undergo a revolution, though I'm not sure you'll understand terms like 'economy' and 'government' as a revolutionary system. But there are still groups of people who hate each other for their ancestor's reasons."

"I think I would need to know Above-world history to understand that." said Nikhall. "But we cannot all undergo 'revolutions', as you call them."

"Well, I just hoped that this would be one less step to take on the road to peace." said Drake. "Have a good night, Golaran… er… Nikhall."

"You too, I suppose, Above-worlder."

Drake went to bed, feeling that at least some of his messages had sunk in. Yet again, he felt that peace was now more possible just for doing that. Drake still supported the Hekeni in all their endeavours – but he had a new perspective on right and wrong. The Golarans were certainly the worst of all the tribes, but as Drake learned, it was not their fault. They were driven to it. He had always thought of Prehistorcians as a race with values and beliefs above those of the earthbound countries. However, it seemed they were more human than he thought. Now he understood why Dave had always told him that they were worse than they would like to believe. But did this mean that all Humans truly were inherently evil, as many philosophers thought? No, Drake thought, they weren't. He decided that Humans were good at heart, but lacked the courage to do the right thing for whatever reason.

But then again why did the black Stone have no light? Was it really a sad metaphor on mankind, or was it just coincidence? Drake listened more closely to the land than he had ever listened before.

He searched for a feeling. In fact, he demanded one. Soon, he got one. He felt, suddenly, as if everything was going to be okay, and that this was just a grand plan too complicated for mortals to understand.

Everything was working out the way Prehistorcia wanted it, and that was all Drake needed to know. He drifted off easily into a dreamless sleep.

*****

In the morning, he awoke to Al's yelling. He saw Al screaming at Nikhall, holding the mammoth-skin blanket Drake had given to him.

"Al, what's wrong?" he asked.

"This piece of vermin stole our property!" he yelled.

"I did not!" yelled Nikhall.

"You did to, don't lie, Golaran scum, we know you —"

"I gave it to him." said Drake. When Al didn't listen, he yelled it. Al turned to him in disbelief, a look of pure venom on his face.

"What?"

"I gave it to him." Drake repeated, though less confidently. "He may be a Golaran, but he's still a human being. He has done nothing to earn our disrespect, though his tribe has. Will you hold him accountable for his whole tribe? Doesn't every human have the basic right to respect?"

"He's a Golaran!"

"And you're a Hekeni!" yelled Drake. "Those are *your* values I'm yelling back at you! Try practicing what you preach!"

Al gave Drake a look of utmost loathing. "Traitor." he said.

"What?" asked Drake, genuinely surprised.

"You heard me. You are no longer a Hekeni. Get out."

"But —"

"OUT! Leave this expedition, Drake Burgess, and join the Golarans if you think they deserve respect! Get out of this tribe, and out of this holy land! You are a traitor! Get out!"

"You... you're serious!" said Drake.

"You have five seconds before I throw you out myself."

It was perhaps very lucky that Harry and Dazz had heard the conversation. They came over, and stood between Al and Drake.

"Al, you don't want to kick him out." said Harry.

"Yes, I do!"

"No, you don't! He's your friend, Al and there's no harm in treating the Golaran like a human. Drake's right, he deserves at least a little respect."

"I'm Sekka, Harry, that goes for you too. Dazz! If I say he's out, he's out!"

He lunged for Drake, but Dazz and Harry held him back.

"Drake is a Hekeni!" yelled Harry. "Once a Hekeni, always a Hekeni! Al, you and I have been friends for years! Listen to me as a friend. You don't want him kicked out!"

Al took deep breaths. "No.. no, you're right. You're still in the tribe, Drake. But you and I are no longer friends." he said it with such conviction that Drake was sure he meant it. Al walked away towards Nemeli.

"Thanks for sticking up for me, guys."

"Drake, that was a foolish thing to do." said Harry.

"What? But you said –"

"I said it to keep you here with us! But Al is right, he's a Golaran! They have never done anything to earn our respect. I don't think you should try to make friends with him."

"But, Harry–"

Harry held up a hand to silence him. "Do not make friends with the Golaran. Also, remember that logic does not guide us in the way it guides you. Under the circumstances, I think it's better not to be seen with you." he walked away.

Drake sighed. It seemed impossible that just ten hours earlier he had felt hopeful. His confrontation had caused a scene the whole tribe seemed to see. Just great. If he was doing the right thing, why did he feel like such a complete fool? He walked over to Jane.

"You don't think I'm wrong, do you?"

"Well..."

"Jane!"

"Well, no, Drake, you should treat the Golaran like a human!" she said. "But these people aren't a logical society, they don't let science and logic guide their beliefs. The Hekeni and the Golarans hate each other, like the Israelites and the Palestinians. You need to be careful, Drake, or you could get yourself into a lot of trouble! More than today! You're lucky Harry and Dazz came to help you, but you could see even they were disappointed. You might not agree with their decisions, Drake, but you must understand that they still have consequences on you!"

Drake sighed. "I guess so. But Al is usually sensible. Wouldn't he at least have taken it a bit easier? More like Harry did?"

"To be honest, Drake, I think Al's mind is clouded by the Extinction Stones."

Drake scoffed. "Yeah! Come on, there's no real power in them!"

"Drake, sometimes you can be an idiot! There's no real power in the Holy Grail either, dumbass!" she flicked his nose. "You may not believe in the power of the Stones, but *they* do, and you have to understand the magnitude of that belief!"

"So you're turning against me, too?"

"No, Drake, I'm not, but..." she sighed. "I think Al will come to himself, but don't push it to that point again! You're always listening your brain. Now try using it!"

Chapter 30 – Triassic Desert

The group left the Stone Hills, and began the march out to the Triassic Desert, just a short ways south. They followed an empty riverbed, which, in the warm season for the Icy Peaks, was flowing with water and renewing the life in this arid desert landscape.

The desert itself was hot, with reddish sand and twisted trees and cacti dotted the landscape. Rocks and old logs were more common here, too, as this was a more of an Australian desert than the Drought Lands, which more resembled the Sahara, and the possible climate during the Permian just before the massive extinction.

Drake rode Tenethax close to the back of the group, away from Al, looking behind the truck of the army jeep, Where Ahrzi was chirping at him happily. If only the little Utahraptor understood. He sensed Tenethax knew there was something wrong, but he kept quiet, as he always did. Drake felt that Ahrzi and Tenethax, at least, were still friends with him. No Extinction Stone could corrupt their minds.

He reached into the bag for some meat for Ahrzi, and threw a small strip at him. He caught it with ease. In just one month he had grown substantially, and was now as high as Drake's hips. His feathers were becoming softer, and they seemed to be disappearing. It was then he realized that Al had removed the Extinction Stones from Tenethax's back. Whether that was a sign of corruption or no more friendship, Drake felt even worse.

Sam, on the other hand, was now as long as John was tall. As the two of them had rightly suspected, dinosaurs grew up fast, even here.

He looked up at Al; he was separated from Drake by at least twenty people. Alol was next to Al, speaking Hekeni to him; Harry and Dazz were next, followed by John, Jane, Steven, and Nikhall. Drake was sure Nikhall was even less welcome up there than he was, but the Golarans used blackmail.

As the day wore on, and the sun got higher, it became John's turn to reflect on events. He totally agreed with Drake, but he could not stand up for him. He did not want to meet the same fate.

He adjusted his hat, and began looking around the desert for signs of life. It was flat ground, but even so there were very few animals. At least there were no rattlesnakes. They weren't travelling very far when a distinct roar met his ears.

John was such an avid fossil-hunter, and so obsessed with his passion, that he had learned, like the Hekeni, to distinguish the cry of one dinosaur from another. He could identify all types of ceratopsians he had heard, of the hadrosaurs, and he could distinguish between the cries of Stegosaurus, Kentrosaurus, Lexovisaurus, Paranthodon and Wuerhosaurus; he could distinguish the call between dromaeosaurs, and the calls of T-Rex, Allosaurus, Neovenator, Abelisaurus, Gasosaurus, Baryonyx and Cryolophosaurus; but nowhere in his large repertoire of memorized sounds had he heard this. This was a new sound.

It roared again – it sounded menacing, and large, like something Nemeli would be no match for should she come up against it. He looked towards the source of the noise.

"Al, what was –?"

"No... it can't possibly be. Not now."

"What?"

"They live in swamps, for crying out loud!" he said. "No, it's impossible! It's absolutely impossible! There's no swamp for a hundred miles every direction!"

"Al, what is it?" demanded John.

"One I learned the name of, because it's just about the scariest one thing to run into. *Spinosaurus aegyptiacus*, the one thing in all of Prehistorcia that, when it teams up, can take down anything it wants."

"Spinosaurus?" asked John.

Al nodded. "The Deremahrzi."

Deremahrzi… John pieced together his small knowledge of Hekeni… it meant 'demon-claw'. But then again, he already knew it was a Spinosaurus.

Sure enough, there it was, ahead of them, watching them – it was huge! Sixteen metres, or fifty-one feet long, with a nine-foot-tall sail. Its mouth was elongated, but only slightly. It looked like the head of Nemeli, only bigger, and only slightly longer. The Jurassic Park movie did this wrong, too, as the Spinosaurus, while it had an elongated snout, it was a small elongation in comparison to the size. The thing it did get right was that this dinosaur would slaughter a T-Rex, and Nemeli, too, if it wanted to. Its arms are three-clawed, ultra-sharp killing machines, thought to be used for catching fish. But whether it caught fish or not, Al was right – it lived in swamps.

Then he saw the glowing red eyes.

He had never been so scared in his life! What a monster! And this demon was a guardian of the final temple, meaning it was out to kill them! He would have run, but so far the Spinosaurus just stood there, blocking the road.

Al, thankfully, stopped about a hundred feet away, and stared at it, as if willing it to move. John could have easily walked under it, just as easily as he had walked under the Supersaurus. He could have walked between its legs as easily as he could have walked through a door! Not that the Spinosaurus would be as content for him to try it as the Supersaurus had been.

"Look at the eyes!" said Steven.

Al got Nemeli to back up. She was much too small for it. That Spinosaurus would kill her as easily as it could kill any of them.

The Spinosaurus, tired of waiting, lunged at them, roaring loudly as it charged them. Al and Nemeli ran, and John ran, too, following the other Hekeni. He was several fast-paced seconds away until he turned around. The Spinosaurus was held at bay! Drake, on Tenethax, was fending him off. Tenethax, the three adult Styracosaurus, along with the two Ankylosaurus, the Dromaeosaurs, the two Kentrosaurus and the Stegosaurus all formed a massive defensive wall even a cursed animal could not penetrate. Nemeli ran back and helped them out. All the Hekeni were getting behind the defensive wall.

John ran to get behind it, too. He wasn't the only one. The Spinosaurus turned, seeing all the Hekeni returning. He ran forward, and ate a Hekeni who couldn't run fast enough. He turned around, and charged in John's direction – he might make it, but the Spinosaurus was faster.

"John, get back here!" called Drake.

"Screw it, I'm not beating that thing in a foot race!" he had already turned and ran before he finished his sentence.

He heard the Spinosaurus pursuing him with all its speed, and it was gaining. But what was he thinking? There was no place to hide! It was the open desert, not a hiding place in sight!

By luck, he came upon a small cliff which would be a small waterfall in the wet season. There was a crack under it – but could he fit? It wasn't like he had much of a choice. He made a sharp turn, making the Spinosaurus stumble, and he just barely squeezed through.

He screamed with fright. A rattlesnake! A snake had made its home here! Its rattle was shaking menacingly, which John knew was a sign to back off. But there was nowhere to back off to!

But even the snake was distracted. The Spinosaurus's nose was directly at the ground, sniffing it. The snake stopped rattling at once. This made John very scared – this animal was so big, even the snake knew it didn't stand a chance! He decided he would have to run for it. Now, at least, the Spinosaurus was distracted. He got himself into the best position he could.

The Spinosaurus began sniffing the far end of the crack. As soon as it did, John used a burst of strength he had never before had to launch himself out of the rock, get up, and run clumsily forward. The Spinosaurus only vaguely realized this was happening.

But what speed! Surely no dinosaur could go so fast! Surely some demonic madness from the Stones must have possessed it! Even Spinosaurus could not be that fast!

Yet it was. It was gaining on John, this time much closer. It snapped down, and narrowly missed. It took one step for every six of his. The next bite would be fatal.

But then he heard a sound far scarier but surprisingly, it was more welcome. It was the sound of a machinegun! The Spinosaurus faltered. John looked around, and saw Drake driving an army jeep, with Kevin standing in the back, operating the machinegun installed on the roof. He fired round after round at it, and the Spinosaurus didn't seem to take any hits. Drake pulled up as the Spinosaurus walked away, recuperating.

"Hurry up and get in, before tha' thing comes back!" said Kevin.

John didn't need telling twice. He hopped in the passenger seat and Drake hit the gas.

Drake got massive speed out of the jeep, and they outstripped the Spinosaurus before it knew what had happened! They got back to the Hekeni.

"Good thing it gave up when it did. I was outta bullets." said Kevin.

"You okay?" asked Drake.

"I'm fine. I'm actually more worried about you." he replied.

"I'll be fine. You just shouldn't be seen with me for a while. I don't want to drag you down with me."

"You were right, for the record, about the Golaran. Don't tell Al." John hopped out.

Drake smiled, in spite of his feelings. Finally there was a person totally on his side. He knew he could always count on John, when it really came down to it.

Al sniffed in, taking a deep gulp of air. "We're getting close." he said. "The temple is too small for that guardian, so he sits here to guard it. But we are close! I can feel it! Final, undisputed victory over the Mayztecs is near. Onward to the final Extinction Stone!"

Drake turned the jeep off and set it in neutral again. He hooked it up to the dinosaurs, and they continued forwards. The three Coelurus scampered around him, last in the line, playing with Ahrzi, who was only slightly larger than them. They ran around the Lufengosaurus, ahead of him, and came running back, as if nothing out of the ordinary had happened.

Al patted Kevin on the back. "I knew this stuff would come in handy! Good job, Kevin."

Kevin thanked him and looked back sadly at Drake. He shrugged. Drake didn't blame him – what could he do? Kevin hadn't been here long, and with Al's mood, he might not consider Kevin to have ever been a Hekeni and banish him if he stood up for Drake.

But, despite Al's estimates, the tomb was not close. It took them three hours to reach it, and it as sunset when they finally glanced it. Al insisted on camping at the very base of it, so they could go in bright and early tomorrow morning.

Elmerik the Extinctor's tomb was carved into a great desert monolith. The entrance stood eight feet off the ground, and it could only be reached by hoisting yourself up or by climbing the twelve, steep stairs. The difficulty was not supposed to prevent people from going up – it was to prevent animals going up. The entire tomb was a rough rectangular rock, and it looked like Ayers Rock, only much smaller. The only indication that it was a tomb was the staircase, the perfectly rectangular, ornately carved entrance, and the flattened platform carved above the stairs as a kind of front porch to the temple.

They set up camp directly under the entrance. It was dark when they had finished, and Harry, today, told no stories by the fire.

Tonight, everyone was filled with anticipation and dread at the day ahead. But Drake found it a relief. Perhaps, when the sixth Stone was recovered, Al would forgive him.

Chapter 31 – Elmerik the Extinctor

The sun rose, casting orange light over the reddish-brown desert. It was going to be a bright day with no clouds, and Drake was woken up by the sun shining in his eyes. He got up, and saw that no one had bothered to wake him, though the expedition was already preparing to go inside. He looked around and saw Harry walking up to him.

"Good, you're up. I was just coming to wake you."

"Uh-huh. Sure."

"I was. Al may not like you at the moment, but you're still one of the few people who can touch the Extinction Stone and not feel overwhelmed by its power."

"Your mind isn't corrupted by the power." said Drake.

"No, Drake, but do you know how strong a mind I need? I felt the power, Drake, and it felt so *good*! It was as if I had the power of Prehistorcia at my fingertips! It was as if I could do anything, destroy or create anything! Do you know how much willpower it took for me to let it go? And then there's Al, who was much younger than me when we got lost here, and so even more attached to this place!"

"So what does Al need to do to snap out of it?"

"Let's hope finding this Stone is it." said Harry, though he didn't sound hopeful.

Drake walked over to the staircase. Al sneered at him, but said nothing. Drake was rather heartened, however, that Nikhall got a truly evil look that Drake had, thankfully, never seen pointed at him.

"Come on." said Al. He made small clicking sounds, and the three red-orange Coelurus came to his feet. "Pick them up. They might come in handy."

Drake picked up one – it was quite dainty, and light.

"You have the stuff?" asked Al, directing his question to Kevin.

"All of 'em righ' here." he held up a sack.

"Good."

In the expedition were Kevin, Dave, Tom, all the paleontologists, Nikhall, Al, Alol, Harry and Dazz. The final Stone, Drake supposed, was a sight no one wanted to miss.

Al led them up the stairs to the platform eight feet above. The platform was perfectly flat, with residual dust from a millennium of erosion. The platform was actually quite wide, large and deep enough for them all to stand on comfortably. Set into the wall, in the middle of the platform, at the thickest point, was a rectangular limestone door, lighter than the surrounding reddish-rock of the region. In was ornately carved, with an Ankylosaur carved in the centre, from a side angle, its tail up as if to strike a predator's face.

Around the ankylosaur were Mayztec symbols, and around the edge, very small drawings had been carved in. This time there was much more turmoil in them – a massive army with shields and spears were attacking an army of dirosaur-riders, each carrying their own spears, some with bows and arrows. It was just these drawings, except at the four corners, where a great round stone shone brightly at the backs of the armies. This was the holy war, for lack of a better word, over the Extinction Stones, when the rebels finally decided they would take no more, and overthrow the tyrannical power of the Mayztec Empire.

Alol read the inscription, while Harry translated: "The tomb of Elmerik the Extinctor, ruler of all the land, greatest king of his time, and true master of the Extinction Stones.'

Even Alol's voice became very offenced at this. He snarled at it. Harry snorted, too.

"Not anymore, you stupid old bastard." said Al. "Come on, help me get this door open!"

Dazz and John went and he ped pull the door back. It looked a lot heavier than the others, probably because it was much thicker. Drake and Harry went in to help. The door was very thick, but with the help of crowbars, they lifted it out of the way, and set it aside. They walked in.

The room was wide and spacious, though the only illumination was by the ray or light from the sunrise pouring in. The tomb was still dark. Al handed out flashlights to everyone, but deliberately avoided Drake's eyes when he handed him one.

He flicked it on. Now this was an amazing temple!

Its ceiling was high, so high that it reminded him of a castle entrance, the thing that made people tremble in awe at it. Everyone moved their flashlights around. At the far end of the room, and it was a very wide room, there was a high cliff, as high as a palace balcony, with two sets of straight, moderately-angled steps, one on each end, which led upwards to a further hallway. All around the room were carvings and paintings, all of great armies fighting each other, with the rebel forces on the backs of powerful, deadly animals – Allosaurs, tyrannosaurs, bears, and ceratopsians, or sometimes ordering the animals forward, animals like big cats and dromaeosaurs.

"What a place to die in!" exclaimed Tom.

"If this is how they spend death, how did they spend life?" asked Drake.

The lights shone further around the room. At the walls there were several skeletons, every one of them with shattered ribs, spine, and/or skull. What had done that?

But they had forgotten the guardian. It happened to be in this room, and they heard it from a grunt. Between the flashlights and the rays of the sun, most of the room was illuminated, except for the front corners, in which the guardian lurked.

It emerged. It had glowing red eyes, just like all the others. It was only as high as Drake's hips, but it was nearly six metres, or eighteen feet long, and it was very heavily armoured, with spikes along its sides and knobs across the back. There were two large spikes over its shoulders. Its head had two short horns at the back of its head, and two more jutting downwards below its cheeks. It had a long tail, the end of which was stiff, and it was tipped with a large, bony club capable of delivering a bone-shattering blow to even the mighty Spinosaurus, not that it lived in the same place or time.

It was a Euoplocephalus (yoo-oh-plo-seff-al-us), so heavily armoured that even its eyelids had armour. The only way to kill it would be to somehow avoid the club, and flip it over to its soft underbelly. Euoplocephalus weighed more than two tons, so even with its tiny brain, it was more than a match for even the smartest predator.

"What is that?" asked Tom.

"Euoplocephalus, native to North America. The most heavily armoured dinosaur ever." said John.

"Ever is a big word." said Al. "But yes, in essence, it is the most heavily armoured dinosaur here. You'd be hard-pressed to find a more impenetrable one."

"It's the fortress of the dinosaur world. Built like a tank." said Drake.

The Euoplocephalus cut off their way to the stairs, and swung its tail menacingly. Al clicked his tongue once, and the small Coelurus came running. He ordered them to do something in Hekeni, and the rushed off.

They began hissing, and running around the Euoplocephalus. They were no match for it, but they were like annoying flies, and he wanted them gone. He turned around, trying to find them. He swung his tail madly, slamming it into the ground every time it heard the chirp. Based on the dents it was leaving, Drake was sure it could shatter the human ribcage, and cause instant death. That must have been what happened to those explorers sitting as skeletons at the sides of the walls.

They chirped and ran around, the Euoplocephalus swinging wildly every time. But still it stood its ground, even though the Coelurus tempted it to move.

"Alright, plan B." said Al. "Kevin, make it move!"

Drake found this an incredibly trivial command, as it would not move just because Kevin told it to. However, that was before Drake saw what was in the bag.

He pulled out grenades! Judging by the bag, he had about a dozen grenades in there. He threw one at the Euoplocephalus.

It landed under the animal's underbelly and exploded. The animal screamed in pain, and took a step back. Kevin threw a second, and the grenade exploded, causing the Ankylosaur to move even further back. Kevin threw a total of five grenades until the Euoplocephalus stepped away enough for them to run up the left-hand staircase. Al clicked his tongue, and the Coelurus leapt up the steps after them.

They moved forward, through the hall, which was shaped like an arch, and was lower than the first roof, made of massive red-stone bricks. Again, carvings adorned the walls. Some of them had faded paint. They got near the end of the hall, and saw a skeleton with torn clothing, and a green-feathered arrow sticking out of his eye.

"Hmm. Shot by a Hekeni." said Nikhall. "He must have been a Golaran."

"Oh, please..." said Al. "You think a Golaran would be clever enough to make it this far?"

"This must have been part of the last expedition." said Harry.

"Yeah, but he's kind of creepy." said Jane. "Let's keep moving."

They reached their next obstacle. It was not an end to the hall, although it was an end to the floor. A huge, gaping pit had been dug, and Drake was not sure how deep it went. He was sure that it was not shallow, and looking at the walls, they were too smooth to climb up if one did survive.

"How do we get across this?" asked Steven.

"We've got the rope." said Dave, who had indeed brought a rope in his bag.

"Anyplace you can find to tie it to?" asked Drake.

"That's why we brought this." said Harry.

They looked. Kevin pulled, out of his bag, a hammer and a metal tent peg. With a good pounding, it went into the ground easily; they tied the rope to it.

"I wonder what the last expedition used." said Harry.

"Well, whatever it was, we know it worked for them, right?" replied Dave, tightening the rope. "Right, since I'm the mountain climber, I'll go down, and climb back up, and pound in the second stake."

"Can you get back up? The sides are very smooth." Nikhall commented.

"Aw, worried about the poor little Hekeni?" asked Al.

"No, I'm worried about the Stone. We have to get it out somehow."

Dave took the rope, sent it over the edge, grabbed onto it, and used it to go down after placing his flashlight with Al. After a while, they heard him call up:

"It's really not that deep; quite a few bones here, though. I'll try to ignore them."

"Can you find your way up?" asked John.

"No worries, a mountain climber can always find a few handholds!" he said. "Ah, yes, here they are! I'll be up in a jiffy, then!"

Dave's fingers were trembling as he reached top of the other side, the rope in his teeth. He was having real problems holding on, but he flipped himself over, and stayed limp like a dead fish.

"That's a workout, that is!" he said.

"Ready for us to throw the hammer over?" called Al.

"Give me a minute, Al, I still have to rest!"

"Rest later, tie it up now!"

Dave got up, and picked up the hammer and peg as they were thrown over. He pounded the steak in, tied the rope, and knotted it tightly. It was military-strength, so it wouldn't tear easily.

"I wonder how the Mayztecs got across this?" asked John.

"When I was down there with the bones, I saw three or four long, rotten planks of wood. I think they put it there to rot, and when the explorers stepped on it, it broke, and they tumbled down below."

"That's possible." said John. "Were they thin?"

"Very much so. They were so thin that I think the Mayztecs even had to go across one at a time, and carefully." replied Dave.

The Hekeni were careful, too. They each gripped the rope, and swung across as if on monkey bars. It looked incredibly difficult to Drake, but the natives, including Nikhall, didn't have a problem with it. Soon, Alol was last, with the Coelurus. He picked them up, placed them in an open army backpack, and gripped the rope himself.

"Can a man that old and frail make it across?" asked John.

"He'll have to try." said Al. "But a man like that? No not a chance."

But Alol did make it, though he was slower than everyone else. Harry and Dazz hauled him up, and walked down the path. This time, at the end of the path, was their destination.

But it was covered with skeletons! There were literally dozens of human skeletons before the door of the burial chamber; some stuck with arrows, others with smashed bones, but mostly they were all just there, empty eye sockets, staring blankly into nothingness. It was one thing to see them in movies, but there was something about them that made Drake nervous – these were once real, living people, all killed for the power of the Extinction Stone they failed to retrieve.

"Well, at least we know where the original expedition came." said Harry.

"Yeah... let's make this fast, okay?" asked Drake.

The hall ended in an abrupt wall, with another, smaller, ornately carved door, this time with a Mayztec drawing of Elmerik on it. Drake could barely make out the features, as someone had scratched them out.

"Uh…" he turned to Harry.

"This expedition was so recently after the fight that many of these people may have remembered the Mayztecs taking the Stones when they were children. They must have hated him even more than we do today."

Al and Dazz pushed the door inwards, and it swung in easily. The chamber was totally dark. Bones were scattered all across the floor, more victims of Norral's last expedition. There was the large, stone coffin of Elmerik at the end of the wall, flanked by two great golden Spinosaurus. And there, at the foot of his coffin, clutched in the long-dead hands of a rebel, was the red Permian Extinction Stone.

Chapter 32 – The Truth at Last

Drake, Al, Nikhall, Alol and Harry were the first to step through. They were followed by everyone but Steven, who had a small phobia of human dead bodies; he could stand them, but he hated looking at them. They crowded around the mummified body – the only non-skeleton.

"He's been mummified." said John. "The old air must have preserved him."

"Everything else here is decomposed." said Drake.

The mummy was sitting with his knees bent into his body, holding the Stone between them and his chest. He was dressed in leathery, hairy clothing. His head was bent down over the Stone, with blank eye sockets and yellowed teeth. At his feet was a ring made of bone with just one very old feather and the claw of a Dromaeosaur in it. He had a long, grey beard and long hair. Nikhall gasped in horror.

"If you don't like dead bodies, wait outside with Steven." said John.

"It's not that." said Nikhall. He picked up the head and tilted it back. "This is Norral!"

"What?" asked Drake.

"It is; this is the dead face of Norral! See, the Sekka-hat here?" he pointed to the bone ring, "and this face, it's old, and mummified, but it is still recognizable! This is Norral! Every Golaran knows the face of the man who ruined us!"

Drake turned to Al. His mouth was gaping, at a loss for words.

"So this is Norral?" asked Harry. Everyone's face was shocked now.

"You said he perished." said Drake.

"We thought he did, in the flames." replied Nikhall.

"Wait!" said Al, finally finding words. "Wait! This can't be Norral! Norral returned from the tomb, alive, to live with the Rooloer Tribe for another year before the Golaran attack."

"This is Norral." said Nikhall.

"So he put the Stone back..." said Harry. "Why?"

"I think I know." said John. "Norral, when he appeared to the Golarans posing as the chief that day, took the opportunity to flee. He knew the Golarans would never stop hunting, so he came here, and put it back where he found it. But something killed him before he could leave, or, judging by his position, something that trapped him so he *couldn't* leave."

"That sounds possible. It even sounds probable." said Nikhall.

"No, it doesn't!" said Al. "Why bring it here, when he could flee anywhere?"

"A last act of evil." said Nikhall. "He hated the Golarans. He hated what we'd done to him. He brought it back, knowing the Rooloer Tribe was extinct, so that when other people came to verify the story, everyone would realize the Golarans were lying. But he never got out himself."

"Why?" asked Drake.

This time Harry spoke. "Prehistorcia has a lot of unexplained magic. Perhaps Norral, when he got here, truly did feel sorry. Or it could be that the tomb sealed him back in."

"The last one." said Nikhall.

"But he's perfectly preserved." noted Drake. "How?"

"That's no mystery." said Harry. "The Extinction Stones have kept Prehistorcia the timeless, ageless land it always has been. They keep Prehistorcia alive, keep it unchanging, allowing the animals' life and preventing extinction. Norral has been holding it for seven hundred years – some of its power must have rubbed off on him."

Al was still speechless. He stared at the mummified body of Norral with a kind of detached consciousness, as if he was seeing it, but thinking about a million other things.

"So... the Golarans were... innocent?" asked Jane.

"No, they were still guilty." said Harry. "But no guiltier than the rest of us."

"Wow..." said John. "So much hate... because of one little man."

"It's not the first time that's happened." said Drake.

Al began to mouth words silently. Dazz pulled the Stone from Norral's hands – he clung on hard, based on the effort Dazz went through. Finally, though, it was wrenched free, and Norral's body crumpled to a heap on the floor. When Drake saw the Stone, he saw there were two black, hand-shaped marks.

"There's something on it." he said.

Dazz tried to wipe them off, but he couldn't. It appeared they would stay there.

"They not come off. Try water." he said.

"Outside." said Al weakly.

Nikhall shifted in place, and looked at Dazz. "Hekeni, may I... have the Stone of my tribe? Please? It is our right. I won't force you to give it to me, but I would not withhold the Triassic Stone from you."

Dazz thought about it for a moment. He handed over the Stone.

Nikhall took it swiftly, and held it like he had just found buried treasure he did not want to share. They all walked out of the burial chamber.

They reached the rope. Alol swung across first, followed by Steven, Dave, Kevin and Harry. Soon, it was only Nikhall, Drake, Al and Jane on the other side.

"Don't wait for us!" called Al. "Get out now!"

The group walked away, waving goodbye. Only Jane remained behind, but she left the area, too, when Drake waved her on.

Meanwhile, on the other side, Al was next to Drake. They stared at each other awkwardly, until Al deliberately averted his eyes. He felt along the chamber wall, as if suddenly very interested in the carvings. Nikhall was more noticeable, and he turned to Drake.

"Your turn, Above-worlder."

"I'm the Sekka, I'll go before him!" called Al.

"Fine." said Nikhall. He leaned against the wall where an Ankylosaur was carved, waiting. It sunk inwards, to everyone's surprise, and the burial chamber door closed behind them. There was a rumbling, and the Euoplocephalus carving fell out. Behind it was a long peg. Nikhall looked in.

"I think that was a key structural point in the foundation!" said Nikhall. "Those *Derem* Mayztecs! They actually built a self-destruct button!"

"Seriously?" asked Drake. It seemed impossible.

"Yeah, I can see it now." he said, staring at the hole. "This is Mayztec plaster, and when it ruptured, all these tiles they used to make it will collapse, too! They look like bricks, but they're tiles! Come across, quickly!"

Al ran forward, gracefully balanced on the rope, and got to the other side. Nikhall walked slowly ahead of Drake. Drake swung across getting there slowly but surely. The walls began crumbling. He was nearly there.

But at that moment, the roof cracked. A massive brick fell from the roof, snapping the rope just behind him! He and Nikhall swung forward, and their faces hit the dusty rock wall. Nikhall was above Drake, Extinction Stone in one hand, rope in the other. Al came forward.

"Golaran." he said. "I can't lose the Stone." he extended a hand.

"If I reach for it, I fall." said Nikhall. "Besides, I don't trust you!"

"Just hand it to me, I swear by all six I will pull you up!"

Nikhall hesitated only a moment. He began sliding slowly down the rope. He handed the Stone to Al.

Al put the Stone aside, grabbed Nikhall's hand and hauled him up. Nikhall rolled over onto the ledge. Al extended his hand down for Drake. But Drake could see the rope coming untied at the peg. He climbed up, and grabbed the ledge with his hands, just as the rope came loose. Al began tugging up Drake. Drake was a fair bit heavier and weaker than the thin, wiry Golaran native.

"Nikhall, help me!" Al called.

Drake saw the Golaran's face clearly, even in the low light of Al's last remaining flashlight. It was a grin of uttermost evil, the face of a villain. The kind Golaran was gone.

"*Rahalah*, Hekeni."

"What?" cried Al, dropping Drake. "You traitor! You Derem! You Golaran!"

Nikhall picked up the Stone and ran down the hall.

Al looked like he was going to chase after him, but Drake's grip wasn't good, and he began slipping. He tried getting himself up, but it was no use; he was only loosening his already feeble grip.

"That Stone will be ours, Golaran!"

"Al!" Drake gasped.

Al looked down the hall, then back at Drake. Drake's grip was loosening as Al struggled with himself. Finally, he turned back to Drake, knelt down, and extended his hand. Drake looked up at him, confused.

"But, Al... the Stone..."

"It's not important."

When he said that, Drake felt exponentially happier. He looked in Al's face – his smile was wide, friendly, and welcoming. It was as if the last couple of days had never happened. When Drake saw Al, he knew it immediately – Al was back – the real Al, not the one obsessed and corrupted by the Extinction Stones. Drake reached up and took his hand.

More bricks fell. Drake pushed up with his feet on the end of the cliff. In a massive surge of strength from Al, Drake was hauled up and over.

"I'm sorry." said Al, picking him up and hugging him.

"It wasn't you." said Drake, as they pulled away. "It was the Stones."

"But I let them get to me." he replied. He looked on the verge of tears. "I'm so sorry."

A brick fell, and landed right between them.

"We'll save it for when we get out, shall we?" asked Drake.

"Agreed."

They ran down the hall, finding some paths totally blocked by bricks. It was a primitive, but effective, self-destruct mechanism. The passage would still be here, but it would crush everything inside of it. That was why the tunnel was bricked! They reached the massive room, looking out over the top. The door was closed.

Al shone the last remaining flashlight around the room. The Euoplocephalus was back in the corner, but it was just standing there, motionless.

"Can we risk it?" asked Drake.

"We don't have much choice."

They ran down the opposite stairway from the one they took to get up. It was furthest from the Ankylosaur. Al and Drake hit the door at top speed, and pushed with all their might. It was a large brick, or so it felt like it. The Mayztecs built their tombs too well. They pushed for what felt like hours, never giving up, until they saw light coming through the crack. In just a few seconds, the door opened up. It seemed much easier now. That was because Dave, Dazz, and Jane stood at the other end of it.

"We saw the door opening." said Jane. "Nikhall said the temple destroyed itself, and you were buried in the rubble."

Drake saw Jane had been crying. He couldn't stand the thought of her being sad over his death, but at the same time felt warm inside, knowing there was someone who would be sad at his passing. He'd have felt the same way about her, too, he knew.

"We almost were, thanks to him!" said Al angrily. "Where is he?"

But he didn't wait for an answer. Al ran forward. There was Nikhall running in the distance.

"Nemeli!" yelled Al. *"Ghret na Golaran!"*

Drake knew that command well enough – eat the Golaran. Nemeli bounded forwards, and grabbed Nikhall by the back of his clothing.

"Wait, wait, wait!" he pleaded.

"Lo smar. Kramm." said Al, which meant 'not yet. Soon.' "What?" he asked.

"You can't let her eat me! I still have the Stone! She eats me, you won't get it back!"

"Oh, we'll get it back." said Al with a dark smile.

"Nikhall, why? Your tribe was vindicated!" said Drake. "Your story was proven to be true! Why did you leave us there to die?"

"It was regrettable to leave you, Above-worlder." he said, dangling two feet off the ground, but no longer squirming. "But it was more pleasurable to leave him." he looked at Al.

"But still... why?"

"The Golarans come above all else! I am bringing them back their Stone!"

"No you're not. Drop it, or you're dead!" said Al.

"I'm dead anyway!" he screamed. "Besides, you don't think I would die for the Extinction Stone?"

"Fine, here are your options." said Al. "Option one: you drop the Stone, Nemeli drops you, and you run back to the Golarans. Option two – I kill you, and we get the Stone anyway."

"How can you kill me without losing the Stone?"

"You think I can't order her just to bite off your empty head?"

Nikhall dropped the Stone, utter anger in his eyes. Al snapped his fingers, and pointed down. Nemeli dropped him, but not gently. Nikhall stared at them hatefully. Al picked up the Stone.

"Leave my sight." said Al.

"This isn't over." muttered Nikhall.

"No, it's not. But it is over for you. Go, Golaran." Nikhall continued to stare maliciously at them, immobile. "Fine. Nemeli... *Kremma* ('now')."

Nemeli licked her lips. Nikhall's face turned to fear and he ran. Nemeli chased after him, snapping at his feet. Al laughed at them until Nikhall was out of sight.

"Will she really eat him?" asked Drake.

"Nah, she'll just fool around with him and come back when she feels like it." said Al.

"I guess I was wrong about him." said Drake.

Al sighed. "No, you weren't. Perhaps f we'd treated him better, he'd have been better towards us. I suppose you were right after all. I'm sorry, Drake."

"I should have realized the hate between your two tribes runs too deep."

"But that was no excuse for how I acted towards *you*. You come from the Above-world, and I should have realized you were still getting used to our ways. But fact is, you didn't deserve it. You're a Hekeni, and you're also my best friend."

"What about Harry?"

"Yeah, don't tell him that."

There was a small chuckle, and a period of silence. The sun was now high in the sky, and they could make out Nemeli's silhouette coming back.

"Well, now you have all six Stones." said Drake.

"Yeah... but it doesn't feel as good as having my friend back."

Drake smiled. "So the Mayztecs lost."

"Yes, the Mayztecs lost." said Al with a smile. "They've finally been beaten, after eight thousand years. I only wish that Norral was beaten, too."

Drake sighed. "If only. Maybe he won't have to be, now that the truth is out there. Maybe, for the first time in a long time, there can be peace between all the tribes of Prehistorcia."

"Yeah... maybe."

Chapter 33 – Back to Turtle Lake

Al and Drake went back to the foot of the entrance to Elmerik's tomb, followed by Nemeli, where the Hekeni were assembled and packing for the trip home. The Hekeni saw the red Stone under Al's arm, and greeted them with applause. Al bowed low, but Drake remained awkwardly standing, feeling out of place. Al held the Stone above his head, and yelled:

"*Na Mayztecs ser RANATH!*"

The Mayztecs are now completely and utterly defeated, or so it translated loosely into. The Hekeni cheered at this, too.

"So you and Drake are good now?" Harry asked.

"Yes." said Al. "Thanks for stopping me from doing something I would have regretted."

"It's my job. I see you got the Golaran's Stone."

"Yes, but we'll have to give it back. For once, I think, I'll be honest. We'll tell them that both mine and Nikhall's mind were corrupted by their power, and I took it back as a principle."

"Do you think that will keep them from coming after us?"

Al sighed. "Maybe it will. Peace is a two-way street, and eventually we'll need to make the effort, too."

There was a long silence. Finally, Harry spoke: "So, are we going to unite them?"

"Unite them?" asked Drake.

"Sure, I don't see why not." replied Al.

"Uh, I do!" said Drake. "You can't unite the Stones! All that power in your hands would corrupt you again! You'll end up just like Elmerik, crushed and destroyed by the power of them! Do you really want to risk the fate of Elmerik the Extinctor?"

"They called him *Elmerik na Ehralah*, or the Extinctor, because he stole the Stones and were then destroyed by them." said Al. "He used them for the wrong reasons. I won't."

"What are those right reasons you'll use them for?"

"I won't use them to crush my enemies. I'll unite them here, to see them work. Then I'll use them to make peace, and hold friendship among the tribes."

"But –"

"Too late. Here are the Stones."

Five Hekeni carried the Stones, and placed them in a circle around Al's feet. First, the Ordovician Stone. Then, the Devonian Stone; Al placed down the Permian, while the others placed down the Triassic Stone, the Cretaceous Stone, and finally the Pleistocene Stone.

"Here we go." said Drake, unable to turn away, though he wanted to.

All the Stones began glowing bright white, and they suspended above the ground, hovering at Al's chest. The light left, and they each displayed an animal – Anomalicaris for Cambrian, Dunkleosteus for Devonian, Dimetrodon, a sail-backed lizard-like carnivore for Permian, a Coelophysis for Triassic, a T-Rex for Cretaceous, and a woolly mammoth for Pleistocene. Drake watched in awe as the lights faded.

They all turned into balls of light, and entered Al. They began orbiting around him, and Al looked almost ghost like himself.

"I can feel the power! I can feel it!" he said in an other-worldly voice. "Feel my power!"

He raised his hands, and clouds gathered around as if out of nowhere, large dark clouds with rolling thunder. Lightning smashed down around them and rain drenched them, but Al stayed miraculously dry. He smiled and laughed, and the rain came down harder.

"See? I can bring water to this dry wasteland! And I can make the mountains move!"

"But you won't, right?" asked Dave. "You said Prehistorcia was wonderful just the way it was made!"

"There's always room for improvement!"

"But not from you!" It was Kevin that yelled it. He had a pistol in his bag, and shot away at the Stones, using all six bullets and blasting away every Stone. Every time a Stone was blasted, lightning struck.

Al fell over, the Extinction Stones rolling away from him as the rain still poured. He began getting up. Kevin dropped his pistol.

"And *that* is why I was brought here." he said.

"Really?" asked Al.

"You said we'd know. Ah know now what ya meant. Ah was brought here to go with y'all on the expedition, and stop ya from unitin' the Stones."

"Prehistorcia really does think of everything." said Al, weakly. "We should never unite the Stones again."

"We won't." Drake promised.

"I told you the Stones had power."

"You did." replied Drake, nodding. "And here's a bonus for you, Al. I'm now a believer. I believe in the power of the Stones, even though I can't see an explanation for them."

"You don't *need* an explanation." said Al. "They are here. That's all you should care about."

*****

They packed up and started off. After a few minutes, Al's rain had stopped. The Stones, miraculously, remained unhurt, and perfectly intact. The rain washed off the black marks of Norral's hands from the Permian Stone, but there was still some grey there that Al said might never come off.

They walked towards the riverbed, finding that water had filled it. The river was running on what little rainwater had entered it, but it was still there. It didn't provide too much of an obstacle, though. It was shallow and slow, and the waterfall John had hid under was now just a small trickle, no bigger than a faucet on its highest setting flow rate. Those that did not fill their water pouches during the rainstorm filled up here.

Ahrzi and Sam were now responding to every command given to them. Al said they may even be better trained now than they would have been in the camp.

"I wonder how Gary's doing with his Stegosaurus." said John.

"Probably fine." said Jane. "I wonder what he'll name him... or her... whatever it is."

"I don't know." Drake replied.

Steven sighed heavily.

"What?" asked John.

"I never found a dinosaur to train." he said. "You, Drake and Gary have one, Jane is getting one, but I don't have one."

"That was your choice." said Drake.

"I know, but I just couldn't find anything that drew me to it. Besides, they all look so hard to train, and I know so little about infant dinosaurs."

"We all know nothing about infants. Are you really going to let that stop you?" said John. "Sam practically trained himself after a few months."

"Same with Ahrzi." added Drake.

"You always overanalyze." said Jane. "Just pick a dinosaur and train it! I don't know what it's like yet, but I'm sure the Parasaurolophus must have laid eggs by now. I'll probably have one waiting for me when I get back. You should tell Al what you want to train."

"But that's the thing. I don't know. Nothing intrigues me."

"Well, you'll find something, I'm sure." said Drake.

They walked up the west side of the river, on the opposite side of where they encountered the Spinosaurus. They saw no sign of it anymore. No sign of anything. They continued upstream, and camped by the riverside. The next day, they would meet up with the Flimzoak again.

This time, as they walked up, they did meet something. As they got to within sight of the Stone Hills, there was a sad, desperate sort of moaning coming from the left. Al sent a team to investigate it. When they told him it was a dying mother, he led the whole group there.

Of course, Drake had heard 'mother' in the Hekeni term, but the sense he heard it in, as he soon learned, was a dying mother dinosaur. It was actually a rather sad sight, to see it so badly hurt.

"What species is it?" asked Tom.

"I could tell you that." said Drake. "Gorgosaurus."

"No, no, you might think so, but it's not." said John. "It is, in fact, *Albertosaurus sarcophagus*, though many species of Albertosaurus have been reclassified as Gorgosaurus, for reasons even I can't fully understand on some of them. But see, here? This is the same skull of the original fossil described in 1905."

The animal was a tyrannosaur, and ruled North America before Tyrannosaurus, seventy-five million years ago. Named for Alberta, Canada, where it was discovered. It had an oval head with a sharp snout, a long, S-shaped neck, two arms each tipped with two claws; its legs were thick, like tree trunks, and well-muscled. The entire animal was about ten metres long, or thirty-three feet. It was grey, with brown vertical stripes and covered in protofeathers. Its face was bloody with scars along the neck and body, and it was moaning painfully.

"What did this?" asked Jane.

"It must have been our Spinosaurus friend." said Al. "Nothing else would attack a mother Albertosaurus, not in this region."

"But it was cursed! Why kill this if it was a guardian?" asked John.

"I don't really think it matters. It might have run into her, and killed out of anger."

"But still, it was only a guardian."

"Even a guardian has defensive instincts." said Al.

"Hey, look here!" said Steven.

They all gathered around. Twelve eggs lay huddled in a circle in a dirt nest. The mother growled, and they backed off. She went down again. She wouldn't last long, even if they had the equipment to try and heal her.

"Where's the father?" asked John.

"He might have been killed earlier, perhaps defending the nest, or even by the female." said Al. "After all, there's no law they have to hunt together. He could have done something wrong, and she chased him away so she could raise the eggs alone. Or maybe he just left on his own."

"What'd the bloke do, cheat on her?" laughed Dave.

"This is a serious matter, Dave. Her children will be left parentless, if these eggs survive at all to hatch."

"So why don't we take them?" asked Steven.

"What?"

"You said there are no domestic carnosaurs this size in Prehistorcia. Let's take them and raise them. I think I could raise these, I already feel a connection to the dinosaur."

"Are you sure?" asked Al.

"Why not? Isn't that how it worked with Nemeli?"

"Well, Steven, if you think you can raise them, go ahead and take them. But wait until the mother dies, because she still has some fight left in her."

It took only half an hour for the poor animal to die. Drake wanted to help it, even if it just meant putting it out of its misery, but there was nothing they could do. When she died, Steven took the eggs and placed them gently in a nest of straw the Hekeni had made from their dinosaur food stores in the back of the truck.

Again they left the area, leaving the dead mother there. There was nothing they could do. They moved towards Turtle Lake.

But as they got closer to the tree line, they met another sight, this one not as sad, but much less preferable. It was the Spinosaurus again, his eyes glowing red, still affected by the Extinction Stones' power. He stared at them, and John was sure it recognized him. It roared, and ran towards the group. Once again, the defensive dinosaurs got into position to protect the Hekeni.

He was swayed back, but he did not leave.

"We can't get past him!" said Jane. "What do we do now?"

Al turned to Drake. "Do you think you can draw him off?"

"How?"

Al nodded towards the jeep. Drake understood. They put the fake brown Extinction Stone in plain sight in the back of the jeep, and John, Drake and Kevin got in, with Drake driving. He shifted gears, and hit the gas. He caught the Spinosaur's attention, and it turned away from the group.

"Now what?" asked Drake to John.

"I suppose we didn't think that through totally."

Kevin, standing behind the gun, dropped the fake Stone and twisted the turret behind them. He looked at them as if the answer was obvious, and pulled the trigger.

Nothing happened.

"It didn't work!" said Drake.

"I know it didn' work! This must be the one I used up all the ammo on!"

"So what do we do?" asked Drake.

The Spinosaurus was catching up, snapping at the fake Stone. John saw that the supernatural strength it had was wearing off, but it would still catch them.

"Only one thing to do." he said. "Bail!"

He leapt out. After staring at each other in surprise and confusion, Kevin and Drake jumped out, too. They rolled on the hot sand, and the Spinosaurus ran right past them, chasing the jeep. John was behind them, running towards them.

"You think he can catch it?" asked Kevin.

The Spinosaurus lunged, and grabbed the gun on the roof. He picked up the whole jeep, shook it, and threw it away. The roof of the jeep and its cannon was wrenched off, and it landed on its back a few metres away. The Spinosaurus dropped the mangled gun and began chewing at the vehicle.

"I'd say yes." said John.

The Spinosaurus sniffed at the brown Stone, curiously, taking a break from the constant tearing of the jeep. It seemed to realize it wasn't real.

"I say we get out of here before it finds us." said Drake.

"Agreed." the other two said in unison.

They backed away as fast as they could without causing a disturbance. They met the Hekeni group coming towards them. Al waved.

"You made it!" he said.

"We did." said John.

"Aye, and what a wreck tha' is!" said an unfamiliar voice. They turned to see Alol.

"Did you say something?"

"Aye, I did laddie. Didn't know I could speak the language of the Above-world, did ye?"

"So… you understood us every time we spoke English?" asked Drake.

"Aye." he grunted. "Me dad was a Scottish sailor, back in fifteen eighty-one. Me dad brought us to the New World, that is me mum, and me brother. When they crashed near the Gulf of Saint Lawrence, we were swept into a cove. The minute they entered it, it collapsed, and they find themselves here!" he gestured around. "Three months later, me mum gave birth to me. So, what was it ye called me? A frail old man?" he smiled.

"I, uh, I didn't..." began Drake.

"Didn't think I could understand ya? Well, I can, laddie, and yeh'd've realized tha' if ye followed the clues. I speak English just fine. I speak it a hell of a lot better than you speak Hekeni!"

"Sorry. I didn't think it mattered that much."

"Aye, I be getting' old. But no harm done, laddie, all is forgiven."

"Alol, your father was a colonist?" asked Steven.

"Yes, he was, or rather, was going to be. I've also heard I'm the politician here."

"Sorry." said Al.

"Nah, ye be right, as an elder, I am technically the politician. I'll also be tellin' ye right now, I'm much less frail than me looks suggest, but ye never seemed to realize that."

"Well, we won't make that mistake again." said Drake.

"Aye, ye won't." said Alol. "But this don't get ya a bad reputation with the elders, Drake Torvosaurus. We still think highly of ya, though Al I'm not so sure about."

"What? What did I do?"

Alol looked at him very seriously. It was the look a parent gives to a child when they'd done or said something stupid.

"Oh... right." said Al. "That's over now."

"Aye, it is, but as of now I'm makin' the decisions for the group, and that goes for the elders, too. We'll return the Stones, no arguments. The only Stone we keep is the green one. Got it?"

"Yes, sir." said Al.

"Good. No hard feelings, lad, you're still a fine leader when you're in your right mind."

"Hey, was 'Alol' your actual name, or one you chose?" asked Drake.

"Me name's always been Alol. Me parents thought it's be nice to name their new child for the land he'd grow old and die in. Me original surname was Mclan, but today I be Alol Albertaceratops, and that's what I remain. Tha' earthly name isn't mine anymore."

He let Al move on ahead of him, smiled widely, and walked along. Harry walked up next to Drake, still trying to figure it out.

"You know, I knew he spoke English."

"What?"

"Yeah, he told me in the Zolgaf camp. We thought it'd be funny to see you make fun of him in a language you thought he couldn't understand. And it was! That look on your face when he first spoke English was priceless!"

"Glad you had fun."

"Aw, come on, Drake, it was just a joke, besides, you've been forgiven."

Drake sighed. "So I'm assuming he's passed the historian role onto you?"

"Sort of. When he dies, he's making me the official historian. That's not the point, though. He actually has a good sense of humour. He'd be disappointed if he didn't get at least one good tease."

"Stupid old goat." said Drake.

"I can understand ye!" said Alol.

"I'm aware of that, but we're still in a free society, and I can say whatever I want." said Drake. Alol laughed heartily, and then replied:

"No ye can't! Ye did nay vote!"

Chapter 34 – The Journey Home

The Hekeni camped with the Flimzoak again, telling them of their adventures out in the desert. They listened attentively, and made large pots of soup made from animals found in the lake. They saw the final Extinction Stone, and the Hekeni left the next day, refreshed and recovered.

The Albertosaurus eggs were, according to the Hekeni, at the perfect temperature. They stayed nestled in the back of the remaining jeep. Now they would have an Albertosaurus colony at the Hekeni camp, something that had never been seen by any Hekeni still alive, not since the great battle that killed off the Mayztecs. Even now the oldest of the old only knew of the Mayztecs from their parents, and were too young to remember anything more than the Last Expedition.

They walked slowly through the Teratornis Hills, as though they were deliberately stalling. However, late in the day, a few dots appeared on the distance. Al moved the group quickly towards them.

It was the Trontoll expedition from a week ago, returned from their mapping of the region. Al greeted the Trontoll Sekka, a Neanderthal, and he returned it.

"Greetings to you, Hekeni leader." he said. "We meet again."

"Yes. How was your expedition?"

"Quite successful. Am I to assume yours was, too?"

"Yes. Well, uh, see you lat–"

"Al!" said Drake.

Alol patted him on the shoulder. "You can do it, lad. Let it go."

"Uh... let what go?" asked the Trontoll.

"No, I can't. Drake, you'll have to do it."

"What?" asked the Trontoll again.

"You see, Trontoll, we weren't honest with you last time. We did meet the Flimzoak, but we had another goal. We were... uh... we were getting... Drake..."

"We were retrieving this." said Drake in broken Hekeni, holding out the Extinction Stone of the Trontoll Tribe.

The look of shock on all the Trontolls faces happened so fast and in unison that it was almost funny. The Sekka got down on his knees, taking a deep gasping breath of awe. He held his hands out, as if he was trying to gently catch a slowly descending star. Everyone's eyes were fixed on the Cretaceous Stone, and after only a few seconds the lead Trontoll got up, and smiled.

"Our Extinction Stone!" he said with a gasp.

"Yes. It should remain yours, too." said Al. "All we ask in return is eternal friendship."

"You have it already my dear Hekeni friend!" the Trontoll leader hugged Al, lifting him into the air. "This is a historic day in Trontoll history! Prehistorcia praise the Hekeni! May Zog have mercy in the monsoons! May Hagoth forever smile upon you! May Thellina bless you with a million years of good fortune!"

"Yes, we get it, a thousand blessings from a thousand gods." said Al, a little bitterly. "Just take the Stone, and we'll leave with eternal friendship."

He took the Stone gently, not forcefully, although Drake could tell he was eager to have it. "Is all you really want eternal friendship, Hekeni? Such a small price for so great an object?"

"It is, but it may seem harder than you realize." said Al. "The Golarans will try to lie to you, and tell you we did not give you the real one. But I assure you, it's real. As for the Golarans, I learned something about them since last time. I think we need to make peace with them, too."

"Peace with the Golarans?"

"Yes, I've learned a terrible truth about history. We'll be happy to tell you about it, if you would be willing to camp here for a night."

The Neanderthal stared around at the group, and at the Extinction Stone. "I think that can be arranged."

So the Trontolls stayed the night. Harry and Alol told the story in Trontoll, not just of the final temple, but of the whole journey. Drake barely remembered much of it anymore. He remembered the plane coming down from the sky like a comet and the Tomb of King Zolgaf as though they were distant memories. The Drought Lands seemed so far away, and when he reflected on their journey, he realized they journeyed, step for step, farther than they had a year ago, when they had gone to rescue Hekeni prisoners from the Golaran camp. It had been longer, too, lasting roughly two months to get from the Hekeni camp to this point.

The storytellers put great detail into the moments from the time they last saw the Trontoll. They especially emphasized the Golaran points of view of the old histories, and it was even more shocking when those versions of history turned out to be true. It was late in the evening when they started, but well past midnight when they were finished.

The Trontoll had just one animal with them, a brown Triceratops asleep with the Hekeni ones. Drake was asleep, too. When they finished speaking, the Trontoll leader stood and began speaking to Al in the Hekeni language:

"I understand now. The Golarans may not have been treated unfairly, but it is wrong to keep them away now, hundreds of years later. Their histories are right."

"As near as we can figure, yes." said Al.

"But why did you not give us our Stone a week ago? Why did you lie to us?"

"I think hearing the story, you'll agree this was a very holy quest. My mind, and the mind of many Hekeni, was corrupted by not only the thought of getting ours back, but by uniting them. I am very sorry we did not give it to you, but you have it now. Can we forget it, and move forward?"

The Trontoll smiled. "We've all seen what happens when people do not have a chance to tell their side. I think we can forget it, Hekeni, and we will do our best to try and cooperate with the Golarans. We have it now, anyway, with no harm done!"

"Thank you. I assure you, that is the real Stone."

"Yes, I'm sure it is. It has an inner light, and inner warmth that no human hands can duplicate. May Morkmak bless your tribe with wisdom, Hekeni, as he has today. We will be friends, hopefully forever."

"I think that's all anyone really wants."

*****

When everyone woke up, Al explained they were following the Trontoll north, until they broke off to go west. They would go north of the Mammoth Mountains, through Megatherium Pass, which would put them on the Smilodon Hunting Grounds, the same plains that Jane had travelled over to get to the Hekeni village a year ago with Dazz. The reason they went through Pterosaur Canyon was because it was more efficient, because all the tombs seemed to line up in that road.

Needless to say, the way home would be shorter and quicker simply for that reason. The Trontoll, however, would split off and go east for about three days, to the shores of the Forked Lake where their tribe had been for almost as long as they had existed.

So, Al led the group along the northern ridge of the Mammoth Mountains, and the Neanderthal, carrying the Stone in a bag on their Triceratops, took his two dozen Trontoll and led them northeast. Al said it would only be a week before they would get back, once they got to the pass.

There were no animals on the way back, except for a few that stayed in large herds or flew. The Mammoth Mountains loomed in the distance for three days until they reached the pass, where giant ground sloths roamed over wide fields with periodic forests. Ground sloths actually had armour underneath their hair, so as a result it was hard for any non-dinosaur carnivore to kill them.

Like Valley, Pass had a different meaning in Hekeni. In Hekeni a Pass could be a way through the mountains, but with such places like Allosaurus Pass and Megatherium Pass, the meaning also meant a way between two mountains ranges close together.

As they walked, Drake asked Harry: "So what is the whole story of the Mayztecs?"

"You mean the whole history?"

"Yeah."

"I can't explain it briefly. The biggest parts you already know."

"But what was life like under Mayztec rule? You say they're descended of earth civilizations. but that could mean anything."

Harry sighed. "Well, I suppose I can give you a shortened version. Look, life then was harsh and cruel, probably more so than it ever was, and hopefully more so than it ever will be. They had a hierarchy, and even the life at the top was harsh. Of all the Mayztec Emperors, which were forty-one dynasties, only a handful ever died of old age. Some of them died of disease or animal attack, but the vast majority were killed by rebels, assassins, usurpers or they died in battle.

"But even so, life as an emperor was good, no matter how bad the record was. His servants didn't have it too bad, either. They were usually paid well, with good perks, and if they got really good, they could kill the emperor in his sleep and take the throne until some other guy came to kill him. There was the middle-class, which were soldiers, scholars and merchants and scribes, and basically anyone rich or with an education. That, honestly, would have been the best class to be in, but that's just my opinion."

"And the peasants?" asked Drake.

"The peasants had it very bad, they were dragged through the mud. They did the dirty work, with little pay, but even so, they carried a certain amount of respect, being Mayztecs, and most of them lived lives – dirty, overworked lives, but still, they could find enjoyment, take their small pay, and have their own property, and possibly enough for the lowest class of all – slaves."

"The Mayztecs had slaves?" asked Drake.

"Oh, yes, and they were almost always not a native Mayztec. They were rebels, some taken in battle, some just the descendants of prisoners. They were also other species, such as the Australopithecus, the Homo erectus, and the Neanderthals, although the Neanderthals, if they were Mayztec-born, could be permitted peasant status. One dynasty of emperors was even Neanderthal, but they went pretty fast from old prejudice.

"Even a pygmy was king, once, but they, too, had very limited rights. Most of them were slaves, and they did all the dirty work, with no pay at all, and very little food or rest. They were so beneath the common Mayztec that a noble would literally yell at his slaves to help even the lowest, most penniless peasant, though they were usually too selfish to do so."

"But I remember you said King Zolgaf's grandfather sent the Zolgaf Tribe five hundred *Homo ergaster* soldiers. Wouldn't they get middle-class status?"

"Many of them were slaves anyway, but something else to know, Drake, is that King Zolgaf's dynasty was actually a fairly good one. They made peace with rebels, they believed in equality, their ideas were very much based on those of King Rilowin. It wasn't until a thousand years before its fall, when the Mayztecs began shrinking, that any non-sapiens of Mayztec birth could be made actual citizens.

"Besides, while many of them were slaves by birth, their government wasn't so... feudal, though I'm sure there's a better word for it. A man could move up, if he worked hard, and like I said, there was even a dynasty of Neanderthal rulers."

"They sound remarkably like my society, except up above, they won."

"I know, and that's a sad fact. Fortunately, down here, the pacifists, if you want to call us that, prevailed. That's another reason we're different from Native Americans — we didn't wait for the war to be brought to us. We advanced and progressed all the time, we used tactics, we stole technology, we scrapped morals. It might not have been nice, but it was necessary. We became a Mayztec society, except ours preached equality and love of the land... and we never really built temples.

"There were wars waged against us for eight thousand years, because we resented Mayztec rule. There was one massive war four or five thousand years ago that killed millions of people and lasted four generations, ending all lines to the Mayztec throne for three hundred years, but at the same time driving all the rebel tribes into hiding with what little numbers were left."

"That doesn't sound good. Why did all this start in the first place if you preach peace?"

Harry laughed at that. "Ah, so naïve about us. I love it. Don't worry, it happens to all newcomers. The sad, hidden truth of it is that we were no better than Mayztecs, in the beginning. We kept no slaves, true, but that was all. Do you really think, after all this, that the Golarans just *gave* the black Stone to the Solg? The only thing that stopped the Hekeni and the Solg warring each other was the Mayztecs."

"I guess I never thought about it."

"No. The Hekeni don't really want that history paraded around, either. The Mayztecs were powerful, and ruthless, and they were a growing threat. So we united to take them down, and by the time we were done, we were friendly. Not that you'll hear elders admitting it. We're not always so… selective in our killing, either. Do you remember what Al showed you, your first week here?"

"Lagosuchus Rock? Yeah, he said it was the last place anywhere to find Lagosuchus. That the Mayztecs killed them off."

Harry smiled. "Think about it. If the rebels controlled the north, how could they have been so wiped out? Why is it that even now the south has more diversity than the north? Because we've been living in the north much longer. We're better now, yes, but we learned the hard way."

Drake hesitated for a long time, before finally asking: "So were there other tribes created and destroyed by the Mayztecs?"

"Yes, during their rule, fifteen tribes were created, two of them being extinct now: the Ratnik Tribe, created by escaped slaves, and then destroyed by the Mayztecs after a few thousand years. Then there was the Rooloer Tribe – we know how that one turned out."

"But that would make only nineteen tribes in Prehistorcia." said Drake, counting up. "Right now there are twenty. What's the twentieth?"

"Well, the Mayztecs were absolutely huge." said Harry. "We waged the war to wipe them out for almost three decades, and even still we missed the peasants and some middle-class runners. They're now a nomadic tribe known as the Nemnar, but they have forgotten the old ways, and while they still worship Mayztec gods, they have not tried to reclaim their old land, nor have they tried to destroy the rebels. They're excellent traders, and they even helped us on the last few expeditions to retrieve the stones, hoping it would be a good apology."

"So they've been forgiven?" asked Drake.

"Yes."

"But not the Golarans?"

"I know." sighed Harry. "Another thing we didn't do well. Funny little world we live in, when one can forgive their enemy for a lifetime of cruelty, but not their friend for a bad mistake."

Chapter 35 – Back Home

Drake, John and Steven had not seen the Smilodon Hunting Grounds before, and while Jane just stared around, remembering things, they looked around intently, though there was much less action than Jane had seen a year and a half ago. Then again, this group had fifty dinosaurs and eighty people, with a vehicle. When Jane crossed here, all she crossed with was Dazz, Flutt, and two other men, one of which was at the Hekeni camp, and the other would follow Jorge up onto the Above-world.

Once again, as they crested the hill, Jane met that sight she had seen so long ago, looking over the vast, prehistoric valley with extinct plants, and a wide expanse of open wilderness. They would camp one night in the forest, although it seemed Al would have them walk through the night.

"Why the rush?" asked Jane, when he announced his intentions. "We're getting there."

"Yes, me agree." said Dazz. "What is real reason?"

"Aren't we all a little homesick?" he asked.

"Yeah, but what's one night?" asked Steven.

"Well, for finding the Stones, we may very well not have to do any work ever again, right? Don't you want to head home and start the life of luxury?"

"Who are you trying to kid?" asked Drake.

"Alright fine. I'll use the old excuse, then – because I'm Sekka, and I said so!"

"Alol?" asked John.

"I follow the Sekka, I have promised to nay interfere with his decisions."

So they walked through the night. When they reached the first bit of Hekeni territory, Al dropped to his knees and hugged a tree. Drake had a feeling he was more homesick than he liked to admit.

There were six villages in the Hekeni territory, and there was one big one with more than half the tribe's population. Al led them down an alternate route from where Jane was taken, towards a small border town, with about a hundred and fifty houses, and one large one for the appointed leader, who was appointed by Roggan.

A *Homo erectus* turned to him, and waved, and they began speaking Hekeni. Al smiled wider than Drake had seen him do since his near-death in the last temple. Al didn't stay long, however, and they were back in the main village before noon.

*****

Two days had passed, and Al was summoned to the elders, and Drake, John, Steven and Jane were invited along. Yet again Drake found himself in the large room with the elders sitting at their seats, and Head Elder Muthwag sitting at the head. Once again, Elder Skarg was absent. He was absent so often the joke was that he'd died and no one noticed. Drake looked around and found Alol. When he saw he was looking, Alol smiled at him. Drake knew then he was not going to be in trouble. Chief Roggan Spinosaurus was absent this time.

"*Tehrah*, elder Muthwag." said Al.

"Alan Triceratops." Muthwag replied. "I believe you know why you are here."

"The recent events of the past three months?" he asked.

"Yes. Alol has told us much of your exploits, Al, and he speaks... fondly of you." replied Muthwag. "We have heard the accounts of key people in the expedition, except for you four," he gestured to the four paleontologists, "and Nikhall, of course. We have heard accounts from Dazz, Harry, Dave, Gethref, and of three people of outside opinions. We've heard some... interesting... things."

"Are you referring to the Golaran side of the story, or to the events in the temple, or about the tribes we visited?" asked Al.

"A bit of everything. We were informed you tried to banish Drake Torvosaurus from the tribe."

Al sighed. "That's correct, sir."

"It was not a question. You do not have the authority to do such a thing, Al."

"I know. As Elder Alol has hopefully told you, I was not in my right mind at the time. I was obsessed with the power of the Extinction Stones; we all were."

"I wasn't." said Drake.

"No, you weren't." said Al. "That's what made people in the same position as Drake, such as John, Kevin, Steven and Jane in ideal positions to retrieve them. I was mad at Drake because he was thinking for himself. His loyalty is not in question."

"We're not questioning the loyalty of *Drake*." said Muthwag.

"I know. But as I said, I was not in my right mind at the time. I am very sorry."

"A leader must always be in his right mind, Al, or they're not a good leader. However, you are only human, and we all agreed that, under the same circumstances, we would have made the same decisions as you."

"So, I'm forgiven?" asked Al hopefully.

"Yes, but that is not our only matter concerning you. We have heard that you gave the Cretaceous Stone back to the Trontoll. Am I correct?"

Al nodded.

"We did not give you permission for –"

"But I did, Muthwag." said Alol. "That is nay a matter concernin' Al here. In fact, if it wasn't for tha' action, we may have had a great war.

Now the tribes'll simply be wantin' their stones back, with no violence."

"I appreciate the sentiment, Alol, but it will not prevent war. The Golarans are angry, and they have had their Extinction Stone stolen again. Which leads us to our final matter concerning you: the Golaran's story. After the events in the Temple of Elmerik the Extinctor, do you still believe them... verified?"

"There is no other explanation for what we saw." said Al. "And even Alol will tell you it corresponds to the history, from another point of view."

"I'm aware of that."

"Uh, if I could interrupt a moment...' said John. "Why are we here?"

"Ah, yes, you. Head Trainer Mexila?" Muthwag directed their attention to a very old woman.

"The animals you have trained are more responsive than we've seen in the early stages in a long time." she said. "John and Drake, your animals could grow up, if they stay the course, to be the most obedient ones in the land. The fact that after only a few months Ahrzi escaped to be with his true master suggests a bond found only in the greatest of Hekeni trainers. You are here so we can congratulate you."

"Uh... thanks." said John.

"Yeah, thanks." agreed Drake.

"That's not all." said a man at the end of the table. "You have done so well that the chief has decided it will be better for more animals to be trained in the field, just as a test. However, we are making the two of you official Trainers."

"What's that mean?" asked Drake to Al

"Every Hekeni trains a dinosaur, but very few are Trainers. Some are hunters, some are gatherers, some are doctors, some are scholars, but the best Trainers, like me, are given the official title."

"What comes with it?" asked John.

"You have full access to all animals, young and old." said Muthwag. "You will help Hekeni train their animals, you will look after the animals, you will make sure they are all looked after, and that the ones with no one companion are taken care of as if they had one. Basically, you are in charge of the animal pens, under the Head Trainers Mexila and Rekko, and others they have appointed as leaders of certain pens." he gestured to an old woman and an old man opposite.

"Wow, that's... that's an honour!" said John. "It's funny, as a kid I dreamed of doing this, and now I actually get to do it!"

"Yes, but there is one other assignment for you." said Muthwag. "One of you will take Kevin Shales, the newcomer, and let him choose an animal. I believe he's earned it. The other will help Steven train his spirit animal."

Steven looked up. "I don't have a spirit animal."

"Yes, you do." said Muthwag. "Alol tells us you had a powerful connection with the Albertosaurus. Does that not feel like your animal?"

"I didn't think about it." Steven smiled. "I guess that is my spirit animal! I'm training one?"

"You're training as many as you like." said Mexila. "You found them."

"I think one is all I can handle." said Steven, still smiling.

"So, elders, why am I here?" asked Jane.

"You're here because we're tellin' ya in person." said Alol. "The Parasaurolophus laid their eggs. Go out and pick 'un out to train."

"Uh... now?"

"Or whenever. But do it before they hatch." said Muthwag.

"Okay, so, back to the original matter, then?" asked Al. "You know, about the Golarans?"

"Ah, yes." said Muthwag. "We put it to a vote. After strong deliberation, we have at last determined, with the agreement of Chief

Roggan Spinosaurus, that the Golaran in question, Nikhall, was lying. His stories are not to be believed. You may go now."

*****

"Stupid, two-faced, idiotic, useless old farts!" yelled Al when they were out of earshot. "Those spawn of *Derem*! Those clueless fools! How can they believe the story was a lie?"

"Now you're sounding like me, back when you tried to kick me out." said Drake.

"I saw the evidence." Al growled. "We all saw it. Nikhall was a Golaran, but he wasn't lying to us, I'm sure of it. I saw his face when we saw Norral – he was just as surprised at the truth as we were!"

"But he's still a Golaran, and he did try to steal the Stone."

"Of course he did! He was a Golaran, taking back the Golarans' Stone! His mind was just as messed up as mine was! The power of them took him, too!"

"But Al, the tribal differences here run deep." said Drake. "We don't live in a logic-based world. The elders are the children of the people the Extinction Stones tore apart. Of course they don't want to believe that their parents, or even themselves, are wrong."

"Well, look at you. Now you're sounding like me." he replied.

"I know. Great minds think alike." said Drake. "But the story will spread, and hopefully it will make the Hekeni people think. The greatest weapon, is, ironically, one that does no damage. Thought can prove the greatest weapon of all, but it's also the only one that does any good. The Hekeni will think and reflect, and I suspect some of them will believe you and me and Nikhall. But until then, what do we do with the other five Extinction Stones?"

"Return them." said Al. "They're too dangerous, whether as an actual object or as a religious force. There's no other choice but to return them."

"I agree." said Drake.

They stopped, and watched three Hekeni mount the fastest of all the trained animals, the Ornithomimusaur. They were the large, ostrich-like ones. They galloped off at top speed down the southern path.

"Where are they going?" asked Drake.

"To make peace. There will be a war, but we're trying to get a message out first. Hopefully, we can prevent one." said Al. "They'll come to claim their Stones, and we can have all the tribes meet again, and discuss the situations. Perhaps there can be friendship again."

"I hope so."

"Well, everything will work out. It always does."

Drake sighed. "Al, when I listened to the land, I felt like an intruder, like I don't belong here. Do you know anyone who's felt that?"

Al smiled. "Everyone does at some point, Drake. Don't worry about it. After all, it brought you here. So we can assume the land must want you here."

Drake smiled. They walked into the medical tent, where Kevin was. He was talking to the pilot of the plane, who was now awake and sitting up, though he was heavily bandaged. He had dark brown hair, which was trim three months ago, but now was long and unkempt. He had a thick beard, and his pilot's clothes had been replaced by the dinosaur-skin Hekeni clothing. Kevin looked up and waved them over.

"Hey, you two, this is my captain, Louis Wight." he said.

He grinned uncertainly. "Uh, hello." he said shakily. "So you're uh... heh... cavemen?"

"He is. I'm not." said Drake, pointing to Al. "I came here a year and a half ago. Don't worry though, the Hekeni are nothing to be scared of." he looked at Al. "Trust me."

Al looked at him confusingly, trying to work out if he'd been insulted.

"So, why're you here?" asked Kevin.

"I've just been made an official Trainer!" said Drake. "And guess what, they've assigned me to take you out to the pens, to train your own animal!"

"Really?" Kevin's face lit up. "Ah, man, sorry Lou, I gotta go!"

"Wait, wait, I want to see!"

"You know you can't. Come on, Drake, let's see what they got available!"

They half ran from the room "What's wrong with him? Why can't he come?" asked Drake.

"He's temporarily paralyzed from the crash. His legs are returnin', thanks to Hekeni acupuncture and some other tribal remedies. He'll heal. But righ' now, all I care 'bout is findin' me a dino and ridin' it."

"Yeah, I remember when I was naïve enough to think it was that simple." sighed Drake. "Well, take your pick. Anything at all in the camp. What did you have in mind?"

"Geez, I never thought 'bout that up 'til now. Maybe a Stegosaurus?"

"No, you don't want those." said Gary, approaching them. "They're so damn hard to train." he had a baby Stegosaurus tied to a leash. "Hey, Drake, I heard the news from John. You both have been made official Trainers now?"

"Yep." he smiled.

"That's good. What do you plan to do with that?"

"I don't know, but I do know it'll be a big responsibility, and a lot of work, but I really want to do it. Have you named the Stegosaurus yet?"

"Oh, right, you haven't met yet. This is Thellina."

"So it's a girl?" asked Kevin.

"No, that's the sad thing!" he laughed. "Yes, of course it's a girl! Named after the Hekeni goddess of the environment, so it's a big name to live up to. I think the Stegosaurus is my spirit animal now.

But there's a lot of responsibility in training. Are you sure you're up for it?"

"You know me, Gary. I've never been more up to anything in my life!" he replied.

The three of them walked into the pens, each of them a little more experienced with the Hekeni, each of them with a new perspective on Prehistorcia.

Perhaps this was a new road to peace. The Golarans would be angry, but they had been angry at everyone for centuries! Drake watched as another peace delegation went by, two people on the back of a Parasaurolophus. No matter what, the Hekeni would be well prepared.

For whatever comes…

www.ingramcontent.com/pod-product-compliance
Lightning Source LLC
Chambersburg PA
CBHW021943170626
46808CB00001B/9